Dreams of
SAVANNAH

Books by Roseanna M. White

LADIES OF THE MANOR

The Lost Heiress

The Reluctant Duchess

A Lady Unrivaled

SHADOWS OVER ENGLAND

A Name Unknown

A Song Unheard

An Hour Unspent

THE CODEBREAKERS

The Number of Love

On Wings of Devotion

A Portrait of Loyalty

Dreams of Savannah

Dreams of SAVANNAH

ROSEANNA M. WHITE

BETHANYHOUSE
a division of Baker Publishing Group
Minneapolis, Minnesota

Published by Bethany House Publishers
11400 Hampshire Avenue South
Bloomington, Minnesota 55438
www.bethanyhouse.com

Bethany House Publishers is a division of
Baker Publishing Group, Grand Rapids, Michigan

Printed in the United States of America

Library of Congress Control Number: 2020944634

ISBN 987-0-7642-3747-8 (paperback)
ISBN 987-0-7642-3820-8 (casebound)
ISBN 978-1-4934-3001-7 (ebook)

Scripture quotations are from the King James Version of the Bible.

This is a work of historical reconstruction; the appearances of certain historical figures are therefore inevitable. All other characters, however, are products of the author's imagination, and any resemblance to actual persons, living or dead, is coincidental.

Cover design by Koechel Peterson & Associates, Inc., Minneapolis, Minnesota/Jon Godfredson

Author is represented by The Steve Laube Agency.

21 22 23 24 25 26 27 7 6 5 4 3 2 1

Chapter One

Savannah, Georgia
May 1861

Cordelia Owens had dreamed of this day a hundred times. This moment. This story just waiting to happen. While the picnic was in full swing, she slipped away to her favorite spot in the backyard. The live oak towered here, its Spanish moss dripping inspiration. The music from Old Moses's fiddle danced through the air, setting the stage perfectly. A better setting for a romantic tale she couldn't possibly imagine. She swayed a bit to the music, relishing the feel of her hoops and petticoats moving along with her. She wore her favorite pale blue-green dress, with its tier of white lace matching her gloves.

Maybe today, finally, she would get to play the part of the heroine. Her true love would find her here and sweep her off her feet before he charged into battle, swearing that his undying devotion to her would see him through the months ahead.

Yes, it would make the perfect story. Only one thing was missing—the hero of the tale.

"Miss Delia."

For a second—one glorious, heart-pounding second—she

thought it had really happened. That all the dreams, all the tales she'd whispered to herself when sleep was but a haze on the horizon of her mind, had finally come true. Phineas Dunn, newly signed up in the Confederate navy, had finally shown up to her family's annual barbeque, and he'd sought her out here in the back garden, just as she'd always wished he would. She'd turn around and find him in his beautiful uniform of pearly gray, his eyes positively gleaming . . .

She turned. And saw indeed a man in a gray uniform. But his hair was three shades too dark, his frame two inches too tall, and his girth a bit too burly. She sighed and pasted a polite smile onto her lips. "Thomas Bacon. How good to see you."

"Before I go, you mean." Thomas strode to her side. "I'm going to miss you so. But thoughts of you will get me through each battle. I'll imagine your beautiful face and be capable of anything."

The words were right. Perfect even. Nearly exactly what she'd imagined Phin saying to her. But the right words couldn't change the fact that it was the wrong man saying them.

Of course, Phin couldn't exactly deliver the right line of dialogue when he didn't even bother to show up, could he?

And now look at the pickle he'd put her in. How was she supposed to be kind to Thomas Bacon and yet make sure she didn't send him away with false hope? Somehow she'd have to give him a picture to cherish without either crushing his spirit or lifting it too high. She'd just have to act like Ginny, that was all. Her older sister never had a problem answering with that modest tone that left a man utterly clueless as to whether she was simply being polite or in fact felt some affection.

Delia attempted Ginny's demure grin, which was undoubtedly ruined by her squinting into the sun, since she had left her bonnet on the blanket. In her story, Phin had brushed his fingers through her golden curls and mentioned how they shone like the very sun—and now, of course, reality was making a mockery of her imaginings. And, given a few more minutes, she'd probably break out into awful freckles, too, which would send Mama into a tizzy. She could already hear the admonition that would come. *Oh gracious, Cordelia, why can you not maintain clear skin like Lacy? Your sister's complexion is like magnolia blossoms, while yours is freckled as a strawberry.*

She turned to present her profile to Thomas, largely to relieve her eyes and also because that's what Ginny would do. Ginny never held a man's eye for more than a few seconds. "Oh, Mr. Bacon, you flatter me so."

He pivoted to face her again. "It would have to be untrue to be flattery."

False. He ought to have said it would have to be *false* to be flattery, the alliteration would have been—

"Oh!" Whyever was his head lowering toward hers with such determination? Thank heavens he hadn't dared to slip an arm around her waist. She sidestepped him and tried to head for the front garden again. Ginny never reported *this* happening.

He stepped into her path.

Cordelia planted her fists on her well-cinched waist. She didn't want to crush a poor young man's heart before he headed off to war, but to try to steal a kiss, then not allow her to leave? A true gentleman would relent. "Mr. Bacon, do remove yourself from my way."

"Now, Miss Delia, just one kiss is all I ask. To sustain me through the long war ahead." He gave her a smile he probably meant to be charming, though it made her wish she had stayed on the blanket with her sisters and not chased a silly dream.

"I'm afraid I'm not in the habit of giving out kisses to every young man who enlists." She lifted her chin and dared him to take a step closer to learn how hard she could slap. Not that she'd ever had to slap anyone, but she surely possessed surprising strength for someone of such small stature. A proper heroine always did. "Now, I suggest you make way. I don't *want* to turn you into a villain, Thomas Bacon, but I will if I must—and best of luck finding another young lady to give you the time of day after I've finished my tale."

"No need for that." He backed up a step, a smile still teasing the corners of his mouth but with his hands lifted in surrender. "Can't blame a fella for trying, though, can you? You *are* the prettiest thing in all of Georgia. May I walk you back to your sisters?"

Well. At least his good breeding had come to the surface again. "You go on ahead." She'd stay here a moment and compose herself before returning to the picnic and its crowds of friends and neighbors.

Thomas gave her a short bow and hustled away, leaving her to draw in a deep breath. This was *not* the way she had hoped the afternoon would go. But then, nothing ever went like she imagined it would in her stories. Why, just once, couldn't reality play along?

"Don't you know you're supposed to wait for your hero to rush to the rescue? I had it all worked out, but you handled it yourself too quickly." This new voice came from the garden's opposite entrance and sent a sweet trill of pleasure tripping through her veins.

So, Phineas Dunn apparently *had* deigned to come.

He stood under the trellis, sporting his new Confederate uniform. And, if she might say so, he wore it a far sight better than the dreadful Thomas Bacon. His hair glinted the perfect shade of honeyed cypress, and he stood at the ideal height—a full head taller than she, but no more.

Now *there* was a man worth telling a tale about. She had no need to force her grin as she sashayed his way—she couldn't have stopped the lifting of her lips had she tried. "Why, Phineas Dunn. We were beginning to think you had already left for New Orleans."

"Without saying good-bye?" The warm—no, no, *simmering*—

smile he gave her made anticipation dance a quadrille in her stomach. "You know me better than that. Even if you *did* just withhold the chance for me to play your hero."

Oh, that would have been perfect. Her, distressed and desperate, him rushing in ready to duel for her honor. Not that her honor had been in particular peril, but still. "Well, had I known you were here . . ."

Perhaps the situation could yet be redeemed. While he sauntered toward her, she debated what pose she might strike to set *his* heart to pattering. Ought she to twirl one of the curls spilling over her shoulder? No, too flirtatious. She could fold her hands and wait quietly as Ginny was wont to do. But no, he would never believe that of her. Should she lean over to smell one of the few blooming roses? Worth a try, she supposed.

"Too studied." Phin chuckled as he grabbed her around the waist and twirled her once so that she had no choice but to shriek with unladylike laughter. "There. Much better. You can tell all your friends that I swept you off your feet."

Was it any wonder he filled her every dream? Cordelia laughed again as she tucked her arm into his. "Mama would faint dead away."

He hummed and led her into the dappled shadow of the oak. "Luckily, she always has her smelling salts at hand."

"Ah, but then she'd launch straight into a rant about how I hadn't been sent to the Female Academy to learn daydreaming and childishness." She bit her lips as she looked up at him, partly to tamp down the smile, partly so they would redden.

That mischievous light shone in his eyes, the one that had lured her into terrible scrapes when she was a girl. "No, you were sent there to learn how to catch a husband. Any success?"

Had he posed the question to Ginny, she would have demurred and recited something about how ladies never spoke of such things until a formal announcement could be made.

Utter fiddle-faddle, of course. And far too dull. "I'll have you know that I received a proposal just this morning, Phineas Dunn, from a . . . a *sultan*."

His deep laughter made the garden gleam brighter, the colors more vivid. "A sultan, is it? What happened to that emperor you told me about last month?"

Oh, that tale had been one of her favorites. She had spent an entire day in her room writing it down, which had thrown Mama into a conniption. "He was reunited with the love of his youth, so I graciously stepped aside."

The way Phin's hazel eyes sparkled made her wonder if perhaps all those stories she had let herself imagine about him had a hope of coming true. "That's my Delia, as gracious as she is lovely."

His Delia? She could scarcely catch her breath. Never in her life had she fainted, but she felt downright lightheaded now. "See there, I *did* learn something at finishing school."

With another chuckle, he wove their fingers together and gazed upon them for a long moment. "I'm going to miss you." He angled his eyes up, a half-smile tilting his mouth. "When I get back, am I going to find you married to some planter's son who can claim more slaves and acres than anyone in four counties?"

"I . . ." Was he asking her to wait for him? No, no, she mustn't let herself get carried away. Though that would be a dream come true—Phineas Dunn dropping to his knee and proposing. They could marry before he left, under the magnolia blossoms . . .

Cordelia drew in as deep a breath as her corset would allow and hoped her smile didn't wobble. "I shall miss you, too."

He used their joined hands to pull her closer. She prayed her thudding heart wasn't audible to him. "How much?"

As if a lady could answer such a question! As if there *were* an answer to it, a quantity one could assign. *I shall miss you two quarts and three-fourths a cup*. Her gaze moved from the gleaming buttons on his coat down to the handsome gold braid at the cuff and landed on the sword strapped to his side. A shiver coursed up her spine. "Don't go, Phin."

He snapped upright, amusement and incredulity replacing the warmth in his gaze. "What's this? I thought you would be happy to see me go off to war. Just think of all the stories I'll bring home for you, Delia. All the Yankees I'll outwit, and adventure on the high seas to boot, aboard the *Sumter*."

She traced one of the loops of braid with a light fingertip. Happy? No. Proud, perhaps, but . . . "What good will that do me if your ship is blown to bits by cannonballs? Or capsized in a hurricane? Or attacked by a giant squid? Or . . . or eaten by a whale?"

"Eaten by a . . . Delia, really, that's about as likely as me getting mauled by a tiger."

Her eyes went wide. "Are there any of those around? I heard they are going to open a zoological park in New York. What if you end up fighting the Yankees up that way and some exotic creature escapes and stalks you?"

Phin chuckled and lifted her hand to his mouth, pressing a kiss to her knuckles that made them tingle. "I will be fine. And I will come home full to bursting with the most exciting tales you've ever heard."

I'd rather have you. The words twisted themselves around her tongue. A lady would never set them loose, not outside the pages of a book, but neither could a more appropriate response squeeze past them. Though she probably looked like a complete ninny just staring at him, silent.

Her pulse hammered when he pulled her closer still and angled his head. His mouth remained turned up in that beautiful smile of his. "Are you going to pull away from me like you did Bacon?"

She should, to be sure. Much as she yearned to linger in his arms, it wouldn't do to be caught, and there were far too many guests clamoring about the barbeque tables to think this bubble of privacy would last long. Besides, Phin had no intention of marrying her before he headed to war, given that he left tomorrow.

Would it be such a terrible thing, then, to give him a farewell kiss to send him on his way? She hoped not, because she couldn't bring herself to pull away, and he drew slowly nearer.

"Delia? Are you back here? It's time for Daddy's announcement." Ginny's voice rang through the garden as light and clear as a chime. "Delia? Is that you?"

Cordelia pulled away so she could wave at her elder sister. "It's me, Ginny. I'll be right there."

Ginny stopped a few steps into the garden and smiled. Her radiance came, no doubt, because in moments Daddy would let it be known that his baby girl would marry Charlie Worth within the fortnight, before Charlie joined up. "Do hurry, Delie-Darlin. I'm too excited to wait a moment longer than necessary."

"I'm coming."

The promise was enough to send Ginny on her way, though Cordelia wasn't sure whether she ought to follow now or say something more to Phin.

He answered the question by catching her around the waist and pulling her against him. "Not yet, you don't."

That intoxicating smile of his flashed again. How would she survive without the promise of seeing it regularly? "Phin, we—"

"Shh." He brushed a thick curl over her shoulder and then slid his hand under the locks, anchoring her head. Oh, how she hoped he couldn't tell how he affected her. She tried to commit every detail to memory as he tilted her face up, inclined his own. The way his gaze tangled with hers and his lids half-shuttered his eyes . . .

But then their lips touched, and her mind went foggy and incoherent. She couldn't have said how long that first gentle kiss lasted before he deepened it. All she knew was that no words in the world could have captured this magic, the feeling of a puzzle clicking into place at long last, the swell of a heart that hadn't realized until then what it meant to truly feel.

When he pulled away, it took her a moment to realize her arms had locked around his neck. And for the life of her, she could think of nothing clever to say.

Phin's smile looked adorably smug. "Will you save me a waltz?"

"Today?"

"Every day. Every ball. That ought to guarantee you remember me while I'm gone."

As if she could forget the man who embodied all her dreams. "*Every* waltz. But you had better come back to me, Phineas Dunn."

"I sure intend to." He spun her around like in a country dance and then caught her by the hand and pulled her toward the rest of the guests. "Will you wait for me?"

Not exactly a proposal, but the question nevertheless made her grin. She could only pray she managed to put a bit of sophistication in it. "You know I will."

"How long?"

The music from Old Moses's fiddle was joined by the rest of the band, who must have just arrived, earning a hoot of approval from the crowd in the front. Cordelia tucked her hand into the crook of his elbow. "Forever."

Hopefully that would be promise enough to deliver him safely through the war. And hopefully it would be over soon—she had no desire to wait forever for him to hold her again.

Chapter Two

Off the Isle of Pines, Cuba
July 3, 1861

Day had long since faded. The sun's fire was extinguished in the water to the west, and clouds obscured the heavens where moon and stars should abide. Phineas Dunn stepped into the heavy, humid darkness and sighed. Behind him, his best friend edged onto the deck too.

"Not exactly what I thought it would be," Spencer said, his voice barely a rumble against the Caribbean breeze. A pulse of humid silence beat between them, and then Spence elbowed him in the side. "You'll have to exaggerate aplenty to turn this into a tale for your sweetheart."

Phin breathed a laugh, not sure yet how he'd take the events of the afternoon and make them anything worth telling Delia about. He'd come up with something, though, just as he'd been doing every week—not that he had any idea when his letters might reach her. Regardless, he sent them as often as he could, ignoring the teasing of the other men of the crew. They didn't tease because he had a girl to write to—no, they teased because he hadn't had the good sense to marry her or at least propose before he left. *A dang fool*, Spencer had labeled him the first time Phin had drawn Delia's photograph out, before the *Sumter* had even left port in New Orleans.

If only it had been a simple matter of choice. Though now he'd best push all thoughts of Delia aside and focus on the task at hand. "I'll report to Hudgins."

"Good. He likes you better." With a laugh, Spencer turned toward a few other members of the prize crew, who were pushing trunks toward the starboard rail. "I'll give them a hand."

Phineas nodded and strode toward the officer in charge. Hudgins turned at his approach and offered him a smile. "Anything of interest below, Dunn?"

"The hold's empty, sir. I daresay the sail and rigging are the only things worthwhile we'll find on her." Still, he cast a glance over the lantern-lit deck of the *Golden Rocket*. She was a fine merchant vessel, one not unlike his uncle's, where he had learned all things maritime.

Hudgins nodded. "Would you report that to Commander Semmes and get his instructions on what we ought to do with her?"

"Aye, sir." When he spun away, his glance snagged on the Union flag that was carefully folded nearby. He had watched the ship strike her colors a couple hours before, had known pride and relief when she raised a white flag in its place.

The first prey of the CSS *Sumter*. The first victory of the Confederacy's first cruiser. And hopefully the first blow to the Yankees. There must be a way to focus on *that* in his letter to Delia. Make it seem a glorious conquest instead of the anticlimax it had been.

Phin headed for the rowboat that would take him from the *Golden Rocket* to the *Sumter*. A wisp of the blowing trade wind caught the Stars and Bars that waved over his ship and cooled the perspiration that had gathered under his collar in the *Rocket*'s hold. He climbed over the rail and down the rope ladder to the boat.

He ignored the twist in his chest.

This was *not* Uncle Beau's ship. It was an enemy vessel. And the long-faced commander was certainly not his uncle, the man who had instilled in him the love for the sea that had led him to New Orleans and the cruiser, when all his friends from Savannah were happy to join one of the many Georgia militias.

Phin dropped into the rowboat and settled in, grabbing the oars. He'd become friends with the rest of the crew quickly, especially Spencer. They understood him like his Savannah friends never had—heard the sea's siren song, felt the need to feel a ship's deck rocking beneath their feet, knew the satisfaction of seeing the world on a chart and reading the map of the stars. Perhaps the crew were almost all merchant sailors, not military, but they all shared that love of the sea. And being the very first Confederate sailing crew had bonded them together quickly. He knew well that these men would be his brothers for life.

No moonlight illumined his watery path, but the lanterns aboard the *Sumter* led the way. He cut through the water quickly. A few minutes and he was scrambling up to the teeming deck of his floating home. His gaze searched out Commander Semmes and found him at the rail, watching the *Golden Rocket* with hands clasped behind his back.

Saluting, Phin stopped at his side. "Evening, Commander."

"Dunn." Semmes turned his way, lantern light catching the white of his teeth as he smiled. "How fares the prize crew? Anything to report?"

"Only that the Yankee captain was truthful, sir. There was nothing in the hold, nothing at all on board of interest to the Confederacy or to make her worth towing in for the prize. Some provisions, some sail and rigging you may want to keep for repair purposes." Though they did their best to rely on the *Sumter*'s steam rather than sail. But if coal ran low . . . "Hudgins sent me over to seek your orders, sir."

With a hum directed out at sea, Semmes held his silence for a moment, then nodded. "Burn her."

"Aye, sir." He saluted again, though when he spun away, that twist tightened in his stomach. Not an unusual reaction for a soldier's first witnessed casualty in war, he supposed. No one would think less of him for considering it a shame to destroy such a finely crafted vessel.

Still, he didn't intend to let them see the conflict. While he climbed back into the rowboat, he set his mind on what words he'd put to paper for Delia instead. The ship would have to be twice its actual size, of course. Perhaps captained by a pirate with a beard that reached down to his belt. And instead of them burning it, maybe it would have to explode, the *Sumter* crew barely escaping with their lives . . .

Soon the rowboat bumped against the hull of the *Golden Rocket*, and Phin reached for the ladder, climbed it quickly. He found Hudgins right where he had left him.

Hudgins greeted him with a lifted brow. "Tow or burn?"

"Burn."

The officer sighed even as he nodded. "Seems a shame, doesn't it?"

So he *wasn't* the only one. Still, Phin offered a confident smile. "I imagine we'll find prizes aplenty worth keeping, sir."

"I imagine so—if we can find ports into which we can tow them. Well, nothing for it now. Spencer! Gleason!"

As Spence and another of their friends hurried over to hear the order, Phin took a step back and made himself useful. He lugged another chest of provisions toward the ladder, then gathered the assorted sails and ropes that had been drawn aside to be taken. Spence joined him in time to help lower it all to the rowboat, and Gleason climbed down to welcome the booty into its transport.

"Think Semmes will give us leave in Cuba if we land to take on coal?" Spencer picked up a rope.

Phin slanted a grin at his friend. "Well now, I'd say it's probable. I know we'd all like the chance to post a few letters. Eat a decent meal."

"Find some fairer company." Spencer tied the rope round about the trunk and handed one end of it to Phin, an impish grin on his mouth. "At least those of us who *don't* have letters to post to the prettiest girl in all of Georgia. Maybe I can find a pretty señorita to write to, *sí*?"

Phin snorted a laugh. "You know very well you're going to end up married to Mabel. You might as well stop fighting it and declare yourself."

Spencer made a face at the mention of the neighbor from home he alternately growled about and thought longingly of. Apparently today was a growl-about day. "And have to listen to her nagging for the rest of my life? No thank you. If I'm going to have a nagging woman, she might as well nag me in Spanish so I have an excuse for ignoring her."

Shaking his head with another laugh, Phin took his end of the rope and they eased it over the side, lowering the trunk slowly into the rowboat and Gleason's waiting arms. "We both know you're not looking for a señorita to *marry*."

Spencer chuckled. "No, I imagine I'll marry one of the girls my mother listed as acceptable for me. But she never said I couldn't enjoy an evening with anyone else."

As if Mrs. Spencer—a fine Louisiana lady—would ever speak so crassly. Phin rolled his eyes. "Just be careful in what you say, will you? You know well Semmes expects gentlemanly behavior from the crew. Especially when in port."

Though his expression was shrouded by the shadows of night, Spencer's snort came through clear enough. "Seems to me he worries too much about how we entertain ourselves in port. With everything else he needs to consider, we should hardly warrant his attention, so long as we don't get into trouble with the law and report back on time."

The trunk settled on the floor of the boat with a thud. Phin loosed his rope and coiled it on top, then reached for another armload. "Semmes is an intelligent fellow. He's more than capable of worrying about it all."

At least the snort held a little laughter this time. "You'll join me, won't you? Gleason said he would. He's been to every major Cuban port before, so he can lead the way."

Phin had been, too, but Uncle Beau had never led him to the particular parts of town that Spencer had in mind, and he'd never sought them out on his own either. The Dunns had their flaws, sure enough, but Father had raised him to embrace the very moral creed that Semmes was insisting on from his men.

Women were to be treated with respect. Protected at all costs. Not taken advantage of. He'd grown up pretending he was a knight, ready to do battle for the fair damsel's honor.

It was no wonder he'd always been charmed by Delia's stories.

To Spence, he simply said, "No thanks. I'll just stay on the commander's good side and focus on finding a decent meal, if we get shore leave, and—"

"Everyone in unison now . . ." *Everyone* was Spencer and, from below them, Gleason, but the two singsonged the rest of Phin's words, " . . . post my letters to Delia."

If they meant to irritate him, they'd have to try harder. Phineas laughed. "Well, we haven't had the chance to post anything since we left New Orleans, which means I haven't sent the one where I exaggerated our narrow escape from the *Brooklyn*." He tossed his armload down to Gleason.

"The only one that wouldn't have required much exaggerating." Spencer waited for Gleason to extend his arms again, then tossed down a section of tied-up canvas. "I was beginning to think we'd never see open water and would be stuck in the Mississippi for the duration of the war."

Phin picked up the last of the gear. "Better than sitting in the marshes outside Savannah with my cousins. The letter that reached me said the fevers were far more deadly than the Yankees offshore."

Hudgins strode up, gaze landing on Phin. "Is that everything?"

"Aye, sir," Phin said with a nod.

"Good. Spencer, join Gleason in the boat, if you will, and be ready to row the second our boots hit the floorboards. Dunn, you're with me. Time to light this *Rocket*." The midshipman spun away with a beckoning motion of his head.

Phin exchanged a glance with Spencer, just long enough to see a spark of jealousy on his friend's face—quickly gone as Spence nodded his acknowledgment of the order. They'd been lucky to be chosen for the prize crew from the one hundred and forty sailors on the *Sumter*. Phin ought to take it as the highest of compliments to be chosen for this, too, the first real action of their maritime war.

Yet splashing the deck and rigging with the kerosene Hudgins handed him didn't feel much like a battle. And holding high the torch that would set it ablaze sure lacked that sensation of victory.

The fumes from the fuel curled around him, burning his nose. He'd known the war would be different out here on open water. Wanted it to be. But it was going to take some getting used to.

Hudgins motioned him to the rail. Phin took up position to scurry over it even as he reached for the torches. After handing them over, Hudgins opened the lantern and held it out. Phin lit first one torch, then the second.

Their glances held. Just for a moment, little more than fleeting. But enough to know that the prize crew's leader once again shared his thoughts. Felt, too, that bare tingle of excitement smothered by a reality not so adventurous, not so romantic.

Well, as much as it might disappoint Delia if he wrote the

naked truth to her, war wasn't a pretty story. It was just day after day, month after month of doing what had to be done.

At Hudgins's nod, Phin hurled the first torch as far as he could toward the aft. A second later, the lantern hit on the fore end of the deck, shattering in a whoosh of expanding flame. Phin launched the remaining torch far starboard, away from them, and turned before he could see where it landed.

"Over we go!" Hudgins's voice fought the wind and the quickly mounting thunder of rising flame but still made it to Phin's receptive ears without trouble.

He was already halfway down the ladder and soon landed in the rowboat. Even as he took his position, Hudgins landed, too, and shouted, "Row!"

Spencer and Gleason sliced the water with the oars in a rhythm fast and smooth, propelling them toward the *Sumter* and away from the *Golden Rocket*. By the time they bumped against the familiar hull of their ship, the Yankee vessel had ignited into an inferno.

Phin followed Spencer up the ladder and helped pull up the rowboat so they could unload it. But his gaze, like the hundred others on the deck, held fast to the blaze across the water.

After all the crew's talk about the blasted Yankees and how hard they hoped to hit them, after all the laughing dreams of glory and prize money, no revelry sparked the air. No cheers went up. A strange silence held the sailors immobile as the dancing, crackling glow beyond entranced them.

A few heads shook. A few deep inhales signaled unexpected emotion. A few shuffling feet seemed inclined to leave yet remained rooted to their spots. Until now, most of the crew had served on ships much like the *Golden Rocket*, with her once-billowing sails.

Just like Phin. He took a spot shoulder-to-shoulder with his friends of a few months and stared at the flaming ship that seemed, in many ways, more familiar than the *Sumter*. Maybe he was still green. He had taken well to the military training Semmes had been instilling in them, but the point remained that he wasn't a naval officer. Just a businessman who loved the sea. And this wasn't the kind of business he was used to.

Across the water, a great snap split the air, and the mainmast of the *Rocket* came crashing down. The ship tilted. For now, the heat from the blaze still touched his face, heightening just slightly the temperature of the balmy Caribbean night. But soon enough it would slip under the concealing waves. Disappear, the heat along with the substance.

Commander Semmes turned from his spot at the rail. As always, his shoulders were squared, his chin level, his spine straight. "Yonder sinks the testament to our mission, men. May she be the first of many. And may her loss be a blow to all Yankee-doodledom."

A chorus of muted agreement rippled through the gathered crowd. Phin whispered his "Hear, hear" along with the others and watched the ocean consume the flames. When the last tongue of orange disappeared beneath the waves, when darkness reigned on the sea once more, he turned and headed down to his hammock.

Lantern light cast a steady glow over their cramped quarters, the shadows sharp and deep. Phin settled into his hammock, tired but not ready to sleep. So instead he pulled out the book into which he'd placed the photographs he'd brought from home.

The first was of his parents. They looked staid and somber here, but Phin smiled at the memory of the pride in their eyes when they saw him off. His father had tried to talk him into gathering a regiment and staying near home, but hunkering down in the marshes held no appeal. Instead, he had let his mother pull all the strings her family's connections gave her to secure this appointment aboard the Confederacy's first commissioned cruiser.

The next photo revealed the face of his baby sister, Sassy—Saphrona might not be a baby anymore at seventeen, but she had certainly lived up to his nickname for her. Her parting instruction had been, *"Go defeat some Yankees, Phin, and make me proud. I shall die if I have to claim a coward for a brother."*

He slid those two back into their spots and smiled at the third picture, the one that had come in the first packet of letters he received in New Orleans. The prettiest features in all the Low Country dimpled up from the paper. Even in a photo, her grin conveyed imagined mischief. Her eyes seemed to gleam with that laughing light that was pure Delia.

Spencer, in the hammock above his, leaned over and grabbed the picture from his hands. "Haven't you memorized this by now?"

Phin clamped down on the urge to leap out of his hammock and instead folded his arms behind his head. "Spence, one of these days you're going to snatch something from the wrong man's hands and get a fist in your nose."

Spencer chuckled, then sighed. "If Mabel looked like this, I'd have married her before I left. Still not sure why you didn't at least put a ring on her finger."

He would have, if he could. Cordelia Owens was everything he'd ever wanted in a wife, and more besides. He'd always liked her, had long considered her the best of his sister's friends. But when she'd come home from finishing school so beautiful . . . well, every man in Savannah had been vying for her attention, and who was Phin to win it? Sure, their families were friends. The Dunns were respectable. They owned a beautiful house in the city and a plantation on Tybee Island off the coast.

But some of the other men seeking her favor owned far more—and Mr. Owens had made it quite clear that he intended to approve only the offers for his daughters that would be financially advantageous to him. With no sons to his name, Owens meant to parcel off his own holdings to his daughters, with the goal of their being able to add his land to their husbands' lands and build an empire. Create some of the biggest, most successful plantations in Georgia.

Hence the quick marriage between Ginny and Charlie Worth before Charlie went off to war. His plantation in the hill country abutted the Owenses' rice plantation. Every man in Georgia knew that Cordelia's dowry would be the indigo plantation her mother had brought to the marriage, nearer to Atlanta. And Lacy would be left with the house in Savannah someday.

It was all he could do to force the smile to stay on his lips. "Frankly, I'm not sure her parents would have allowed it had I tried. When I asked permission to write to her, her father made it quite clear he didn't intend to encourage her to wait for me."

No, he'd rather gotten that hard glint in his eye and said, *"I like you, Phineas. I like your family. But Tybee?"* And he'd shaken his head.

All a man was to Reginald Owens was what he owned.

But Delia was Owens's soft spot, and he hadn't been able to deny her request to correspond with Phin. For whatever reason, she favored *him*, it seemed. Of all those other men . . . He didn't know why. And he wasn't about to question it too much. She favored him, which meant there was some hope she wouldn't already be married to someone else by the time he got home. So, he'd just have to make sure her affections stayed strong—hence the letters sent home every time he could manage it.

"Are you joking?" Spencer's face appeared again, upside down and incredulous. "Why wouldn't he approve of you? You're . . . you're a Southern *paragon*, man."

"Hardly." The word emerged on a laugh. "The Dunn holdings are rather modest compared to Owens's. He owns two enormous plantations, plus the house in Savannah."

Either Spencer looked a bit troubled by this, or Phin was just no good at reading upside-down expressions. His friend handed the photograph back. "Maybe you should have stayed close to home, then. Raised a regiment like all your friends and cousins. You'd probably still be stationed in Savannah, or near it, and could see her once in a while."

"And miss the chance to share a narrow little room with all these fine sailors and marines?" Grinning, he swept an arm out, encompassing the rows of hammocks three high and running the length of the room. "Never."

Gleason looked up from his repose across from him. "Spencer has a point. Seems to me you'd have been more inclined to stay in your own territory, with your slaves to do the work for you."

The suggestion grated. He was one of the few sailors aboard who even owned slaves, which made the others look at him in a certain way. He'd never tried to explain that it wasn't a situation his family particularly liked, but there was nothing they could do about it, aside from sell everything off. Georgia law no longer allowed a man to free his slaves.

"That's not what I was looking for in a war experience." Phin pulled out pen and paper. If they did land in Cuba, he'd have a whole packet of letters ready to post. "Frankly, I would have taken up the call for privateers if it had seemed logical. But with the blockade, my uncle advised against it. Considered becoming a runner, but my mother begged me not to, to join up instead. So, this was the best alternative."

"Even though it pulled you away from your ladylove."

Ladylove. He shook his head, his fingers penning her name with care. Bachelorhood had treated him well thus far. Free to sail wherever he pleased, to take his tour of Europe. Ma said he had itchy feet, which was true as not.

He hadn't planned on giving all that up any time soon. Certainly not with the uncertainties of war upon them all. But then he'd seen Delia again that spring, and suddenly he was happy to keep his feet on the ground for a while and started wondering if she'd perhaps enjoy life on the island. Imagined how he could turn one of the parlors into a writing room for her. If he promised her endless paper and pens and ink and novels, maybe that would be enough to convince her to spend the rest of her life by his side.

"Forever," she had said. Promised. And she was too much of a romantic to go back on that. He'd just have to convince her father it would be advantageous somehow. And with a little luck, the *Sumter* could help him in that. They'd all get a cut of any prize money they earned. If the war lasted long enough and the booty was big enough, maybe that would earn Owens's respect. Maybe.

He traced a finger over Delia's image, grinning at the ink stains that inevitably marked her fingers. Then he went back to the letter.

After finishing and putting his supplies away, Phin settled back in his hammock and closed his eyes. Orange flames seemed to lick at him; black smoke filled his nose. He shook it away. Spanish moss dripping from tall oak limbs, that's what he would think of. The fragrance of magnolia blossoms, too sweet, too heady. Delia in his arms, her hair its own golden fire, her eyes as green as a lush field. Rosy lips parting, gleaming. Whispering.

"Don't go."

His breath caught in his throat, and he half turned toward the wall. Even in his daydreams, Delia surprised him. But he knew her. Knew that, when it came down to it, she was like any other Savannahian woman. She might miss him, and in that way not want him to go—which was fine by him. But she'd have no use for a man not willing to fight for his country. More, she wouldn't want one who sat itching his bugbites in the trenches for a miserable year.

She wanted a hero.

And he intended to be one for her.

Chapter Three

Cordelia bolted upright in her bed, swiping at the perspiration trickling down her temple. Her nightdress clung to her, and her thin cotton sheet was tangled through her legs. What a terrible dream. Hissing flames and acres of water, darkness pressing in on every side. Then—what had it been? More water, a storm. Something bad, something dangerous. Pain, searing and throbbing. Then the gritty taste of sand in her mouth.

Silly—but then, the impressions were so intense. Taste, feel, sound . . . all well formed, vivid. Why, it could have been a pirate story. A shipwreck, perhaps. A desert island. Maybe—but no. That wasn't right. Something else, something . . . maybe some*one* . . .

"Morning, Miss Delia." The melodic voice sounded from the corner of the room.

Hearing it was no surprise, though hearing it so early made Cordelia plant her hands on her hips and frown. "Did you sleep in here again? Salina, let me talk to Daddy. Maybe he can have a word with Big Tom."

Her maid—and dearest friend in the world—waved a hand and bent over one of Cordelia's dresses, needle flashing in the morning sunlight. "Don't you be fretting about me, Miss Delia.

Don't want no trouble, especially when you said I could sleep here anytime he gets too forward."

Sighing, Cordelia sat on the bottom of her bed and studied her maid. A colorful turban wound round her head, but she happened to know it covered hair a few shades lighter than the midnight black of the rest of Salina's family. Her skin, too, was a fairer brown, her features fine.

And beautiful. Beautiful enough to earn the attention of the male slaves, whether she wanted it or not. "You ought to marry, Salina. If you had a husband . . ."

Salina glanced up, her apple-cider colored eyes sparking with muted determination. "A fine idea, exceptin that your daddy done gave me to you and said I'd go with you when *you* marry. And I ain't much for the thought of takin a husband only to leave him soon as Mr. Phin gets back."

Phin. Usually the mere mention of his name made a grin spring to her lips and her cheeks flush with the memory of that stolen kiss in the garden. But just now those sensations of fire, darkness, and pain surged at the thought of him.

What if *his* ship had burned, sunk? What if he was hurt? Or . . . no, she wouldn't even entertain the possibility of an *or*.

"You all right, Miss Delia?"

She shook her head, reached up to smooth away the golden locks that fell in her face. "I had a bad dream, and I think it might have been about Phin. Something with a ship burning, water everywhere. Pain." She blinked and shook her head again, forced a smile. "My fears at work, no doubt."

But Salina frowned and set the dress aside. "Was there sand, too, in the mouth? And the pain—in the leg?"

Though her heart gave a terrified thud, Cordelia inclined her head and beat back the panic. "Was I talking in my sleep?"

"I had me the same dream." Salina abandoned her sewing entirely and came to sit beside Cordelia.

Mama would scold if she saw it, but they'd been friends as

long as Cordelia could remember. Long enough that she held out her hand and felt a breath of comfort when Salina took it between hers.

Though the difference in color was unmistakable, their hands were the same size. Same long fingers, same pronounced knuckles that Mama said looked prone to rheumatism, ones that would turn knobby and gnarled when she got old. *"This is why we marry when we're young,"* she had said. *"And still beautiful."*

Some things it was better to keep Mama from knowing, lest she dampen them with her dour predictions. Like this unbalanced friendship.

Cordelia squeezed Salina's hand. "All the same? A ship, fire? Water and darkness? Pain and sand?"

Salina shivered. "The Lord must have sent it to us both, like as not so we'd pray for him. All that water—I don't know how he can like it, Miss Delia, sure and I don't. The spirits must surround them sailors day and night."

Cordelia very nearly rolled her eyes. "Salina, you're a Christian now. You ought to know better. The dead do *not* come back into the land of the living through water." Though last year Cordelia had written a wonderful story speculating on what would happen if they did. Full of dark shadows and cold chills, the rotting smell from the rice and indigo fields . . . it had been one of her best stories and had given Ginny and Lacy nightmares for a week.

Mama had strictly forbidden her from ever writing such tales again, an order Cordelia had obeyed rather happily. She'd given *herself* nightmares for a week too.

"If water don't give the dead a way to live, then what's the point of baptism?" Brows arched in a way that would have earned the ire of the elder Owenses, Salina stood again and moved over to the door of Cordelia's dressing room. "And if the pastor at Third African teaches it right, the graves done opened up when Jesus died, didn't they? The dead went walkin."

Cordelia grinned. "Ah, but there was no water mentioned in that story."

Salina snorted a laugh and disappeared into the closet, emerging a moment later with Cordelia's chemise, corset, and hoop. "We best get you ready. You're going with your mama and Miss Lacy to that aid meetin, ain't ya? Then there's the picnic for the Fourth later. You'll want to wear your new white dress with the blue sash for that, and I'll have it ready for you."

Some of the residual tension in her chest eased at that thought. Mama and Mrs. Young had promised her that she'd be allowed to plan a series of *tableaux vivants* to help raise funds for the war, and she knew just what she wanted to do. As a unique take on the usual portrayal of classical artwork, she would weave the living pictures together with a story she'd written. Considering how to pull that off was far more fun than thoughts of the picnic that Phin would definitely *not* be attending.

She stood and changed from her nightdress into her chemise, washed her face with water from the basin—water devoid of ghosts, she noted—and then hooked her corset, still tightly enough tied that Salina wouldn't have to redo it. But as she stepped into the circle of petticoats waiting for her and her gaze settled on the rumpled pillows, her newly won ease fled.

"What do we pray for him, Salina?" She'd never gotten divine direction on anything before, so far as she knew. How was she to know what to do with it? The Owenses attended church solely as a matter of course. They certainly didn't belong to that class of planters who looked down their noses at their neighbors for not being holy enough. She believed all that she had learned through the sermons, but . . .

Salina lifted the skirts into place. "Seems to me there either be danger brewin or danger done. So we ought to pray protection for him. Breathe in."

Cordelia sucked air in, and Salina tied the petticoats in place. Under her breath the servant muttered, "And we ought to be grateful River done snuck a talisman into Mr. Phin's bag."

"River—Phin's valet?" She tried to turn, but it was hard to manage with Salina working at her waist. "Why would he do that?"

"'Cause he cares about his master, that's why."

Cordelia opened her mouth but then decided against offering any response. The Negroes couldn't be argued with when it came to the beliefs that had come with their forebears from West Africa. Daddy said their minds weren't suited to reason. Cordelia could never agree with that, knowing Salina so well, but they sure were stubborn folk. Best to be grateful Salina had abandoned most of the ways of her conjurer aunt in favor of the Savior and leave it at that.

Salina took a step back. "I'll fetch the dress."

"Thank you."

A few minutes later, her dress had been lowered into place and buttoned, and Salina had her curls arranged in perfect order. Cordelia flounced toward the door but then halted when her gaze snagged on her secretaire. She'd scribbled the end to a story last night before bed and itched to reread it now to see if it was as much fun in the light of day.

But if she didn't come down to breakfast on time, Mama wouldn't let her do the tableaux vivants.

She gathered the papers together and turned with an exaggerated plea on her face. "Salina, would you read this for me and tell me what you think?"

Salina pressed her lips together and glanced at the door. "I'll try to get to it between my chores. Maybe once your mama's away from the house. You know she said if she caught me reading again, she'd send me to the fields."

"No she won't. Daddy won't let her. That's why he gave you to me. And *I* need you to know how to read." She set the story back down and grinned. "Be brutally honest and put a note by anything you think I should change."

She left her maid with an amused look on her face and hurried downstairs to the breakfast room.

Lacy, early as always, sat in her usual seat, and Daddy at the head. Mama, thank the Lord above, hadn't arrived yet. Cordelia took her chair and couldn't help but miss her elder sister when she noted Ginny's empty seat across from her. "Morning, Daddy. Lacy."

Her father smiled, the light from the window gilding his silver hair. "Morning, Delie-Darlin. How's my sunshine this morning?"

"Just fine." She grinned at Lacy, then nodded toward Ginny's abandoned chair. "Have we heard anything new from Ginny?"

"She's well settled with the Worths at their home in the mountains and planning a visit to Twin Magnolias to see how everything fares," he said, referencing the Owenses' rice plantation. "Are you certain you girls wouldn't like to accept her invitation to join them? You've never summered in Savannah before."

Lacy's chin went up, her blue eyes sparking. "We'll not abandon the city in her hour of need, Daddy. Not without you and Mama."

Daddy chuckled and glanced from Lacy to Cordelia. "Well, it's still safe enough here, if a bit overrun with soldiers. Though I'll warn you both again—the first case I hear of yellow fever, you're leaving."

"Yes, Daddy," Cordelia murmured in unison with her little sister.

Mama glided in just then, dressed for their outing in indigo blue. "Morning, darlings. Cordelia, do you have your plans for the tableaux vivants ready? We must be at the Youngs' promptly at ten."

"I'll be ready."

"Good." Mama studied Cordelia as she sat, examining each curl, ruffle, and fold. She nodded and turned to do the same with Lacy. "Lacy dear, do take off that ribbon. You may wear it to the picnic later, but not to an aid meeting."

"Yes'm." Lacy quickly untied the ribbon from around her neck, shooting a glance at Cordelia that conveyed amusement and frustration both.

Cordelia hid her grin behind the cup of coffee that had been waiting for her. She took a sip and let her mind wander to the fun of the tableaux they'd put on, to the picnic that afternoon. But then a cloud passed before the sun and cast a shadow on the table, and she couldn't subdue the shudder that worked up her spine.

Where was Phin today? On a grand adventure, no doubt. Perhaps in some exotic port. Dining with a dignitary, convincing the locals of the nobility of their cause. He could be helping revolutionize the design of a weapon that would scare all the Yankee ships out of the water.

Or he could be engaged in a heated battle, with cannon smoke filling the air and a watery grave yawning wide. Fleeing for his life, grabbed with every step by verdant overgrowth out to capture him, hold him until wild creatures could devour him.

She squeezed her eyes shut and hoped for the first time in her life that his day was dull and boring.

Never before had Phin beheld such quiet contemplation on the Fourth of July. He stood with Spence, Hudgins, and a dozen others along the rails, gaze latched on the two ships that had been mere specks on the horizon at daybreak and which the *Sumter* was now nearly upon.

Semmes strolled the length of the deck and stopped behind Phin and Hudgins. "Strange, isn't it, gentlemen? To realize that on this day in 1776 our forefathers were all fighting together for the right to govern themselves, and that now we're fighting our once-neighbors for that same right, again?"

Hudgins sighed and nodded.

Phin drew in a long breath. "A sad realization indeed, sir. Makes you wonder what has happened to the concept of freedom. The Yankees sure don't recognize ours."

"And now they call us *rebels*—just as the British once called us all. Yet they deny being tyrants." Semmes shook his head and turned away. "Not the sort of Independence Day we are used to celebrating, to be sure. But we will win our right to celebrate our independence anew, make no mistake. And perhaps those two ships ahead of us will help with that most noble goal. Hudgins, you have the first of the prize crews again, and I want you with him, Dunn."

"Yes, sir." Phin saluted, smiled . . . and darted a glance at Spencer, who didn't look so happy.

Then Hudgins turned their way with a grin. "Spencer—you'll come again too. And . . . Davidson, let's give you a chance this time."

Having Spence included rekindled Phin's smile for a moment, but it faded when the commander strolled onward. Phin had woken up this morning thinking of Delia, of those wide green eyes begging him to stay. Worried about whales and tigers and giant squid.

How could that make him want to laugh at the same time it made him go tense and alert?

Hudgins looked back at the ever-nearing sails. "What do you think? Will they surrender as easily as the *Golden Rocket* did yesterday?"

Phin studied the lines of the ships, the size and outfitting. "They're both merchant vessels. They won't be well enough armed to fight. They'll surrender."

A few minutes later, the warning shot boomed out from the *Sumter*, landing off the bow of the nearest ship. A few minutes more, and the Union vessel struck her colors and raised the white flag.

Hudgins straightened and jerked his head toward the rowboats. "That would be our cue. Let's make it quick, gentlemen, so the *Sumter* can meet that second ship too."

Phin's feet pivoted, obedient and quick. But Delia's imploring face flashed before his mind's eye again. Her voice echoed in his ears. *"Don't go."*

He shook his head to clear it and clamped down on the tide of emotion that swamped him. They'd all felt regret last night, watching the *Rocket* burn. They all probably wondered if today's tasks would be any easier.

But letting such doubts linger would only hurt them. He couldn't hesitate, couldn't let himself put a pretty face on his fear and use it as an excuse. Better to use that image as inspiration.

He climbed into the rowboat with his friends and grabbed an oar. A little exertion was exactly what he needed. Grinning, Spencer followed behind him and took up the other oar. The other three members, two marines and then Davidson, looked every bit as happy.

Phin blinked away another image of Delia's imploring eyes.

At Hudgins's nod, Phin and Spencer stroked the oars through the water, headed for the now-anchored ship bearing the name *Cuba* on its hull. No surprise, then, to see her so near the port of Cienfuegos. The only questions were whether she was registered in the Union and to whom her cargo belonged.

Their boat bumped against the *Cuba*, and Hudgins led the way up the ladder, Phin close behind. When his boots hit the deck, he felt the glowers of the vessel's crew upon them. One of the elder members stepped forward, thunder in his brow. "What is the meaning of this, gentlemen?"

Hudgins sketched a bow. "It is my honor to inform you that you have been apprehended by the CSS *Sumter*. Might we see your papers, please?"

The captain folded his arms over his chest. "Confederates."

"At your service, sir." Hudgins lifted a brow. "And you are?"

The captain growled low in his throat but motioned another man forward with a few leaves of paper. "Captain Stroud. You will see we are of the everlasting state of Maine."

Hudgins's lips hinted at a smile. "Yankees." He took the papers and handed them off to Phin, apparently unwilling to break eye contact with the man opposite him.

Stroud made a mocking imitation of the midshipman's bow. "At your service, sir. Now I demand you let us go. It is Spanish cargo we carry, of no concern to you."

Phin flipped through the papers. "Well, you are from Maine and your cargo belongs to Spain, sir, we grant you that."

Hudgins inclined his head. "Which means we have the honor of offering you a tow to Cienfuegos, Captain Stroud, where we can turn your cargo over to the proper authorities and deliver you to a United States consulate before dealing with your ship."

Sputtering, face gone red, Stroud took one menacing step toward Hudgins. "Pirating rebels!"

Given the tic in Hudgins's jaw, the prize master didn't take kindly to his years at the Naval Academy being tainted by such a misnomer. Phin edged forward, putting his shoulder just a bit in front of Hudgins, and fastened on a smile that would hopefully calm his superior even as it taunted Stroud. "Perhaps if you mean in the tradition of the Sons of Liberty."

"How dare you liken yourselves to the Patriots?" The captain rolled back his shoulders and tugged down his coat, gaze sizzling. "Those who prey on innocent merchant vessels simply because of the flag they fly are pirates, pure and simple."

Hudgins's hand landed on Phin's shoulder. Friendly and tense all at once. "Dunn, see to the tow. I'm going to escort Captain Stroud and his crew to his cabin, where they will remain under guard until we can deliver them to their consulate."

Phin turned, but not before the disdain seething through Stroud sent a frisson of warning up his spine. He glanced at the two marines with them, at Spencer and Davidson.

They'd have to be well on their guard until they reached Cuba.

Chapter Four

Salina stifled a delighted laugh at the closing line of Delia's latest story, covering her mouth with her hand to keep from being overheard. How did she come up with such things? Grand adventure, sweet romance, enduring love . . . such fanciful ideas. As idealistic as their author.

Completely outside Salina's experience, but still she loved to hear Delia read them to her or—better still—read them herself.

Though she'd been prepared to make notes of any outright mistakes, she straightened the papers without leaving a mark. Sure and there were some notes she could have made about the characters and their viewpoints, but why point out the ugly side of things that Miss Delia couldn't see? She'd ignored them because she didn't know nothing about them, and Salina would just as soon leave it that way. She'd tell her the story was perfect just as soon as she got home.

In the meantime, work enough waited to keep her busy. Salina gathered up the clothes ready to go to the laundress and employed her hip to open the door. A spiritual hummed its way out of her throat, the same one her *murruh* had always sung to her on the Owenses' plantation.

With the missus and her daughters out for the morning, the house had relaxed, its gray bricks all but sighing. Salina padded down the back stairs without caring whether she made any noise, smiling at the loud Gullah banter that came from the kitchen. When she entered, both the cook and the laundress looked up.

"Is you bringin me mo work there, Salina girl?"

She grinned at the hired laundress, who was sorting through a mound of rumpled cotton while she and the cook gossiped. "We can all use more work, ain't that right, Fanny?"

The wiry cook snorted and nodded toward the pile. "Sure and right, gal. Put it on down for Emmy and git yo'self out the way. Them there roses Miss Delia favors be bloomin, and I reckon she'd like it if some was waitin in her room."

"You be a smaa't one, Fanny." She added Delia's clothes to the pile and waved her farewell as she stepped out into the blistering July sunshine. She sure missed going to the mountains this summer. But she wouldn't complain, no sir. If she gave the missus an excuse, she'd be in the rice fields yet, where death came so slow you wished it would hurry, and so fast you never got to meet your own children.

My, but she wished Mr. Phin had married Delia before he went off to fight the Yankees. Then she'd be away from here. To a place with its own set of problems, sure enough. But it couldn't be bad as this, with a snake ready to bite her heel if she took a single misstep.

"Salina."

Speaking of missteps . . . She sighed to a halt halfway to the rose bushes. Ought to have known Big Tom would be out here, it being his domain, but he was usually tending the flowers round the front of the house this time of day. "Tom, what you doin back here?"

The young gardener emerged from behind the trellis, his straw hat casting a shadow across his handsome face. Salina forced a swallow down her parched throat. When the master bought Big Tom last year, she'd thought him the best looking man she'd ever set eyes upon. He wasn't so tall as his name might make you think, but he was broad with muscles, and so intense all the time that he seemed bigger than he was.

She always felt like corn mush around him, though she wasn't about to let him know it. He had half the maids in Savannah sighing over him, and rumors abounded about the trouble he led them willingly into.

She didn't mean to be one of them.

He slid to her side, closer than he ought to have gotten. No, he wasn't so tall, but still he towered over her. She took a step back, folded her arms over her chest, and prayed the good Lord he wouldn't see what his nearness did to her.

"I's right where I s'pposed to be. Question is, where you disappear to last night, ooman?"

Salina straightened her spine to make up for the fact that her knees went plumb weak when that smooth, deep voice of his wound its way into her ears. "I had to check on Miss Delia."

She shouldn't have glanced up into his eyes—those warm cinnamon depths sparked with knowing. He eased a little closer. "Now, Salina, we both know Miss Delia don't never need you that late. Not skay'd of me, are ya?"

Scared? Not in the way he meant. Her eyes slid shut. "Tom, I done told you to keep your distance. Ain't nothing gonna come here."

"Why?" His fingers brushed her cheek. They smelled of warm earth and green life. "You kin't tell me you don't like me, sweethaa't. I see it in yo eyes—when you dare to look at me."

"Don't matter what I like." She pulled away because she had to, even turned toward the roses again, and reminded herself of all the reasons to stay clear of him. "'Tain't allowed."

His snort followed her, his shadow keeping pace and holding her in its arms as she walked. "Massuhs don't never mind if their slaves get married, Salina. You breed, you just give 'em more slaves."

His voice went flintier with each word, and his shadow settled beside her, arms stopping at the elbow like they were crossed. She didn't dare look at him again and focused instead on the roses—though she hadn't thought to bring anything to cut them with. "Married, is it? That what you said to Abbie and Josie and—"

"Ah, that different. *Yo* different, Salina. Give me the word, and I settle right down. Give the massuh more slaves."

She shook her head. Even if she wanted to believe that—and she wasn't enough of a simpleton to—it wouldn't have mattered. "Ain't the way it is for me. The master—"

"Tell me he don't touch you." Tom grabbed her shoulder, spun her around. His eyes burned bright as the summer sun. "If he do, I . . . we kin get away, Salina. I heard them Yankees will welcome any of us that can reach their lines, welcome us wif open arms."

"No. Tom." She gripped his wrists and prayed her words could convey even a portion of the unease that idea sparked inside her. "You run away, the massuh don't just wait for you to come back and laugh it off as a lark, give you a few days in a holding yard when you wander back. You run away, you get kilt. Ain't worth the risk."

"Ain't it?" He pulled her closer, bent down till their noses nearly touched. "Don't you wanna be free?"

Free. A stranger word she'd never heard. How many songs had she learned as a child that spoke secretly of an elusive freedom? How many covered the desire to escape the master, using the words of spiritual freedom that the white man couldn't argue with, since he was the one who taught it to them?

But it wasn't so simple. Not for her. She drew in a deep breath and met Big Tom's probing gaze. "My murruh always told me family be the most important thing in the world. That freedom ain't worth two cents if you can't share it with the ones you love."

He nodded. "'Course. But you ain't got no family here, Salina.

I asked Fanny, and she say yo aunt's yo only family left, and she's on a rice plantation somewheres."

The Owenses' rice plantation, to be exact. "I got family here." When he frowned, she wet her lips and wondered if she dare speak the words that ought never be spoken. Seeing the determination in his eyes, she suspected it might be the only way to convince him to let his fool ideas go. "The master don't never touch me, Tom. It was my murruh he wanted."

His hands fell away, and his eyes went wide. And flat. "Mass Owens be yo' . . . but . . . they say you didn't come here till you was ten."

"From his plantation. I lived there with Murruh till she died, then he brought me here."

He backed away a step. "I knew . . . ain't no secret you a mulatto, bein so light. I jest didn't . . . yo' his blood."

And there, that was the single fact that made her life less her own than any other slave in the house. They at least had the dream of freedom, of escape, of the whispers from the North, of that big long word that the whole South was willing to fight against—*emancipation*. But even if slavery were no more, Salina knew she wouldn't leave. Couldn't. Not when her best friend who might not even know they were sisters was still here, still needing her.

Not when her mother's people kept backing away when they realized she was the master's child, and that he acknowledged it enough to keep his promise to her murruh to see after her. To make sure she was never sold, never put in hard labor. When he gave her to the daughter she most loved and said she could stay right there beside her all her days.

Assuming he didn't die anytime soon, or the missus would send her away in half a flicker. She knew who Salina's father was, for sure and certain. And hated her for it.

Tom slid another step away but then halted, and his face went more determined than ever. "Still. If'n you *wanted* to—"

"I don't, Tom. I can't."

Footsteps sounded from the direction of the house, and when the master stepped into the garden, Salina was real glad Tom had dropped his hands and stood a good space away now. Especially when Mass Owens arched his brows in that way that meant you better answer just as he wanted. "Is there a problem, Salina?"

Tom swept his hat off, bowed just a bit, and put it back on. "No suh, Mass Owens. I jest goin to get her some shears for them there roses for your Miss Delia is all."

"Then you might as well cut them for her too and deliver them to the kitchen. Salina." He held an arm outstretched toward the door he'd just come through. Command masked in invitation.

She didn't even dare look at Tom to send him a silent goodbye, just tucked her head down and hurried toward the house.

Mass Owens fell in behind her but stopped her a ways from the door with a gentle hand on her elbow. "Look at me, Salina."

A deep breath was needed before she could manage it. She made a conscious effort to keep the Gullah from her speech, since he had asked her repeatedly not to speak her mother's language in his presence. "Yes, sir?"

He glanced at the garden again. "Is Big Tom giving you trouble? If he is, I can send him elsewhere."

She measured out her response like a coveted spice. Not too fast, not too slow. "No, sir. I've taken care of it. He meant no harm and won't bother me again." Even if some silly part of her, the part just like Abbie and Josie, wanted him to. Wanted, at least, to go squealing to a friend that the most handsome man in all Savannah had offered to run off with *her*.

Mass Owens seemed to hear what she didn't say as much as what she did. "I know best, Salina. It may not seem so to you, but I do. And the best thing for you is to go with Delia."

"Yes, sir, I know." She did, when it came to that.

But it was the part that always came next that dimmed her every tomorrow. The part she saw even now boiling behind his eyes.

He drew in a long breath and inclined his head. "And even then, you're not to wed a Negro, you know that. I won't be your master once she marries, but I'll still be your father, and you'll honor my wishes. You hear?"

He'd said it before. The first time hearing him call himself her father had been such a thrill—he'd never put voice to it before—that she'd scarce paid any mind to what it was he commanded.

But the meaning had struck harder each of the three times he'd reiterated it. Murruh had apparently been good enough to bed, but he couldn't bear the thought of his blood being bound to a black man—though heaven knew he'd never sanction her wedding a white man neither. No, she'd pay for his sin by being forever on the outside looking in, not suited for the people of either of her parents.

Oh, to be in one of Miss Delia's stories, with all her happy endings, where the uglies didn't exist or were neatly defeated by the end of the tale. Oh, to be a bird that could fly away and build its nest wherever it wanted. Oh, to be either black or white, to have a place.

"You'll have a good life with Delia. Rich and full, she'll see to that." Mass Owens looked as though he might reach out and touch her cheek, or maybe chuck her under the chin. He didn't, of course.

"I know she will, sir. And I wouldn't want to be no—I mean, anywhere but with her." Not to say she wouldn't like to be with her and have a family of her own too. But it would have to be enough to be Delia's companion. Maybe mammy to her children.

It would have to be enough . . . even if it wasn't.

He nodded and preceded her into the house, apparently satisfied that his orders would be obeyed. As always.

Salina sighed and let her gaze move beyond the gardens, out to the sandy street with its folk bustling by. You could always spot the longtime Savannahians by their hunched shuffle, a result of plodding year after year through the foot-deep sand that served as pavement. Seemed most of the men out and about these days were soldiers or militiamen, decked out in their spiffy uniforms.

Whenever Miss Delia and Miss Lacy had other young misses over, they talked of little but the floods of handsome bucks, who in turn seemed more interested in courting the few reputable ladies left in the city than in protecting anything from the Yankees stationed off the coast.

Maybe Miss Delia would fall for one of them, one who would marry her now. Maybe . . . oh, who was she fooling? There wasn't anyone for Miss Delia but Mr. Phin. Salina could tell that sure enough by the way her green eyes went all dreamy whenever his name came up. And all her stories lately seemed to have a certain type of hero.

Her sister was in love. It made Salina grin, at least for a moment. Until that terrible dream swept over her again. Put her in mind of the tales her aunt used to tell, though she knew now such happenings came from the Lord Almighty, not the spirits Aunt Lila used to talk about.

She closed her eyes and let the dream images wash through her mind. "Protect Miss Delia's man, Lord God above. Lift him out of those troubled waters, fly him far away from danger and sorrow. Bring him back to her, if you please. Bring him back so he can take us away. Far, far away from danger and sorrow."

"This is the stupidest piece of nonsense I've ever read, and I will *not* make a fool of myself by being in it."

Cordelia's eyes went wide with disbelief when Annaleigh Young snatched up the copy of the tableaux vivants that Cordelia had copied with painstaking care for her. Coffee-brown curls bouncing, Annaleigh sneered at the story and rent it in two. The paper seemed to weep as it ripped.

Or perhaps that was Cordelia. She covered her mouth to keep her gasp from being followed by a squeal. It was only paper and ink. Never mind that the ink formed *her* words, *her* story, and that it had taken an hour to transcribe each copy.

Annaleigh tossed the shreds to the ground and stomped to the window, her bell skirt swaying.

Hateful creature. Petulant child.

"Annaleigh!" Sassy Dunn swished her fan before her and scowled at Annaleigh's back. "What a mean thing to say. Especially since we all know it isn't the story you have a problem with, only the fact that you will not be in the center of the stage so much as Lacy."

Cordelia's sister rolled her eyes. "Fiddle-faddle. We can trade parts if that will make you stop this nonsense, Annaleigh."

Cordelia's chest went tight as the girl raised her chin and turned just enough to look down her nose at them. She looked the perfect villain. All cool disdain over that roiling venom that flowed where her blood ought to have been.

"You could not persuade me to take part," the villainess said on a long drawl, "were you to offer me *all* the places. It's nothing but a bunch of romantic claptrap, unsuitable for young ladies to be reading at all, much less portraying before all Savannah. Why, I shouldn't even *look* at some of the artwork we're supposed to be presenting in live form, and with that story she wrote to tie them together . . . it's as bad as a novel."

Try as she might, Cordelia couldn't keep her eyes from narrowing, her lips from pressing into a thin line. And now that she thought of it, Annaleigh's hair wasn't coffee brown at all. It was dark as murderous midnight and would be better suited to having snakes curl through it rather than ribbons and lace. No doubt she had a vial of poison hidden in the bodice of her gown too.

Lacy's sigh carried a note of exasperation. "Oh, Annie, don't act this way. It's not for our own good we're doing it, after all—it's to raise funds for the soldiers, for the Confederacy. Who's to say if our contribution doesn't pay for a weapon that turns the tide of a battle? Or even the war?"

Annaleigh sniffed. Probably mentally murmured some ancient curse to fall about poor Lacy's head too. "I shall consider it. That is all I can promise." No doubt those innocent words were code for something far more sinister—she was probably calling her minions down upon them even now.

When the door squeaked open behind her, Cordelia jumped and half expected to see her imagined toadies marching in. But no, it was only a black woman with a tea tray in hand.

The new figure ought not to have garnered any attention, but Cordelia found herself watching her. And not just because of Cordelia's silly fancies. There was something in this woman that made her think a story lurked. Something about the stick-straight posture, the defiant roll of her shoulders, the stubborn light in her eyes. Not at all what one usually saw in a servant. She didn't move with the silent motions meant to go unnoticed, nor did she slide the tray onto the table without a clatter.

No indeed, she all but plunked it down, and then she turned to Annaleigh with a brazen lift of her brow. "Do ya be needin anythin else, miss?" She spoke in an accent Cordelia hadn't heard before. Not the Gullah from the Low Country, not the more structured patterns some in the city used.

Annaleigh didn't so much as glance at the tray. "Lemon."

"There is some there already."

"Bring more, then."

The black woman's lips parted, gleaming with disgust, but then she clamped her mouth closed and nearly stomped from the room.

Yes, definitely a story there. Though it might be as simple as being fed up with a surly mistress.

"Stupid creature." Annaleigh flounced back over to her seat beside Sassy. "I do declare, Pa ought to have sent her to the rice fields rather than keeping her here—and will yet, if I have anything to say about it."

Sassy turned her face Cordelia's way and gave her a wide-eyed stare that begged her to change the subject.

There was nothing in the world like shared emotions to restore Cordelia's cheer. She grinned. Why pass up even the smallest opportunity to play the role of heroine? "Have you heard from your brother lately, Sassy?"

"Not directly, no." But she smiled and smoothed back her sleek, honey-colored hair, though it needed no smoothing. "Daddy read a report that the CSS *Sumter* finally broke through the blockade, though, and is in open water. Apparently it caused quite a fuss among the Yankees."

"Blockade running!" Annaleigh snapped open her fan and gave it a vigorous swish. "Oh, it's so dangerous. I hate to even *think* of dear Phin in such a situation."

Dear Phin? Why, if that little ninny had any designs on him . . . well, it didn't matter. He was Delia's beau. She was the one with the right to dream of him, she was the one he was writing to, she was the one he'd asked to wait for him. Cordelia tilted her head a bit and folded her hands in her lap. "Really? But just imagine the adventure he's having. I hear the mouth of the Mississippi is a treacherous place, unable to be navigated by any but the most experienced pilots. And it can't have been easy to find one, what with the Yankees patrolling the waters."

She leaned forward, a smile tickling her lips. "I imagine he and his crew had to sneak by them in the dead of night. The sultry, brackish air would have been hanging heavy over them, the eerie light from the full moon shining down on their deck. And they'd have been praying for a cloud. A whole bank of clouds to block that traitorous moonlight."

Sassy lifted her hoop just enough to make a quick move from

Annaleigh's couch to Cordelia's. "Did it come? Or did they have to make a run for it?"

"They could see the cover they needed building on the horizon, but it was still hours away. '*Gentlemen*,' their captain said as he paced the deck before them, '*it is time to beseech the Almighty for a way to be made for us—and to go out and search for our prophet who can lead us toward it. We must find a pilot*.' And so he appointed a scouting party to put down on a little island close by." She paused, frowned. Were there little islands in the mouth of the Mississippi? "And at the head of it, of course, was the favorite among the crew—Mr. Phineas Dunn."

Lacy gave a little clap and edged closer, expression enthralled. "Keep going, Delia. Did they find their prophet-pilot?"

Oh heavens, she hoped so. And that no giant squids were involved. Pasting on her most mysterious smile, she pitched her voice low. "Well, he led his men into the thick undergrowth of the island, with only that cursed moonlight to illumine his path. . . ."

Chapter Five

Phin tossed a few more pieces of jerky onto the tray and deemed it good enough for the prisoner crew. He made no pretense of being a ship's cook, and so they'd have to settle for what was on hand—a few hard biscuits, the jerky, and a couple shriveled apples.

Unfortunately, the prize crew would have to settle for the same until they made it to Cienfuegos and rejoined the *Sumter*. For the sake of his friends aboard the second ship they'd captured, he hoped they had better fare on the *Machias*.

He strode from the galley toward the captain's cabin, where the *Cuba*'s men were being held. Spencer had been assigned the task of guarding them, along with Davidson.

Yet the passageway outside the cabin was empty. Where the devil were the men?

He didn't know whether to be relieved or irritated when he heard Spencer's voice coming from within the cabin. "Do I have your word as a gentleman?"

"You do." Stroud's voice, calm and low.

Phin snorted even as something went tight in his chest. He didn't know what Spencer was talking to this man about, but he sure hoped his friend realized that no Yankee really knew the meaning of the word *gentleman*. Each and every one he'd met put higher stock in his own goals than in honor—which was why they were now at war with them. Had the Northerners abided by their word to let the South live as it desired, to determine its own laws and fix its own mistakes and live its own way . . .

He toed open the door and set the tray down upon a table with a bit more clanging than necessary, then sent his closest friend an arch glance. "Everything all right in here, Spence?"

Was it his imagination, or was Spencer's smile too bright? "Just fine, Dunn, just fine. Davidson and I were asking the captain about the, uh, company to be found in Cienfuegos. Not sure he's directed us to the right place though."

He glanced to Stroud, whose mustache twitched. The man was seated at his desk, unbound, on the assumption that he could do no harm without a weapon. Like saying a snake couldn't harm you if you had it by the tail, in Phin's opinion.

He scanned the rest of the room, not missing the way Davidson seemed to find the ceiling so very interesting. Then Phin nodded at Spencer. "You'd better get back outside before Hudgins comes by."

"Good idea. Gentlemen, enjoy your . . . meal, if that's what we're calling it. This the best you could do, Dunn?" Spencer's grin looked right this time, natural.

Maybe it *had* been his imagination—or maybe the man was just embarrassed at having been caught talking to a Yankee about where to find intimate company in Cuba. He *ought* to be . . . but that wasn't his usual way.

Phin mustered up a smile of his own. "Careful, sir, or you'll offend my honor and I'll have to call you out."

Spencer laughed and slapped a hand to Phin's shoulder that propelled him out the door. "I'll guard my tongue. Captain, gentlemen."

The three stepped into the hall, and Spencer pulled the door shut and turned the key in it.

Phin shook his head. "You're lucky it was me who came by and not Hudgins."

"Probably. But no harm done." Spencer reclined against the door. "Please tell me there's better food than that for *us*."

"I'll do what I can." With a smile and wave, he headed for the stairs leading topside. Before he headed back to the galley, he needed to get this foul taste out of his mouth. Thankfully, he spotted the prize master at the rail. "Hudgins."

His superior turned around with a welcoming smile. "Dunn. All well below?"

Phin leaned onto the railing, bracing his forearms against it. Another cloudy night hovered over them, blocking the light of the moon and holding in the muggy heat. "Probably fine."

Hudgins arched a brow.

Phin sighed. The last thing he wanted to do was get his friends in trouble, but he needed to hear the prize master tell him all was well. "It's just Spencer. He and Davidson were in the cabin talking to the captain. Harmless, according to Spence, but it makes me uneasy."

"Hmm." Hudgins pursed his lips and stared out at the *Sumter* just ahead of them. "Not the wisest behavior, to be sure. But he's just a sailor, a merchant—not accustomed to the ways of war."

"I'm a merchant sailor myself, sir, and you wouldn't find me having an amiable conversation with the enemy."

The midshipman chuckled. "I tend to forget you're not trained in the military. You've taken to it better than the others. We'll keep an eye on Spencer and Davidson and make sure they don't act that way again. For now, why don't you get some sleep? I'll take first watch, and then you can relieve me."

"Yes, sir." Phin straightened, saluted, and headed below once more, happy to let someone else deal with meals for the prize crew—for his part, he had no appetite. But as he settled into the borrowed hammock, he couldn't shake the feeling that rest wasn't what he needed either.

Delia's face crowded his mind when he shut his eyes, those big green eyes gleaming, her kissable lips set in a concerned frown. How was it that he'd left home so many times before and never missed any one person more than another, yet now her image was always there? A bittersweet ache took up residence in his chest.

He let himself relive that moment when he drew her into his arms. Her tiny waist under his hands, the scent of lilac water drifting to his nose. The look in her eyes—hope and desire, surprise and fear.

Was she waiting for him like she promised? Or had her father already persuaded her to bestow her sunshine smiles on someone else?

He felt himself drifting off with that question spinning round his mind. His dreams were a muddled jumble of swaying skirts and her light laughter, and of other uniformed men pulling her into a dance or under that live oak in her garden. *Their* tree. He tried to move forward to reclaim her, snatch her from the faceless man's arms, but he couldn't find his footing. It was like the ground had become an ocean.

"*Sumter* men! On deck, now!"

He jerked awake, and it took only a second to realize it was the Caribbean heaving under him, not the rich Georgian soil. Phin leapt down and raced topside, where the wind gusted hot over him and waves pounded the *Cuba*'s hull.

Hudgins motioned him over. "They cut our line—the *Machias*'s tow snapped, and the *Sumter* had to catch her. They signaled us to continue into Cienfuegos on our own. Take the wheel, Dunn, heading north by northeast."

"Aye, sir." He spun toward the wheel—and came up short when he saw the muzzle of a pistol pointed at his face.

"Belay that, Mr. Dunn." Captain Stroud cocked the gun and stepped into the circle of lantern light. "I'll be taking my ship back now."

Phin heard a curse from behind him but was a bit more concerned with the pistol just now. He sketched a bow, sweeping his arm out in a grand gesture. But rather than just tuck it to his chest, he grabbed his own sidearm and came up with it leveled at Stroud. “It’s my honor to inform you that you’re mistaken, Captain.”

Hurried footsteps sounded from every direction, and Hudgins darted across Phin’s periphery. “Davidson! Spencer! Get those prisoners back belowdecks!”

But when Spencer stepped up behind Stroud, weapon raised, he didn’t point it at the Yankee captain.

He leveled it on Phin.

Hope sank into his stomach and turned to wormwood. “Spence?”

“Sorry, Phin.” His friend gulped and stepped up beside the Yankee. “It’s nothing personal.”

Nothing personal? His closest friend was betraying all they stood for, and he called it *nothing personal*? Phin edged back a step. “Call me antiquated, but I’m afraid I do take it personally when someone holds a gun on me.”

More running footsteps reached his ears, along with the crash of a wave. From the direction of the mainmast he heard one of the marines call, “We’re with you, sir!”

So the treachery was limited to Spencer and Davidson. Small comfort.

He had to get clear of Stroud and Spence, make his way over to Hudgins and the marine. They’d have a better chance of regaining the upper hand if they could cover one another. Hopefully that wouldn’t require him raising *his* gun against his friend. Spence might have no difficulty doing so, but Phin sure would.

Before he could determine a sound plan, a gunshot blasted from near the wheel. Lightning echoed it above them, its slice of light illumining full-blown panic on the deck. Not exactly the opportunity he had hoped for, but he wasn't about to let it pass him by.

He lunged away, his glance raking the deck as he went. He spotted Hudgins climbing the mainmast, no doubt so he could see the rebelling crew all at once. Their marines stood in position below him, one firing at whomever had taken a shot from the wheel.

"Phin, stop!" Spencer shouted into the wind.

"Let him run." Stroud's words slicked over him like ice.

His party was only twenty feet away. A few more seconds, a few more running steps.

He saw the wide eyes of one of the marines as he looked over Phin's shoulder. Heard the crack from behind. Felt the impact in his leg, the pain exploding like a cannonball as flesh ripped away.

A scream wrenched its way from his throat. He tried to catch himself, to put his weight on his good leg so he could keep moving. But he slipped, his boots finding no purchase on the spray-soaked deck that even then pitched on another swell. Was anyone steering the brig through the rising waves?

Lightning flashed again. Brilliant, blinding. Thunder rolled through the heavens and from the guns.

His pistol fell from his hand as he crashed into the rail. His fingers curled around the wood. The ship rose again, forcing him to hold on or be sent tumbling still more.

His leg throbbed in time to the night. Was it his vision that went blurry, or just the darkness and ocean's spray that made it seem so?

Another bullet tore into the rail, inches from his fingers, and he jerked away. Tried to put weight on his injured leg.

Stars burst before his eyes as he buckled. Dizzy, so dizzy. He couldn't tell where the water came from, or where the wood under his feet had gone. Blackness seemed to wait everywhere when those stars faded.

Delia's fingers were in his hands again, her eyes bright and glistening. *"Don't go."*

He tried to hold on to her—had to hold on. But he didn't want to pull her down with him, did he? Not here. Not into the gunfire and convulsing sea. He relaxed his grip.

"Dunn! No!" Hudgins?

No, Delia. *Don't go, Phin. Don't go.*

The water enfolded him, warm as a dream, and silenced the thunder of traitors.

"Not in there, Cordelia. Not today."

Cordelia came to a halt on the sidewalk, unable to tear her gaze away from the shop specializing in books, old and new. "But, Mama—"

"*Please*, daughter." Mama lifted a hand to her forehead and adjusted the angle of her parasol as their servant boy waited behind them. "Do I not indulge your unfashionable whims often enough? Do you not spend a shameful number of hours each day closeted up with your inks and papers and novels? You needn't drag me in these places with you when we are supposed to be seeing what silks the runners have managed to bring us."

Guilt pricked her as she noted the flush on her mother's cheeks and the genuine distress on her face. Yet she *needed* the written word, needed it like Mama did her smelling salts. Especially on a day like today, when a second dream, identical to the first, wouldn't leave her mind. Was a few hours' escape such a terrible thing to ask? "But, Mama, I've read all the ones at home, and Daddy said I may buy a new one."

"Not today." Mama's eyes snapped and crackled like blue flames. "I do declare, Ginny never asked me to take her such places, and Lacy wouldn't either, if you didn't drag her along wherever you go. Don't you realize people are talking, Cordelia? Why, according to Ellen Young, the Dunns hope Phin does, in fact, *not* propose to you, as you're so eccentric. She claimed Willametta Dunn said as much last week."

Eccentric? People really thought her eccentric just because she enjoyed reading and telling stories? Cordelia's throat went tight. Not everyone, surely. People always seemed so entertained by her tales, and she didn't lack for friends—friends who often *asked* her to regale them with a yarn. And there, right across the street, was a band of officers staring at her. She wouldn't lack for beaux either, if she encouraged any of them.

But then, the Dunns' opinions meant more than those of any random passersby. If Mrs. Dunn had really said that, if it weren't just the sour musings of a dour-faced Mrs. Young, then Mama was right to be concerned. She'd never considered that her reputation may be in danger because of her love of literature.

"I'm sorry, Mama." Her voice came in a hush, no doubt as low and pained to her mother's ears as to her own. "I didn't realize."

Mama sighed and reached over to brush a gloved hand along Cordelia's cheek. "What the Dunns think is not all that important—there are better men out there for you than Phin—but you must take care. In proper measure your oddities can be endearing, but you must remember to temper it with the grace and breeding we have worked so hard to establish in you, and not ruin it by too-frequent trips to bookstores."

Better men than Phin? Never! Yet if anyone's advice on what would keep a man's attention could be trusted, it was Mama's. Emeline Owens was still regarded as an outstanding beauty and had grown only more elegant with age, according to the portraits in their home. Daddy had been the catch of the generation, she knew—and Mama had captured his heart with enviable skill. Even foul-tempered Great-Grandmama Penelope had liked her, which was such a feat that stories were still told of it at family gatherings.

"I shall endeavor to do better, Mama."

"That's my girl." Mama fastened on a smile and nodded them onward with a huff. "Oh, this wretched heat. It's livable only to the slaves. How I wish this dreadful war hadn't ruined our summer plans."

"I'm sure Daddy would be happy to send us elsewhere." She said it largely because she knew exactly what reaction she would get.

Mama didn't disappoint her. She rolled back her narrow shoulders and lifted her sculpted chin, looking as though she could face down the enemy army singlehandedly. "Fiddle-faddle. It's one thing to summer elsewhere when all is well and we are free to enjoy ourselves, but let it never be said that Emeline Owens flees from trial the moment it presents itself. No Yankee fleet will force me from my home, and if I must remain in it to be certain it remains mine, then so be it."

Cordelia smiled, though her eyes went unfocused. Mama could make a perfect heroine with a bit of editing. She could see her now, standing on a . . . a windswept moor. Or perhaps a bluff overlooking the sea, an ancient castle behind her. Yes, that was it—a crumbling castle that had stood long and proud on the promontory, held for centuries by some noble family, of which she was the sole survivor. An enemy king had his ships just outside, and an army surrounded her on land too. But she would go out to face them down, her golden hair tossed by the wind, eyes glinting with a brave determination that would, obviously, capture the warrior-king's heart.

"Cordelia!"

She snapped back to the present and saw that they had arrived at her mother's favorite shop, and that Mama stood impatiently in the doorway while their boy held the door open. A flush heating her cheeks, Cordelia rushed past young Micah and decided to be grateful that another lecture wouldn't be forthcoming inside the store.

When had she last come in here? Definitely not long ago, but she nearly gaped at how bare the shelves were. They'd felt no lack in matters of food, produce arriving from the plantations without hindrance, but the blockade was obviously interfering with the textiles and lace Mama so loved.

Mama muttered a choice phrase about the Yankees that included a word Cordelia had been forbidden to use under normal circumstances. Somehow she suspected she'd be forgiven its use in the same context.

Of course, she would have to deliver it correctly. Could she muster such total disdain in two little words? Convey such antipathy in the syllables of *Yankee*, and condemn them to the devil with such calm assurance? She would have to practice to get it right.

Except she wouldn't dare. Perhaps she could compromise with *Blasted Yankees*. Though even that was a stronger word than she was wont to use.

Mama motioned her over and held up a bolt of pale pink silk under Cordelia's chin. Then shook her head and replaced it. "Blue or green would suit you better, but they haven't any. What are you planning to use as costuming for your tableaux vivants?"

"Lacy and I were going to have Salina help us remake some of Grandmother's old gowns. Assuming it goes ahead, which it may not if Annaleigh won't take part."

"Oh, never mind her." Mama waved a dismissive hand and sorted through the sparse selection of lace. "She'll never allow herself to be excluded, so will fall in line. And your father promised he would see about having it at the Pulaski House."

The thought of her tale being performed in the city's most famous hotel was enough to send her into palpitations. "That would be . . . if we could, I . . . words fail me."

Mama laughed, bright as a chime. "Now that, my dear, is a landmark event. Come." She headed toward the front of the shop again. "There's nothing here worthwhile. Let's head over to Pulaski House now to remind ourselves of its layout, and we can have a lemonade while we're there. I do hope the Morgans will have delivered Lacy home by the time we return."

The sun beat down with frightful intensity when she stepped outside, so blinding that she flinched and squeezed her eyes shut. She heard Micah opening her parasol for her, but it was movement from the other direction that brought her eyes open again, just as a collision sent her skirt swaying.

"Oh, pardon me!" The voice was deep and genteel, though when Cordelia looked up, she could scarcely make out anything about the man except that he wore a Confederate uniform. The sun cast all else in deep shadow. "My deepest apologies, miss. I wasn't watching where I was going."

He had a nice voice, even if it lacked that perfection that was Phin's. Cordelia called up a smile and was grateful when Micah held out the parasol. "No harm done, sir. I shouldn't have stopped as I did."

The man angled a bit to take in Mama, and in so doing revealed a nicely chiseled face. He bowed to them both, then frowned as he regarded her mother. "Pardon me, ma'am, for being so forward, but could it be that you are Emeline Owens?"

Mama arched her brows and allowed the barest of smiles, though Cordelia saw the sparkle in her eyes, the one that enjoyed being recognized by complete strangers. "I am, sir. May I ask how you know me?"

When he smiled, the officer revealed a row of perfect white teeth. "You bear a remarkable resemblance to my mother. I am your cousin—distantly, I grant you. Georgette's son, Julius James. When we realized I would be posted in Savannah, she gave me your name and address, though I'm afraid I haven't had the chance to call formally. I only just arrived on Wednesday."

Mama's eyes lit so brightly that Cordelia got a tingle of warning up her spine. That particular glint only surfaced in her matron's gaze with the emergence of matchmaking possibilities.

Oh, Lord above, let it be Lacy she thinks him perfect for.

"Julius, of course! How wonderful to see you again—why, it's been so long I'm embarrassed to name the number of years. My darling Delia here was only a babe."

His gaze meandered her way again, those white teeth still gleaming. Really, who had teeth that white? And a jaw so square? And she had no use for shoulders quite so broad.

Though he *would* make a fine model for the warrior-king in her mother's castle story. She would have to make the heroine resemble Lacy more than Mama, now that she thought of it. But with their mother's strength and wit.

And piercing glare.

Had she missed something? Cordelia cleared her throat and snapped open her fan. "I'm afraid I don't recall any visits with your cousin Georgette, Mama. Though I do enjoy hearing her letters."

Apparently she hadn't missed anything vital, as Mama smiled and relaxed, then motioned toward the street. "Would you walk with us a ways, Julius? We were just going to treat ourselves to a lemonade at Pulaski House before heading home. You could join us, if you have the time."

Surely he wouldn't. An officer newly arrived in the city—he must have scores of tasks to attend to. Men to order around. Weapons to polish or clean or whatever it was one did with them so they might shoot at the Yankees. The *blasted* Yankees. The d—no, she couldn't even think the word.

"I would be delighted." His words were aimed at Mama, but his gaze was on Cordelia.

Drat. And her mother looked far too pleased. But never mind. She would remind Mama later that she had promised to wait for Phin and nudge the more eligible daughter forward. Lacy would fawn over Julius's fine features and bat her lashes at him just so when he visited their house, which would in turn win his devotion.

Yes, a perfect plan after all.

He offered them each an elbow. Mama preened while she tucked her hand into the crook, but Cordelia managed only a polite smile.

"How fortunate that I came across you this way. I did dread the thought of showing up on your doorstep without invitation."

Mama laughed. "Oh, family needs no invitation! Georgette's son is always welcome in our home and at our table. You must dine with us the first evening you have free. Mr. Owens will be very glad to make the acquaintance of another fine officer who can feed him gossip on the war, and of course my daughters will be pleased to get to know another cousin. Isn't that right, Cordelia?"

"Of course, Mama." All the more so if that glint in her eyes would just *go away*.

Julius angled a smile Cordelia's way that was nearly as warm as the July sun. "I'm certainly looking forward to making the acquaintance of my lovely cousins as well. You have three daughters, Mrs. Owens, do you not?"

"Indeed I do, Julius dear. Our Ginny just wed in May—a hurried event, as you can well imagine, before her Charlie signed up. She fled Savannah with her husband's family last month. But Cordelia, Lacy, and I are determined to stay as long as Mr. Owens does."

"Admirable, ma'am. Thus far my family feels secure on our plantation outside Atlanta, but I know my mother would be hard-pressed to leave her home as well." His gaze wandered Cordelia's way again. "Do you still find enough by way of amusement in the city, Cousin, now that most of your friends would have left?"

Amusement? A war was on, and he thought she cared only

for her own amusement? Cordelia lifted her chin. "That is hardly my primary concern these days. Even so, those dearest to me have remained." Both Lacy and Sassy would be taken with him, she knew. No doubt he would be taken with one of them as well, once he met them.

And wouldn't that be a most delightful twist to the story? The warrior-king could have first met some other young lady nearby, perhaps a lady-in-waiting. He would be intrigued by her for a moment, but only until he met the lady of the castle, and then he would realize the other's beauty held no candle to the noblewoman's. Or perhaps it was the inner workings of the lady's character that would win him. That strength, that spine of steel.

No doubt Julius would admire Lacy's sweet disposition as much as her magnolia-fair skin. Unless, perhaps, he was the type to be more drawn to Sassy's wit and clever tongue, which would be equally acceptable in Cordelia's eyes, though Mama might protest. She tended to be possessive of possible matches for her daughters, and if Cordelia recalled correctly from cousin Georgette's letters, that branch of Mama's family owned the estate next to Belle Acres, the indigo plantation Mama had brought to the family as her dowry. Daddy would no doubt find that an alluring prospect. He went ever on about the need for more Southern families to build up empires that the North couldn't crush.

"We shall look for you tomorrow, then." The pleased finality in Mama's tone pulled Cordelia back again. "You can ride with us to Mr. Dunn's birthday ball. I'm afraid you'll find that social gatherings are not what they once were, but we are all determined that the Yankees shan't steal from us all of life's pleasures."

What? Mama had invited this stranger-cousin to Phin's house? Granted, he wouldn't be there, but still. It seemed wrong somehow.

Julius turned them toward Pulaski House when Mama indicated it. "It sounds delightful, ma'am. Are you sure it won't be an imposition for me to come to this ball?"

"Oh, the Dunns are good friends who would welcome another member of our family. I'll just send Willametta a note this afternoon."

They entered through the grand doors of the hotel and headed toward the dining room, where a servant soon showed them to a table by the window and promised the lemonades would be out directly.

Cordelia waited while Julius pulled out a chair for Mama, then lifted her own hoops just enough to sit without making them spring up.

Julius sat last, dwarfing his chair. "I must say, ma'am, it has been a true pleasure to familiarize myself with your fine city these past two days. It's a beautiful place."

"Why, thank you, Julius dear," Mama said as if she herself had designed each graceful brick building. "We are quite proud of it."

Certainly Savannah was lovely—but it was *home*. Cordelia would enjoy seeing a more interesting place one of these days. Like London or Paris. The Scottish Highlands, with that castle on a bluff, perhaps. Italy, where the Renaissance masters had thrived. Oh, maybe Istanbul or Arabia.

Or, if she must remain closer to home, the islands in the Caribbean would be enough of a change, or out on the Western frontier. Daddy read them the most amazing stories from out there.

New Orleans. New York.

No, not New York. Even in her daydreams she wasn't stupid. She'd find no happy welcome in the North.

At the warning cough from Mama, Cordelia refocused her gaze and pasted attentiveness on her face. Now, how could she give the impression that she was the boring and homely sister?

She put a bit of a hunch into her shoulders—hopefully not so much that her mother would notice it, just enough to contribute to an overall picture—and lowered her chin.

Probably too subtle. Ah! She had just the thing, borrowed from a secondary character in her last story. Which was, in turn, borrowed from a friend who had fled the city a month ago. Barely controlling a telltale smirk, she snapped open her fan, then snapped it shut again. Open, shut. Open, shut.

Mama blinked, long and meaningful. "Of course, Julius dear, both Cordelia and Lacy would be happy to save you a dance."

Open. "Of course." She put on Ginny's smile, the one that was all demure sweetness, which didn't suit Cordelia at all. "I'd be delighted." Shut.

Julius's smile had a nice charm to it, she had to admit. He and Lacy—or Sassy—would make a fetching couple. "I don't know how I shall properly thank you for your hospitality, ma'am."

Open, shut.

Mama smiled, though when Julius looked back to Cordelia, her smile was overshadowed by a glare so pointed she may as well have had a bayonet in hand.

Open—she lost her nerve and just fanned herself.

Small talk dominated the conversation as their lemonades were brought out, Mama and Julius updating each other on pertinent family news. Cordelia tried her best to keep from drawing the officer's attention with any sudden movements, since it seemed to take him far too long to look away again once his attention was on her. It was a relief when they all stood and he bowed his farewell.

"May I claim a waltz with you, Cousin?"

She made her smile tight and, she hoped, ugly. "I'm afraid I've promised them all already."

"Then I shall have to make do with a country dance." With another bow on his part, they parted ways.

Tomorrow night she'd be sure to wear that pink gown that didn't well complement her complexion and let Lacy borrow her pale green silk that she had been begging for.

"Oh my." Mama put extra gusto into the swish of her fan as they started for home. "I hadn't realized what a handsome man Julius had grown into. Isn't he delightful? And Georgette married into one of the best families in Atlanta. Their cotton plantation does quite well, and they own at least a hundred slaves. Julius is quite the catch—I can't imagine how the Atlanta ladies let him get away without one of them marrying him."

Cordelia accepted her parasol from Micah with a nod. "Perhaps he has some fatal flaw they all know of but we don't yet. Kleptomania, maybe."

Mama sighed. "Cordelia, really."

"Or pyromania."

"Cordelia!" Only Mama could manage to yell in such a hushed tone. "He suffers no kind of mania, I am sure."

Cordelia raised both brows and chin, just like Mama did when she was being condescending. "Well, of course we wouldn't think so after so short an introduction, but if there's a sudden rash of theft or fires . . ."

A low, muted chuckle slipped out before her mother's face regained its placidity. "Utter fiddle-faddle. He is a fine man from a fine family, and you would do well to consider him if those glances he sent you continue."

"Mama. I am all but betrothed to Phin."

"*All but* does not keep tongues from wagging, nor does it provide one with security and well-being." A hard gaze arrowed into her. "I'm not saying you must go back on your word to Phin here and now, mind you. Only that it is a wise woman who has a secondary plan."

A sigh slipped past her lips. "Don't you think Lacy will like him? And I imagine he will like her even better than he could me."

"I will not have my youngest daughter marrying before her elder sister. It would be a blight you may never live down, and if something were to happen to Phin . . ."

"Nothing will happen to Phin." She kept her tone strong, confident. But uncertainty quaked through her stomach, and she tasted the grit of sand in her mouth, felt that searing pain in her leg.

Oh, Phin, where are you today?

Chapter Six

Awareness crept in, slow and throbbing. The noises struck Phin first—waves lapping shore, gulls crying. Then the smell of salt air and rotting vegetation. Somewhere in the recesses of darkness, he had the impression that he ought to hold on to sleep as long as he could. Hold on to the night. Hold on to the oblivion with the same strength with which he vaguely recalled holding on to a bobbing piece of wood.

But an innocent shift made pain tear through his leg and send a wave of agony through him. He rolled, trying to escape the torment, but that only lit more fires that made him scream. Or try to scream. The sound that emerged from his parched throat was more of a groan that ended on a whimper. He coughed, spat out the grit of sand.

The wave of pain dulled just enough that he became aware of heat on his face. The flames of hell? Had his life not been good enough? His heart not clean enough? Was this how he would pass eternity?

Never in his life had he wished so hard he had paid more attention in church, or to his father's nightly reading from the Scriptures.

But he'd never heard of the afterlife being filled with seagulls.

Phin pried his eyes open, though the lashes were stuck together and it took considerable effort. He had to blink a few times to clear his vision.

But opening his eyes flooded his mind with far more images than what was in front of him. The dark of the night, a pistol leveled at his face. Spencer, traitorous Spencer. Hudgins up the mast, the rail he crashed against. Then a black gulf in his memory. He must have fallen overboard. He'd come to at some point when something slammed into him, but the ships had been out of sight, either because of distance or the storm.

The something that'd hit him had no doubt also saved him. He didn't know what it had been, other than wood. He'd had just enough energy to crawl halfway onto it and hold on, then . . . then . . . what?

A mottled sky stretched above him, clouds even now overtaking the sun and casting the world in cooling shade. He turned his head a bit to the right and saw a canopy of green leaves nearly over him. Palms and a few evergreens he had no great need to name. To the left crashed the ocean, emerald green swirling through sapphire blue.

The Caribbean. Or so he would guess. He couldn't have been washed to an entirely different tropic. Though, frankly, he had no idea how he'd held on long enough to wash up on any beach, alive just enough to think he shouldn't be.

He tried to move, but the pain roared, and Phin sagged right back down into the sand. His mouth was so dry, his skin cracked and tight. The ocean hadn't killed him, but the sun would. He had nothing. No water, no compass, no idea where he was or how to get where he needed to be.

Lord God above . . . Even his brain felt parched. He knew how to pray. Maybe he hadn't done so often enough, and never with the devotion his parents tried to inspire in him, but surely he hadn't forgotten. *Lord God. If you're there . . . if you know where I am . . .*

Wrong, all wrong. He squeezed his eyes shut and dug his fingers into the sand. *Help me, please. Save me.*

Water rushed over his leg, warm but nonetheless shocking. And when it curled up his thigh and into the wound, the pain burned so bright he convulsed, back arching against it. He had to move. Had to get out of the way of the tide.

Phin rolled onto his good side and tried to pull himself up the beach. Panting, screaming, each movement seeming to take every last drop of his strength and yet accomplishing nothing. He managed to drag himself a foot, then another, before his arms gave out and he fell facedown into the sand again. At least his head was now under the covering of a leafy green branch, hanging low overhead.

It wouldn't be enough protection to make any difference. But it would have to be, for now. He closed his eyes and tried to catch his breath. Tried to calm his frantic pulse. Tried to tell himself his leg was not really on fire.

After a moment, he could hear beyond his own ragged breathing. Was that . . . humming? It sounded close. Somewhere within the trees.

Yes, humming. Humming that turned into a song, the disembodied voice deep and true.

> "O God, our help in ages past.
> Our hope for years to come.
> Our shelter from the stormy blast,
> And our eternal home."

"Help!" Phin scrabbled around to face the direction of the voice, tried to clear his throat. "Help!" Little more than a croak, certainly not audible over the singing.

He could see a figure now, though, big as his voice. When the man emerged from the tree line, Phin waved an arm.

The black man came to an abrupt halt. He was tall as a

mountain, or so it seemed from Phin's prostrate position. Well dressed, which meant he must be in a high position with his master. He surveyed him for only an instant before coming his way.

"Please." Phin could only pray the rasp of his voice was at all understandable. "Help."

The man crouched down, a frown etched deep in his forehead. "What has happened to you, my friend?"

Friend? River was the only slave in his acquaintance who would call him that, and only because of a shared childhood. Why would a black man who was a stranger think to use such a title? Phin scowled. And the man's accent was all wrong. Granted, not every slave the world over would speak with the Gullah patterns with which he was most familiar, but he had heard plenty of Caribbean slaves talk too—and this wasn't how they did it. Though those here in Cuba might have a Spanish accent. Was this a Spanish accent? His brain refused to tell him.

When Phin opened his mouth, his words didn't much resemble what they were supposed to either. More like ill-formed screeches that dissolved into a fit of coughing.

A canteen appeared before him, and hands the size of frying pans unscrewed the top, then held it to Phin's lips.

Never had water tasted so sweet.

"There now, that should help a bit at least." British. His accent sounded, of all things, British. And there was something far too sure about his gaze. "I've never seen such a uniform, sir. To whose military do you belong?"

"The Confederate States." At least his voice sounded more like his own now, if still hoarse.

The giant retracted the canteen and stood so fast it made Phin's head swim again. "Then may God have mercy on your soul."

"Pardon?" It took him a long moment to process what was happening when the man spun away, his booted heel spraying sand all over Phin. "Don't leave me here! Please, man, take me to your master—I will make it worth his while, and yours too."

The mountain spun around again, cold fury pulsing in his neck. Phin couldn't for the life of him think how he had caused it. "Worth my while?" the man echoed between gritted teeth. "And how, pray tell, do you intend to do that?"

Phin tried to push himself up a few inches, which sent the fire through his leg again. The man had a point—for the first time in his life, Phin wasn't in a position to help anyone, to do anything. He was completely at the mercy of this volcano ready to erupt, with no idea what he might do to make the explosion come.

He clenched his jaw against the pain and cleared his throat. "I . . . I have accounts in Cienfuegos. I'll repay your master fully for helping me and will stipulate that you're to be given some too. Please, man. I need help. I will do whatever I can in recompense."

The man snorted his opinion of that, but then he stilled, closed his eyes. His larynx bobbed. When he opened his eyes again, calm had overtaken him. "From where do you hail?"

"I don't see what—" He cut himself off with a groan when his leg took up a new throb, as if hammering home that he was in no position to question the fellow's right to seek answers of him. "Savannah."

When the man rolled back his shoulders, he seemed to grow another foot. And the calm, cool gaze he directed Phin's way was even more intimidating than the mystifying anger had been. "Savannah, you say. The Lord Almighty has obviously washed you up on my beach for a purpose, rebel. I'll help you—on the condition that you help me."

"I'm no rebel. I'm . . . Mr. Phin." Through the cloud of agony, Phin caught a glimpse of how the strange pieces of this puzzle fit together. He fell back into the sand and closed his eyes. The British accent. The too-sure attitude. The way he called it *his* beach. "You're free."

"Any man who breathes the air of England is free. And I've been breathing it since the day I was born."

An unamused laugh coupled with a groan. Most people in his acquaintance said regularly that there was no creature more dangerous to all that the Confederacy stood for than a free black. They stirred up things best left untouched, made discontent those who'd never grumbled before. Phin had never particularly agreed with that idea, but this man sure seemed like he'd live up to the reputation. *Not the help I had in mind, God.*

He wanted to ask what it was this man would demand in return for his aid. Wanted to argue against being called a rebel. Wanted to make it clear that his cause, the Southern cause, was about far more than just slavery—it was about the rights of a people to govern themselves.

But the overcast sky fell atop him, and the world went gray and nebulous. The earth swung under him even as unspeakable weights pressed his limbs down. At least the pain lessened, faded away, and he could see Delia's face more clearly now. Or perhaps it wasn't *now* but *here*—in some netherworld beyond the pale.

Maybe he'd just stay here for a while. Delia would understand.

Luther heaved a sigh as the rebel soldier's head lolled to the side and his body went lax. He winced at the oozing wound in the man's leg, at the raw patches on his neck and the ripped clothing. Somewhere deep inside, sympathy stirred. Deep, deep inside.

But on the surface the anger still boiled and seethed. "Really, Lord?" he whispered into the sultry breeze. "*This* is why you sent me down here this morning? Not for news of Eva, not to commune with you, but for this? This man who thinks himself my natural superior?"

What had he said his name was? Mr. Phin. Well, Luther had no intention of referring to him as that. He was happy to use a "mister" if he had a last name to go along with it, but not with a first name, like one of his slaves. For now, *Phin* would have to do.

He knew well what the Lord expected of him—he had to get this sorry young chap back to the bungalow and see to the wound. Fetch a doctor, no doubt. Nurse him back to health, if possible. Put his search on hold that much longer, as if months hadn't been wasted already.

But the Lord had His plan, had His time. And this was obviously part of it.

Savannah.

Luther flexed his hand and stared at the unconscious soldier. True, he couldn't be sure Eva had ended up there, but he knew it's where the ship had gone. It's where she would have been sold. If he could but get into the city, he could discover to whom she had been sold and follow her trail from there.

Except that entering Savannah was impossible for a free man of color, thanks to the laws of Georgia forbidding them entrance into any port. He had already tried and been sent back to Cuba, his name put on a list assuring he'd be barred entry if he tried it again.

"*We don't need any uppity coloreds sowing dissent and troubling ideas about freedom,*" the official at the dock had said.

Was it any wonder so many of these unfortunate black people from America's South held England as an ultimate goal? Yet here Luther was, desperate to gain entrance into that land of bondage and misery.

For Eva. Only for Eva.

As for now, this Phin chap. Luther indulged in one more

sigh and then stepped back over to his side. Crouched down, scooped the fellow up.

A long, guttural moan brought Luther's sympathy a little closer to the surface. He hadn't thought to ask how Phin had come to be on this out-of-the-way stretch of Cuban beach with a bullet in his leg. But then, the answer wouldn't matter all that much. He would help him in any case.

Though he'd let the rebel think it conditional for a while. Maybe it would inspire the boy to discover a way to get Luther his Eva back.

He settled the young man as best as he could against him and turned back toward the path through the trees. Luther had trod this same little footpath morning and evening for too long. It was supposed to have been a holiday. A few months away from his church, from his students. A chance to not only meet Eva's beloved Grammy, but to purchase the old woman's freedom and take her home with them.

A good deed, born of love.

He ducked under a low-hanging bough and tried to ignore the ever-present question tickling the back of his mind. *Why didn't you warn me, Lord? Why didn't you tell us not to come?*

No, the better question to ask would be why men treated each other as they did. Why such evil still prevailed in hearts that claimed to know Him.

A colorful bird swooped across his path, and the smell of ripe fruit teased his nose. Luther strode over the uneven ground and glanced down again at the injured man. He had a face tanned from days in the sun, but not burnt, which meant he hadn't likely been on that beach for long. Salt water had dried to a white crust on his jacket's fancy gold braid and buttons. The holster on one side of his hip was empty, but the sword on the other banged against Luther's leg with every other step.

Luther's bungalow came into view, a tiny little hut more part of nature than shelter from it. Even after months in its diminutive walls, he couldn't quite fathom how Grammy had lived there for decades, how Eva had grown up in its negligible shadow. He still couldn't help but contrast it to his tidy flat in Stoke Newington, on the outskirts of London.

Yes, he missed his silver tea service. His favorite chair. The new curricle he had commissioned not yet a year ago, along with the fine pair of horses to pull it. And oh, those shelves of books, leather-bound spines all facing outward with gold-leaf type marching across them. He missed his books most of all.

That, and the feel of a cool breeze on a foggy morning. How he yearned to be *cool* again, a sensation he hadn't felt for six months. Hard to believe he had been looking forward to the tropical climate when they first planned this trip, that he'd enjoyed these balmy breezes for the first few weeks.

Now each hot wind felt like a mighty hand squeezing the life out of him. The very air was heavy, the earth ready to rear up and erase all evidence of man.

He didn't dare look at the freshly mounded grave as he strode over the small clearing before the bungalow. It would only remind him that he hadn't been quick enough, hadn't been good enough.

The door stood partially open. Luther toed it to a wide gap and ducked down to clear the threshold. He'd forgotten that crucial move a time or two and gotten a sore forehead for his forgetfulness. This whole house gave him a crick in the neck, given that he couldn't stand upright in any part of it.

He covered the distance of the floor in two steps and knelt in the corner by the single cot. With care he'd be certain not to admit when Phin came round again, he eased the man onto his stomach on the straw-stuffed mattress.

Had he mentioned that he missed his feather bed? The one large enough for his frame? He ventured to guess he would come to miss this cot, now that he'd be relegated to the floor.

The soldier groaned again as Luther positioned his injured

leg on the ticking. His head thrashed from side to side, but his eyes didn't open. Just as well. If that oozing leg hurt as much as it looked like it would, the fellow would be better off unconscious.

Luther fetched a lamp, lit it, and set it on the rickety bedside table, which he scooted toward Phin's leg. Light aplenty spilled through the window, but he wanted to get the best possible look at the wound to determine if he should go fetch the doctor. When he leaned in close and saw the way the fabric from the man's uniform was stuck to the wound, even after what must have been hours in the water, he suspected he had his answer. To be sure, he rolled the lad gently onto his side.

No exit wound in the front, as he'd thought. Which meant the bullet was still lodged inside. This definitely fell beyond Luther's expertise. He hated to leave him alone long enough to fetch Dr. Santiago, but he had little choice.

After removing the lamp well out of range of flailing limbs, he moved the table within reach and set a tin cup of water upon it. If Phin awoke, he would no doubt be more concerned about water. And in case the pain gave way enough for the lad to realize he needed food, he set some bread and cheese there, too, covered with a cloth.

Then Luther knelt beside him, held his hands above the wound, and closed his eyes. "Father God Almighty, I cannot know your will or your purpose in washing this young man up on my beach. But knowing you love him even where I cannot, I pray that you touch this wound, that you set a barrier against infection, that you help this boy keep his life and his leg. I pray the healing wrought by your precious Son upon him and claim his life for you, Lord. Please lead me as I care for him, and give Dr. Santiago your wisdom and grace. In the name of Christ Jesus, amen."

He withdrew his hands but stayed on his knees for a long moment, studying this unwanted guest. A Confederate soldier, of all things. A young man fighting to keep Luther's entire race bound by slavery.

Yet he couldn't ignore that murmur that moved through him, the one that forced his eyes open to see more than the uniform. This young man in his twenties must be at least ten years Luther's junior, perhaps more like fifteen. And knowing the life pampered young men tended to lead—to which class he obviously belonged, given that offer of bribery on the beach—he had likely never known hardship or toil. Luther sighed. Phin was little more than a child, even at his age. Untested, never put upon, seldom taxed.

Until now. The war between the Union and the Confederacy may have only just begun on American soil, but this young fellow had received an early taste of its realities.

Luther stood, his neck bent at its habitual angle in this low-ceilinged house. "Well, young man, I don't know if you can hear me, but if you can, rest assured I shall return as soon as possible, with a well-trusted doctor. There is food and drink here for you. Try not to fear."

Phin made no response, so Luther turned and exited the house, stretching the discomfort from his neck as soon as the sky towered overhead. Oh, for soaring cathedral ceilings, for scrolling plasterwork several feet above him. For windows with glass panes and brocade curtains.

He must get his head out of the realm of wishes and into the present though. With another silent prayer to underscore the urgency that crept into his consciousness, Luther hurried to the little lean-to he had constructed to house his horse. Gulliver wasn't exactly the fine horse he had waiting for him in England, but the large gelding was the best he could manage here. And he would traverse the two miles to the doctor's home easily enough.

How often had they made this same journey together over the last months? Too many. Far, far too many. But at least the frequent interactions with the physician had resulted in an unexpected friendship. And an improvement in Luther's Spanish.

It took him only a couple minutes to saddle the bay, hoist himself up, and urge him into a trot down the overgrown lane. The road wound past Hacienda Rosario, on which Luther refused to gaze. He didn't have to. He knew well how the Big House sprawled gleaming white in the glaring sun. How the rows of tobacco plants marched along, acre after acre. But whether he looked or not, he could hear the chants of the slaves. If any dared glance up from their tasks and see him, he would be able to feel their burning gazes too.

At the crossroad, he turned right and headed for the home of the physician-planter. Dr. Santiago had a house far more modest than his neighbor, with far fewer slaves. And a far fairer mind. Still, it had taken months for Luther to earn the doctor's respect.

He rode through a copse of trees, dense but brief, and then looked out over Hacienda Santiago. "Lord, let him be at home."

Here, the slaves greeted him with cool glances—absent any welcome, but also absent the hatred he found at the Rosario operations. To them, he was nothing but an outsider, rather than an outsider they thought should be among them. He nodded an acknowledgment to the nearest field hand, who summarily ignored him.

Gulliver clip-clopped up the drive and went without prodding toward the stable. The stable boy was one of the few on this cursed island who smiled when he saw him. "Señor Luther! *¿Cómo está?*"

"*Bien*, Juan." Even with so short a reply, his Spanish felt as smooth as a rusty hinge. He switched to English, knowing the boy understood it as well as Luther did Spanish, anyway. "Do you know if the doctor is at home?"

"Ah, *sí*." He motioned toward the Big House.

"Thank you. That is, *gracias*." He'd nearly said *merci*. Why couldn't Eva have hailed from a French quarter? He would have been far better at communicating with them.

He handed over Gulliver's reins and strode toward the back door. It stood open to receive the breeze, but he nevertheless knocked on the frame even as he filled it.

One of the house slaves looked up and offered a polite smile. "*Buenos días, señor.*"

"Good morning. I need the doctor—it is an emergency. *Emergencia.*" He nearly rolled his eyes at himself. He only knew the word because it was a cognate—and since it was, the servant would have been able to understand his *emergency* quite well enough.

The man looked doubtful—probably wondering whom Luther had to seek medical aid for—but nevertheless motioned him down a hallway that let out near the doctor's study.

Luther waited while the servant knocked, stepped inside, and introduced him. When he was given leave to enter the study, he found Dr. Santiago standing with a sober smile. "Good morning, Luther. What is the matter?"

Luther waited for the servant to exit. "I found a man on the beach this morning, Doctor. He is in a bad way—a bullet in his leg, no exit wound. He seems to have been in the ocean and is unconscious more than not, in terrible pain. It goes beyond what I am able to tend without instruction."

Already reaching for his familiar black bag, the doctor shook his head. "Curious. Is he from Cuba?"

"No. Georgia. He is a Confederate soldier of some kind, though I got no more out of him before he fainted again."

"Curious indeed." Santiago took a moment to run his fingers down his beard, then charged toward the door. "Well, let us not tarry. How old a man, do you think? Generally strong of physique?"

Luther knew only too well how age could affect affliction. "Young. I guess midtwenties, and he looks otherwise healthy."

The doctor led the way out the back, calling out in rapid Spanish over his shoulder to the servants he passed, no doubt telling them where he could be found. A few minutes later, Juan had saddled a horse for Santiago and led Gulliver out for Luther.

Once they were underway, Santiago looked over at him. "Have you any idea how long ago he was wounded?"

Luther shook his head. "I can only guess that it hasn't been long. I walked the beach last night and saw no evidence of him then."

"He is in much pain?"

"He seems to be, yes."

The doctor nodded, lips in a grim line between his beard and mustache. "How is his color? If he is pale, it may mean he has lost much blood."

To that, Luther had to shrug. "It was difficult to judge, as he seemed to be rather tan."

"He gave no indication of where he had been?"

"No, Doctor." Luther shifted in the saddle and cast his gaze in the direction of his makeshift home, as if he could see it from here. "Said he was Confederate, from Savannah. Offered to repay me—or rather, my master—if I helped him. That was all he said before he went under."

Santiago sent him a look of knowing amusement. "Knowing you as I do, Señor Bromley, I am certain you took that assumption with the utmost, how do you say . . . deplume?"

"I believe you mean *aplomb*, Doctor." Luther's lips twitched, but he held down the smile. "Assuming that you assume I handled it with grace and not with lack thereof."

Santiago chuckled. "It depends on my level of sarcasm, which I meant, I think. No?"

"*Oui*. I mean, *sí*." He sighed and rubbed his eyes. "I admit to feeling a bit of insult when he referred to my master. I ought to have simply agreed and let him hand over a tidy sum to the church, since the Lord is the one I serve."

A low hum came from the doctor's throat, then another thoughtful glance. "Savannah, did you say?"

"*Sí.*"

"Is that not . . . ?"

"It is." Luther's fingers gripped the reins until his knuckles ached.

"A strange coincidence."

He only nodded and held his tongue as they finished the trip.

Soon enough, they were back inside his bungalow, and Santiago, able to stand upright under the low roof, had pulled over what he needed—the lone chair, the rickety table, the lamp. "*Agua, por favor.*"

Luther jerked a nod and fetched the bucket of water he had filled from the well first thing that morning. Santiago dipped some up and poured it over the wound. He made a ticking sound with his tongue and muttered in Spanish.

Not knowing what else to do with himself, Luther crouched down beside the cot. "Is it bad?"

"The usual problem with a gunshot wound—the bullet pulled fabric into the leg and is itself lodged inside. If I miss a piece, it will fester. More water, if you please. We will get it nice and wet, then cut the pants away."

At home in England, it was always Eva who played the part of nurse when a parishioner was ill. Luther far preferred reading to them, talking with them, praying for them. But he had grown accustomed to giving such medical care here in Cuba. He poured a generous ladle of water over the wound, his breath snagging when the prone man groaned in his sleep. When Santiago brandished his scissors, Luther helped pull the cloth gently away from the flesh wherever he could, until the soldier's leg was bared to mid thigh.

"Now the work begins." Santiago affixed a pair of spectacles to his nose and bent over the leg. "If he begins to awaken, you must hold him still."

Luther nodded—and prayed the Lord would be merciful and let Phin remain unconscious.

For an hour, the doctor painstakingly removed sliver after sliver of blood-soaked fiber, then set to work digging out the bullet. At this, fresh blood gushed out in earnest, demanding Luther move from his defensive posture of a lazy arm restraining Phin to pressing rags all around the leg to catch the river of red. When at last he heard the metal *ping* of bullet hitting pan, he took his first breath of relief.

It fled, seeing the shake of Santiago's head. "The damage is great. His bone . . ."

Dread cinched tight in Luther's chest. "Fractured?"

"*Destrozado*. Shattered. If he lives, he will have a long recovery ahead of him. You must pray the *gangrena* does not set in. I do not look forward to coming back here to amputate, but it is *muy probable*."

Luther stared down at Phin's face, tense even in sleep, his distress obvious. He had symmetrical features, a straight, narrow nose, a cleft to his upper lip that Eva always teased was exceedingly handsome on a man. All the young belles back in Georgia no doubt swooned when he entered a room. He was so young, undoubtedly full of vitality before this.

Yet now he was cut down. His life hanging by a precarious thread, his leg likely lost. Abandoned by his compatriots on an unfamiliar island with no friend to pray him back to health.

What matter was the uniform he wore? Under it was a man who, if he lived, would be hurting from far deeper within than that bullet had pierced.

Santiago stood. "I will make a splint. He must not move the leg. It must be braced."

So must *he* be. Luther closed his eyes and gripped Phin's shoulder. "Father God, again I commend this young man to you. Sustain him, Lord. Save him."

The patient's breath hitched, then eased out in an agonizing moan. His eyes fluttered open, though they remained unfocused before his eyelids came down again. "Delia. Didn't tell Delia . . . tell her I love her."

Luther gripped his shoulder a little tighter. Who was this Delia? Wife? Sweetheart? Either way . . . either way. "You'll have the chance to tell her," he swore, so low the man likely didn't hear through the haze of his pain. "Rest now, my friend, gather your strength. I'll get you back to your Delia."

And maybe—if the Lord smiled on him—he would find his Eva too.

Chapter Seven

Cordelia fastened the pearls into place around Lacy's ivory throat and viewed her little sister in the looking glass before them. "There." She couldn't resist a grin. The pale green dress set off Lacy's coloring perfectly, and with those blooms of excitement giving her cheeks a becoming rose, she would be irresistible to all the young men.

One Julius James included.

Lacy tried to mute a squeal, but the punctuating bounce wouldn't be contained. "Oh, Delia, it's been too long since we've had a good ball. Are you sure this cousin of ours will like me? And he's handsome? As handsome as Phin?"

She felt a bit like Jane Austen's Emma. Or some other selfless, beatific, matchmaking heroine. To that effect, Cordelia pasted on a patient smile and smoothed Lacy's skirt a little better over her hoop. "Well now, I can't say as *any* man is as handsome as Phin—but I daresay you'll find him to be so, yes, and he'll just adore you."

Lacy spun around and threw her arms around Cordelia. "Oh, Delia, thank you for letting me borrow your dress. Now I'll leave you to get ready before Salina pushes me out the door."

Salina grinned. "Now, I'd never do that, Miss Lacy. Leastways not unless you got in my way while I'm trying to curl Miss Delia's hair."

Lacy laughed and flounced out. The room felt quiet in her wake, a bittersweet semi-peace. Cordelia drew in a deep breath and sank down onto the stool of her dressing table.

Salina got to work with the curling tongs, hot from the small fire that had been built to purpose. "And what you gonna wear, Miss Delia, now that you done gave your best new gown to your sister?"

"Oh, any old thing. It hardly matters, since Phin won't be there." She kept her head straight but let her gaze wander to the flowers on the wallpaper. Wouldn't it be something, though, if he just showed up without warning? Perhaps his ship was fighting the Yankees off the coast and they were given leave in Savannah. Or his captain could have a dispatch so crucially important that it must be hand delivered, and naturally he would choose his most trusted man to dispatch it.

Yes, Phin could be on his way to the city even now. Braving the Yankee offensive, slipping through enemy lines.

Captured. Shot. Taken prisoner and carted off to one of those dreadful prisoner-of-war camps she had heard horror stories about. Where he would starve, get eaten by lice, be tormented by dreadfully large rats, left to waste away in a . . . a *dungeon* somewhere, with no one to visit him, no one to dab his sweat-soaked brow, no one to even talk to.

She squeezed her eyes shut against the dark images. "Do you think he's all right, Sal?"

Salina drew in a long breath and wrapped a length of hair around the tongs, tugging softly. "I don't rightly know, Miss Delia. But I been prayin for him."

"So have I. But I can't escape those dreams. The feeling he's in danger."

"In danger don't mean without hope though." Her fingers

rested a moment on Cordelia's shoulder, warm and familiar. "You keep clingin to that, and keep on prayin. To my figurin, the Lord wouldn't bother givin us dreams about it if there weren't something we could do, if all hope was lost."

She would have nodded, but Cordelia had learned long ago not to do such a fool thing with hot tongs at her head. "An excellent point. I shall keep praying, keep hoping." But she would also resign herself to not seeing him tonight, or any other time in the near future.

"And keep thinkin on what you wanna wear tonight, 'cause if you don't look your best, your mama will send you straight back up here."

Cordelia met her friend's reflected gaze in the mirror and smiled into the knowing glint. "She likely will at any rate. I always seem to neglect something she insists upon. But I think I'll wear the ivory-and-pink striped one."

"Pink?" Mirror Salina arched a brow. "You really don't care to impress this Mr. Julius, do you?"

A laugh bubbled forth. Any other servant would assure her she'd made a fine choice, say what a beautiful gown the silk and taffeta had turned out to be. But Cordelia much preferred Salina's honesty. "I really don't. Though Mama assures me that a gown so lovely can't *help* but flatter me, no matter how ill-suited it is for my complexion."

Salina let loose a dubious hum that worked its way into a song as she continued her task. Cordelia relaxed into the familiarity. Many long minutes later, the mirror began to reflect the carefully crafted image Savannah would see tonight. Golden curls, set just so, laced through with ribbons. Green eyes that Cordelia would work hard to keep free of worry. Cheeks that Mama would no doubt pinch some color into before they exited their carriage at the Dunns'.

What would Phin say if he saw her tonight? Would he think her pretty, even in pink? Would he draw her away from the crowd for another stolen kiss if he were here? Would a light of jealousy enter his eye if he beheld Julius claiming a dance?

He hadn't looked particularly jealous after seeing the scoundrel Thomas Bacon try to kiss her. But then, he had been too amused at her taking a stand as she had. It may be different now that she had promised to wait for him though. He must think of her now as his and wouldn't take kindly to another fawning over her.

Not that Cousin Julius had been *fawning* yesterday, but why get particular over word choice? If she were dreaming Phin were here, she could very well dream he was delightfully jealous—just enough to whisk her away from all the other doting men, off to some quiet corner where he would gaze down into her eyes, a storm of passion in his own, and lean down, so slowly and delectably—

"Miss Delia, are you going to step into this gown, or do you want me to go to the ball in your stead?"

Cordelia started and looked over to see that Salina had put away the curling tongs and gotten out her hoop and gown, which she had spread out on the floor, awaiting her. All while she sat here dreaming of another kiss from a man who was undoubtedly hundreds, if not thousands, of miles away. She chuckled at herself and stood, shrugging out of her dressing gown.

Salina held out a hand to lend her balance while Cordelia stepped over the splayed skirt and into the opening. Once within, her maid raised up hoop and dress and fastened them, cinching tight the sash around her waist.

Cordelia watched the gown smooth into place in the mirror and sighed. Such lovely fabric, in such a flattering design. It really was a shame the color didn't suit her well and that, if it had, Phin wasn't here to see it.

When Salina's face appeared beside her, eyes narrowed in scrutiny as she fussed and tugged, Cordelia grinned. "You know, I do believe it would look better on you, Sal. We ought to try it on you sometime."

The maid's eyes went wide in terror—and something even darker. "Don't say that, Miss Delia! If your mama caught me in one of your gowns . . ."

"Oh, pooh. What could she possibly say if it was my idea?" Yet the darkness in Salina's eyes took on a name.

Resentment.

Because Delia had what she couldn't? But that had never come between them. What, then? She pursed her lips. Perhaps it was the reminder she resented. Or the fact that Delia would suggest something that could get her in trouble.

She sucked in a long breath. Was it cruel of her, even, to suggest Salina step for so brief a moment from her role? To remind her of those games they used to play, where a prince came to steal Salina away?

When they were children, she couldn't quite fathom that one of her dearest friends was doomed to servitude forever. She'd thought surely, *surely* freedom waited on the horizon for her somehow. But reality told a very different tale than her own imagined ideas of justice. "I'm sorry, Salina. I shouldn't jest so, now that we're all grown up."

Salina's smile looked forced and a touch sad, but at least that flare of resentment subsided. "Ain't your fault, Miss Delia. Your mama just don't like me much is all, and I don't want to do nothing to make her mad."

"Nonsense. How in the world could Mama not like you? You're sweet and smart and pretty."

A strange look crossed Salina's face, then flew away. In its place settled a determined mask of good humor that Cordelia knew from experience was as impenetrable as it was false. "Well now, if anyone be sweet and smart and pretty, it's you, sure enough. What necklace will you wear?"

"Hmm." She studied her reflection, giving up the argument

solely because she knew she'd get nowhere with it. "I think perhaps I lent Lacy my pearls prematurely."

"No matter, I know just the thing." Salina turned to her jewelry box and came up with the delicate cameo that had been Great-Grandmama Penelope's. "Wear this and you'll be just like that Lucy in the story you wrote last month, the one who saved the whole kingdom by decoding those picture-words, all thanks to the number of curls engraved in her cameo."

And how could Cordelia help but grin at that? "Perfect."

Salina no sooner got it around her neck than the door opened and Mama came in. "Hurry, Cordelia. Julius just arrived, and we must repair to the Dunns'."

"Coming, Mama." She stepped away from Salina and twirled. "How do I look?"

Mama pursed her lips. "Why didn't you wear the green and give Lacy the pink, if she wasn't content with her own gowns? The other would have complemented you better. Not that this isn't a lovely dress, mind you, but green brings out your eyes so very well."

"As it does hers." Cordelia tried on her sweetest smile, though it rarely worked any miracles on Mama. "She's been begging to wear it, and I didn't know how many other chances she'd have, what with more and more of our friends leaving the city."

The way Mama opened her mouth and narrowed her eyes, Cordelia knew a lecture was coming. She would no doubt point out that if Lacy could find no other time to wear it, then when would Cordelia? And that as the elder daughter left unmarried, it was her responsibility to find a husband quick as she could. That she ought to know better than to try to sabotage herself. And did she really think Julius would be dissuaded by something like a dress? Men seldom noticed such details as color anyway.

But it was about the picture they made, and Lacy would

make a glowing one, feeling as lovely as she did tonight. Which Mama was astute enough to realize.

She was also apparently astute enough to realize that making such arguments would take time they didn't have. She closed her mouth again, set it in that way that said she all but bit her tongue in the interest of peace, and lifted her golden brows. "How very kind of you to lend your favorite new gown to Lacy. Now if you're ready, darling, do come down and greet your cousin."

"Yes, ma'am." As soon as Mama's back was turned, she winked at Salina, then pulled on her gloves, scooped up her fan, and exited her bedchamber.

Voices reached her ears from the parlor before she even arrived at the bottom of the wide staircase. Daddy's laughter, and the deep baritone that belonged to Julius. Then the soft, higher giggle of Lacy. Mama, she saw a moment later, was just going in.

Cordelia took her time traversing the hallway, keeping her steps slow and giving undo attention to her posture. Long gone were the days of balancing books on her head—she didn't really have to give any thought anymore to whether her spine was straight, her shoulders square, her chin up to that perfect angle. But focusing on it always made her measure her pace.

And she was in no great hurry to join the others. Instead, she kept to the wall so that she could peer into the parlor without being seen. Daddy and Julius both stood with snifters in hand, their attention on the females. As always, Daddy's smile looked proud and warm as he glanced from Lacy to Mama.

Julius, though he bowed when the lady of the house entered, kept his gaze almost entirely on Lacy.

A smile bloomed on Cordelia's lips. Excellent. The warrior-king had forgotten all about the lady-in-waiting now that the princess of the castle was before him. He would certainly prefer Lacy's fair-as-the-moon skin. Her half-an-inch smaller waist.

Her wide-eyed, guileless regard, the way she focused entirely on every word he spoke.

What man wouldn't like such attentiveness from a pretty young woman? Julius would no doubt remember how absent-minded Cordelia had seemed to be at the Pulaski House and think Lacy the better-witted sister, by far. Anyone would.

Except Phin, of course, who knew to whence her imagination always flew and never begrudged her those flights of fancy.

She edged just a bit closer so she could hear what tale of Julius's enthralled Lacy so thoroughly.

"We've had our share of problems, too, Mr. Owens. Especially at Christmas last year. Mother tried to talk Father out of giving alcohol to the slaves, but he feared the reaction if he didn't. Turns out he should have heeded her warning—it's always been raucous with the Negroes all drunk, but last year . . ." He paused, looked again at Lacy, sighed. "Well, let's just say things got more out of hand than usual. Mother swore she would never again be on the plantation for the holidays."

Cordelia indulged in a frown, since Mama wasn't looking her way and so couldn't admonish her about wrinkles. Were they having problems with their slaves on one or both of the plantations? Hopefully not Twin Magnolias, which Ginny would be folding into the Worth holdings now. She hated to think of her good-hearted sister being faced with that sort of trouble.

She eased forward another step, but apparently the tale was done. Just like that. No scintillating morsels, no sense of excitement or danger whatsoever. All Cordelia's alarm came from that "too" at the beginning of his speech, and it was her own concern, not his. Yet there were the makings of a true tale of desperation in whatever had happened on his plantation at Christmas.

One no doubt unsuitable for Lacy's ears, she would grant.

Still, he could have hinted. Added a bit of inflection to his tone. A gesture to indicate it was more than an unfortunate fact seven months past.

Daddy sipped his drink and nodded. See there, *he* knew how to load a simple move with untold contemplation. He looked so very serious, so very sorrowful at the state of affairs. "I have often said the Negroes are like children—they need our guidance and care. And like children, when we allow it, they run rampant, until we check them and rebuke them."

Well, this was as good a time as any to make her entrance, before Daddy waxed verbose on how he ruled his slaves with a firm but fair hand. Cordelia had heard him and his friends debate the topic ad nauseam already. Full of feeling though he was, she had no great desire to hear the whole argument again. Especially since she'd made the mistake of indulging in a roll of her eyes once and had received a twenty-minute-long chastisement for the display, never mind that Salina was perfect proof that the color of her skin had no bearing at all on the state and strength of her mind.

Cordelia slid into view, her slippers silent and skirts a mere whisper, and stepped into the room. She headed for Mama but directed her smile to the company at large.

Daddy stepped over to her with a bright smile. "There's my sunshine. Delie-Darlin. You met your cousin Julius already, didn't you?"

"Yes, sir." She barely glanced Julius's way, but it was enough to see that he smiled at her with too much warmth for comfort. Even as he stood so near Lacy, with her looking up at him as if he bejeweled the heavens with each shining star.

Were it possible, Cordelia would have straightened her spine even more. Perhaps cool distance would put him off where clicking fans and hunched shoulders hadn't. Though in all likelihood, time would accomplish it on its own. She was still the first one he had met, and so he would feel a lingering attachment. But it would dissipate. The flame of Lacy's adoration would burn it away like fog. Like chaff.

Or perhaps like gunpowder, given that flash of temper in Lacy's eyes when Julius left her side and came over to take Cordelia's hand. Oh bother. The last thing she wanted was her sister to be angry with her, and over a man Cordelia had no interest in.

"Cousin Cordelia." Julius bent over her fingers, lingered three seconds too long. "You're looking even lovelier tonight than yesterday, which I thought impossible."

She enjoyed a good dose of flattery as much as the next lady, but she happened to know he was lying through his teeth. Yesterday's pale blue day dress had, quite honestly, looked far better on her than this ornate pink evening gown. She kept her smile polite, reserved. "How nice to see you again, Julius."

Her coolness seemed to have the desired effect. When he straightened, his eyes snapped in a different way, with acknowledgment. "Likewise." He turned so that he could see Lacy again. "I just had the considerable pleasure of making your sister's acquaintance. Had I any idea my Owens cousins were so charming, I would have journeyed to Savannah long ago."

Lacy's cheeks went pink, her lips curling into a happy-again smile.

Cordelia mentally nodded in satisfaction and decidedly ignored the clearing of Mama's throat. Much preferred was Daddy's oblivious smile. "You are a pretty picture tonight, Delia. I imagine you've been wishing your Phin were here, hmm?"

Oh, how she adored her father. She tucked her hand into the crook of his elbow and grinned up at him. "I had the same thought, I confess. When will this dreadful war be over, Daddy, so he can come home?"

A few months ago, he would always say, "Soon enough, darlin, just you wait and see. We'll scare those Yankees back to the North in no time."

Now he sighed and patted her hand. “We’ll get the best of them. Your tableaux vivants will no doubt be a big help with the revenue generated. I’ve been promised that we have the Pulaski House for it, so you see that your girls are organized, now.”

She bounced a little, let out a muted squeal of excitement. But at that particular moment the reaction was solely for his benefit. Where had his confidence gone? Why the quick change of subject?

Perhaps she ought to pay more attention to news of the war.

She hadn’t long to consider it, for a few moments later they were told their carriage was waiting and together went outside to find Julius’s horse alongside it. When he vaulted into the saddle, Lacy leaned close with a sweet little sigh. “He’s magnificent.”

Thankfully, her sister moved away too quickly for her to answer, accepting the footman’s help into the carriage. Cordelia eased forward a step to follow her but paused when a tingle raced over the nape of her neck.

A glance to her left proved that Julius had settled onto his mount and now watched them—or rather, Cordelia—intently. He offered a handsome half-smile, but it did nothing to warm her insides. Nothing to make the evening glow brighter. No, all it did was magnify the ache.

Directing her gaze to Mama’s back, Cordelia waited her turn to be assisted into the buggy. She missed Phin. How strange it was to long for someone so intensely, so completely, when his previous absences hadn’t had that effect. But then, things had changed between them. And he wasn’t off on holiday, touring Europe, or enjoying a business jaunt with his uncle. He was at war.

How did everyone else do it? They all had husbands and sons and fathers and brothers and beaux at war. Did they all feel this pang? This terrible dread, born of uncertainty?

But Phin couldn’t even send letters regularly, being at sea.

Maybe that was why it hurt so much. She couldn't know. And in the absence of knowing, she imagined.

A brown hand appeared under her nose, and she put her fingers into it, let the footman help her up. Settled on the seat beside Lacy. Oh, why couldn't she be more like Ginny? Ginny never wasted time on imagined fears. She just had faith that the Lord would protect her Charlie and did what she could to assure the general welfare of the soldiers. According to the letter Mama had read last night, she and the other Worth ladies spent every spare moment organizing aid, knitting socks, embroidering sashes. Whatever they could to benefit the cause.

Daddy climbed in last and sat beside Mama. A moment later, the buggy rolled forward. All around them swirled the hot evening air, damp and somehow pulsing with the colors of the declining sun. Lacy opened her fan with a flick and waved it before her face, but Cordelia just gazed out the side—the one beside which Julius was *not* riding.

She supposed she could spend more time with a needle and thread. Produce something useful. Mama would be pleased if she would, especially if it meant giving her fingers time to lose the ink stains. Though she always wore gloves out of the house anyway, so she failed to see why it mattered so much if she had a bit of a callus on her middle finger and a blue-black tinge that couldn't be scrubbed out of her cuticle.

And it wasn't that she disliked sewing. She had immense respect for it. Why, just last month she had come up with a story about a seamstress whose meticulous work was single-handedly responsible for saving an entire orphanage of destitute children who were nearly trapped in a fire—the very day before a generous, handsome donor saved them all from the poorhouse.

The generous hero, of course, had hair that perfect shade of cypress. Hazel eyes. A mouth that could quirk up into the most charming smile in the world, one that was unafraid to be amused. And that turned so soft and intoxicating when he drew the heroine close. . . .

The Dunns' house loomed before them, and the driver pulled the horses to a halt a goodly way from the doors. Every respectable family left in Savannah seemed to be here, half of them lining the drive in front of the Owenses'.

"What a lovely ball this is going to be!" Lacy fanned herself more vigorously as she surveyed the crowd. Her gaze lingered on the scores of men in uniform. The shades ranged from blues to grays, dependent on what regiment they belonged to and the wealth of those who paid for the commission.

Cordelia's eyes were drawn to the ones adorned with gold braid and epaulettes, though each new one she found only made her want to sigh. Not Phin. Which she knew. But still, hope refused to wither completely.

Julius drew his horse to a halt directly beside her but said nothing. Perhaps he wanted to speak with Lacy but didn't care to interrupt, given that she and Mama were talking, their attention out the opposite direction.

A fine idea, except that he seemed content to look at Cordelia rather than her sister.

Bother. How did one fight off a warrior-king?

Chapter Eight

Though the darkness shifted and ebbed, it wouldn't go away. Try as he might, Phin couldn't push his way through it, couldn't find the light. His limbs felt like lead, his whole body seemed to ache and throb. His face burned hot, his hands cold.

He blinked a few times and drew in a long breath. And realized this darkness was night, not the endless pit in which he had been swimming for . . . eternity, it seemed. There, pale silver light illumined a window, absent glass. It crept a few feet across the floor—dirt?—before the night swallowed it. He could make out the outline of a table. A chair.

Insects buzzed and chirped, a cacophony that he must have been hearing for a long time. The sound seemed familiar somehow, though when he focused on it, it set his teeth on edge. A flex of his fingers told him he lay on a lumpy mattress covered in coarse cotton.

Where was he? He had no recollection of arriving in any hovel like this. No thought of where he could be, of how he got there. Of who had applied the binding that wouldn't let him move his leg.

No, wait. Voices—he remembered voices.

"My son, attend to my words."

Several voices, hadn't there been? He had a feeling he had heard conversation. Debate, even. But mostly there had been the one voice. Deep enough to be memorable. Though he couldn't place the memory.

"Incline thine ear unto my sayings."

When he tried to gather together his thoughts, put some time frame on them, all he could dredge up was that disembodied voice. He had the feeling he had heard a lot of it. Hours, surely. Upon hours. Perhaps days. Beyond that . . .

"Let them not depart from thine eyes."

British, the voice had been British. Which, again, seemed to hit upon a memory. What was it? He knew no one from England. There were Irish aplenty in Savannah, but—but he wasn't in Savannah. The *Sumter*. The *Cuba*.

Spencer. Stroud. He had been shot. Fallen overboard. Ended up . . . where? How?

"Keep them in the midst of thine heart."

Spencer. Phin squeezed his eyes shut. He'd thought they were friends. The best of friends, brothers, destined to serve out the war together and then remain close for the rest of their lives. But clearly that wasn't true. If they'd really been friends, he couldn't have turned on him like that, without so much as a word about the doubts he must have been having.

Why? Why had he done it? It was true that Spence didn't have as much invested in the Confederate cause as some did—his family didn't own a plantation, had only two slaves. But he'd understood that it was the whole way of life they were fighting to preserve, hadn't he? The agrarian lifestyle. The focus on the land instead of cities and factories—as if *that* offered a better way of living to the hordes of overworked, starving immigrants who struggled to survive in the North. And above all, they were fighting for the right to decide for themselves how their states ought to be governed, rather than being dictated to by someone thousands of miles away who didn't understand the first thing about life in the South.

But Spence must have decided that it wasn't worth the fight after all. Perhaps he'd decided *nothing* was worth the fight. Was that it, maybe? The war itself, the cost of it, that had gotten to him so quickly?

Apparently a months-long friendship wasn't enough to counteract that. Or maybe . . . maybe no friendship ever was. Maybe no man could be trusted beyond the moment.

Phin's fingers dug into the prickly mattress under him. Was that breathing he heard from the other side of the room? He could barely make out the sound above the infernal insects, but he was fairly certain. Which would make sense. He was obviously under someone's care. Someone had carried him here. Someone had bound his leg. Someone must have been giving him water, at least, for he felt only slight thirst.

A British voice. The man on the beach. That was right—the free black. But *he* wouldn't have taken Phin in. His hatred had been obvious.

"For they are life unto those that find them, and health to all their flesh."

That was definitely the voice he had been hearing though. Praying. Singing. Reading. That accounted for those fragments of verses filling his mind now. Were they from the Psalms? Maybe Proverbs? Memorization of Scripture had never been a high priority.

At least part of the mystery was solved. Motives may be beyond his grasp, but it had to have been the black man from the beach who brought him here, who had been tending him. He must have taken pity on him.

Well, Phin would see he was repaid for his effort. And get out from under this wretched roof soon as morning came. Perhaps dawn was near even now. He pulled himself up to try to get a better view of the window, to discern the angle of the moon.

Pain ripped, screamed, sliced through him. A guttural groan tore unbidden from his throat.

The breathing in the corner hitched and shifted. Then a lantern flamed.

Phin wanted to look, wanted to say something, but it took all his concentration to keep from crying out. He couldn't convince his back to relax from its arch. Couldn't convince his fingers to let loose the sheet under him. He pressed his head as hard as he could into the pillow, clenched his teeth. And waited. Just waited for the agony to pulse its way down to a manageable throb. Only once it had was he aware of how ragged his breath sounded, puffing out of flared nostrils.

If he ever got his hands on Spencer . . .

A *clunk* sounded near his head, inspiring him to pry his eyes open again. The lamp now sat on a small table within reach. It cast its light on a shadow of a man who seemed to go on and on, up and up, all the way to the ceiling.

Phin made an effort to slow his breathing. "You again."

"Luther Bromley." He sloshed some water into a cup and held it at Phin's mouth. "I'm afraid I only caught *Phin* the other day."

Phin took the cup, though his hands trembled. "Phineas Dunn." He tried to drink with some dignity, but he shook too much and couldn't lift his head enough. Water splashed out, dripping down his arm and onto his chest.

One of Luther's meaty hands gripped his and helped steady the cup, the other sliding under his neck to prop his head. "Well, now that you're coherent, Mr. Dunn, allow me to correct a few of your mistaken assumptions from the other day. I am no one's slave, nor have I ever been. I will not pretend otherwise merely for your ease of mind."

Phin took a sip of lukewarm water that did little to calm the pain-ridden irritation. Free or not, what gave this man the right to assume he knew Phin's mind? Solely to irritate him in return, he asked, "Then why are you serving me?"

Was that a hum or a growl that came from the man's throat? "Like so many of your kind, you mistake Christian duty for a natural station. Let me assure you, young man, that I read all the philosophers at Cambridge, I know from whence your ideas come, and they are sadly misconstrued. If you're going to advocate a monstrosity like slavery, do so honestly—just say outright you want cheap labor. Don't try to dress it up with a nonexistent morality." He leaned close, his dark eyes gleaming like firebrands. "It only makes you look like an idiot."

"Watch yourself." How many times had he heard his father's friends expound on the dangers of offering education to colored people? They said they came away with ideas that could do them no good but get them into heaps of trouble. Phin had never put much stock in that idea, had in fact made certain River was able to read and write and do arithmetic. But he'd also cautioned his valet never to let on that he knew as much as he did—no matter the right or wrong of it, it *could* land him in a heap of trouble. A lesson this mountain of a man had clearly never had cause to learn but which was undoubtedly as true in Cuba as it was in Georgia. He tried again to push himself up and was rewarded again with an agonizing spear of pain in his leg. Through clenched teeth he said, "Help me up."

Luther arched a sparse brow. "Did your mother teach you no manners?"

"What?"

The other brow reached up to match its mate. "I am happy to help those in need, but even the beggars in the streets of London have the good graces to say *please* when they ask something of me. Don't tell me they are better taught than a pampered planter's son from Georgia."

Phin slammed his eyes closed. As if he'd been able to get out anything but those three words through the pain. Though now, after a few deep breaths, the tension eased. "I'm beginning to wish you had left me on the beach."

"And I may yet return you there." Luther crossed his arms, thick as most men's thighs, over his barrel chest.

So be it. If this high and mighty Englishman was going to act this way, Phin would just have to get on without his assistance. His leg couldn't be that bad. He would just sit up. Swing his feet to the floor. Hobble his way out of doors and find someone somewhere who wouldn't assume that every word to fall from his lips was meant to be an insult.

He got so far as to move his lower leg halfway off the cot when the ferocious pain made the world spin and go gray. A distant scream echoed in the recesses of his mind. Not until the ache registered in his throat did he realize it was his own.

It seemed half of forever that the room kept rocking, that every sound was far away and nonsensical. When at last his senses settled, Luther was dabbing Phin's brow with a damp cloth, his mouth set in a grim line.

He was stuck here. At this giant's mercy. Unable to move at all. He swallowed back the fear-tinged anger and forced out a whisper. "It's bad, isn't it? My leg?"

"Dr. Santiago fears he may yet have to amputate. The bullet shattered your femur." The rag left his brow. "What happened to you?"

Phin kept his eyes closed and let the darkness take him back. "I'm one of the *Sumter*'s crew."

"The what?"

He blinked his eyes open, though only for a moment. Why would he expect this man to know about his ship? "The CSS *Sumter*. The Confederate States' first cruiser."

Luther pursed his lips. "A pirate ship."

"Absolutely not! We are a duly certified ship of the Confederacy—"

"Whose sole purpose is to prey on virtually unarmed merchant vessels. That makes it a pirate ship."

He may yet lose his leg, but he hadn't lost his honor. Phin gripped the sheet under him. "Cruiser."

"Semantics." An infuriating half-smirk mocked him.

"Depriving our enemy combatants of vital goods and resources is not an act of piracy, especially given the blockade they have on every Southern port, attempting to deprive our wives and children of the same."

The giant leaned forward, bracing his forearms against his knees. "Delia is your wife, then? You have children?"

The question punched him in the stomach. Phin pushed himself up on one elbow to fight it, gritting his teeth against the pain. "What do you know of Delia?"

"Calm down, Phineas." He used a single finger to push him back down to the pillow, no doubt to illustrate how weak Phin was right now. "You mentioned her the day I found you. Seemed rather distressed that you hadn't told her you love her."

Flames sprang to life on the back of Phin's neck. "How long have I been here?"

Luther just studied him. Did the question really require that much contemplation? "Not married, I'm guessing, or you wouldn't be so embarrassed. Betrothed?"

If only. "We have an understanding. How long? A day? Two?"

"Four. You were speaking in general, then, about the Northerners depriving the wives and children of the South." Luther nodded and leaned back. "And so, you were aboard a ship called the CSS *Sumter*, attempting to deprive the United States of valuable resources."

Phin's eyes slid closed again. "How could it have been four days? I have no recollection of any of it after waking up on the beach."

"You've been in such pain that Dr. Santiago has administered morphine regularly. Was the *Sumter* near here? I've never heard of it."

"We were off the Isle of Pines. Captured two ships, and I

was on the prize crew aboard one. Seas were rough, the second prize broke free of its tow, so the *Sumter* had to tend to it and cut ours. Two—" He had to pause, suck in a long breath. "Two of our sailors turned on us. Freed the ship's crew, and . . . I don't know what happened. Our officer was up a mast, shooting broke out. I was struck, hit the railing. I fell overboard and managed at some point to find a piece of wood to anchor myself to, though I remember little other than that."

What had become of Hudgins and the others? Had they retaken the *Cuba*? Rendezvoused with Commander Semmes in Cienfuegos?

What had happened to Spencer? Had he been killed? Arrested? Would he be tried for treason? Or, the unthinkable—what if that treason had been successful? Would his friend end up in the North? Would he . . . would he fight for them? How could he go through life knowing he'd bear the badge of a turncoat forever on his soul? How would his sense of honor allow it?

Maybe he didn't *have* a sense of honor. Maybe that was the problem.

A breath whistled past Luther's lips. "The Isle of Pines, you say? I wonder how you made it all the way here. The Lord must have held you in His hand."

The Lord? It seemed that if the Lord was going to be so active as to save him, He could have intervened a little earlier and stopped the treachery. "Where am I? Near Cienfuegos?"

Luther straightened and frowned. "You're in the Pinar del Río province. Nearly three hundred miles from Cienfuegos, if my Cuban geography can be trusted. Which, granted, I don't know nearly so well as British, but . . ."

But he was right in this case. Phin scrubbed a hand over his face. Those three hundred miles might as well be a thousand in his current state. He couldn't walk. He had no horse and suspected this Luther fellow didn't either. There must be a town around here somewhere sizable enough to have a telegraph . . . though from what he'd read, Cuba's telegraph wires were undependable. And wasn't there some law about only Spanish messages being allowed? A telegraph office certainly wouldn't help him get word home. It may, at best, allow him to get a message to Uncle Beau's contacts in Havana.

Or to Cienfuegos. Maybe Semmes was still there. They didn't need any repairs yet, having only been on the open ocean a few days, but the commander would most likely take the opportunity to seek more coal for the boiler. Perhaps give the men shore leave. It was possible he was still there. If Phin could get him a message, maybe he would wait for him.

Oh, who was he fooling? The *Sumter* couldn't wait for one lost sailor as low in the ranks as Phin. Especially one who would be confined to his hammock until they could reach some other port to put him off at.

He would be a liability. A mouth to feed that couldn't earn its own keep. Trouble. Nothing more.

Still, he must get in touch with someone. Let them know he was alive, see what became of Hudgins and the marines . . . and of Spencer. Get instruction on what he was to do. Failing the help of a telegram, he'd simply resort to letters.

Luther stood, took a single step. Banged a few pieces of metal together, presumably pots or cups or whatnot. He came back a minute later with a tin plate covered in fruit. "Can you eat?"

Phin eyed the offerings and tried to query his stomach on whether it was empty or not. Nothing looked appetizing, even though all appeared fresh and juicy. He shook his head.

Luther nodded and sat again, sliced off a piece of mango. "You aren't even going to ask, are you? It hasn't occurred to you to wonder. Perhaps it's the pain. And the morphine. I shall give you the benefit of the doubt and assume so."

The scent of the mango, tangy and earthy, only made his throat tighten. "Ask what?"

"What an educated black man from England is doing in a filthy little hovel in Spanish-held Cuba. I'm certain if you were yourself, it would strike you as odd. I know it still strikes me so on a daily basis."

"Well, now that you mention it." He had noted from the moment he first caught site of the giant that he was well dressed. Too well dressed to belong in this place. "You obviously have a story." And it would obviously be full of what Luther would term injustice, which he'd probably expect Phin to defend. It sounded utterly exhausting. "Perhaps you can tell me about it tomorrow. I'm afraid I'm worn out."

Luther sliced another piece of mango. "You're going to listen now, young man, before you fall into another few days of opiate-induced delirium. Go ahead and close your eyes if you're too taxed."

He may have clenched his teeth until he felt the muscle in his jaw throb, but Phin kept his eyes decidedly open.

A chuckle was his reward. "That's what I thought. But it isn't really my story that has brought me here. It's Eva's."

The name meant nothing to Phin, but the tone as Luther said it made him instantly aware of what kind of story this would be, at least in part. The kind that brought Delia's face to mind, made his lips remember the feel of hers. The kind that made his chest ache in a way completely separate from the pain caused by bullet and battery.

The kind he wasn't sure he could stand to hear right now. "Luther—"

"She was raised here, right here in this little bungalow, by her grammy, who was mammy to the master's children. Her mother died when she was too young to remember, but because her grandmother was such a beloved house slave, my Evangelina was always treated well while the old master was alive." Luther made another slice, this one with all the precision of a surgeon with his scalpel, and with just as much concentration.

"The young master . . . well, you know how these things work, being a young master yourself."

He knew how they could, yes. But he didn't like the implications. Phin swallowed. "My family has never been of the mind that slave women are to be treated as concubines, Luther. My father taught me to respect all women, no matter their race or station."

Luther grunted, raised the slice of orange fruit, but then sighed and tossed both whole mango and piece to the plate. "Think what you will about us, Phineas, but we're not born with souls meant to shoulder such burdens. Eva . . . it nearly broke her, but praise be to the Lord, she and her grammy saved enough money to buy her freedom. She came to England. I met her mere days after she arrived, when she came into my church. It didn't take us long to court, to marry."

Phin tried to shift without causing a new wave of pain, and without interrupting Luther. The man stared into the flame of the lamp as if it held all the mysteries of past and future both. The light gleamed off his shining brown scalp.

"Ten happy years we had together. But the moment we step foot on this godforsaken island, it's one loss after another."

Phin's brows knit. "Did she die?"

"No." Luther looked up, eyes sparking. "At least I pray not, though I've not seen her in months." He surged to his feet, turning his back to Phineas. "He took her from me. Her old master took my Eva and put her on a ship bound for Savannah, as if he had the right to do so. And no one dared listen when she screamed for help. Why would they? A white man claimed she was a troublesome slave, and she didn't have her papers on her."

All Phin's attention was stuck on that one word. "Savannah."

"Savannah."

Phin shook his head. "But the slave trade has been closed for nigh unto sixty years. He couldn't send her there to sell her."

"You think there's never a way around that? That a white

man from Virginia never buys a slave in Cuba, where he's been living, and then takes her home with him when he goes—or claims that, anyway?" Luther's nostrils flared. "I tried to go after her, managed to get past the blockade. But they wouldn't even let me step foot in port."

"They wouldn't, no." Phin sighed and finally let his eyes slide shut. "Free blacks are considered rabble-rousers in the city."

"*Your* city." Luther's voice had moved closer, coming from just above him now. "You can find what I can't, Phineas. You can find where they sent my wife. And if you promise you will, then I promise I'll not let you die."

Who was he to make such a bargain, such a promise? God? An unamused laugh came out on a breath. He tried to blink his eyes open, but they were too heavy. As if any man could promise life. All he could promise was not to hurry death. Was that what he had meant?

No. The darkness settled on him again, warm and comfortable. He didn't sound like that type, no matter the fact that he could break every bone in Phin's body with his bare hands, if he so chose.

But he'd said something about *his church*, in a way that seemed to be more possessive than a mere parishioner. And Cambridge. He'd said something about Cambridge.

Phin turned his head just a bit. Oblivion retreated a tick, just enough that he realized it had been closing in.

Strong fingers gripped his shoulder. "Promise me, Phineas. Give me your word."

"My son, attend to my words; incline thine ear unto my sayings. Let them not depart from thine eyes; keep them in the midst of thine heart."

Luther wasn't God. Just a man of God.

Close enough. "I promise."

The fingers released him, and he melted back into that place where the pain could ebb away.

Chapter Nine

Salina peeked through the narrow opening, careful to keep it unnoticeable to those within the room. The white folk liked the idea of the slaves being able to move about the house without being seen, sure enough. But no doubt the collection of twenty ladies within would get their petticoats in a bunch if they paused to realize that the passageways built behind their rooms could be used for purposes beyond serving them.

Not that Salina had any nefarious goals, no sir. She just wanted to see Miss Delia's tableaux vivants, and heaven knew she wouldn't be making an appearance at the Pulaski House next week. So, she'd hurriedly given instructions to the visiting maids who had come to help with the costuming and then taken up a place in the dark little cubbyhole behind the drawing room.

After all, she needed some inspiration if she was going to create the best possible costumes for the tableaux.

"Perfect, Annaleigh," Miss Delia said, her smile sweet and encouraging.

Though in Salina's opinion Miss Annaleigh was the worst model in the group. So why she was the central figure in each tableau . . . Miss Delia must have switched some of their parts for the sake of peace. She never wanted to offend anyone and would no doubt do whatever it took to make the collection of young ladies as happy as she could. A losing battle. One of these days, Miss Delia would have to learn that.

Annaleigh tossed her curls over her shoulder with a look so haughty Salina would have liked to take a nice wire brush to it to try to scrub away the contempt. "Well, as perfect as one can expect, anyway, given the limitations of the narration and the uninspired choices of paintings we are representing."

Why, that nasty little shrew! Salina had read every word of Miss Delia's script, and it was such a creative way of going from one classic work of art to the next, telling a story as she did. Since it was going to be seen by all of Savannah, Salina had even worked up the nerve to offer some actual critique. Better her now than some high-falutin' lady later, right? And Miss Delia had received it graciously.

Though no doubt if Annaleigh knew a slave had helped with any of the words, she really *would* storm off and never return.

Which was sounding better and better.

"Don't be that way, Annaleigh." Miss Lacy sighed and moved back to the spot on the floor she would occupy when the curtains were raised. "It isn't becoming."

Sassy Dunn smirked in a way that most young ladies couldn't get away with. "It's the only way she knows how to be, Lacy."

"Be as mean as you like, Saphrona, it won't change the fact that I have twice the beaux you do." Miss Annaleigh spun the other direction, toward a group of girls busy controlling their grins at the argument. Salina could well imagine the look that would be on her face. Superior and taunting, with only the thinnest covering of sugar. "And the Owenses' handsome cousin sure seemed to find my company pleasant at your daddy's ball last week."

Miss Lacy's face turned pink, but Miss Delia put a hand on her sister's arm and smiled. It was what she called her Ginny smile, all politeness and modesty, and as fake as those curls of her rival's. "We thank you, Annie, for helping our cousin feel at home in Savannah. He certainly did mention your family's hospitality when he came to call on Lacy the next day. Now, we had better run through the script one more time before Salina and the others arrive with the costumes."

The glance Miss Delia sent toward the crack in the wall said that Salina's hiding place was known by at least one of the occupants. Luckily, though, the one who wouldn't care. She smiled to herself and vowed to hold her spot for just one minute more. Then she'd rush back to the sewing room, where the gathered seamstresses were hard at work.

In the drawing room, a flurry of skirts flashed while all the girls took their places again. Only five were "on stage." They each struck a pose that Salina knew was meant to imitate some great painting, though she couldn't recall which one. She had only seen them once, in the book Miss Delia had brought up to select paintings from as she wrote the tableaux.

Miss Annaleigh, of course, stood in the center, looking as though she were holding two combatants apart. Right funny, given that she usually *was* one of the combatants.

The other girls stood off to the side, awaiting their turns. Miss Delia nodded for another of her friends, who had been given the part of narrator, to begin.

"When the dawn of time was still soft and misty, when the great land of Greece was a sun rising over the horizon—"

"Oh, stop." Annaleigh let her arms flop to her side. "*Must* my little cousin be playing the part of a man?"

Said little cousin flushed scarlet. "Annie—"

"Someone has to, and you insisted she be beside you in each scene." Miss Delia's Ginny smile looked strained around the edges. "We can hardly have young men playing the parts with us; it wouldn't be quite decent."

"And at least she isn't all but nude, like in the painting." That helpful observation came from Sassy, of course, and nearly made Salina snort with laughter.

"I like the part just fine, Annie." The cousin smiled and patted Miss Contrary on the arm. "I love the scarlet cape I'm getting for it, and the shield. Just never you mind. Let's keep going."

They did, but Salina slipped down the passageway and out into the servant quarters, knowing she had better make sure all was going as it should with the costumes. Given that the actresses spoke not a word, their clothes had to tell the story of the paintings.

It was great fun, really, having such a big part in the production. Not that anyone else would likely see it that way, of course, but Salina would know. She'd know she had done her part, helped her sister's show be a success.

Six other servants had been enlisted to help, one from each of the families represented in the drawing room. The room she typically used for sewing was crowded with four of them, and the other two were in her closet of a bedchamber. Workspace was precious indeed in any house in Savannah. Wasn't like on the rice plantation, no sir, where each slave family had its own little cabin and there were rooms aplenty inside for them to use. To work in the Savannah house, most of them had to rent their rooms in Yamacraw or Currytown.

She got a shudder even thinking of those sections of town. Maybe she ought not to fear them so much, given that many of the residents were her own kind. But crime pranced through those streets to the merry tune of the dance halls, and Salina had no desire to step foot in time to it. Besides, there were as many Irish there as blacks these days, and they didn't take kindly to one another ofttimes. Or so she'd heard.

After checking on the two in her room and fetching them some of the fabric they needed, she settled in with the larger group. "They gonna be needin us soon."

One of the women in particular attacked the cloth in her lap with renewed fury. Salina hadn't caught the woman's name, though she looked to be in her late twenties.

Another older woman laughed. "Look at Vangie, workin hard to prove she been workin, though we all know Miss Annaleigh ain't gonna believe it no matter what she bring out."

"Oh, you be one of the Youngs'?" Salina reached over to pat the woman's shoulder. "Ya have my sincerest condolences."

Vangie breathed a laugh and paused a bare moment to tuck a spiral of hair that had come free back into her turban. "There is no pleasing the young miss."

"Don't waste your time tryin, then." Old Bess snipped a blue thread with her teeth, then threaded her needle with red. "Now, my Miss Sassy will be happy nuff with my work and will have her fun in it. The Dunns run a good house." She looked over at Salina and smiled. "When you come with Miss Delia when she and Mr. Phin marry, we make you right at home."

"Y'all hear any more from him lately?" Salina poked some white thread through her needle and set about finishing Miss Delia's costume, one of pure Grecian white. Or would it be Miss Annaleigh's now? If so, she may just set the seams crooked.

"Naw, not since his last letter from N'Orleans. He ever write to your miss? I know her daddy done give him leave to, if he had a mind."

He had, though according to the talk she'd heard from Mass Owens's valet, he hadn't been exactly happy about it. He didn't have the heart to turn down Miss Delia though. If she'd set her sights on Mr. Phin—which she'd clearly done—then Mr. Phin it would be. "Quite a few, there at the start. Full of sweet nothins and tales as big as the sea." Her lips quirked up, then settled again. "Miss Delia worries for him somethin awful. She been havin these dreams. . . ." No need to mention that Salina had shared them. That would put too dark a meaning on them.

Old Bess's hands stilled. "What kinda dreams? Good ones? Nonsense and love?"

Salina just shook her head.

Even that was enough to make Old Bess raise her hands and let out a shout. "Lawd of Mercy, keep yo hand on our boy. And don' let it be his ghost a-visitin Miss Delia."

"Now, stop. There be no call for that kind of thinkin." Salina knew the glare she sent wouldn't do any good. Old Bess had too many decades under her apron to give a lick about the opinions of a girl Salina's age.

"Don' you be tellin me what I've call to think, missy. Young, lovestruck girl like Miss Delia havin forebodin dreams of her man . . . that be bad news there, you mark my words." Old Bess shook her head and jabbed her needle into a pincushion. "Bad news, I tell ya."

"Well, we be prayin rather than frettin." Salina finished attaching the translucent blue cloth, not sure what to call the filmy, scarf-like thing, but content that it would do a fair job at imitating the painting.

"Wise girl." Vangie winked at her, then shook out the garment in her lap and held it up to survey it. "Might as well see what in particular she finds to complain about before doing more."

All the others reached stopping points as well and gathered up their things. The young ladies would all need to try their costumes on in the privacy of the guest bedchambers, but knowing them, they'd like the chance to flutter over the dresses together first. With a smile, Salina led the way down the hall to the drawing room.

She paused outside it when deep voices came from within. A peek through the door showed that a collection of uniformed men was inside, laughing and flirting with the girls. Now, where in the world had *they* come from?

The housekeeper, Pearl, slipped out and motioned the seamstresses in. "G'on, g'on. They knows you be comin, and the menfolk be ready to have some lemonade while the ladies is gone."

Salina nodded and sidled through the partially opened door. She spotted Miss Delia in the corner with Sassy, their gazes on Miss Lacy and a tall, broad officer who matched the description they'd given of that new-come cousin of theirs, Mr. Julius. Salina traced a path along the edge of the room to get to her mistress.

Miss Delia greeted her with a warm smile. "Oh, are they finished? Let me see. Though I suppose I shall have to trade costumes with Annaleigh now." She took the dress from Salina's hands, then glanced over to Miss Contrary, who was giving poor Vangie a tongue-lashing. "Lovely. But I think perhaps I'd better go make the trade. You just stay here out of range of her shrapnel, Sal."

Miss Sassy chuckled as Delia moved off. Salina pressed herself back against the wall so as to stay as removed from the goings-on as possible.

A few others sashayed to Miss Sassy's side, their hoop skirts swaying in a way no doubt meant to mesmerize the menfolk. Salina suddenly wished she hadn't worn her new, bright turban with its rich blue color today. Had she wrapped the old faded one around her head this morning, she would have blended into the wallpaper far better.

Best to let all the attention go to those who wanted it. Those who viewed the gentlemen in their gold-braided uniforms as potential husbands, not potential masters. She'd just pray Mr. Phin home again—according to Old Bess, the Dunns never touched their slaves.

"I do wish Delia hadn't invited Annaleigh to be part of the tableaux." Mary Mercer snapped her fan open and swished it in front of her face. "She spoils everything."

"Especially when Delia gives in to her every demand like she does." Mary's sister Sarah sniffed and raised her chin. "If she had but stood firm—"

"Then Annaleigh would have stormed out, her four cousins with her, and we wouldn't have had enough girls to complete the display." Miss Sassy smoothed the sash around her tiny waist with what looked like an absent gesture.

Miss Mary harrumphed. "If you ask me, Delia just can't stand that Annaleigh doesn't like her and does whatever she can to win her favor."

Sassy lifted a brow. "Nonsense. She knows well that Annie just doesn't like anyone."

That much may be true, but Miss Delia would be sore upset to realize that Miss Mary and Miss Sarah had such opinions of how she handled the tableaux. It hurt her something fierce when all the hard work she put into something, be it a story or a situation, went unappreciated. Salina may have had the same thought minutes earlier, but she'd never *say* it like that. Why did society girls always think their own opinion was all that mattered and never take into account anyone else's feelings?

Was it possible Delia heard their catty exchange, or did she just glance back for fortification? Given the shadows lurking in the green of her eyes, Salina had to think she'd caught at least part of the Mercer sisters' words. But Miss Delia knew better than to face down an enemy with uncertainty cloaking her, Salina had to give her that. She squared her shoulders, lifted her chin, and took the last few steps to Miss Annaleigh's side.

Salina buried her smile when her sister reached straightaway for the pretty gown Vangie was getting the what-for about and exclaimed loud enough for the whole room to hear, "Oh, it's perfect! I do declare, it makes me not at all miss the roles we switched, though I'm hard-pressed to part with my Salina's masterpiece, I must say. What a talented seamstress you have, Annaleigh. It's no wonder your new gowns have been so lovely."

Miss Contrary was obviously torn between accepting the

flattery and arguing the point of Vangie's competence. Lips pursed, she took the gown Salina had made. "Well, this is—"

"Perfect for you, I know. The color will suit you so much better than it would me, I do confess." Miss Delia made a shooing motion toward the doors. "Go try them on, everyone, and then we'll do the tableaux again in costume."

The assembly broke up, ladies and slaves exiting together, chattering over the costumes. Miss Annaleigh was, of course, the loudest. "So little fabric! I swear I don't know how our grandmothers could countenance wearing so little. No flounce, no hoop, no . . ."

Thank heavens, she exited the room there. Miss Delia came Salina's way again, looking like she would have shaken her head were it not for the audience.

"Well handled, Miss Delia." Arms held out for the gown of Vangie's making, Salina smiled. "Just like that snake charmer you wrote about last year."

Miss Delia's laughter rang through the room and brought half a dozen male gazes her way—and one cousin striding for her only seconds after Miss Lacy headed for the door.

Salina tried to disappear behind the wide skirts of her mistress and let her impressions of Mr. Julius settle in her mind while her eyes focused on the rug. Easy to see why Miss Lacy had been all aflutter over him. So tall, shoulders so wide, hips so narrow. And his face—well, he was handsome, for sure, but she preferred the strong features of her African side to the too-pinched noses and lips of the masters.

And this master in particular had far too many features in common with the mistress. Though it wasn't the fair hair or straight nose, which the misses Owens boasted too, that made Salina uneasy—it was that hard ice in his blue eyes.

"Delia, allow me to wish you a most pleasant afternoon."

Though Salina couldn't see Miss Delia's face, she recognized the tension in her shoulders right enough. "Thank you, Julius.

I must say, I was surprised to see you and your friends here today. I thought for sure you'd have maneuvers or training or Yankees to fight off."

Did the gentleman hear the censure in her tone? Salina glanced up and indeed saw that his answering grin was strained. "I assure you, we have already drilled, and no Yankees would dare show their faces on the Georgian mainland."

Miss Delia only hummed and took a step to the side, her aim obviously the door.

Mr. Julius halted her with a hand on her arm. "Have I done something to offend you, Cousin Cordelia? It seems whenever I'm near, you're eager to be away."

Her face was the perfect mask she'd learned to put on at the Female Academy. Her posture was straight as an arrow, her chin at that level that would let Salina stack books upon her head. But the fingers of her right hand curled in that way she always employed when trying to hide the ink stains from her mother—the one sign that she was defensive and bothered.

"Not at all, Cousin." Though her tone was as sweet as the mistress could wish it, Salina still detected the tension that Miss Delia was trying to keep hidden. "We're glad to have you in Savannah. Why, Lacy—"

"I was speaking of *you*, not your sister." Mr. Julius stepped closer—too close, but what could Salina do to help? "Delightful as she is, you are the elder—"

"And spoken for." Miss Delia took another step away. Much as she could manage, anyway, with his hand still gripping her elbow. "I do hope you'll forgive me if I've seemed a bit distracted in your company. It's only that my mind is so often on Phin."

He released her, but so slowly that it was obvious he wasn't convinced. "Hmm. I wonder that you'd have such loyalty to a man who was fool enough to leave without marrying you."

"A situation that will be remedied as soon as he returns, I assure you." Smiling, Miss Delia stepped clear of him. "Do enjoy your lemonade, Julius. Now, excuse me—Lacy and I must be fitted for our costumes."

Miss Delia motioned for Salina, though she wished she'd been allowed to stay unmoving behind her. Soon as she stepped forward, Mr. Julius's gaze swept over her, from turban to sandals. She didn't much like the light she detected in his eyes, but it weren't exactly unexpected. How many times had her murruh whispered into her ear, *"I wish you weren't so pretty, baby girl. No good never came from a slave girl being so pretty"*? But then he shifted to watch Miss Delia glide away, and that gleam didn't change, not one little bit. And it should have—that was a lady he was watching with such a predatory gaze, not a maid who'd been raised to keep a keen eye out for such a look so she could do her best to avoid it. What was the point of social standing if it didn't come with a bit of respect to protect you?

She darted after Miss Delia, drawing near once they were in the hall. "I don't like that Mr. Julius. He don't look at you like he should."

Miss Delia's smile wobbled a bit before sticking in place. "Nonsense. He just hasn't yet fully realized how preferable Lacy is. But don't worry." In a move that would have sent the mistress into a faint, Miss Delia reached over and gripped Salina's hand—there, in the hall, in plain sight of anyone who might walk by. "When Phin comes home, no one will question anymore."

Salina gave those lovely ivory fingers a squeeze, then pulled her hand away before they both landed square into trouble. Why didn't her sister ever consider such things? She sure hoped Miss Delia was right about the cousin. But couldn't help but fear she was wrong. That Mr. Julius had a plantation near the one the missus had brought to the marriage, didn't he? Which meant that Mass Owens would find him a fine match for the daughter who'd inherit it.

And that daughter wasn't Lacy. It was Cordelia.

Cordelia tossed the red scarf over her shoulder and struck her pose. Then struck it again upon remembering that she needed Annaleigh's pose, not the one she had perfected before the mirror in the preceding week.

She glanced toward Annaleigh, who stood, as always, in the center of the room. Where she completely failed to capture the spirit of the painting they were embodying. Oh, she would be the ruination of the entire tableaux, but there was nothing Cordelia could do about it. Not without losing five key models who had places in each of them.

Look at her, her smile smug and hateful. And why did her little cousins do her bidding in all things? If it were only Annaleigh in danger of quitting, Delia may just risk offending her and shoving her back into her original roles. Kicking and screaming, if necessary.

But no. This wasn't about the tableaux themselves. It was about raising funds for the Confederacy, for the men out there fighting. For Phin. Why, Daddy said the efforts of the ladies in Savannah put food in the soldiers' mouths, boots on their feet, and weapons in their hands.

Annaleigh hardly mattered at all when pitted against such a cause.

At least the costuming had come together. Cordelia glanced around at the other girls, all arrayed in redone dresses borrowed from their attics. The simple styles of the early part of the century worked perfectly for the paintings of ancient scenes and battles she had selected.

And despite what Annaleigh said, everyone else seemed impressed by the story she had written to draw the works of art together. No one *else* had implied there was anything lacking. Or unsuitable.

But what if they were thinking it? What if they had laughed

over her story when they were in the spare chambers, changing into their costumes? What if *all* of Savannah laughed? Or, worse, thought it somehow indecent?

Cordelia's arm slipped down a notch. At least until Mama shot a hard glance at her, pointed at her lazy arm. She raised it again and glanced at the other mothers and officers draped over the furniture around the room. All the girls had been excited to have a small audience to practice in front of.

Though, for her part, Cordelia would have been happy for it to be limited to their families and not include all these men.

At least Julius kept his gaze mostly on Lacy, where it belonged.

Mostly.

Their narrator read through the first bit of the story, her voice sure and melodious. Cordelia had definitely made a sound choice in selecting Maybelle Gregory to do the reading. Once that portion was complete, Maybelle paused to signal the change of tableau.

The girls did a quick but graceful switch. Most of them moved off to the side to make room for the second group, and the servants went to work quickly altering the accessories of their costumes to prepare them for the next painting represented. A moved sash here, different color shawl there, quick let-down of hair.

Maybelle was halfway through the second installment of the story when the drawing room doors banged open and a servant boy charged in, breathless. "Mrs. Dunn! Mrs. Dunn! This just come." He waved a folded paper in the air, one that bore the mark of Savannah's telegraph office.

All motion in the room ground to a halt. Except for Willametta Dunn, who stood and, like a statue, held out an arm.

Her servant hurried forward to place the paper in her hand, nearly tripping over Julius's extended feet in the process. "With the mister away, I rushed here fast as I could, ma'am. The delivery boy say it be real important."

The sound of a quickly drawn-in breath reached her ears. Sassy, just behind her. Cordelia slid backward and put her arm around her friend. Tried to still the trembling that began in her stomach and coursed outward.

"It can't be Phin," Sassy murmured as she gripped Cordelia's hand. "It can't be. He isn't on the front lines, isn't really *fighting*. It's probably a business matter for Daddy. Mama will scold Lyle for bursting in here, and that will be that."

Cordelia nodded. Hoped. Wanted to believe Sassy was right.

Mrs. Dunn flipped the folded paper open. As her eyes moved back and forth, her lips pressed into a thin line. She drew in a long breath. Then another—or tried to. Somehow Cordelia wasn't surprised when the lady's face washed pale and her eyes rolled back.

"Mama!" Sassy shrieked and rushed toward her mother, even as Mama and Julius both jumped to be of assistance. Young Lyle managed to break his mistress's fall somewhat but made no protest when Julius took over the task of supporting her.

For a long moment, Cordelia felt suspended, as though she were watching a play unfold, a drama that had been written out and rehearsed. Not real, surely not real. Just a play.

But when Mama waved her ever-present vial of smelling salts under Willametta's nose, the lady came to just long enough to exclaim, "Phin!" before swooning again.

Cordelia's feet acted before she realized she'd told them to, propelling her over the floor to the gathering. She stopped and crouched down beside Sassy, who was lifting her mother's hand.

"Read it to me, Delia," her friend bade in a murmur as tears coursed down her cheeks.

Her hand shook as she took the telegram that Sassy had slipped from her mother's fingers. As if drawn by a magnet, her gaze went straight to the two most important words.

Phin . . . lost.

She cleared the emotion squeezing her throat shut, determined not to need those nasty smelling salts waved under *her* nose. "It's from your Uncle Beau, Sassy. It says, 'Been in Cienfuegos. *Sumter* arrived with prizes, Phin not on board. On prize crew of ship that has been lost. Hope ship will arrive soon but all fear the worst. Pray.'"

The worst. Cordelia lowered the paper, but her eyes remained focused where it had been. Lost. They all feared. But what was the worst? That the ship sank, Phin along with it? That he had been taken prisoner and would be handed over to the Yankee courts? What might they do to him, if that were true? Did Yankees believe in torture?

"No. No, no, no." Sassy squeezed her eyes shut and gripped her mother's hand with what looked like bruising strength. "Not Phin, it can't be. Uncle Beau must be mistaken. Phin can't be . . . *missing*."

So she wasn't the only one, then, for whom the not-knowing felt as terrifying as certain loss.

Cordelia put her arm around her friend again and let her eyes slide closed.

Darkness. Tossing waves, searing pain. Sand in the mouth, under the fingers. Desperation. Agony.

Were they real, those dreams? Sent from heaven like Salina said, so that they would know to pray—perhaps even *how* to pray? Were such things possible outside the pages of a book?

"He's all right." She whispered the words, as much for her benefit as Sassy's. "The ship he's on must have simply encountered a delay. They'll arrive where they should any day now, and Phin will rejoin his crew."

Julius cleared his throat. "Well now, I don't mean to discourage. But the *Sumter* won't long wait in port, I'm sure. Lord willing, your brother will indeed make his way there, Miss Dunn. But even if so, he and the rest of the prize crew will likely then have to find their own way home, where they can check in with the admiralty and get new instructions. Seems as though his tenure on the *Sumter* is at an end either way."

Cordelia opened her eyes so she could glare at him. "Not particularly inspiring information, Cousin, given how difficult it will be to make it past the blockade."

The lift of Julius's brow screamed a challenge. "I am only offering reality, my dear."

"Reality? What use is *that*?"

"Cordelia!" Mama's admonition came out on a horrified gasp.

Cordelia bit her lip to keep from saying anything else that would earn her censure. To be sure, she hadn't meant to let *that* slip out. And given the whispers she heard coursing around the room, she wished she could draw the words back in.

Willametta's lashes fluttered open, her eyes glassy. "Phin. My darling boy."

Sassy's breath caught on a sob, so Cordelia took it upon herself to lean closer to the woman she would someday call *Mother*. "He's all right, Mrs. Dunn. I know it. He is."

The lady's hazel eyes, just like Phin's, focused on Cordelia's face. Was that pity within them? No, it couldn't be. Just fear and grief. "He is lost."

"Off adventuring, no doubt, since the opportunity presented itself." Maybe her grin wobbled, but she pasted it on. "You know how Phin loves his adventures."

"He does, at that." Willametta looked as though she may say more. So much swirled through her eyes that Cordelia couldn't hope to decode—thoughts and wishes and regrets. But after a moment, the woman shook her head and looked to her daughter. "We had better hurry home, Sassy, and get word to your father on the plantation. He'll want to know."

"Yes, of course." But Sassy glanced with watery eyes to Cordelia. "Might Delia come with us? I mean, unless you need to oversee the rest of the rehearsal."

At Mama's nod of permission, Cordelia offered a smile. "Of course I'll come. You needn't even ask."

She couldn't have said what all happened in the next minutes. A flurry of activity as the crowd surged upon the Dunns with their promises of prayers, a general push toward the door. But somehow or another, Julius ended up at her elbow.

"Hope may flame eternal, Delie-Darlin, but you must face facts at some point." His voice was low, no more than a murmur. And sounded like curses to her ears. "Your young man could very well be gone."

Her answer was to stride away with steps too large to be ladylike.

Even so, she couldn't outpace the roiling darkness of fear.

Chapter Ten

Seven long days had dragged by since his charge had last awoken. Luther sat in his usual spot in the too-small chair by the too-small cot, with the too-dim light from the lamp shining upon the most precious belonging he had on this side of the Atlantic.

The Bible felt like home in his hands. Its worn leather cover had earned each crease and fold and scuff honestly, by continual use. He had thumbed through the pages so often that most of the gold leaf on the edges had come off. This book had gone through Cambridge with him, had been the volume he placed on the pulpit when he gave his first sermon. Its words were familiar, dear.

Yet, they barely dulled the edge of the knife he still felt so acutely in his side. Eva, his Eva. He needed her, missed her in ways words couldn't say. His beautiful hart, with her natural grace and vigor. She had come to England unschooled, untrained in anything but how to keep a master's house. But he had taken one look into her endless gray eyes and had known there was more to her than that.

So, so much more.

"Delia! Delia, no. Delia."

Luther sighed and picked up the dampened cloth, blotted

Phineas's forehead with it. "It's all right, Phineas. Delia is all right. You'll go home to her soon."

The thrashing eased, though only the Lord above knew if Luther's words had any effect or if it was pure coincidence. He splayed a hand over the pages open upon his leg. Eva had always marveled at how, when he did that, the page disappeared entirely. Her delicate little hands couldn't cover half the surface.

And she had been so quick with her words when she first saw him do it, though her English had still been rough. "*The Scripture you read on Sunday said we ought to hide the Word within our hearts—you said nothing about hiding it under our hands.*"

Luther's lips tugged up at the memory of the sparkle in her eye. He had known that very day that she was the one the Lord had ordained to be his wife. His companion, through all the trials. Working beside him, toiling in the dirty streets of London, ministering to others—many of whom were fugitives from America's South.

God Almighty, let someone be caring for her now, as she has cared so well and so long for others. As I care even now for this stranger.

Though the stranger had become less of one over the nearly two weeks he had lain on Luther's cot. He was seldom awake and hadn't been coherent since that night ten days ago, but his mumblings revealed more about the man than his conversation had. Luther felt almost guilty at all the private thoughts that spilled from the boy's lips.

His love for the girl named Delia.

His fear he was disappointing his parents.

His respect for his commander, Semmes.

His anger at a man named Spencer, who had been a friend but had betrayed him—all of them—on the *Sumter*.

He had learned names, of both places and people. Some dear, some seemingly despised. Even a description, now and then, as if he were reciting it for some reason, and exaggerating it besides.

A picture had begun to emerge. A picture of a young man with a lot to live for.

But fever raged through his body, and Dr. Santiago said pneumonia had settled into his lungs. Whenever they tried to lower his dosage of morphine, he would be out of his mind with pain.

Luther still couldn't fathom how the lad had managed to keep afloat over all the miles from the Isle of Pines to his beach. It was a miracle, nothing less. God's doing. He must have set a quick current to carry Phin and his life-saving piece of wood so far in so short a time.

And if it were truly a miracle that he lived at all, surely that meant healing would not elude them forever.

"Father in Heaven," he prayed softly, but loud enough that it might slice through the cloud of Phineas's mind, "place your hand on young Phineas. Heal him, Lord, by the power of the blood of Christ Jesus, who has died so that we might live. Let this young man stand again, walk again. Go home again to the family he misses so much."

He opened his eyes and would have sworn the shadows shifted at the edges of the room. His imagination, in all likelihood. Or the swaying of the tropical foliage outside his window. Still, it made his nostrils flare. He looked down to the page his Bible was open to and began to read where he had left off earlier.

"'Bless the Lord, O my soul: and all that is within me, bless his holy name. Bless the Lord, O my soul, and forget not all his benefits: who forgiveth all thine iniquities; who healeth all thy diseases; who redeemeth thy life from destruction; who crowneth thee with lovingkindness and tender mercies.'"

A hard knock sent the door rattling so forcefully, Luther was afraid it would fall from its makeshift hinges. He stood, Bible closed around his finger. But he didn't so much as take a step before the plank door swung wide.

A man far more despicable than any Confederate soldier filled the space.

Luther straightened his neck until his scalp pressed against the ceiling. "Rosario."

"Bromley." Hatred gleamed in the man's coal-black eyes. "I told you one month, no? You are still here."

"My deepest apologies. I assure you, I do not want to be, and I will be glad to find a room in the nearest town, just as soon as my . . . guest is well enough."

"Your guest? *¿Invitado?*" He took another step into the room, gaze on the bed, and sneered. "Who is this?"

Luther crossed his arms over his chest, Bible now tucked against him. If a wall he must be, then so be it. "A planter's son, injured and marooned. Santiago has been caring for him."

"Santiago. *Imbécil.*" Rosario spat onto the dirt floor.

Luther didn't give him the satisfaction of looking down at the newly made mud, nor of letting his disgust for the action show. "Unless *you* have some medical experience, Señor Rosario, he is the only physician for miles. I see no reason to complain about him."

Rosario strode past Luther to survey Phineas. Noting, Luther was certain, the fine gold hilt of the sword that lay beside the bed. The exquisite embroidery on his uniform, the once-fine braid and epaulettes. He would see in a glance exactly what Luther himself had noticed—the young man came from wealth.

A sound that bore an uncanny resemblance to a growl came from Rosario's throat. "I will send slaves with a litter. We will move him to the Big House for proper care."

"No." Not until the word was out of his mouth did Luther realize he had any intention of arguing. That he intended to be the one to see Phineas back to health, back onto his feet. "I have cared for him this long; I will continue to do so."

Rosario spat out a Spanish something too rapid for Luther to follow. He caught only *idiota*.

A groan from the bed stole his attention before he could attempt to make more sense of the diatribe. Luther spun around to find Phineas's eyes open, his breath coming in fast, panicked gasps. Luther dropped to his knees beside the bed and, when the young man tried to sit up, held him down with a gentle hand. "What is it, Phineas?"

His hazel eyes were glazed with fear. "Don't . . . don't let them take me. I don't want to die. Don't let me die. I don't . . . don't let them carry me off. Out of the water, I'm out of the water. Not gonna die, I'm not. You promised."

Rosario shuffled behind him, and Luther glanced over his shoulder to see the man had taken a step back. "He is *loco*."

"It's only the fever." Luther reached for the tin cup on the little table. "Don't worry, Phineas. You're not going to die. I promise. Here, drink."

He drank, then relaxed against the pillow again. His eyes slid shut. "Spirits in the waters, they say. Always laughed—superstition. But they were right. It carried me off. Carried me right away toward Hades."

"No, Phineas, it carried you to Cuba." Luther quirked a brow toward the slowly retreating planter. "Which may *seem* like Hades often enough, but you're still in the land of the living."

Phineas's hand landed on Luther's arm, stealing his attention again. "You promised. Promised I won't die."

"I know I did. I intend to keep that promise." Luther covered the lad's pale, cool fingers long enough to give them an encouraging squeeze.

The door creaked open. "Keep him here. Stay with him." Orders issued, Rosario retreated, his footsteps the next sound from that direction.

A shudder worked through Phineas, and his hand slid back to the mattress. "And I'll keep mine. I'm a man of honor. I'll help you. I will. Soon as I . . . I will."

"I know you will, Phineas Dunn." Luther sighed and settled

his Bible on his knee again, rubbed a hand over his face. "I know you will. Just as soon as you can."

Luther slid his eyes closed too. *How long, Lord? How long?*

When the houses turned from brick to wood, Cordelia shifted a bit on her seat. It wasn't often she ventured past the fashionable areas of Savannah. Occasionally, of course, her eyes would set upon the wooden façades that denoted the shift from wealth to mere subsistence, but never in her life had she ventured into the bowels of Currytown. Mama preferred to focus her charitable works toward other sectors and only permitted her daughters to participate in the drawing-room portion of them. The stitching and sewing and embroidering. Not the delivering, no sir.

Willametta Dunn, however, looked undaunted as she sat in the partial shade of the buggy, en route to one of their slaves who had fallen ill. Sassy had declined joining them, but seeing the look of disappointment in Mrs. Dunn's eyes at that, Cordelia had volunteered to accompany her.

It was, after all, a chance to spend some time with Phin's mother. Win her favor. Convince her that Phin hadn't made a poor choice by asking her to wait for him.

Beside her, the matron drew in a long breath. A frown creased her brows as she looked to the horizon, spurring Cordelia to follow suit. A plume of black smoke billowed in the distance.

Up her spine danced a chill of dread. One couldn't grow up in Savannah without a healthy fear of the destruction fire could wreak in the city. "Are we headed that way?"

"No, praise the Lord." Willametta motioned to the left even as the driver steered the carriage around a corner. "River rents a room yonder. The fire looks to be in Oglethorpe Ward somewhere. Probably Yamacraw."

Cordelia nodded and, given the woman's scrutiny, hoped the

intense summer sun hadn't burnt her face already. She had a bonnet on, of course, and the buggy provided some shade, but the sunlight still reflected off the sand of the streets.

"I do appreciate your joining me this morning, Delia." Willametta's smile was sad and strained, as it had been each day the past week. "It's always so good to have company on a trip such as this, but Sassy cannot abide the slave quarters, neither in Savannah nor on the plantation."

"Oh, I'm happy to come." And why would Sassy mind the slave quarters on the plantation? Those she had visited before were tidy little cabins with carefully tended garden plots, squawking chickens, and oinking pigs. A veritable home within the larger home of their master's. Quite cozy.

Though when she'd said as much one time, Salina had given her a strange look. A look that said maybe she hadn't seen everything.

As for the slave quarters in Savannah, she knew well this side of town could get less than savory. Sassy's reticence to travel here she could understand well enough, but Cordelia would be certain not to let any unpleasant thoughts show on her countenance. She would be the figure of grace, just like her companion.

Perhaps when she got home, if she had time before the tableaux tonight, she would pen a story about a philanthropic heroine who risked life and limb to rescue the downtrodden. Who, perhaps, even braved the smoke and flame of a town ablaze to save the life of a particularly precious beggar, perhaps even coming away disfigured—though of course whoever the hero turned out to be would love her all the more for the reason behind the scars.

Willametta's hum brought her back to the present. "I'm sure Phin would appreciate it. River has always been so dear to him; they've been together since they were boys. Much like you and that mulatto girl of yours, I imagine."

"Salina, yes. She's a—" *friend*. But Cordelia could hardly

say as much, not to anyone but Salina herself. "She's a favorite. And when Phin comes home, he'll certainly be glad to know River was well cared for."

Willametta's hazel eyes went damp. "It's the uncertainty of his homecoming that has rendered poor River ill, I suspect."

"We mustn't think that way though. He'll come home, I know he will." Over the past week, Cordelia had perfected her brave smile, in spite of the fearsome images that would spring up in her imagination at odd moments. In spite of the dreams that woke her most nights, dreams of giant alligators snapping their jaws at him, of man-eating sharks circling him, of ogre-faced Yankees tossing him into the dankest of prisons with rats baring their teeth at him.

Willametta reached over and patted Cordelia's hand. "I do appreciate your optimism, Delia dear. But the truth is, we can't know if Phineas will ever come home. I'm proud of him for going, for joining the Cause, for . . . but I wish I knew. I just wish I *knew*, knew whether he was alive or dead. Do I hope, or do I resign myself?"

With a squeeze of Willametta's fingers, Cordelia forced away the images of gators and sharks and Yankees and held tight to that smile. "We are nowhere near resignation, ma'am. Had your brother not happened to be in Cienfuegos, we wouldn't even know of this missing ship—and if the navy hasn't seen fit to contact you, they obviously don't deem it worth worrying over yet. So of course we hope."

The lady's lips wobbled. "But it's so hard to hope when there's so much wonder. Don't you wonder where he is, Delia?"

"Well, I . . ." Cordelia drew in a sharp breath and rolled back her shoulders. "Why, I'd wager he's in the Everglades, down in Florida. There was a storm that night, you see, a terrible gale that whipped the ship off course and landed them there rather than in Cuba. It was a frightful night—the winds howling, the waves roaring—but the good sense of the crew landed them on a deserted stretch of beach. They all escaped injury except for the ship, which was beyond repair, given the resources at hand."

A small smile emerged on Willametta's mouth. "Wondering is an entirely different pastime for you, I think. You can turn it into something more than worry."

Except for those moments when she still tasted sand in her mouth, felt that agony in her leg. "Sometimes."

A nod from the older woman drew Cordelia's attention to a row of clapboard housing. A few people walked along the street, scarcely casting a glance their way, but otherwise the place was empty. No doubt those who rented rooms here were all about their masters' tasks.

When the buggy rocked to a halt in front of a building like every other, Willametta gathered her basket and her skirt. The moment the footman offered a hand, she put hers into it and descended. Was it eagerness to help, for a distraction, or was she determined to complete her task and get out of Currytown?

Cordelia followed her companion to the street level, unwilling to attribute any less-than-gracious motives to Phin's mother. Once her feet were upon the packed sand, she smoothed out her skirt and drew in a long breath. Willametta was already making for the door, though she paused at the threshold to wait for Cordelia to catch up.

The doorway was narrow, so much so that their skirts both pressed to a bell as they went through and sprang back out once they were in the dark, odorous entryway. Cordelia followed the woman up a set of creaking stairs, the footman bringing up the rear.

After going halfway down a hallway, Willametta knocked upon a door. "River? It's Mrs. Dunn."

"Comin, ma'am. I's a-comin." A shuffling came from within, then the sound of a bolt sliding. The concerned face of Phin's valet greeted them a moment later. "There be news?"

Willametta's face went soft. "No, River, I just came to see how you were feeling."

Relief filled his face. "Now, ma'am, you don't need to bother yoself with me. I be back to work tomorra."

"It wasn't concern for your work ethic that brought us here, but rather for your health. May we come in?"

River only then looked beyond his mistress and spotted Cordelia. She offered him a small smile, but he made no response, not to her. Just directed his gaze back to Willametta, nodded, and opened the door wide.

The apartment was roughly the size of Cordelia's bedchamber, and seemed to house at least four people, given the cots lined up against the wall. She could hardly imagine trying to live in such little space—but then, how often were the occupants even there? Only at night, in all likelihood.

River rubbed a hand over his close-cropped hair. "I feel a far sight more better now than I did this mawnin, ma'am. I real sorry I didn't come in today—it jest . . . well, there ain't nothin for me a do right now nohow, and I felt plumb sick after that dream I had last night."

Had a chair been handy, Cordelia would have sunk right onto it at those words. Surely it wasn't uncommon for any number of folks to have bad dreams when someone dear to them was missing. But still, the mention of it was enough to bring Cordelia's back to her. All those imagined monsters, all those desperate feelings.

Willametta touched a hand to the young man's shoulder in what looked to be a soothing, gentle gesture. "What kind of dream, River? Of Phin? A distressing one, I presume?"

River gave one quick jerk of his chin and turned his face toward the lone window in the place, which had a stunning view of the wall of the next building. "All shadows and daa'k, and some bad devil spirit speakin in tongues. But it was a-threatenin him, I could tell."

Cordelia opened her mouth to question him, to ask if he'd had any other dreams of Phin—perhaps any similar to hers. But when she saw the sheen of moisture in Willametta's eyes, she bit her tongue.

The lady sniffed, then raised her chin in an obvious effort to force composure upon herself. "I can certainly understand why that would upset you, and I don't begrudge you the time to digest it. Especially since, as you say, there is little for you to do with Phin . . . away as he is." She cleared her throat and wove her fingers together, resting them on her skirt. "But I daresay we will all fare better with busy hands. My husband and I have been talking of how to keep you occupied, and we both agree that you should act as bodyguard for Sassy. With so many soldiers about, I don't feel comfortable letting her out of the house without an able-bodied male to accompany her."

River rolled his shoulders back and gave another quick nod. "I be honored, ma'am. Until Mr. Phin come home."

"Yes . . . until then." Willametta pivoted on her heel, her skirt swishing and swaying. "If you are feeling up to it, you could begin tonight and escort us to the Pulaski House for the tableaux vivants."

"Sho thing. I come round the house soon as I git cleaned up some."

"Take your time, so long as you are there by supper." Willametta paused with her hand on the knob. "And, River, I am glad you are not ill. But very sorry you were so disturbed by this dream of yours."

In his gray eyes gleamed respect as he dipped his head. "I sho do appreciate you comin all the way out here, ma'am, to check on me. Yo good folk."

"Well. It's the least I can do." Willametta blinked a few times and motioned at Cordelia. "Come along, Delia. I had better get you home so you can prepare for your tableaux."

Well, that certainly hadn't been so bad. She didn't know why Mama forbade them to come here, or why Sassy had refused. Cordelia moved to meet her chaperone at the door, River close on her heels to open it for them.

He cleared his throat once his mistress was through. "Miss Delia, if'n you had yoself the fancy to tell Salina I say hello, I wouldn't argue none."

"I reckon I can manage that." Her smile flashed, then faded. And Salina's words to her after their bad dream found their way to her lips. "River . . . he has to be alive for someone to threaten him. There's solace in that."

"Less that water done swallow him up and ketch him to the spirit world, and it the devil hisself doin the threatenin." River shook his head, his eyes focused on a spot above Cordelia's head. "Got me a bad feelin bout all this."

"He's alive." She kept her gaze steady on his face until he met it. "Believe that."

He looked ready to express more doubt but then just nodded. "You best mind yo pace, Miss Delia. The missus is waitin."

She turned, followed Willametta back down the rickety stairs and out into the sun that tried its best to blind her. Half expecting some form of chastisement for her exchange with the slave, Cordelia climbed into the buggy with the footman's assistance and settled into her place.

But Mrs. Dunn said nothing. Not when she sat down, and not when the driver clicked up the horses. Not as they trundled back out of Currytown or even when they reentered the familiar part of the city with its terra cotta, sandstone, and bricks of gray, white, and red.

Not until they pulled up in front of the Owenses' house did she finally turn to Cordelia and offer a hint of a smile. "Thank you for coming with me, Delia dear. Perhaps . . . perhaps next time you visit you can tell me what adventures Phin is finding in the Everglades."

"I'd be happy to." Cordelia settled her fingers briefly over Willametta's hand. "I'll see you tonight, Mrs. Dunn."

The footman helped her down, and the front door swung open to receive her. Cordelia hurried into the blessed coolness of home, her aim the library.

"There's my sunshine." Daddy stepped from his study with arms wide for an embrace. "And how are the Dunns today?"

Cordelia walked into her father's arms and breathed in the comforting scent of pipe tobacco and sandalwood. "As well as can be hoped. Daddy?" She tilted her face up so she could see his. "Have we any books on the Everglades? I have some research to do."

Chapter Eleven

Phin couldn't bring himself to open his eyes, much as he tried. They were too heavy, just like his limbs. He felt as though someone had buried him under a whole season's worth of rice, making it hard to breathe, impossible to move, difficult even to think.

But the pain was only a dull thud. The agony clawed only at the back of his consciousness now, a monstrous memory that he clamped down on, pushed aside.

His mind felt hazy, as if he'd spent too long letting it waste away. Images flashed, but none would settle long enough for him to focus on anything but the discomfort.

"He is *moribundo*." That voice . . . he had heard it before but couldn't remember what face might go with it. It was smooth. Smooth as oil and bitter as dandelion root.

A deep rumble sounded from beside and above him. "He is *not* dying." Authority deepened the already-bass voice.

An image flashed. The man-giant. Frowning, sneering. Tending, soothing.

Luther.

Comfort trickled over Phin . . . then off him.

Another image caught hold. Another frown, cold eyes that fell short of apologetic. Another voice echoed in his mind. *"Sorry, Phin. It's nothing personal."*

A supposed friend, casting his lot with the enemy.

A supposed enemy, acting the part of a friend.

Could anyone in this world be trusted? Was there any honor to be had anymore?

Golden hair, eyes as green as hope ready to shoot forth. Lips still rosy from his kiss, a delicate form meant to be cherished. Delia, there was always Delia. She was waiting for him. She was home.

A Spanish curse blistered the air. "He is *loco*, he is *moribundo*. I want him gone."

Phin's tongue knotted around words he couldn't make sense of long enough to spit them out. Words that wanted to affirm soundness of mind and body. Words made a mockery by his inability to grasp them.

"Soon." Such surety, such calm. Deep as the ocean that had swallowed Phin.

The smooth voice lashed and spat, an unintelligible rhythm of consonants and vowels. Did the speaker question Luther's declaration of "soon," perhaps?

Phin tried to work through his mind, add together impressions to guess at how long he had lain here already. But he had no way to gauge the passage of time. It had been only endless, fathomless pain. No days at all, only that one long, forever night.

"Do cease your whining, Rosario. I have offered you payment for our tenure here, and you refused it, no doubt solely that you might try to lord over me. If you want to try to physically force us away, then be my guest." The scraping of a chair over packed dirt grated, and a shadow fell over Phin's face. "Please, I beg you, *try*."

A growl sounded, then the smack of a loosely hung door against a frame. After the blustery release of a sigh from above him, the chair creaked and groaned, and the warmth of sunlight bathed Phin's face again.

Something else in the room shifted, something not so easily defined. It wasn't shadow and sunlight, or noise and silence. No, it seemed to have more to do with tension and relief. With a perception that had nothing to do with the senses.

Whatever its source, he could now relax the fingers he hadn't been aware he'd curled and draw in a long breath. Still, he couldn't rid his heart of the feeling of an enemy lurking nearby. Not the man from the door, and certainly not Luther. But something, somewhere. Within him, perhaps, hidden in his own limbs. The source of the pain, of the lack of memory. This thing that wanted to devour him and send him to his death.

Born of a bullet.

Wrought by betrayal.

Though the sunlight still heated him, a chill crept up his spine.

A rustling came, delicate and familiar. Paper. Pages in a book—thin ones, thin as rice paper. Luther cleared his throat. "We were in Second Corinthians chapter nine, Phineas. Now, what was the verse before Rosario arrived . . . ?"

Phin felt he should know the answer, though he wasn't sure why. If he could only push aside the curtain of mist, he maybe could not only tell his caregiver the number of the verse, but recite where he had last read.

Odd. He had never excelled at quoting Scripture.

"Ah, here we are. Verse six. 'But this I say, He which soweth sparingly shall reap also sparingly; and he which soweth bountifully shall reap also bountifully.' I imagine a saying such as this would make sense to a planter, would it not? You reap what you sow."

His lips wanted to move, wanted to wrap themselves around the question.

What had he sown that reaped betrayal? What had he done

to deserve the fate he'd received? Nothing—he had always been a good friend, a good son, a good master.

Hadn't he?

"'Every man according as he purposeth in his heart, so let him give; not grudgingly, or of necessity: for God loveth a cheerful giver.' Now, there is a difficult command. Would I help you so willingly if you could not help me?" A deep hum made the question sound even more private than the musing had, and even that had been spoken so lowly, so softly that Phin had to assume Luther thought him unable to hear. "I would have, though I likely would have made you think it grudgingly. Which no doubt says something about my character, that I make such use of the fear men hold me in because of the way the Lord fashioned my bodily shell."

Had he been able, Phin would have shaken his head. He'd never assumed that black men were incapable of intelligence, like some of his acquaintances did—but he'd also never expected to hear one speaking like this, musing on Scripture and philosophy in a way his own friends never even tried to do. Though suddenly he wasn't sure if that said something about the nature of Luther or of his own choice in friends.

"And what of you, Phineas Dunn? Were I not the one spooning broth past your lips and cleaning your wound, would you have offered me your aid?"

The only response Phin could manage was a curling of his fingers—and his mind was so sluggish he had no idea what meaning he hoped to attach to the minute gesture. Would he have helped? His first response would certainly have leaned toward no. It was never a wise idea to interfere in the dealings of other masters and slaves.

And yet, he and his family prided themselves on being different. They did not bed their slave women, as this Rosario apparently had. If one saved up the money to purchase his freedom, they did not withhold it—in the days when it was still legal to do so. Certainly they would never cheat a freed slave by claiming he was still in bondage and then ship him—or her—away from his family. Families not only *ought* to be but *had* to be preserved in order to guarantee a workable community. Had it been possible, his grandfather would have freed all their slaves upon his death, and that was a decision Father had fully supported until the law prohibited it.

He had no qualms about calling this planter who didn't want him here a villain—but in some ways he was more Phin's brother than this towering black man. They shared a race, a way of life.

But, heaven help him, nothing more. And if one's peers did not insist upon justice, then who would?

He would help, as he had promised. He would help. But was it only because Luther had secured the promise, only because it was a debt, because he had already received aid in return? Would he have sought that justice of his own volition?

The sea seemed to toss around him again, black waves and white froth. The bed beneath him spun and dipped.

Maybe he would have helped, maybe he would have acted.

But suddenly he wasn't so sure if *maybe* was enough.

Applause thundered in Cordelia's ears like the sweetest music in the world. Though she wasn't on stage for this last tableau, it hardly mattered. She twisted the vivid material of her scarf before her and let the tide of anxiousness give way to elation.

They loved it. They loved her creation. Her careful selections, her painstaking narration. Her choreography and design.

Annaleigh fluttered and bowed as if *she* were the one to whom all honor was due, but Cordelia wasn't about to let that affect her. Especially since everyone in the room must also be able to see the girl's skin turning green as her monstrous nature burst forth and her nose sprouted three—no, *five*—unsightly warts.

A wave of rustling came from the crowd, and when Cordelia peeked out she saw the audience stand. "Bless my soul." She reached over and grabbed Sassy's hand. "Is that more than politeness?"

Her friend laughed and tugged her toward the stage. Cordelia nearly pulled away, until she realized that Maybelle had called them all out. She loosed the crumpled fabric she'd been clutching and glided from behind the curtain with Sassy and company, taking a place for herself beside Lacy.

Maybelle stepped away from her podium and joined hands with one of the girls nearest her, and everyone else followed suit. Sandwiched between Lacy and Sassy, Cordelia gave their hands each a hearty squeeze and curtsied when everyone else did.

That was apparently all the longer her friends could manage to keep from their families. They all but surged down the stairs and into the crowd in the next moment, no doubt eager to receive their due adulation.

Cordelia lingered for a heartbeat, so long as Lacy and Sassy did. She had no desire to trip over the others thronging the steps off the stage, but neither did she want to draw attention to herself by staying up here too long.

"It was perfectly executed, Delia." Lacy linked their arms and beamed over at her. "And look at that crowd! We will have raised a sizable sum for the Confederacy here tonight."

Her heart seemed to rise up in her chest. But she ought not to feel pride for her own sake, merely for the good people of Savannah who had supported the cause tonight, and the gracious young ladies who had been willing to bring her idea to life.

"Let's go down now, shall we?" Sassy led them into the crowd, and within seconds the milling Savannahians had come between them to congratulate each on her role.

Cordelia thanked the elderly lady who had grasped her

hands. When she looked for Lacy a moment later, she found her engaged with Julius, a happy flush to her cheeks as their cousin grinned down at her. He had tucked her hand into the crook of his elbow and was leading her toward the refreshments.

Excellent. When he had seen Lacy strike her last pose, the fallen victim of treachery, then no doubt a desire to protect and love her had swelled up inside him. Thank heavens Annaleigh the Dreadful had only insisted on taking Cordelia's roles and hadn't coveted Lacy's.

"One of the best tableaux I've seen."

Cordelia paused, trying not to be obvious as she looked to see who spoke. When she spotted Mrs. Gilmore talking with her esteemed husband, her pulse doubled.

"Without question," Mr. Gilmore replied. "Such a clever way of drawing them together. Miss Owens always did have a knack for storytelling, did she not?"

"Oh indeed. Her mother goes forever on about her, and obviously for good reason."

Would it be terribly unladylike to squeal and bounce? Probably, given the company. And she certainly didn't want to let the couple know she had heard them, as that would be terribly ungracious of her.

Still, she had to tell *someone* that a leading family thought the tableaux so grand. Lacy was out of the question, so she turned to find Sassy.

If she weren't mistaken, Sassy's skirt was the one swishing out the hallway that led to the necessary. Well, Cordelia would head that direction too and catch her friend upon her return.

It took her a few minutes to slip through the crowd, and she made no attempt to keep the smile from her lips as she overheard praise upon praise. Even those who were usually snide, and from whom she expected to hear Annaleigh's sentiments echoed, seemed pleased with the performance.

When finally she gained the quiet of the hallway, Sassy was

out of sight, but the silence was a welcome respite that allowed the evening to solidify in her mind.

Everything had come together. The costumes had all been perfect, and she had loved seeing the pride in Salina's eyes at their final fitting. Once they arrived at the Pulaski House, Cordelia had discovered that Annaleigh was nervous enough—and hence quiet—to be nearly tolerable. The house had been full, each change of tableau had gone smoothly, no one had tumbled off the stage . . . success tasted sweet indeed.

But oh, how she wished Phin had been here to see it. Cordelia glanced around to make sure no one watched her and then indulged in a lean against the wall. Relaxed her posture, closed her eyes. Called up that handsome, beloved face. Hair the color of cypress. Eyes of honeyed hazel that inevitably sparked with amusement. That mouth of his, always quirking up in a crooked, mischievous grin.

Where was he? How long before he found his way home, or at least until they heard from him? *Lord, wherever he is, let him know I'm thinking of him. Praying for him. Waiting for him.*

"Has anyone ever told you how lovely you look with that wistful expression upon your face?"

The words were right, but the voice was all wrong. Knots cinched tight in her stomach as her eyes flew open and beheld Julius standing a mere three feet away. His gaze was not so much on the face he had just complimented as on her figure. Oh, how she longed for her hoop to hide the shape of her hips and legs! However did her grandmother wear this simple style day in and day out without burning at the immodesty?

She cleared her throat and straightened, squaring her shoulders and raising her chin. "Phin made mention of it, yes." More or less. Perhaps. If she combined a few of his observations into one.

"Hmm." He edged closer, his expression now a combination

of pity and . . . well, were she writing about it, she would have had to label it seduction. But she had no intention of calling it such now, given the circumstances. And the fact that it was she to whom he offered it and not her sister.

"I realize, Delie-Darlin, that you'll have to mourn him, even though your match was never official. I'm willing to be patient while you do that."

Had it been Lacy he crowded so, forcing her back until her spine pressed against the wall, perhaps it wouldn't have had such a threatening overtone. Perhaps his lips' turn would be called a smile instead of a smirk. Perhaps, when he reached out and touched his hand to her cheek, it would have been a welcome caress instead of a shocking advance.

But she was *not* Lacy, and she had done nothing to invite such attention. Nothing. She had made it clear from their first meeting that she was spoken for already.

Phin. Where was he when she needed him? Why could he not now come sweeping in and rescue her, like he had been ready to do in the garden with Thomas Bacon?

She jerked from Julius's hand and tried to dart away with some grace, but he planted a hand on the wall beside her to halt her. Of all the audacious—Cordelia huffed out a breath and narrowed her eyes. "Forgive me if I've done anything to mislead you about my affections, Cousin. Though I cannot think how, from my words and actions, you could *possibly* think me interested in a pursuit. I will not be mourning Phin because he is not dead. And so I will wait for him. Your *patience* is better applied to a willing recipient."

"And your loyalty is better applied to one who is here to appreciate it." Fire snapped in his eyes. Not the smoldering gaze of one in love, but rather the dangerous spark of one ready to consume what wasn't his. "One of these days you'll admit what I knew from the moment I collided with you, Delia. You were meant to be mine."

How had she ever thought him a hero, even in someone else's story? He was no warrior-king, fit to win the heart of the elusive princess. He was the cleverest kind of villain, the kind that made everyone *think* him a hero—a usurper.

"I'm afraid you're mistaken." Why would he not back away, give her room to breathe? "And I'll thank you to remember you're a gentleman and accept my decision with grace."

He leaned closer instead of taking a step back. Surely he wouldn't try to kiss her, here in the hallway of the Pulaski House, with all of Savannah society milling a few feet away. He couldn't possibly be *that* forward, could he?

He seemed to be. Which meant that she may yet have the chance to prove her slap contained surprising strength.

"There you be, Miss Delia."

At the intruding voice, Julius halted, swinging an irritated glance to the side. River stood a few feet away, an oblivious-looking smile upon his face, though she knew well he was not so mindless as he looked.

"Go away, boy."

"Aw, now, I kin't be doin that. I got me strict orders to stay close to Miss Sassy, and she be comin outta the necessary any second." He offered a wide smile that likely didn't fool Julius any more than it did her—and likely infuriated him even as it offered her profound relief. "Kin't be leavin a pretty young lady unattended these days, after all, what with all the good-fo-nutt'n soldiers bout the town."

The insult finally succeeded in what insistence had failed at. Julius stepped away, hands in fists at his side. "Are you insulting the fine men of the Confederacy, boy?"

River's eyes went wide, as if only just realizing how that might sound to an officer. Did Julius see the craftiness? "Not the fine men, no suh. I jest talking bout all the po trash what flooded the city. The folks that ain't got the manners and up-bringin' to know to listen when a lady say *no*."

"I know Sassy appreciates your protection, River." And if Cordelia were a lady worth her salt, her unspoken *And so do I* would come through loud and clear through her eyes.

Julius's knuckles went white, and the vein at his temple pulsed. Then he slid back into calm, even smiling. "It's good to know some slaves in these parts still know their place and are willing to risk their lives for their masters." He pivoted, jerked his head in a cool nod at Cordelia. "I'll see you tomorrow at supper, Cousin. Wear that lovely pink dress again, won't you?"

Cordelia feared her mouth hung open like an abandoned gate. Had he threatened River? Was that what that was?

And had he actually dared tell her what to wear? And, worse still, commanded her to don the least flattering dress in her chifforobe? Her fingers tangled in her scarf again. "That pompous . . . contemptible . . . villainous jackanapes."

River drew in a long breath. "You be careful round that there one now, Miss Delia. He bad folk—you can tell'um by the look in the eye."

Hadn't Salina said much the same thing? A long breath blustered through her lips. "I'm beginning to see that. Thank you for stepping in when you did, River."

"Sho nuff, now, sho nuff. That's what Mr. Phin would want me do. When he . . ." He paused, swallowed, drew in a quivering breath. "When he come back, you gwine be the new missus. So the way I figure it, I best be lookin out for you jest as sho as I look out for Miss Sassy."

Since she had no desire to let Phin's valet see her with tears in her eyes, she blinked a few quick times. "I appreciate that more than I can say."

"You jest be sho and spend as much time with Miss Sassy as you kin, Miss Delia, so's I kin do that for ya." He nodded, held her gaze for half a moment, then looked beyond her. "I best git back. I see yo daddy comin."

"All right. Thank you again." She smiled into his nod, turned halfway around before stopping. "Oh! River—I told Salina you said hello. She flushed a right pretty shade of pink."

"Done she?" He cleared his throat and fiddled with his sleeve. "Thanky for that, Miss Delia. Thanky much. I knows I ain't no Big Tom, but . . ." He cleared his throat and spun away with one more muttered thank-you.

Her smile turned to a grin, then faded. Why would he mention Big Tom like that? Salina didn't welcome any advances the gardener made, and she definitely hadn't made mention of him to the Dunn servants.

Had she? Would she?

"And what is the young lady of the hour doing hiding in the hallway?"

At her father's smiling voice, Cordelia turned to face him and forced aside thoughts of Salina. He looked handsome tonight in his buff coat and trousers, and there was no mistaking the pride on his face.

It did her heart good to see it. She looped her hand through his arm. "I was just waiting for Sassy is all, Daddy. It went well, didn't it?"

"You are a true sensation. You and Lacy lit up the stage." He leaned over and pressed an affectionate kiss to her forehead. When he pulled away, a grin twitched at his lips. "But I could have sworn I saw a certain young officer cousin of yours follow you out here."

"Oh." The heat that surged to her cheeks was more from frustration than anything, but she doubted her father would realize that. "He . . . he just . . . you don't need to worry about that, Daddy. I have no interest in Julius."

The last thing she expected was the frown that creased her father's brow. "And why is that, Delie-Darlin? I realize you'd set your affections on Phin, but Julius is a fine young man. I know he favors you, and his court bears considering."

"Daddy." Him too? She didn't dare pull her arm away, but she averted her face. She couldn't help it. "I don't . . . I can't . . . I don't like Julius, he—well, the way he looks at me—"

"Nonsense." Though soft and gentle, the single word made it clear he wouldn't stand for her disparaging the young man he'd apparently taken a shine to. "He's from a good family, well bred. If you see something in him you don't like, it's just that talented imagination of yours at work. No doubt it's in cahoots with your heart, which won't let you think of anyone else just yet. But, darlin'—"

His large, familiar hand took her chin and turned her face back to his. She found his eyes, bright and blue, looking at her pleadingly as he sighed. "We can't make decisions that affect the rest of our lives based on the emotions of youth. The Dunns are a good family, Phin a fine young man—but Julius would be the better match. If we combined his plantation and Belle Acres, the two of you would become the largest landowners in the county."

Delia was shaking her head long before he finished. "I don't care about any of that, Daddy. If you do, then—then give Belle Acres as Lacy's dowry instead of mine and—"

"I'll hear no such nonsense." That stubborn look entered his eyes, the one he so rarely gave her but which she'd seen often enough in his dealings with others. "We decided years ago who would get what, and everyone knows it. I'll not abide the talk that would spring up if I were to change it all now. No, Delia, Belle Acres is yours. You can't just shuffle the responsibility that comes with that onto your sister because you fancy a man who's likely never to return."

"He *will*." Her fingers dug into his arm a second before she caught herself.

Daddy's head moved in a sorrowful, slow shake. "I don't think he will. I was willing to grant him leave to court you—against my better judgment, since you favor him so—but when the Dunns received that news from Willametta's brother, I made a few inquiries, hoping someone somewhere would have spotted the ship he was on. But the *Cuba* has vanished . . . and there were reports of a storm in the vicinity that night."

Try as she might to hold her tears back by will, blink as she might to clear them away, they still blurred her vision. "I can't give up on him, Daddy. I can't." Her voice came out as little more than a murmur. "And I can't accept another man's court just because you like where his property is."

Daddy thumbed away the droplets that had just spilled onto her cheeks. "I have a bad feeling about this war, sunshine."

Must he make things even worse? "You said it would be over in a few months."

His sober expression didn't shift. "The Yankees are already on the coast, on the islands. The main army is advancing through Virginia. I want to see you safe."

"I *am* safe. They wouldn't dare come to Savannah, not with all the soldiers stationed here."

He pursed his lips, lowered his hand. "Atlanta would be better."

Her chin rose of its own accord. He would never tolerate defiance, but Daddy admired strength. "I will not flee in fear. That isn't the kind of person you raised me to be."

That earned her only a hint of a smile, quickly washed away by sobriety. "If you married Julius, you wouldn't be fleeing there for refuge. You'd be taking a place in its society. Your mother and Lacy could go with you then without argument."

A hand seemed to vise around her chest. "Daddy, please don't ask this of me. I love Phin. I promised him I'd wait."

"But for how long?"

A shudder overtook her. Phin's words, Phin's question, right before the fiddle had struck up at the barbeque. She could still see the hope in his eyes, the ardor, the admiration.

But Daddy's gaze held only cold, hard reality. Expectation.

Logic. He wouldn't like the answer she'd given. But it wouldn't be held back from her lips. "Forever."

Her father sighed. "I can't let you do that, sunshine. I can't let you throw your life away and sully the family name in so doing. Even if you set aside the wisdom of joining your fortunes to Julius's, you know well your mother won't let Lacy marry until you do. Do you want to ruin *her* chances for happiness as well?"

"That isn't fair." Did he even hear the rusty squeak of her voice? Her throat felt so tight. "Younger daughters marry first all the time—"

He rested his hands upon her shoulders and stared deep into her eyes. "Cordelia." He never called her that, never. It was always Delia, Delie-Darlin, sunshine. "You will do what must be done."

"Daddy—"

"Hush now. You may wait for Phin until September. I think that more than reasonable, and it's more than my better judgment wants to allow. I'm granting it only because it's you. If he's alive, we'll hear something by then. But if we do not, then you will accept Julius's suit at that time. Am I understood?"

She forced a swallow. "Lacy would never forgive it."

"You let me worry about Lacy." He dropped his hands and took her elbow, turned her toward the crowd of people.

Her breath balled up in her chest. Let *him* worry about Lacy? Hadn't he just foisted the responsibility for her happiness upon Cordelia? Well, she would do right by her sister, by her family. But that meant honoring the commitment she'd already made. And perhaps steering Lacy away from Julius, too, if he were as much a jackanapes as he had played tonight.

They walked a few steps, and then Daddy looked down at her with an arched brow. "You didn't answer me. Am I understood, Cordelia?"

She always thought of herself with her full name, so why did hearing it from his lips make her want to cringe? But she wouldn't show it. She would be strong, brave. Like any good princess locked away in her tower, waiting for the knight to return as promised. She gave him the smile he most liked and tilted her face so her curls brushed her cheek. "You're understood. Father."

Chapter Twelve

August 7, 1861

Something was different. Something had changed. It took Phin a long moment to realize it was the light filtering through the moth-eaten curtains on the windows.

Light. Vision.

His eyes were open. How long had he struggled to raise the lids? Forever, it seemed. Days, weeks, months, years—time had lost all meaning as he tried and failed, over and over, to will his body into obedience. And now, without even trying, his eyes were open. He saw the dust motes sparkling in the shafts of sunlight. He saw the patterns of brilliance and shadow play upon the walls, the floor. A reflection of water danced on the ceiling. And there, the bowl of it the sunshine had found.

The room was small. Bare. Poor. But it was the most blessed sight he could ever recall seeing, with the exception, perhaps, of the love gleaming in Delia's eyes.

Vision. Sweet, sweet vision. He blinked to clear the grime from his eyes and lifted a hand to rub at them. Lifted a hand! It moved, without pain, without feeling like a lead ball. It just . . . just *moved*, and rubbed, and then held itself in front of his nose while he stared at it, in awe of its obedience.

"I'm alive." He wasn't so sure he had been before, not really. His mind had functioned, yes. Sometimes. Enough to listen, enough to think, enough to hate the fact that he couldn't move, couldn't talk, couldn't do. But he hadn't really *been*. Not like this, alive again. How far dare he push it?

Well, he had to try more than merely rubbing his eyes. Drawing in a deep breath first, he wiggled his toes and, when that worked, pushed up on his elbows. The earth didn't spin, which seemed like a good sign. Though even from that small action, his arms ached.

The door swung open, and a flood of precious sunlight leapt into the room. Silhouetted against it, a giant ducked his head and entered, unable to fully straighten his neck again once inside. He hummed as he entered, setting a sloshing pail upon the floor.

"Luther." The word escaped his lips so easily, with neither a squeak nor a moan. For the first time in however long it had been since they took the *Cuba*, he felt like smiling.

The man's eyes went wide, and he jerked back up so fast he knocked his head against the ceiling. "Phineas! You're awake!"

He nodded and pushed himself up another few inches. "How long has it been? A week? Two, perhaps?"

Luther crossed the room in two long strides and sat down on the rickety chair beside Phin's bed. Its rustle and creak was as familiar as a lullaby. "A month, Phineas. A month and a few odd days since you first washed ashore. You've come to a few times, here and there, but not for weeks now. I was beginning to fear you never would."

"Me too." He made no protest when Luther reached for a new-looking pillow and put it behind him, then helped him find a comfortable position against it. He was now upright enough to see but reposed enough that his muscles sighed in relief. He shook his head. How had an entire month gone by? And what had happened in all that time? Where were his crew, his ship?

Did they all think him dead, either from the bullet or the fall overboard? Undoubtedly.

The bullet—his leg. Had they . . . ? He reached down, patted the limb. Its scream of pain at the contact assured him it was still in place as much as the feel of it under his hand did.

"Still there," Luther said on a chuckle. "Dr. Santiago considered amputation, but he was convinced you wouldn't recover from it if we tried, given how weak you've been. We've avoided gangrene, praise be to the Lord, but it doesn't seem to be healing as quickly as it should. Santiago warned me it would be difficult to get it to set correctly."

Yes, of course. He knew all that. Had heard the conversations, though some of them had been in Spanish. Dr. Santiago's voice had been the soft, doleful one, his Spanish words melodious. Not like that other one.

"Here. Drink."

Phin reached for the tin cup full of water, though Luther's meaty hand didn't release it entirely. Probably wise. Still, he could direct it to his own lips. Tip at his own rate. Drink without a dribble, then hand it back. "I think I'm hungry."

A deep laugh rumbled from Luther's throat. "Praise be to God for that! I've got nothing but broth in you since you arrived. Would you care for some fruit? I'd just prepared a plate."

"Yes. Thank you." A moment later, a platter of pineapple, oranges, mango, and bananas had his mouth watering. He selected a slice of mango and relished the juice upon his tongue, then looked back up into Luther's placid face. "Why did you not give up on me? Turn me over to . . . the dark one."

Luther arched a brow.

Phin shook his head. "Not his color, his . . . I don't know. Whenever he was here, I just thought of him as being dark as the night. His name was Ros-something."

"Rosario." Luther grunted. "You have the right of him, to be sure. I wouldn't turn my worst enemy over to that man."

The mango went down smoothly, so Phin next chose a slice of pineapple. "Am I not that?"

Luther's next grunt sounded amused. "No. Perhaps I thought so, when first I realized *what* you are. But now that I know *who* you are . . ."

"Who I am." Strange, that phrase had never before made him question it himself. "You know that, do you?"

When Luther smiled, his teeth gleamed white as the moon. "You talk in your sleep—or your delirium, as the case may be."

Phin cleared his throat and studied the bright yellow fruit in his fingers. "I suspect I ought to be embarrassed."

"You said nothing of which you need be ashamed." Leaning forward, Luther braced his forearms against his legs and clasped his hands loosely. "It's good to hear you speaking coherently though. To see you awake."

Phin swallowed the last of the pineapple and reached for a banana. His fingers fumbled over the stem, couldn't get it to break so he could peel it. Blasted weak hands. He had to clench his teeth when Luther took it from him and accomplished in a single second what he couldn't manage at all.

It chafed, this needing help for the smallest task. He had never in his life relied on his servants to do what he was capable of doing himself, yet here he was, relying on this man. Who wasn't even one of his servants, obligated to help. No, he was entirely reliant upon and indebted to a freeman who had greeted him with scorn.

Yet Luther's face contained none of the pride now that Phin remembered seeing when first he landed here. And so he didn't mind saying, "Thank you, Luther," as he accepted the fruit back again.

The giant's eyes gleamed. "You've learned some manners in this past month, I see."

"I've learned something. Not quite sure what." He held the banana a long moment, waiting for his arms not to feel so heavy. "I need to get word to my family."

Luther nodded. "I have paper and pen I can fetch. Or if you're not feeling up to writing it yourself, you can dictate it to me."

For a long moment, Phin could only stare. Of course Luther was educated—he was aware of him having read chapter upon chapter, book upon book to him over the last month, recalled the mentions of Cambridge and his church. Still. In Savannah, blacks were absolutely forbidden from learning to read or write. They weren't even allowed to hold a job in a printer's office, lest they pick it up. Some still knew, of course—River included. But it was something to hide, to do in secret, not to offer freely.

Phin shook his head. "We can try, but I have my doubts a letter would reach them, what with the blockade all along the coast. Is there a telegraph office nearby? If I could at least get word to my uncle's contacts in Cienfuegos . . ."

Now Luther shook his bald head. "It would take me two days to get to and back from the nearest telegraph office, and the Cuban lines are terrible. Messages have no guarantee of making it through. I would be willing to try, but every time I start down the drive, Rosario's servants make for the cottage. I don't know if he intends to take you to the Big House or throw you out, and I haven't been willing to risk finding out. I haven't ventured farther than the well in weeks."

"Not worth the risk, then. Especially since I have no way of knowing if my uncle will even make port in Cuba again any time soon." Phin took a bite of his banana. "What of the doctor? Could he help us?"

"Perhaps, had you asked a week ago. But he had to travel to Villa Clara Province to be with his daughter during her confinement." With a sigh, Luther straightened again and passed a hand over his scalp. "I'm afraid we are without allies just now."

The banana stuck in his throat. No allies? No surprise, in a world where loyalties shifted like the wind. But he had to get word to his family somehow. At the very least, they would be wondering where he was, whether he was well. And if Semmes had sent them a letter, then they would think him lost. Dead.

They would be mourning him. Father, Mother, Sassy—they'd be trying to say good-bye, to grieve him so that they might move on with their lives.

And Delia. He squeezed his eyes shut and drew in a long breath. If they'd been told he was dead, then Delia . . . he hadn't even proposed. He had given her no promise, no legitimate reason to wait. Her family would give her only so much time to grieve before they'd begin ushering the other young gentlemen her way.

No. He wouldn't lose her, not because of this. He opened his eyes and met Luther's gaze. Determination would have to shore him up where strength failed him. "Let's try the letters. But God willing, before we know if they got there, we'll be on our way ourselves. As soon as I can walk."

Luther shook his head. "That might take a while, Phineas."

Given how it had hurt even to touch his leg, he cringed at the mere thought of trying to stand. But it must be done. It was the only way to get his life back. "We'll take it slowly, move a bit more each day. And it'll give us time to come up with a plan. Think of the best way through the blockade."

"Ah." With a wide grin, Luther reached down and pulled something from under the bed. A roll of paper, which he unfurled to reveal a map of Cuba, the Caribbean, and the Confederate States. "I've been gathering all the news that makes its way here. From what I can tell, the blockade is cinching ever tighter along here." He traced a finger down the coasts of the Carolinas, Georgia, all the way into Florida. "Runners are still making it through, but it gets riskier by the week. I think a better idea may be to head this way."

Phin nodded when Luther tapped Florida's Gulf Coast. "General Scott's 'anaconda' won't be so tight there, you're right. If we find a ship headed for Cedar Key, we can take the train inland, and then up to Savannah."

Luther's brows arched. "There's rail the whole way?"

"Most of it, at least. I know there's a line from Savannah down to Troupville. Another from Cedar Key that heads northeast and connects with a line due west from Jacksonville, at Baldwin. I think they were building a connector line from that westbound rail to the one in Georgia. It ought to be completed by now."

"Ought to be?"

Phin shrugged. "If there's no rail, there will still be horses. We'll make it."

Luther's nod looked more contemplative than convinced. At first. Then he caught Phin's eye and gave one final, decisive nod. "We shall make it indeed. To your Delia."

"And your Eva."

"Quite so." He stuck out a hand.

Phin just blinked, until the meaning of the action made itself known. Then he prayed his hesitation wasn't too great. Never in his life had a black man offered a hand to shake—but into this particular broad palm he was entrusting his life. It seemed only fair to seal it.

Salina rocked back on her heels and wiped the sweat from her brow with the edge of her apron. The sun hung directly overhead, so bright and glaring she fancied it would burn straight through the earth all the way to the other side. Heavens, but she wished they'd all gone to the plantation this summer. Savannah was near to unbearable.

The ground under her knees was hard and dry, yet the air weighed wet and thick. How must all those soldiers be faring out there on the marshy coast, dug into mosquito-infested trenches as they likely were?

Well, she'd just get rid of these weeds threatening to choke Miss Delia's beloved flowers quick as she could and get back inside.

"Salina? What in the world are you doing gardening?"

She didn't just snap upright at Mass Owens's voice, she leapt all the way to her feet and wiped her soiled hands on her apron. As if that could hide the guilt. As if the guilt was hers to try to hide. "Mornin', sir. I was just . . . well, sir, I came out to pick some fresh flowers for Miss Delia and noticed a few weeds a'growin' is all."

The master narrowed his eyes. First upon her, then upon the overrun flowerbed. His jaw ticked. "And where is Big Tom?"

Surely it was just the heat that made it so hard to find saliva enough to swallow. "I don't rightly know, sir. Maybe he be sick today."

"Today?" Mass Owens frowned at the ground. Pressing her lips together, Salina knew he'd see in a heartbeat that it had been more than a day since the grounds had been tended. When he turned that hard gaze back to her face, she shuddered as if she were the one who had neglected her duties. "Has he run off, Salina?"

"I . . ." What was she to say? That he had offered to do that once, with her, but that she'd heard nothing of it since then? Heard nothing from *him* since he learned she was the master's illegitimate child? That somewhere deep inside she'd known he would make a run for the Yankee line on the coast—and that most likely he'd convinced one of Salina's friends to go with him? "I don't know, sir. I done—I mean, I've kept my distance from him, like you told me to do."

So why did he arch his brow at her like that, like she was lying? She wasn't, and that was the honest truth. She hadn't done more than send a few admiring glances at Big Tom out the window in recent weeks, and even those had been less frequent. He might be handsome as all get-out, but she knew he wasn't for her.

No one was for her. Though she had to say, when Miss Delia had passed along greetings from River . . . well, that had been right interesting. Though she didn't dare think too much about that just now, with Mass Owens glaring at her.

"Salina, I know well slaves talk among themselves. Now, are you going to tell me what you heard, or do I have to ask someone else?"

She latched her gaze onto the ground. "They don't talk to me about Big Tom, sir. I asked 'em not to. Didn't realize that would mean I can't tell you what you need to know."

"Hmm." The hum sounded convinced, at least. And softer than his words had. "You best get inside and cleaned up—Sassy will be here any moment, and Delia mentioned taking you with her today."

"Yessuh." She dashed off quick as she could, flying straight toward her room to exchange her soiled apron for a clean one. She'd plumb forgotten about the shopping trip, so set as she had been on those flowers. They were meant to have been a reminder, something to call to mind that very different dream Miss Delia had said she had a week ago, the one with sunshine and blue skies.

Surely a good sign for Mr. Phin. Surely. Yet as the days dragged by and still no word came, Salina had watched her sister's hope start to shrivel as sure as those flowers would without some water dribbled upon them.

"Lord Almighty, protect Mr. Phin and bring him home soon." She whispered the prayer as she gained her room, apron already untied. Though when she tossed it into her pile of soiled garments, she noted the dirt on her hands and under her nails, and figured she had best take care of that before fetching herself a clean apron.

By the time she emerged again, she heard the Dunn carriage pulling up outside, and Miss Delia was floating down the stairs in the pretty dress of white muslin sprigged with lavender that

Salina had helped her into not an hour earlier. She had the matching bonnet in hand, so Salina hurried over to assist her in arranging it just so over her curls. Secured the utility ties to hold it in place, then tied the wide, silken ribbon in a fashionable bow. "There. Pretty as you please."

"Thank you, Salina." She slipped her hands into her gloves, her smile small. "I would have been tempted to cancel this outing, were I not in desperate need of more paper."

Needing something to do, some way to help, Salina adjusted the bow under Miss Delia's chin to a jauntier angle. "You can't just sit around all day waiting for news."

Miss Delia caught her hands, squeezed them. "Salina," she said, voice low, "August is already half gone. By *September*, do you think Daddy meant the very first day? Or perhaps by the end?"

As if she had any special ability to read the master's mind or meaning. "Lawzy, Miss Delia, you askin the wrong person bout that."

"I know." Heaving a sigh, she headed for the door and motioned Salina to follow.

The sunshine gave them a scorching welcome, and the breeze mustered up a scant breath, hot and heavy. River was just hopping down from his place in the driver's seat. "Mawnin, Miss Delia."

"Good morning, River. Sassy, you're looking fresh as a peach."

River gave the young lady a hand up, and Salina leaned into the buggy just enough to help Miss Delia get her skirt situated. Then she turned to the front, hitched up her own skirt . . . and jumped when a palm appeared under her nose.

When she jerked her head up, she found River grinning at her, obviously amused by her reaction. "Lemme help ya up, Salina girl."

"Oh. Thank you." She set her fingers on his palm, and if she pretended that warm flesh was nothing but a cold iron railing, she figured no one would blame her for it. No use admiring the lively sparkle in his eye or appreciating the way he looked at her—like she was something special.

He boosted her up and jumped up behind. "Woo-ee. I sho do like hearin ya talk, Salina, with yo fine speech."

It took all her willpower to tamp down a grin as she scooted along the bench to make room for him. "I kin talk'um jest like yo, if I wanna." Then the twitch of her lips stilled. "The master don't like it none though."

For a moment, River's brow lifted in question. But soon enough the light in his eyes sparked, and he nodded. "He specs mo of you."

She just nodded, folded her hands in her lap.

River clicked the horses up, their hooves clacking on the stones of the drive before the sound was dulled by the sand-packed street. Her ears focused briefly on the chatter behind her, but Miss Delia and Miss Sassy were just talking about their latest encounter with the mean ol' Annaleigh. Salina had already heard about it—and had said a prayer for poor Vangie, stuck as she was by that she-devil's side, without even an outing like this to bring her some relief now and then.

According to the whispers among the slaves, Vangie was with child, and the minute that had been revealed, Mass Young had all but locked her up inside his house, determined to keep her and the next generation of slave she carried "safe" from any temptation to run.

Them Youngs was something else, that was for sure. Something that made her blood feel all steamed up.

River looked over at her again. "Good to see yo still here, Salina." His words were quiet, quiet enough that the girls wouldn't be able to hear him. Quiet enough that they rang to the depths of her soul and made her forget all about the Youngs.

"Where else would I be? None of the Owenses went inland this year."

He had a way of looking at her that made his gaze seem to bore right through a body. "Ain't what I be meanin. Big Tom . . . well, he say yo his ooman."

Her head snapped his way, and she feared her eyes went wide as the delta. "Can't think why he say so."

"Well, the way he tell it," he said, leaning close and pitching his voice quieter still, "the only thing keepin you apaa't be Mr. Owens."

Only when her nail bit into her flesh did she realize her fingers gripped each other so hard that River had only to look down to see what that suggestion did to her.

If he thought that, it was no wonder he was surprised to see her still here, what with Big Tom running off. Did everyone think the same? Were they all looking at her now, with him gone? Wondering when she'd run to meet up with him?

If Mass Owens got wind of those rumors, thought she knew where Big Tom had gone, thought she'd try to escape too . . . well, she had no intentions of doing that, so she shouldn't worry none. But then, if they looked too closely and saw how familiar she and Miss Delia were, or if they caught her with a book, it could get right ugly for her. The missus could yet have her way, and Salina would wake up one morning in the disease-ridden rice marshes.

Frustration with Big Tom bubbled up. Maybe she'd thought him handsome, but never had she once given him any reason to talk about her like that. She wanted to toss her head back and forth with vehemence enough to get her point across, but she didn't dare. Miss Delia would notice that for sure, and she didn't want to have to explain what got her so riled. Would only upset her, and she had enough on her mind.

So she kept her headshake small, casual. "Ain't so. There are plenty of reasons I ain't involved with him, and that be one, but it ain't the only, or even the most important. I ain't never liked men who flit from girl to girl like he done."

River looked so long and hard at her, she figured she best keep her eyes on the road so as to warn him if anything should jump in front of the horses. "You gwine miss him?"

Did he ask from curiosity? Because he and Big Tom were friends, sharing a room as they did? Or was his interest more personal?

Even if it were, wouldn't matter none. She couldn't let herself wonder, daren't even entertain any thoughts on the matter. River was a fine man, sure enough, handsome in a more understated way than his roommate but no less legitimately. The thought of him thinking of her may have given her a little thrill. But it wasn't to be, no more than Big Tom was. He was still a slave, and she was still the master's daughter.

She wouldn't waste any thoughts on River. And she sure wouldn't waste any more on Tom. "Nah, I ain't gonna miss him. I'm gonna hope he ain't caught, cause I don't fancy seeing him killed, and I'm gonna hope no one else I know is fool enough to risk their necks like that. Don't know why he thought it worth tryin."

Rather than answering, River took up a hum. He didn't use any words, but everyone knew which ones had been put to that particular tune.

Yes, we shall all be free
Yes, we shall all be free
Yes, we shall all be free
When the Lord shall appear.

Maybe that *was* River's answer. The song had been banned—everyone knew "the Lord" meant the Yankees—so what did he mean by humming it? That he hoped for freedom too? Understood why Big Tom would take off like he had?

Salina pressed her lips together. "You ain't gonna do nothing stupid, are ya, River?"

"Me?" His eyes went wide. "No, ma'am, I wouldn't never. The Dunns been real good to me, real good. And Mr. Phin—

well, he help me much as I help him, sho nuff. Reckon I'll keep on there, even if."

Even if. Even if freedom came to call. Even if the Yankees came knocking on their door.

Weren't too many slaves she knew who would stick around if the choice was given. Even the ones with kind masters wanted to be free. Make their own choices. See whatever part of the world struck their fancy.

"Though . . ." He shifted a bit closer, focused his eyes on nothing, cast his voice lower. "I hear me talk. Talk of dem Yankees takin the islands, and folkses aplenty ready to run to em when dey do."

She stretched out her cramping fingers and resisted the urge to wrap her arms around her middle. For a moment she could imagine it—stealing out one night, finding a pilot who knew the waterways, the warm breeze snatching at her hair as she headed for freedom.

A siren's song, that's what it was. And Miss Delia had written a story about sirens last year, so Salina knew all too well how those usually ended. She didn't much fancy being one of their victims, crashed to bits on no rocks, neither. 'Sides, there weren't no tale worth telling that would feature the likes of her. No true love waiting. No prince in disguise. Just a future that would either be cut short by hard work or worn long by loneliness.

No, it would be enough to stay with Miss Delia. She wouldn't be lonesome by her side, no sir. And maybe . . . maybe one of these days . . . well, maybe it would be enough if she realized . . .

Salina sighed. Best not to hope the young miss would figure out they shared blood. Miss Delia loved her daddy something fierce, and it would no doubt tarnish him in her eyes to realize he'd kept her murruh as mistress at the plantation whilst the missus was in Savannah.

River was humming again, this time a spiritual from the

fields that, so far as she knew, the white folk had never uncovered the meaning of. *They'll take wings and fly away*. Buried as it was between words of death and resurrection, no one ever thought anything of it. Not unless they'd grown up hearing the whispered stories from Africa. If Salina closed her eyes, she could still see her aunt leaning over her, still hear her alto voice.

"And the boy, he took on wings and flew like a bird, flew away from hardship. Flew away toward freedom with his magic wings, until he landed someplace safe."

Wasn't heaven the song spoke of, nor was it simply the nether-life with Jesus. The old African lore and spells would always stay woven in—leastways so long as conjurers like Aunt Lila were around.

Salina blinked and shifted to clear her mind. Miss Delia was right—now that she was a baptized Christian and understood better what it meant, understood better what it *didn't* mean, it was best to put away all those questionable things. Focus on the stories she knew were true, and which were just as miraculous.

Focus on the dreams she'd gotten from the Lord above, not the ones her aunt had awakened from in a sweat, with darkness in her eyes.

Laughter rang out from the buggy, jarring but bright.

River leaned close. "What you frettin bout, Salina? Tom? He know how to git where he gwine. He be fine, sho nuff."

"Nah, not him." The shops were just around the corner, and she knew the young ladies would spend a good while inside while she and River waited outside the door. They'd keep an eye on them through the window, but the store was too crowded with shelves for them to all go in. "I'll tell ya in a minute."

His eyes were as gray and beckoning as the morning mist, especially when they sparkled with curiosity like they did now. But he didn't focus them on her long, not with traffic needing his attention. He navigated around the corner, down the street a ways, and found a place to hitch the horses. Quick as a wink, he jumped out to help the ladies down. Salina climbed down too and kept pace behind the girls until River opened the door for them and their hoops swayed through it.

It had scarce shut behind them before River turned to her, his face sober. "I been wantin to talk to you too. That fella what been sniffin around yo Miss Delia—she tell you bout the night at Pulaski House?"

Salina nodded and finally let herself fold her arms over her stomach. "She said you saved her a world of woe. Thank you for that."

One foot shuffled against the sidewalk. "Shucks, Salina, ain't no need to thank me fo doin what's right."

The smile pulled up the corners of her mouth before she could think to stop it. "Don't know what else one body thanks another for."

His grin flashed quick and warm. "True nuff. But I jest doin what Mr. Phin would want. Takin care of the future missus whenever I kin."

"Mr. Phin's what I wanted to talk to you bout." She stepped closer and, though she turned to the window to keep an eye on Miss Delia, leaned in just a bit. "Miss Delia and me, we been havin these dreams bout him. Same time once, same dream. All dark and sinister. But last week she had a dream about him in the sunshine. And I had me one just the other night that was similar. First one what was good."

Horses' hooves thudded along the sandy street, drivers called out, passersby greeted one another. But it was a long moment before River sucked in a slow breath. "Yo got some seer in you, sho nuff. Don't surprise me none. What *does* is that I had me one of them dreams myself. And it weren't the good one. Skay'd me halfway to heaven." She felt him shift, turn toward her. "But if you say the last one's good, then that's good nuff for me."

He believed her, just like that? Was willing to put aside his own fears and doubts? Salina glanced up and fought back a wave of warmth at the way he was looking at her. Wasn't nothing like the way Big Tom always did, no sir. Not like that at all. River's gaze was one of . . . well, if she didn't know better, she'd call it respect. Admiration. But sure and that didn't make any sense at all.

The smile he offered now was slight, and somehow all the more intimate for its smallness, as if it were only big enough for her to see, and no one else. "He'll come on home one of these days, and then him and Miss Delia git'um married." He turned back to the window, but she saw the wink of his dimple nonetheless. "And you be right welcome at the Dunn house, Salina. Right welcome."

Lawzy. She pulled out her little paper fan and tried to swish away the heat. August's heat, that was all. Nothing more. Sure not anything to do with River. Or that dimple of his.

No sir.

Chapter Thirteen

Luther winced when the wagon bumped over a particularly uneven section of road. It was a wince of empathy, and indeed when he glanced over at Phineas, the chap's face had washed pale. The poor fellow gripped his injured leg as if his hand could provide a steadiness that the mismatched horse could not.

What he wouldn't give for his fine pair of grays and the curricle that waited in his stable. Gulliver here was unaccustomed to pulling a cart, and this ramshackle conveyance seemed as though it might fall apart at any moment. It hadn't any spring to speak of, so each bump was magnified. The blankets they had used to pad the seat under Phineas likely did little to nothing.

When his companion's eyes slid closed, Luther sighed. "Are you quite certain you're up for this? It's been scarcely a fortnight since you came to. You've pushed yourself so hard these past two weeks—"

"I'm sure." Phineas's eyes opened again, probably from nothing but stubbornness. "I have to get back. Report in, and let my family know I'm alive."

"I realize that. But another week to regain your strength would be wise."

Phineas shook his head, which was covered in a straw hat that didn't exactly complement the uniform they had painstakingly cleaned and mended together the day before. The boy had looked at him aghast when he handed him a needle and thread, but Luther had only had to arch a brow to overcome his resistance.

Now he fought back a grin at the memory. Amazing how far the lad had come in nearly two months, most of which he had spent unconscious. He suspected the Phineas Dunn of July never would have put needle to cloth—at least not while there was a black man there to do it for him.

"I can't wait any longer." Yet his voice sounded so strained, so full of pain, and the color hadn't returned to his cheeks. "I can't explain it, Luther, but I know it's time."

Luther had the same feeling, but it kept battling against his logic. He'd thought perhaps it was merely impatience on his part. He'd been dreaming of Eva every night, awakened every morning keenly aware of how long they'd been apart.

Then he'd move over to Phineas's cot, see how thin he'd grown, how weak he still was, and think that a long trip was the last thing to be attempted right now.

He glanced over at him now, noting how the gray jacket hung on him, the way his cheekbones had hollows under them—and that after he'd fleshed out a bit in the last two weeks. Before, he'd looked on the brink of death. The pale cheeks brought that impression back again.

Phineas caught his gaze, lifted a single brow. "I'm well."

"Mmm-hmm."

"Don't sound so dubious. It's only a bit of discomfort, that's all."

"Mmm-hmm."

"Luther. Ever pause to consider how odd it is that you're the one fretting?" He shook his head, even chuckled a bit. "What happened to 'Who forgiveth all thine iniquities; who healeth all thy diseases; who redeemeth thy life from destruction'? Trust, my friend. The Lord has delivered me, and I am well."

Luther relaxed his grip so he could look over, his jaw as slack as the reins. "Do you realize that in a single sentence you called me your friend, quoted Scripture, and, in so doing, reminded me to have faith?"

Though the expression Phineas put on resembled the haughty one he'd first employed upon his ignominious arrival, it was rather ruined by the amusement in his eyes. "I most certainly did not. It took *three* sentences."

"Impudent pup."

"Overbearing giant."

A grin tickled the corners of his mouth, but Luther tamped it down. "Unmannerly pirate."

Rather than get angry as he had last month, Phineas let his head fall back in laughter. "Even were I willing to grant that the *Sumter* was a pirating vessel—which I most certainly am not—I cannot think that my brief tenure upon it would earn me such an epithet, you judgmental blackmailer."

"Blackmail? Take it back, you fiend. I most certainly did not blackmail you into anything." But at least the exchange of insults had brought the color back to his companion's cheeks.

Phineas sent him a friendly glare from under the brim of his comical straw hat. "You threatened to let me die if I didn't help you."

Again, Luther's lips twitched. "You are quite mistaken, my good man. I only promised I *would* care for you if you swore your aid. I never once said I wouldn't if you didn't."

"Are you calling me a liar? I ought to call you out here and now."

At that, Luther had to snort. "And am I such a dishonorable lout that I would accept such a challenge, with you in your current condition? Nay, I was not so ill-raised. You couldn't even walk your paces."

Phineas rubbed a hand over his thigh. "Not to mention that you, Sir Giant, could probably snatch a bullet from the air and crush it in your mighty palm."

Luther held up a hand and examined it. "A benefit of having bones made of steel, to be sure. You ought to have invested in some yourself."

A laugh slipped from the lad's lips. "That would have been handy." He, too, looked at Luther's hand, then swept his gaze up, as if measuring him. A new frown puckered his brow.

"Afraid I shall yet crush you?"

"Forgive me." Phineas redirected his eyes straight ahead, his jaw tight again. "It is just . . . your size, while perhaps the greatest I've seen, is on the same scale as a few field hands we have had over the years—and unmatched by any white man I've ever met. I have heard people argue that God would not have designed the black man thus, if not to labor in ways we cannot. I never really gave it much thought before. But . . ."

Luther sighed. "You may as well ask why He gave us a brain, if He intended us *only* to labor in your fields. Or better still, ask if, since the small white man is so perfectly sized for work in the mines, all white men should not be forced into *that* labor."

"It is hardly the same." For the first time in weeks, the chap's voice took on a note of stiffness. "Perhaps our overall smaller stature would make us a good size for the tight shaft of a mine, but we can hardly perform that labor without injury or illness."

Of all the . . . "And the slaves in your fields are never injured? Never ill?" Every muscle going tense, Luther shook his head. "I have prayed over countless blacks escaped from the South, Phineas. I have heard their tales of woe. Workers in your rice fields have a life expectancy of only five years. Over ninety percent of the babes born to slave women on those plantations die; far fewer survive than are needed to replace the workers who fall each year. Is that what you call *well-suited*? If so, I think perhaps I shall purchase a dictionary for you."

"But blacks are all but immune to malaria and yellow fever, which fells any white workers who dare to step into the fields in the summer. Does that count for nothing?" Again, Phineas's hand rubbed absently at his leg. "The work must be done, and so someone must do it, or none of us would have food to eat."

"But there is a difference between choosing to work in those conditions and being forced to." Luther made a conscious effort to relax his grip on the reins. "Your ancestors began enslaving the West Africans because they already had experience growing rice. But in Africa, they *chose* to do it. They were not forced, with a whip always hovering over them. They worked for themselves, for their families, for their neighbors."

"Their neighbors were often the ones who sold them, so forgive me if I ask you to spare me such tales meant to evoke empathy, when the truth behind them sheds as terrible a light on *your* people as on mine." His face had washed pale again, and the muscle in his jaw pulsed.

"Mankind can have black hearts, it is true, no matter the color of their skin."

Phineas didn't seem to hear him. His gaze remained locked ahead, his hand remained on his leg, rubbing, and his face remained tight. "Some of us do all we can to be fair. Our people *do* work for themselves. How do you think any ever bought their freedom otherwise? We allow them to keep their own gardens, their own livestock. They're allowed to barter and sell in the towns. To build their own fortunes, even to find their own employment in the cities and keep most of their wages."

He believed it, Luther could see that. Believed those concessions made it all fair and right. "And because you let them have their own gardens, you think it means you needn't provide them any food. They must toil fourteen hours in the blistering sun in *your* fields, then repair to their own little plots and toil some more. And if their crops fail, well, then they starve. If they can't produce enough to sell, well, then their children have no clothes to wear that winter. Because though their masters fancy themselves guardians and parent figures, they certainly never bother to spend any of their coin on them."

Phineas turned sparking eyes his way. "We are not all monsters just because we own slaves."

"And we are not all beasts just because our skin is of a deeper hue." He motioned to the field beside which they drove, with the scores of bent brown backs tending the tobacco plants. "You think none of those men have dreams, or would if they were given the chance? That none would like to go to sea, or to read a book? Paint a picture, write a symphony? Do you think none would make excellent physicians or solicitors or teachers? But those dreams are the very things you fear. You fear they will steal your workforce away, and so you deny them the chance to know such a future exists for them. You deny them the most basic of human instincts—to *learn*. Aristotle says—"

"I declare, Luther, I can tolerate your incessant reading and quoting of Scripture, it being the Word of the Lord and all, but if you take to quoting some long-dead Greek, you may have this here crutch swinging toward your head."

Luther looked from the crutch propped on the bench beside Phineas to the young man's strained face. He couldn't have said why the boy's anger made him want to smile again. "All right then, no Aristotle. Fair enough, I suppose, since I now have you quoting Scripture. You were a most attentive pupil while unconscious."

Phineas grunted, but his stature relaxed again. "Pupil indeed," he muttered.

Up ahead he could see where the fields gave way to civilization, where the town sprang up between the tobacco plantations and the seaport. Not much longer, and the cessation of the bumps would no doubt improve Phineas's mood, along with his well-being. But in the meantime . . . "If you don't want to discuss the philosophy, then let us examine a specific case. You. And me. Would you deny me the life with which the Lord blessed me?" His question came out as little more than a rumble. "If it were up to you, would you strip me of my education, my freedom? Put me in your fields?"

The glance Phineas spared him was brief, distant. But not as biting as it might have been. "If you don't cease your infernal sermonizing and lecturing once in a while, I just *might* wish it."

Luther pressed his lips together and deliberately frowned to keep himself from cackling in victory. Try as he might, Phineas didn't deny *some* facts, anyway. It was a start.

Though the way the man shifted and turned slightly, the wary look on his face made Luther's suppressed mirth die away. "What is it?"

Phineas blew a long breath through his lips. "You do realize, don't you, that you're going to have to give up the appearance of freedom? There's no way they'll let you in the Confederate States as a free black, even in my company, even if I signed for you. We'll have to get papers forged saying you're my slave, bought in . . . I don't know, Florida or something. Somewhere legal. It's the only way they'll let you in—and we'll have to use a false name for you, too, if they've put your rightful one on a no-entry list."

Luther's hands tightened on the reins again. "All of my thirty-five years I've been free, and now I must *pretend* to bondage?"

Phineas grimaced. "And that accent of yours would give you away in a heartbeat, so you had also better pretend to muteness."

His nostrils flared, filling his nose with the scent of tilled earth and green plants. "My grandfather fought in *your* Revolution with the British so that his children would be free. My cousin was married to the daughter of Olaudah Equiano, the most influential African in England, made so because of the voice he put to paper detailing the horrors of slavery—a book that spurred the abolitionist movement. And you really would have me give up my voice. Give up my freedom."

"No." Phineas's voice was soft. "Only the appearance of it. Only in company. I know of no other way to get you to your Eva."

Eva.

Luther squeezed his eyes shut, summoned up the image of her flawless, beautiful face. She was worth any humiliation. Any sacrifice. "So be it."

"Good, because that plan will have to begin as soon as we reach town. I must be the one to buy the tickets."

Luther managed only a nod.

"And we'll have to find someone to forge that bill of sale too. I don't suppose you know of anyone? I imagine a minister like yourself—"

"I know of someone. I was forced to employ his services for my last attempt to make it onto your beloved Georgian soil, though clever documentation wasn't enough." And his fingers clenched ever tighter at needing to resort to such tactics yet again.

Phineas sighed, shifted. "Luther, I . . . I'm sorry it has to be this way. I am, and I hope you believe that."

He nodded again, but acknowledging that the planter's son beside him possessed a bit of fairness did little to make reality less harsh. "I'll do what must be done . . . gratefully, with thanks to you for upholding your end of the bargain."

"You saved my life." Phineas's voice was soft and held a bit of bemusement. "And you . . . or maybe it wasn't you, but somehow or another, something shifted during the last months. Nothing looks the same anymore."

Praise be to you for that, Father God. "Perhaps nothing *is* the same anymore, Phineas."

"That's what I'm afraid of." He finally removed his hand from his leg, though only to wipe the sweat from his brow. Then he turned his head toward a passing buggy, inside which sat a young couple, the woman's arm looped through the man's as he held the reins. They both laughed, looking caught up in their own tropical world. Didn't so much as look toward Luther's cart. Phineas sighed again. "I should have acted sooner, not been afraid of her father's disapproval. Had I proposed to her before I left—or better still, married her—then I wouldn't be so afraid she's moved on already, thinking me dead. The mourning period would give me time to get home."

Poor chap. Luther at least knew that Eva would never turn to another, not of her own free will. She'd wait for him to find her. She'd know he'd upturn the entire earth if necessary, so she would bide her time. Pray and wait.

Of her own free will, anyway. Though if the master she was sold to in the States was anything like the one she'd been cursed with in Cuba, her will may not be taken into account.

Chest tight, throat even tighter, Luther forced that thought away and committed her again to the Lord. When he found her, they'd work through the horrors, no matter how bad they were. No demons would come between them, and nothing would keep him from reclaiming her, freeing her. Taking her home. With the Lord's help, he'd make it right.

And he'd just have to believe that the same would be true for Phineas. "If she loves you even a fraction as much as you love her, she'll still be waiting."

"I'm not so sure she does." His eyes slid closed, his face reflecting his pain—pain Luther suspected was as much from his heart as his leg. "She loves the man I was—the one who went off on adventures, who was willing to battle the enemy for a taste of glory. The one she could make a hero in her stories."

"Your leg will heal, Phineas. You'll be that man again."

"My leg *might* heal. But I don't know that I can ever be that man again." He winced when they jolted over a bump, hissed out a breath.

Luther did his best to steady the cart. "What is it you don't know if you can get back? The sense of adventure? The yearning for glory?"

"No. The trust. The trust in those supposed to fight beside me." He shook his head and repositioned his leg. "I wasn't just fighting *against* the Yankees, Luther. I was fighting *with* my brothers, for my home. And those brothers turned on me."

"Not all of them. You told me your officer—"

"Enough of them. Two, out of a crew of six. My closest friend included."

"Spencer." Luther loosed a long breath and steered the horse around another groove in the road. "You said his name often. I pieced together that he was the one to turn on you, but I didn't realize you were particular friends beforehand."

"Maybe we weren't. I don't know anymore."

In the past fortnight, as Phineas struggled to regain his strength, to get on his feet, never once had Luther heard such despair in his voice as he did just then. Such defeat. But then again, he'd had something tangible to focus on, and he hadn't had to think about what he'd find at home, just about how to get himself there.

Still, he trusted Luther. He might not yet recognize it, but he did—Luther would be willing to swear to that. Trusted him with his life, and now trusted him with his thoughts. Trusted him to do his part. Surely that meant he could trust his own kind again.

Or perhaps it only went to show that the Almighty had one well-tuned sense of irony.

Chapter Fourteen

SEPTEMBER 15, 1861

"And then," Cordelia said in her most compelling voice, leaning forward so she could pitch it low and still be heard, "they heard a rustling in the swamp grasses. A gentle splash. Then utter silence—no insects chirping, no animals skittering. Nothing. Nothing but the sound of danger thrumming through the air."

"Oh gracious." Willametta snapped her fan open and swished it vigorously in front of her face. "It wasn't a panther, was it? Tell me it wasn't a panther—I've heard such horrid things about those vicious Florida panthers."

"Mama, hush." Sassy giggled but also scooted closer to her mother, her hoops bouncing.

Lacy released the lower lip she'd been gnawing. "A panther wouldn't have splashed in the water, would it? They're a type of cat. Aren't they? And cats don't care for water."

Mama scarcely glanced up from her sewing. "Why don't you just wait and see, dear? I'm sure Delia will tell us in a moment."

Cordelia smiled, even as she mentally kicked herself. A panther, of course—that would have been so much more interesting than the alligator she was about to have fictional-Phin wrestle.

She could see it now, his muscled arms flexing as he subdued the tawny beast. They were tawny, weren't they? Or were they black? No, no, definitely tawny. She had read about them just last week.

But never mind. It was good she hadn't planned the story around a panther, since that's what Willametta guessed. Always best to surprise the audience. Cordelia lowered one shoulder so that her curls spilled over it, tilted her head just enough that she could look at each lady from under her lashes. Presentation was, after all, as important as the story itself.

And her stories had been keeping the Dunn ladies' minds off their fears, at least for a few hours here and there. Helped them, she fancied, take hope, have faith in Phin's ability to get out of scrapes.

After all, if he could defeat an alligator with his bare hands, then no Yankee would stand a chance against him.

Never mind the terrors in her own nightmares—there was no need to worry about sea monsters. Or the Man Mountain, that ape-like creature rumored to haunt the Everglades.

Perhaps she ought not to have researched those wild lands quite so well.

Well, enough of her tactical stall. She drew in a long breath. "The silence stretched for what seemed an eternity, and with each passing second, the men's nerves grew more and more taut. They edged backward, back toward solid land, away from that marsh that seemed bent on swallowing them whole."

In the corner of the room, one of the servant women let out a muted squeal and tossed a hand into the air. Cordelia caught a mutter of "water spirits" and "po Mr. Phin."

Well, Salina had warned her that the slaves wouldn't be much comforted by her putting Phin in such swampland. But it wasn't to be helped—that was the story that had come to her.

She tamped down a smile. "Then up from the water sprang a pair of jaws!" Leaping forward to the edge of the settee, she raised her arms as if they were the alligator. It took all her restraint not to dissolve into laughter at Sassy's and Lacy's shrieks. "The men stumbled, ran, tried to get away—but one fell, directly into the path of the largest alligator ever seen in the Everglades."

"Not Phin." Willametta's fan increased its rate of swishing, somehow.

"Oh no, of course not Phin. But it was his dearest friend that he's written to us about, Mr. Spencer. When he saw Spence fall, he knew he must act, especially since the others had all fled. And so he thought, 'Better to die saving a friend than to live in the shadow of cowardice.'"

"Oh." Sassy splayed a hand over her heart. "That's my brother, all right. That's our Phin."

Indeed. Cordelia reached to her side, unsheathed an imaginary blade. "The only weapon he had on his person was his sword, and paltry indeed it seemed against jaws so powerful. Surely, surely that monster would snap the blade in two with a single bite. But he had to try. With a mighty yell he threw himself between the alligator and his fallen friend, sword extended."

"Oh dear." Lacy covered her eyes, as if that would make the word images disappear. Silly Lacy.

"He thrust the sword at the beast, but it had no hope of penetrating the creature's thick hide. Nay, he watched his worst fear come to fruition as the sword caught, then snapped. Enraged, the alligator turned from the fallen Spencer toward Phin and lunged. Phin jumped out of the way, but in so doing, tripped over the legs of his friend."

"Well, of all the bad luck." Mama tied off her thread, snipped it free. Leave it to her to remain unaffected.

Ah well, at least she had three captivated. Five, if one counted the servants. "The gator's jaws closed with a clap that echoed all through the marsh, missing Phin's leg by less than an inch. But he saw his opportunity, knew that the monster's strength was all focused upon the *closing* of its jaws. So he threw himself at the beast, wrapping himself around its mouth."

Willametta looked as though she may soon need Mama's smelling salts. "Gracious me."

"They thrashed and rolled, locked in a struggle that made them one, through the mud and grass, until no one looking could tell where the monster stopped and Phin began."

Mama smoothed out the seam she'd just finished. "I thought the others had all fled."

"Mama." Lacy turned wide eyes to her. "They obviously came back when they heard the commotion and Phin's yell. Now *do* let Delia tell it!"

She made a mental note to think up some special delight for her sister as a show of her gratitude. "Round and round they went, over and over. All through the Everglades, all anyone could hear was the determined grunt of the man bent on survival, and the throaty bellow of the beast bent on its dinner. Until . . . again . . . silence."

Sassy pressed her hands to her mouth, her eyes as round as parasols.

Cordelia resettled on her cushion, straightened the ruffle on her skirt. Deliberately. Just long enough. "For an eternal moment, no one moved. No one spoke. No one dared even breathe. Until, finally, the fallen Spencer picked himself up and crawled over to the now-still entangled forms. He heard a groan, low and soft, but didn't know whether it came from man or monster. Then, with a bellow that would make your skin crawl, the alligator moved."

"No!" Willametta dropped her fan and grabbed Sassy's hand.

"Yes. It moved, rolled—and then halted, with the broken, jagged sword buried up to its hilt in the beast's single vulnerable spot. Here." She touched above her eyes.

A collective breath was exhaled from all, except Mama, who'd taken up stitching a new seam.

Cordelia sat up straighter. "Up from the marsh rose Phin, more mud than man, streaked with the creature's blood. His eyes gleamed with such fierceness that his friends all took a step back. But those eyes didn't rest on any of them—oh no, he was looking beyond them. He spun, turning a full circle. His hand reached for his sword, but of course, it was no longer at his side. And into the clearing moved, silent as night, a band of Seminoles."

"Natives?" Lacy shook her head. "Oh heavens, Delia. Will it never end for poor Phin? You should send Julius into the story to help him."

That was enough to make her want to wrinkle her nose—and blot out that mental note to prepare a treat for her sister. "All the others unsheathed their weapons, but the band paid no mind to them. They glided past, surrounding Phin . . . and inclined their heads to him. '*Hulputta*,' they said. 'We will call you *Hulputta*. Alligator.'"

Sassy sagged against the back of the couch, then sprang back up. "Oh, he won their respect."

"Indeed. They took Phin and his friends back to their village. Tended their wounds, filled their stomachs, offered their best men as guides to deliver them from the swamp. And even now, a new legend is being whispered among the people of the tribe. A legend of the man who had fought the alligator and come away with its spirit. A man with fierce eyes and the patient wisdom of the most fearsome predator. A man who had conquered the swamp with his bare hands. A man who would be forever known among them as *Hulputta*."

They all applauded, even Mama—though her clapping looked more polite than exuberant. Cordelia smiled and gave a short mock bow, finally letting herself laugh at the instant, amazed chatter between Lacy and Sassy.

Not her best story, in her opinion, but far from her worst. Certainly worth the two hours of sleep she had lost last night as she read and wrote, and the new ink stains on her fingers. She could hardly wait to get home and tell Salina how well the telling had gone.

Willametta rose and, even as Lacy flounced into her spot, came over to the settee and settled beside Cordelia. She took one of her hands in both her own and gave it a gentle squeeze. "Thank you, my dear. Your stories are the only thing we have to look forward to these days, the only thing that keep us from succumbing to our worry."

Cordelia covered the lady's hands with her free one. "He's all right, Mrs. Dunn. I know he is." Even if her faith in that was overcome by her imagination half the time. She had Salina to remind her to cling to hope, and she would do the same for the Dunns.

The girls' chatter halted, and the sudden silence in the room brought a chill to her spine, far too reminiscent of the story she had just told.

Sassy stood, her gaze on the door. "Daddy?"

Cordelia turned just in time to see Mr. Dunn step into the parlor. On the surface, he looked much like Phin. Middling-to-tall height, shoulders just broad enough to be both strong and fashionable. His cypress hair had years ago gone gray, and his amber eyes, though always kind, were usually sober.

But never like they were now. She couldn't recall ever seeing the gentle, quiet man look so very solemn, not in all the years she had known him. *Oh please, Lord, let it be a dead uncle. A slave rebellion, Yankees on their plantation—anything. Anything but Phin.*

Mr. Dunn held out a hand toward Sassy. Horror on her face, she hurried to his side, wrapped her arms around him. He then led her toward the settee, made her sit, and crouched down in front of them. When his gaze touched on Cordelia, she saw the sheen of moisture in his eyes.

No. No.

He grasped Sassy's hand in one of his own, covered the joining of Willametta's and Cordelia's with his other. Cleared his throat. "I've had a letter. From Commander Semmes of the *Sumter.*"

Willametta drew in a shuddering breath. "Telling us he's missing?"

"No, my dear." His eyes slid shut. "Telling us he's dead."

The fingers around Cordelia's squeezed with more power than she would have thought they had within them. Still, it wasn't enough to pierce the haze that fell before her eyes.

It couldn't be. It *couldn't*. Semmes was wrong, everyone was wrong. Phin couldn't, *couldn't* be dead. She would know it. She would have dreamed it. She would . . . she . . .

"No." Willametta's trembling carried into Cordelia's hand. The woman shook her head. "He must be mistaken. Sidney, tell me he's mistaken."

Mr. Dunn sighed. "I wish I could. Phin was indeed on the prize crew that took a ship called *Cuba*. Their towline had to be cut during a storm, and that was the last Semmes saw of them. He only yesterday received word of what happened."

A stifled sob came from Sassy. Her mother squeezed Cordelia's hand all the tighter. "What did happen?"

"Betrayal. Two of the sailors freed the ship's crew in return for immunity from prosecution, but of course fighting broke out. The Yankees regained control of the ship and took the crew—including the traitors—into custody. They're awaiting trial for piracy up North."

Cordelia saw the hope flash in Willametta's eyes, along with the answering dread in her husband's. "Then Phin—"

"He was shot." The words, though soft as fleece, bit like a bullet themselves. "In the melee, by the Yankee captain. Then . . . he fell overboard. He wasn't found, my love. He's—he's gone."

Willametta's hands went lax, her face fell into a mask of

close composure that did little to hide the tears swelling in her eyes. "My boy. My precious boy."

"Poor Phin." Sassy swiped at her cheeks, choked back another sob. "He would have been trying to play the hero. That's probably why he died. Oh—the words I last spoke to him! I told him I'd rather die than have a coward for a brother. What a horrid, horrid sister I am."

When Sassy dissolved into uncontrollable sobs, her father gathered her into his arms and held her tight against him. Willametta leaned into them too, releasing Cordelia's hands.

She could only sit where they left her and stare at the pattern in the rug. It couldn't be true. It couldn't. There had been some mistake, some oversight. A miscommunication, a . . . a cruel joke. This commander could have taken a disliking to Phin, borne of jealousy no doubt, and . . . and . . .

Her eyes slid closed, and the dream, that first terrible dream, came rushing back. Fire, smoke. Then water. A storm. Pain, searing and slicing and biting, but then . . . *sand*. Sand, yes, he had washed ashore somewhere. He must have. He had survived, he had suffered. But then there had been sunshine. Hope.

He was alive. He had to be. Alive, on the mend, coming home. He *had* to be.

"Delia." Mama's voice came from right beside her, and Mama's cool hands stroked her cheek. "I'm so sorry, darling. I know how this must hurt you."

Her eyes opened, but a mist still hovered before them. "No. Mama, he's not dead. I know he's not."

Had there been desperation in her tone? Was that why her mother looked at her with disappointment and pity mixed? "Darling, I understand the desire to deny it. But please, don't say such things. The last thing the Dunns need right now is false hope."

She wanted to argue. Wanted to insist. But the mist cloyed and clawed, and she couldn't wrap her tongue around any words. They had deserted her, those syllables she had always considered her dearest friends. Left her to flounder under Mama's stare. "I . . ."

"Come." Mama slid an arm around her and urged her to her feet. Lacy appeared on her other side. "We must go, must give the Dunns some privacy."

That didn't seem right. Her place was beside them. Beside the ones who loved him. "But—"

"You may return tomorrow, darling, but give them today to grieve together."

Oh, how she hoped one of the Dunns would hear and object, would insist Cordelia stay. Claim she was one of them, even if not made so by law. But they didn't look up when Mama and Lacy propelled her past, didn't seem aware of anything outside their tight, tear-soaked circle.

But she caught River's eye on the way out the door. Saw the incredulity upon his face, side by side with the raw pain, and tried to pull away so she might go to him. Offer him . . . something.

Mama had her outside too fast, and into the carriage. Why was it waiting for them already? Perhaps the servants had anticipated their quick departure when they heard the news. It was, after all, expected that they would give the family space to grieve.

Expected. But still Cordelia couldn't shake the feeling that it wasn't *right*.

"Oh, Delie-Darlin. I'm so sorry." Lacy threw her arms around her the very moment they sat. "I never dreamed you'd lose a sweetheart, not as quick as the war's sure to be. If only he had married you before he left."

"Don't speak such nonsense, Lacy." Mama smoothed her skirts. "If she were now a widow, she would be trapped at home for the next year and a half. If lose the sweet boy she must, it is better by far that she lose him now, when she is still free and need not observe a period of mourning. She is far too young and beautiful to waste her youth behind a black veil. We'll plan a ball, my darling. Something to take your mind off it, something to cheer you."

Had the woman gone raving mad? Cordelia blinked, but the image of her mother, earnest and oblivious, didn't change. "I don't want a ball, Mama. I don't want cheer. I want *Phin*."

"Oh, daughter." As their driver clicked the horses up and the carriage lurched forward, Mama tugged Lacy over to the opposite bench and then took her place beside Cordelia. Her fingers felt bony and cold on her arm. "My dear, you never really *had* Phin. Your understanding with him was so new, based on so little . . . you are in love with the character you have created that shares his name, not the man himself. The sooner you leap into society, the sooner you'll realize your heart did not drown with him. It never *was* with him, it was only your imagination. Let it direct you toward another."

She pulled her arm away. How could her own mother say such terrible things to her? Her voice little more than a hoarse whisper, Cordelia shook her head. "That's not true." It wasn't fictional-Phin she loved—it was the man who appreciated her tales, who indulged her in their telling. The man who had never once rolled his eyes at her or shaken his head at the ink stains on her fingers.

Lacy scooted to the edge of her seat and reached over to take Cordelia's hand. "Oh, Mama, be kind. This is a horrid shock to poor Delia. She needs some time before you toss her back into society."

"She has had time already." The knuckles that stroked over Cordelia's cheek felt hard as stone. "We have known these two months poor Phin was missing, and I am well aware your father spoke to you of moving on, Cordelia. My heart aches for the Dunns, but it is not the end of *our* world. It is time to put your feelings for him aside and focus on the one who is *here*. It is time to accept Julius's suit."

"*What?*" Lacy let go of Cordelia's hand as if it had become a hot iron and pressed herself against the cushion behind her. "Just because her beau is dead doesn't mean you can just give her *mine*."

Her beau is dead. Mistaken as they must be, the words slapped and bruised.

"It is not the end of our world." But it was, if it were so. How could Mama not see that? How could she think her heart, her soul so fickle that she could just . . . just . . . just put him aside?

Her mother, no comfort. Her sister, against her that quickly. Her father would offer nothing more. Only the Dunns would understand, would accept her with this ache inside. Why wasn't she in there with them?

Mama's blustery sigh seemed to blow the mist from before Cordelia—and into its place pounded a blinding, throbbing reality. She had no choice but to squeeze her eyes shut against it.

"Lacy, please, now is not the time for your theatrics. I realize you fancy Julius, but you are scarcely more than a child. You have plenty of time to find another beau, and plenty to choose from."

"Then let *her* choose another from the masses." Could Lacy not hear the petulance in her tone? Did she not realize it proved their mother's point about her childishness?

"Certainly she could, but this match is far better than any other we could hope for, with our Fulton County plantations being so near each other. Her dowry, added to Julius's lands, would make them a formidable couple. I'm afraid Julius has no need for our Savannah properties that are *your* dowry, Lacy." Mama's tone had taken on that ice that always signaled defeat to any who opposed her. "He's already spoken with your father about courting Delia."

"He hasn't! I won't believe you. He is *my* beau! He isn't so shallow that he'd choose her *dowry* above *me*!"

Why was there no escape? Cordelia turned her face away, leaned into the corner, but still Mama's skirt pressed against hers, still Lacy's shoe found a connection with her shin. As if that small pain meant anything just now.

Lord, where is he? Where is Phin?

Mama made that low humming sound that indicated deep irritation. "Oh, Lacy, wipe that insufferable pout from your face. You are only sixteen, and you have ample time to choose another. Even if this dreadful war drags out, you will still be young at its end. Your sister, however, has only a few more years before her looks will fade. She can't afford to waste time, and all those officers could at any moment be called to the front in Virginia with their regiments."

"It isn't fair."

Unfair? Did her sister really want to open a conversation about what was fair? Cordelia pressed her fingers to her eyes. "Lacy, hush. I have no interest in Julius—and frankly, you shouldn't either. He's not only after our dowries, he's an outright cad."

Mama put a hand on her shoulder. Not so much to comfort, she suspected, as to restrain. "That is enough, Cordelia. You are overwrought. Go straight to bed when we arrive home. Rest. Perhaps spend the evening with one of your favorite books. Soon enough, things will look different."

She kept her eyes squeezed closed, rather than indulge in the glare she had a mind to give her mother, which would only land her in trouble. But how, exactly, would things look "soon enough"? Bleaker? Or would hope resurface that Phin would yet come home? Either way, she knew well they wouldn't look as Mama wanted them to. Never, never would Julius look like a good alternative.

She did her best to ignore the continued squabbling of Lacy and Mama for the remaining few minutes of the ride. Not until they'd rocked to a halt did she open her eyes, and she was careful to avoid everyone's gazes as she accepted the servant's help down and headed for the front door.

Let Mama think she was being obedient—she would head directly upstairs, shut herself into her room. Take the excuse to remain there until morning. Salina would be happy to bring her up a tray, and Fanny would no doubt load it with enough food that they could share it together, as they so rarely had the chance to do these days.

But that was where her obedience would end. She would certainly not be spending her hours trying to push Phin from her mind. No, she'd spend the time thinking about him. Praying for him.

Home welcomed her into its cool dimness, and she angled herself for the stairs as Lacy flew ahead of her on a cloud of anger. Any other day, Cordelia would have raced after her little sister and tried to soothe her. Today, though, she just couldn't. Certainly not over the likes of Julius James. Let Lacy go, let her storm and stew for an hour or two.

Overhead, Lacy's door slammed shut before Cordelia even reached the stairs. She must be moving slow as molasses. A brown skirt swished into her downcast gaze. She would have ignored the servant without a second thought had she not recognized the feet as being Salina's. For her, she looked up.

And found her friend's beautiful face marred by a frown. "Miss Delia? What's the matter? You look . . ."

Mama stepped up behind Cordelia, a bit too close. "The Dunns just received a letter with terrible news. Their son was shot and fell overboard. Miss Delia is obviously distressed. Take her up to her room, girl, and see to her comfort."

Cordelia's fingers curled into her palm. Why, after all these years, did Mama still call Salina *girl*, as if she couldn't remember her name?

But Salina didn't seem to note it. Eyes large and luminous, she reached for Cordelia's hand. "Oh, Miss Delia. Now, don't you despair none—the Lord can overcome even news such as this, sure enough. You just keep on having faith that he'll come home to you."

Even as Cordelia opened her mouth to thank her, even as she gratefully squeezed her friend's warm fingers, Mama stepped forward. Quick as lightning, her hand rose. Strong as a tempest, it swung. Loud as a whip, it connected with Salina's cheek.

"Mama!" Cordelia spun on her mother but ended up taking a step back, tugging Salina with her. Never in her life had she seen Mama's face splotched with scarlet anger. Never before had she seen such hatred spewing from her eyes.

She didn't even look at Cordelia, her scathing gaze focused upon Salina. "You! *You* are the one who has been filling her head with such nonsense! I should have known, raised as you were by that African devil and that—that *witch* you call your aunt. I want you out of my house this *instant*, away from my daughters!"

"No!" Cordelia leaped between Mama and Salina, hands out to keep her mother from coming any closer.

Even as she moved, another roar came from the right. "Emeline! Get away from her this instant!" Daddy charged into the scene, grasping Mama by the arm and pulling her a few feet away.

Cordelia's hands dropped, heavy as they were with surprise. It wasn't uncommon for her father to intervene with how Mama dealt with the servants, granted, but never had she seen his eyes blaze at her mother like that—and certainly not over the slaves.

And never had she seen Mama look ready to strike at *him* as surely as she had Salina. "I've been pushed far enough, Reginald! I didn't want the girl in our house to begin with, and I certainly didn't want her with my daughters. I won't tolerate it anymore—she goes back to Twin Magnolias. To the fields, if I have any say in the matter."

"Well, you do *not* have a say." Daddy's nostrils flared, his eyes shot sparks. "She's not going anywhere."

There had been a few times in the past when Daddy had defended Salina in Cordelia's hearing, and she'd always assumed—stupidly, selfishly—that he did it because he knew Cordelia loved her. But just now she couldn't be so blind. Because as she looked at Daddy in profile, and then shifted her gaze to Salina . . . as she saw the hatred, hard and undiluted, in Mama's eyes . . . as Salina tucked her hands behind her back and Cordelia saw again those long fingers, just like her own . . .

The truth knocked the breath from her lungs. Salina wasn't just her friend. Certainly wasn't just her servant. She was her sister.

Mama sneered. "I would say that if she doesn't go then I will, but you've already proven yourself unable to be trusted if I'm not watching you every minute."

No. No, no, no. Cordelia squeezed her eyes shut for one blessed second. One second when she could cling to the thought that Daddy wasn't like that, wasn't like the other men, that it was an overseer who had fathered Salina, not *him*.

But there was only so much denial her mind would permit her. She opened her eyes again, looked to her friend.

Salina's eyes—such a familiar shape, and not just because she'd been seeing them on *her* for so long—were wide with horror. But not with realization. No, there was no surprise in them, which meant that Salina knew well who her father was.

Of course she knew. No doubt her murruh had told her. The secret-keeping tried to bite, but Cordelia shook that away. With the knowledge would have come the caution—that she must never breathe a word of the truth.

No, the horror in Salina's eyes was clearly for her.

"I hope you're pleased with yourself, Mrs. Owens." Daddy's voice, hard and final, rang through the entryway. He turned to Cordelia, drawing Mama's attention to her too. She could tell by the quick breath her mother drew in that she hadn't considered how her angry words would reveal what she'd always tried to keep her daughters from knowing.

Perhaps her father meant his gaze to hold some apology, some explanation. But all Cordelia saw in it was a man she'd never known. Never wanted to know. She edged back a step.

Something flickered in his eyes, and the muscle in his jaw ticked. He glanced at Salina. His other daughter. The one he'd never claim in public, but who he clearly must have acknowledged at least to a degree, to stand against Mama for her. "Salina, take Cordelia upstairs. She's clearly distressed."

It broke over her again, that crushing wave of grief she wanted to deny. Phin, gone. And now this on top of it. Her shoulders sagged, and she spun back toward the stairs as Salina surged to her side.

"Miss Delia." Somehow Salina's tone was both comfort and apology, horror and encouragement.

This, at least, she could count on. Cordelia reached out and took Salina's hand. The mirror image of her own, but for the shade of her skin.

"Cordelia!" Mama's voice, on the other hand, held only censure. "Let go of that girl this instant. You know better than to take her hand like that."

"I don't much care, Mother." Unable to turn and face her parents again, she *did* let go of Salina's hand—but only so that she could weave their arms together. It wasn't defiance, not really. It was simply latching hold of the only thing worth clinging to.

Chapter Fifteen

Salina's hands shook as she closed Miss Delia's door, pushing until she heard the click that didn't mean safety. Didn't mean anything was shut out. Didn't mean the most horrible truths weren't right here inside with them. She squeezed her eyes shut as tightly as she'd pressed the wood into its frame, but that didn't do any good either. Just meant she saw the stark realization in the memory of Miss Delia's eyes rather than in her real ones. Though, sure enough, if she turned around she'd see it again in reality.

She wasn't sure she was brave enough to face her sister again, now that Miss Delia knew she was her sister. And yet how could she do otherwise, when she'd be hurting so from the news about Mr. Phin?

Before she could settle that question inside, Miss Delia obliterated the need for it with a hand on her shoulder that turned her around. Somehow gentle and insistent both. Salina sucked in a breath as she spun, bracing herself for whatever might meet her gaze. Accusation, resentment, sorrow? Or, worse, "understanding." That *this* was why they'd always been able to be friends—because half of Salina's blood was Owens blood. That she was only able to read and comprehend and carry on an intelligent conversation because she was half white—a sentiment she'd heard before, and which never failed to make her temper flare. As if her murruh's side were any less human, any less worthy, any less—

"Sal." The second Miss Delia said her name, Salina knew all those thoughts were wrong. Other people might think that way, might even have tried to teach Miss Delia to think that way, but she wouldn't. Couldn't. Didn't. No, when Salina faced her sister, she saw what she *should* have expected—sorrow, but for Salina's sake. Love. Acceptance. "I'm so sorry."

That tugged out a frown, and Salina found her fingers tangled with Miss Delia's, though she wasn't sure who'd done the reaching this time. "Whatever *you* sorry for, Miss Delia?"

A wash of tears flooded her eyes. "For not seeing it sooner. Not realizing. For . . ." She swallowed, her larynx bobbing and her nostrils flaring in an obvious attempt to keep the tears at bay. "For how unfair it all is."

Unfair. That little word didn't begin to cover it. Didn't begin to make up for all the times Salina had to bite her tongue over the years, stop herself from saying things to Miss Delia that wisdom said she shouldn't. Because she *wasn't* just her sister, just her friend. She was a mistress, destined to own slaves—to own *her*. Just like her own father did.

Salina bit her tongue again now, against the words she wanted to say, and focused on the sorrow in Miss Delia's eyes. It didn't put anything to rights. But it made a difference, the fact that her sister's slights had never been intentional, and that she regretted the situation more now than ever. "Ain't your doin. You been a blessing in my life." Even as Salina spoke, her sister swayed, the trembling that must have started somewhere in her core working its way to the fingers she held. Salina hissed out a breath and shoved her own pain aside once again. "You about to fall straight over. Sit down. Tell me what happened, bout Mr. Phin."

Miss Delia's glassy eyes went downright flooded, and her lips took up a tremble too. "They said he was shot. Fell over—

overboard." A sob interrupted, and Miss Delia reclaimed one of her hands to press against her lips.

Salina's heart twisted. She urged her sister toward the bed, where Miss Delia sank onto the feather-filled mattress, her gaze focused on something only she could see. Salina opened her mouth to remind her again of hope . . . which made her cheek sting with the memory of Mrs. Owens's hand. She swallowed, gritted her teeth together, and lifted her chin. That old viper may be able to dictate what she could do in this life, but she had no power over what she thought. What she whispered to give hope to her dearest friend. "That makes sense then, don't it? With the dream we had? But he survived it. You know he did."

She nodded. But instead of lighting up, her eyes shut. Her head bowed. Her shoulders drooped. "If he did, then where is he, Sal?"

That she didn't know, and she figured her sigh admitted as much. "We'll just keep prayin. Prayin he'll come back to you. And it'll be like one of your stories when he does."

Somehow, Miss Delia's shoulders just drooped all the more. She shook her head. "I'm not so sure it'll matter if he does. They want me to marry Julius."

"No!" The word exploded from her lips far too forcefully, but try as she might to reel it back in with a sucked-in breath, it didn't do any good. Miss Delia's eyes still flew open. Still filled with a sad, dark knowing. Though she straightened, her shoulders still looked too heavy with burden.

"I don't intend to. But . . ." Her golden brows knit together. "I don't know who I'd dare to marry now, Salina. Who to trust. If even Daddy has done such terrible things, then . . . how can I know? How can I know who will be faithful? Who doesn't hide such despicable sins behind a smiling face?"

Salina settled herself beside her sister and squeezed her hand. "This ain't something you should have to worry bout."

"It's something we should *all* worry about!" She surged to

her feet in a rustle of fabric, her chest heaving with another sob. Her fingers were still tangled with Salina's, but she didn't pull her to her feet, just turned to face her. And she looked like one of the ladies in her stories, with earnest tears streaming down her face, curls framing her cheeks, and a desperate light in her eyes. Just like one of those fictional ladies, idealistic even in the face of horror, believing she could set the world to right. Never seeing the world was too broken for that. "I can't bring Phin back. I can't change my parents. I can't do much when it comes to society itself. But I cannot—I *will not*—let anyone treat you as our father did your mother. I swear that to you here and now, Salina. If that means never marrying, then that's what I'll do."

Mrs. Owens would have called it theatrics and scolded Miss Delia for such words. But the knot in Salina's stomach said her sister meant every word. She really was as naïve as one of her characters. She believed in this moment that she'd give up her own dreams of happiness to protect her. Because they were sisters?

Maybe. But not exactly. More because she only just now realized how real the danger was. And she couldn't see the reality that Salina knew too well, that intention in a moment of passion didn't mean much of nothing in the long run. Her mama would wear her down about marrying, or the world would. "Miss Delia, don't you go—"

"You're my best friend, Salina." The words she herself had thought more than once seemed to at once both fill the room and make it contract. "You're my sister. I could never live with myself if my decisions brought you harm. So, if I cannot guarantee your safety in whatever house I marry into, then I won't marry."

Salina swallowed past her tight throat. "The Dunns run a good house. The menfolk—they never touch the slave women." She'd never imagined speaking those words to Miss Delia, who ought never to have had to think about such things.

Her sister winced, sniffed, wiped at the tears with her free hand. "God willing, then, he'll come home soon. We can . . . I'll . . . But if he doesn't . . ." She squeezed her eyes shut again, turned her face away, and pulled in a series of long breaths clearly meant to bring her tears under control. She managed it a minute later and turned shining eyes back on Salina. "If he doesn't, then we have two options. Either I don't marry, ever. Or . . ."

Salina's stomach went heavy as a stone at that look in her sister's eyes. "Or what, Miss Delia?" she whispered, not sure whether she craved or feared the words she could see building in those green eyes.

Miss Delia crouched down, putting her below Salina in a way her mama would have slapped them both for. She leaned close, close enough that she could whisper too. Which she did, giving life to a dream Salina had told herself never to dream. Told herself would turn into a nightmare. Told herself wouldn't do no good.

"Or we find a way to get you to freedom."

Phin cast only one glance up at the ship giving a half-hearted chase, then back down to the Bible in his hands, borrowed from Luther. The Yankee vessel was no great cause for alarm. It had spotted them too late and was too heavy to give proper chase to the light English-made ship designed to run the blockade.

But try as he might to focus on the Scriptures, he couldn't seem to read more than a verse before Delia's face swam before his eyes. Only her lips kept turning into a smile that was full of pity and apology. Her eyes mocked him. And her imagined fingers, stained black with ink, pulled away from his.

He slapped the tome shut and set it on the deck, rubbed a hand over his face.

Luther arched a brow. He stood with his back against the

mast, arms folded. All but daring anyone to approach, with that glower of his. For a man who had complained endlessly about the need to hide his freedom and bite his tongue, he seemed to be having quite a bit of fun at the expense of the blockade runners—and had gotten rather adept at communicating with nothing but facial expressions.

Phin raked a hand through his hair, his hat long since discarded. "The light isn't good for reading."

Luther blinked. Just blinked, but said plenty. Enough to make the truth worm its way to the surface of Phin's mind, though he'd just as soon it stay hidden. "All right, fine. It's me. Me and this fear gnawing away at me that says I'm too late."

Though he looked as though he'd like to say something, Luther just pressed his lips together. Phin ran his hand over his face again, though he couldn't wipe away that tight, thudding feeling inside.

My times are in thy hand.

He grunted a laugh. Even with Luther mute, he could hear his voice in his head, reading. That verse was from . . . the Psalms, if he remembered correctly.

His "guardian" chuckled too—perhaps he somehow sensed what had flitted through Phin's mind.

And why not? For all those weeks, it was Phin who had been struck dumb while Luther spoke, while he shared all his ideas, thoughts, and concerns. Now the tables were simply turned. Except that it was still Luther's thoughts, it seemed, rattling through Phin's brain, so obviously the man would have no trouble divining them.

Although it begged the question of what had become of his own thoughts. What had become of *him*.

He settled his hands in his lap and cast his gaze to sea. The port of Cedar Key grew larger on the horizon, but the open water caught his attention. Largely because it didn't beckon him as it once had. How many times had he looked toward the ocean when on land and felt that itch in his feet? The tug in his gut that said his home lay not in Georgia but on the ever-churning waves of the Atlantic and beyond?

Yet now it was only . . . water. Pretty, to be sure. The sunshine sparked diamonds onto the sapphire blue of the Gulf, and the sky was a perfect upturned bowl of cloudless azure. The deck under his feet should have reminded him of Uncle Beau's, should have made him yearn to stride along it, clamber up its masts, or grip the wheel and steer her safely into port.

Why, then, was he content to sit here in the chair Luther had brought up for him? Why did he want only to reach land? Maybe it was just the need to get home and prove to all that he was alive. Maybe he'd feel the call of the waves again once he had satisfied that, once his leg had healed.

Maybe. Again with the doubts.

Lord, why do I feel as if I died while I lay in that stupor? You preserved my life, and I thank you for that. But it seems now I need you to show me what I'm to do with this gift—the life I left behind feels as distant as the Orient.

Luther moved toward the rail and leaned onto it, his face a storm to contradict the blue above them. There was a decided irony to the fact that they had bought passage aboard an English ship. An English ship pledged to help the Confederacy, at least insofar as it was profitable. An English ship for a man who must deny being English.

Phin watched him draw in a deep breath and then turn to face the encroaching land. Watched the yearning possess his face. *That* was what he had once felt for the sea, for the wide-open world. That very same longing Luther felt for Eva. That feeling that life itself waited yonder.

A new pressure built inside, steady if not too intense. He had no idea how to go about finding the man's wife. If he asked too many questions about one black woman whom Luther described as "the most beautiful creature to ever smile upon man"—very helpful description, that—all he'd achieve would be making Savannah think it his own woman of dubious relations he was searching for.

Luther's nostrils flared, his brows tugged down. Then he closed his eyes, lips moving in what was no doubt a silent prayer, and his face cleared again.

Phin drew in a long breath. To the devil with what anyone thought. He would find the man's wife for him, would purchase her from whoever had bought her—which would be far easier than trying to convince said person they had bought the woman illegally. Then he'd send them both back to England, back to their home and their church.

Lord, I am, without question, going to need your mighty assistance on this one, if you please.

He nearly laughed at himself. Never in his life had his thoughts given way to prayer so easily. Had he not, in fact, lain in agony upon that Cuban beach trying to remember *how* to pray? Yet here he was, doing just that every two minutes.

Something had happened to him. No question about that. He didn't know what, didn't know where the old Phin had gone. But right at this moment, he didn't much miss him. That Phin should have been a bit wiser. Chased fewer adventures and more relationships. And better learned in whom he could place his trust.

The Yankee ship gave up and turned back toward the horizon. Not an hour later, the British crew had maneuvered the blockade runner safely into port, and Luther had gone below to fetch their few belongings. Phin stood, supported by the crutches the doctor in Cuba had provided, and debated the best way to get himself down the gangway.

That was certainly one thing the Phin from last spring had in his favor—the ability to move wherever he pleased. Ah well. He would make do somehow, hopefully without disgracing himself entirely.

The thud of footfalls reached his ears, too heavy to belong to any of the sailors. When the enormous shadow fell over him, Phin sighed. "I'm afraid I may require your assistance in debarking . . . Monty." The assumed name still felt strange on his tongue, but he had to get used to using it. They'd had quite a time choosing what Luther would answer to in Savannah. Phin had first suggested *Mountain*, arguing it would complement River, but Luther had vetoed that idea. He hadn't minded the anglicized version of the French word for it, though.

Luther moved to his side and bent over as if to scoop him up. With a snort of laughter, Phin retreated a step. "I'm not *that* much an invalid anymore, thank you. Just . . . if you could . . . I don't know. You have the reach of a crane, perhaps you could just follow behind me but clasp my elbow to steady me in case my crutches slip on the plank."

Amusement dancing in his eyes, Luther shrugged as if to say, *Suit yourself.*

Phin rolled his eyes and turned to face the captain when he approached. He bowed as much as his crutches would allow. "My humblest thanks, Captain, for the use of your fine vessel in delivering me nearer to home."

"Glad to be of service, my good man." The captain nodded, a wisp of his cloud-white hair floating free of his hat. "You were a pleasure to have aboard."

"I only regret I couldn't be of any use to your crew. I am unaccustomed to sitting idly by when there is work to be done." Phin cast another glance over his shoulder at the men scurrying to and fro, taking care of last-minute details so they could get to shore.

"I wish you a most speedy recovery, so you might be back on another fine deck soon." The captain held out a hand.

Luther stepped forward, scowl in place.

Phin barely held back a laugh. His friend obviously knew the poor old captain was offering no threat, but the way the fellow leapt back . . . well, it was scarce amusements to be had for Luther these days.

Phin cleared his throat and held out his own hand. The captain shook it warily, then retreated again with a mumbled "Quite so. Very good. Farewell."

Once he was gone, Phin let the chuckle build and escape. "You're a cruel man."

A twitch of a smile was Luther's only response.

"Well, we might as well begin this delightful process. Say a prayer, will you?"

That earned him an affirmative hum.

Sweat trickled down Phin's temple within the first minute as he struggled to raise himself up to the plank. It no doubt would have been easier to let Luther haul him off like any other useless baggage, but if he succumbed to that now, that's what he would become.

Not exactly the war hero he had hoped to be when he returned home to Delia.

No, he wouldn't be ruled by his injury. Wouldn't let Spencer's betrayal ruin *him*—let it remain solely on Spence's conscience. With one final heave, he poised himself at the top of the gangplank.

Never in his life had its downward slope looked so terrifying. Phin exhaled a slow breath and willed his pulse to slow. His leg thumped, pain beating in time to each pump of blood. Gritting his teeth, he edged his crutches down a bit. Slid his feet after them. Again and again, making progress so slowly that he could only imagine the impatience of the sailors behind him.

But no one said anything, and he felt Luther just behind him. Ready to help but not interfering. And then, finally, his feet were upon Confederate soil. Or rather, the Confederate planks of the dock.

Luther's sigh blustered out behind him, sounding relieved. He drew even with Phin, then retreated a half step.

Phin took a steadying breath and grinned. "To the depot?"

Luther opened his mouth, then closed it and nodded toward the puff of smoke chugging toward the docks.

Phin had made port in Cedar Key before, with Uncle Beau, and had supervised the loading of their cargo onto the train that made its way over the bridge to the strip of docks. He'd even spent an evening or two in town, had visited the newly commissioned lighthouse. Not that said lighthouse would be operational now. As with most Confederate lights, it would be extinguished so as to avoid helping the Yankee ships that haunted the seas.

"The train comes to the docks for cargo, but not for us." Phin nodded toward the wooden pier that would deliver them to Front Street. "We'll have to take Second Street over to the depot."

Luther frowned at the distance he indicated, then at Phin's leg.

"I'll be fine. The exercise will be welcome." And after a few days' practice on the uncomfortable crutches, he'd mastered the rhythm that would allow him to move at a somewhat normal pace.

He didn't dread that nearly so much as what was sure to be a long, jostling trip home.

It took only a few minutes to reach the sandy solid ground and follow B-Street to Front Street. Phin glanced to his left, where he knew there was a bookshop that would no doubt have a few tomes to make Delia rub her hands together. But first things first. He turned to the right, where the street would lead directly to the rail company's station.

As he swung past a grocery and sundry other stores, Phin's stomach growled. But that, too, would have to wait. For now, he just worked on getting past the clapboard structures and making his way to the depot. When finally he hobbled up to the ticket window, he had no trouble digging up a smile. Home was finally within reach.

"Good afternoon, sir."

The ticket clerk looked up from his task behind the window and nodded a greeting. "Good afternoon. Have you been separated from your regiment? All our troops have been sent east to defend Fernandina."

Phin propped his crutches against the wall. "I have at that, though I'm not with the Florida units. I'm trying to get back to Savannah, where I can let my superiors know I'm alive."

The clerk whistled. "Savannah—that'll be quite the long, difficult trip, young man. Using the stage as well as the train."

"Long and difficult." Phin tamped down a grin. "Given what I've been through these past few months, sir, I daresay this will be a delight in comparison."

"Certainly easier than evading the navy along the coast, I daresay." The man looked to the chart upon his wall. "You'll want to take the train here all the way to Fernandina, then catch the stage to Savannah. Or if you were willing to risk another run of the blockade, you could get off at Baldwin instead and hook up with the Florida, Atlantic, and Gulf Central Railroad to Jacksonville, then try to steam your way home."

He had to shake his head at that. "Now that I've finally made Confederate soil, I aim to stay on it. I'll take the tickets to Fernandina, for me and my man here."

Luther didn't move, didn't shift, certainly didn't speak. But Phin swore he felt him tense at being called such. Which made *him* want to shift from foot to foot, which would have been a bad idea. He settled for casting a glance over his shoulder, one that would hopefully convey his apology for needing to speak in such a way.

He'd known it would be difficult for Luther to play this role. But who would have thought that such a pretense would prove so difficult for *him*?

The hard lines around Luther's mouth softened, though. He didn't nod his acknowledgment of Phin's silent apology, but the acknowledgment nevertheless came through in his features.

So long as they understood each other, understood this was necessity and not personal will, they would get on just fine.

Phin handed over a few shillings to cover the cost—borrowed from Luther, which still felt wrong. The clerk didn't bat a lash at the British currency, no doubt seeing plenty of it with the runners who came into port.

"You'll want to be on the train headed east in two hours." He handed Phin the tickets with an indulgent smile. "Best of luck to you, young man. Godspeed, and I wish you quickly healed."

"Much appreciated." He paused, brows raised. "I don't suppose telegraph lines have made it here yet?"

The clerk chuckled. "Amusing. With war on? No, sir. All those plans came to a screeching halt when conflict broke out. You can post a letter, of course . . . though it would be traveling the same route you'll be on, so if it's Savannah you're hoping to contact, you'd arrive at the same time."

He'd just have to hope the one he'd already sent had made it past the blockade. "Well, I thank you for the information, at any rate." He turned and, with crutches back in place, headed for the sandy road. "Couple more days, Luth—Monty. Just a couple days, and we'll be in Savannah."

His companion drew in a long breath. Under it, he muttered, "Amen and amen."

Chapter Sixteen

Cordelia gripped the drapes and wished they were a portal to another world. That she could disappear behind them and find herself somewhere else. Anywhere else. That they would whisk her away to an island somewhere . . . to another time, perhaps . . . to a place where the reality was not so harsh. Instead, she looked down and saw the Dunns climbing out of their carriage, and her heart twisted.

They all wore black, unrelieved and intense. They all moved more slowly than usual, and their shoulders were bent. Their mourning was still in its infancy, early enough that she was a bit surprised they had come to the ball tonight. But then, the death of a son or brother need not keep one at home. Only the death of a husband did that.

Her throat closed, cutting off all air. All desire for air. Why, *why* was she standing here in a ball gown of shimmering blue? She ought to be in black even darker than Sassy's. She ought to have a veil over her face. She ought to have the right to lock herself in her room and hide herself from the prying eyes of society.

"Miss Delia." Salina's voice came soft and gentle, much like the hand that gripped her arm. "You get on back from that window, now, and get yourself downstairs. There's a crowd there already."

She let herself be pulled away, but she also shook her head. "I can't. Not yet. Not until they make me." To prove it, she sank down onto the feather bed and let it pillow around her.

Salina sighed. "You'll make a mess of your fine silk dress doing that—and you know how long your mama had to look to find any material for you."

Even the mention of it hurt. "I told her not to. I told her I didn't want a ball—didn't even want to attend one." But the last weeks had been nothing but this ridiculous planning. As if with talk of invitations and fabric and what society remained in Savannah, her mother could blot out the callous reaction to the news of Phin's death and the hatred she'd shown toward Salina. As if Daddy could undo all his sins if he spent enough money on musicians and candles and food.

Salina sank to the floor at her feet and gripped the hands that lay limp in her lap. "You can't sit up here staring blankly at the wall no more, Miss Delia, she's right about that much. I hate seeing you like this. Like you plumb gave up. You haven't hardly read anything, haven't picked up your pen and ink since you got the news about Mr. Phin. It's been two weeks."

Cordelia turned her gaze away from that earnest, beautiful face that bade her believe. But how could she keep believing in the impossible, when the whole world said Phin was dead? "I don't know what to write anymore, Sal. I've tried, but all my heroes still turn into Phin. And they keep falling into crises out of which I can't seem to deliver them. And I can't—it's like losing him in new ways each time I close my eyes and try to imagine."

"You ain't lost him at all." Salina squeezed her hands, her voice intent. "Somewhere, under all the fear and the disappointment your family's been heaping on you, you know that. You know the Lord sent us those dreams to encourage you."

Did she know that? Cordelia's eyes slid shut. She wasn't so sure anymore. Maybe they weren't from the Lord at all. Maybe they were just coincidences. Maybe they hadn't even been so similar, their dreams, but they had colored each other's recollection of them in the telling. Maybe, as Mama said, she had imagination enough to convince herself of anything.

The only thing she knew anymore was that Salina was the only one willing to be the friend she needed—the *sister* she needed—right now. She was the only one who acknowledged the pain.

She was the only one who, by her very existence, demanded Cordelia look for the first time at something beyond her own limited world. A calling that weighed as heavily as the tragedy that felt like chains around her heart.

But answers to how she could help Salina were as elusive as a hopeful story. She knew nothing about the shadowy world of runaways. Even less about how to circumvent the law and find a way to free a slave legally. She couldn't shake the conviction that she had to do *something* to grant justice to her friend. She just didn't have any idea what.

"Don't you give up, Miss Delia. I won't let you. You give up, and your mama and daddy will have you married to that Mr. Julius in about half a blink."

"No." The suggestion was enough to straighten Cordelia's spine and bring up her chin. "I still have *that* much fight left in me."

"Do ya?" Salina pressed her lips together and shook her head. "You just sit here and take all they pour over you. Your sister's accusations of betrayal, your mama's insistence that you're out of your head to have any hope, your daddy's worry. You gotta stand tall, Miss Delia. That's what Mr. Phin will be expectin you to do."

Cordelia nodded, but still she had no desire to go downstairs. Thus far she'd managed to avoid society since word of Phin's death spread through town, and she didn't relish going into it tonight. To see the pitying glances and hushed whispers. To have to speculate on the speculation.

"As soon as I go down there, Daddy will push me toward Julius." Her stomach twisted. She forced a swallow through her tight throat. "I'd rather put that off as long as possible. It'll send Lacy into another rage, and I don't look forward to having to tell him *again* that I am not interested in his suit."

Just that morning her little sister had declared with a stomped foot that if her parents encouraged a courtship between Cordelia and Julius, she would flee to Ginny's the very next day to escape them all.

Mama had declared that a fine idea.

Cordelia had wanted to cry. Ginny was already all but out of her life, save for her letters. She didn't want to lose Lacy, too, and over a man she wanted nothing to do with. But it seemed she'd already lost her—or lost the connection with her, anyway.

Yesterday, when her little sister had stormed in here to complain about how their mother was in such a snit and it was all Cordelia's fault, Cordelia had told her why. Told her the truth about what had sparked the latest bout of fury in their mother. Told her—with some strange hope that Lacy would finally be on her side again—that Salina was their half sister, and Mama was just angry that she continued to be a part of their lives.

And Lacy had actually *sneered*. Had said, *"Listen to you! She's not our sister. She's just a half-breed slave. Heavens above, it's no wonder Mama's been so angry with you—and yet still you're her golden daughter, worthy of the best match!"*

How? How could the truth be presented so clearly to Lacy, and yet her little sister looked right through it? How could they have been raised in the same house by the same people, and yet Lacy have no concept of what gave a person value—not the color of their skin, but the color of their heart?

Or maybe Cordelia was the odd duck. Because it seemed

she was the *only* one in their house who looked at each slave now and wondered about their story. Wondered who they were when the masters weren't present. Wondered what dreams they would chase if they had the freedom to chase them. It had started just with Salina, yes. She was only one of many slaves in this house, in this city. One of so many people who had been treated for so long as if they were *not* people—people with stories and dreams.

The world was so twisted. So shadowed. Like a book that had gone down the wrong path chapters and chapters ago, because rather than go back and fix the mistake, the author had just kept on following it, darting down new rabbit trails until they ended up here.

Here. With a house full of guests and parents who expected her, somehow, for some reason, to put aside all the pain and pretend to care about their ridiculous ball. All so that she could impress a man she detested, secure a match she didn't want, and help build a plantation empire she could no longer be in favor of.

Every time she thought of the plantations now, she could only see Salina's mother. Her aunt. Her cousins. A whip hovering always over their backs. Threat their only companion. Every time she caught a glimpse of Julius, she imagined him standing over a cowering Salina, threatening her.

Like Daddy must have stood over her murruh. Demanding what he had no right to demand. And she, knowing well she couldn't object, couldn't argue. How would she dare? He held her very life in his hands.

She closed her eyes again and tried to pull her mind back to Savannah. Back to *this* nightmare. Tried to imagine how the evening might go. No one would notice her entrance, of course, she would make sure of that. She'd skirt the edges of the ballroom, find Sassy and Willametta in the back, where they were sure to be. First, she'd apologize for not being with them more in the past fortnight. Try as she might to spend her time there, Mama had found too many reasons to keep her home.

But she'd use their black skirts as a blind tonight as long as she could. Stand behind them, where the blue of her own gown would go unseen.

Still, Daddy would know where to look for her. No doubt he'd head her way eventually, with Julius at his elbow. Her cousin would have that dreadful look on his face, the one that spoke of arrogance and a desire she wished he would direct elsewhere.

But . . . but . . . something would intervene. Some*one*. Perhaps a handsome stranger would sweep into the room and steal everyone's attention. He would be someone uninvited, of course, but dashing enough to command everyone's gazes.

He'd have hair the color of honeyed cypress. Eyes of a gleaming hazel. Stand exactly a head taller than Cordelia . . .

All right, so it would be Phin. She could scarcely think of any other man, so she may as well give in to her longings, if she were dreaming. Phin would sweep in, and a gasp would run through the room. The whispers would ripple out at that speed that only gossip could ever hope to attain, and Daddy would stop in his tracks—and stop Julius with him. They'd turn, and Cordelia would look beyond them.

The crowds would part, of course. Making a path between them. A hushed reverence would fall over the room, and Cordelia would find herself gliding forward as if on a cloud. A glorious, effervescent cloud of dreams come true. The chandeliers would glimmer like gold and create a veritable halo around them. They'd draw ever closer, each step deliberate and yet measured. But she'd finally be near enough to see the passion shimmering in his eyes.

"Delia," he'd say in that way of his, drawing it out as if savoring each syllable. *"Delia, you brought me through it. Thoughts of you—"*

Without warning, Julius jumped out from the crowd, rage

upon his face. Cordelia opened her mouth to scream a warning, but it was too late. The sound of his sword ringing free of its sheath echoed through the room, quickly drowned out by his scream. She tried to leap forward, but her feet felt caught in a morass.

And Phin just stood there, unable to move in time, unable to avoid the arc of the blade.

A sob tore from her throat, and Cordelia slid from bed to rug as the image of her love crumpling and falling filled her mind's eye.

"Miss Delia!" Salina's hands were on her bared shoulders, but Cordelia couldn't convince herself to uncurl. The storm, so long held at bay, shook her whole body. The sobs came in quick, rolling waves, convulsing her stomach and making her fingers dig into the carpet as if it would offer some anchor.

There *was* no anchor, not anymore. No hope. Even if Phin survived the bullet, survived the water, even if he survived every evil that befell him, there was no way he'd make it home. It had been three months. Three months. If he were alive, they would have gotten word.

But they hadn't. Because he wasn't. Hope had sunk back in July, down into the depths of the Caribbean.

She would wait forever. But it would be an empty eternity, and dreaming otherwise would make her nothing but a fool.

"Cordelia!" Mama's voice this time, and the swish of her satin skirts. She felt them on her arm as her mother crouched down, but she couldn't open her eyes. Couldn't slow the sobs. "Whatever is going on?"

"I don't know, ma'am. One minute she was sittin there, pretty as you please, with a dreamy look on her face, and the next she started screamin and cryin and just fell to the floor."

"Cordelia." Mama touched a cool hand to her cheek. "Darling, you are making a mess of yourself with these hysterics. Really, I expect more of you."

"Maybe she's just not ready for a ball yet, ma'am—"

"Oh, hush up and do something useful, girl! Go fetch a cool compress for her face before it swells beyond all recognition."

"Yes'm."

Cordelia's middle heaved so forcefully she was surprised her corset didn't snap. But no, it just constricted, making it impossible to get a breath. She gasped for one, only to lose it in another shuddering wail.

Mama pulled her up and gave her a shake. "Get ahold of yourself. A fashionable swoon is one thing, but this is ridiculous. You will *not* ruin this ball with your theatrics."

She tried again to draw in a breath deep enough to steady herself. Failed again. Shuddering, convulsing, she could make no response. Had no response to make. She just wished her mother would stop touching her, would stop speaking, would go away.

Mama hissed something and moved around behind her. For a moment, given her mother's hands upon the buttons up her back, Cordelia thought some small ray of hope must have shimmered through, that Mama would command her out of her dress and into bed.

A few yanks, and the pressure around her middle loosened along with her stays, allowing precious air into her lungs. "There. Catch your breath, calm down, and then let Salina repair the damage to your face and hair. I expect you downstairs within the hour."

A few swishes of satin, and the door closed.

Cordelia fell forward again onto the rug and tried to focus on breathing. Part of her wanted to rail at her mother for her lack of compassion, her lack of understanding.

But it didn't matter. Nothing mattered.

Phin was gone.

Daylight was fading by the time the stage rumbled into Savannah. Phin was all but sure he'd worn his teeth down to nothing, clenching and gritting them as he had done all day. His leg hadn't hurt so much since he had regained consciousness, but the constant jarring of the stage had nearly done him in.

Maybe that was why entering Savannah didn't give him the jolt of pleasure he had expected. Why he looked out over the wooden buildings kissed by the red-gold fire of the sinking sun and felt only a vague stirring of disappointment. He could think of no other explanation. Certainly he should have been glad to see all the soldiers in their coats of various grays and blues. Shouldn't have looked at them so cynically, wondering which would betray a brother first.

As the stage drew to a halt at its final stop, he closed his eyes and shook his head. He had thought the bullet in his leg his greatest cause of injury—but that honor undoubtedly went to Spencer.

He felt the thud of Luther jumping to the ground from his place beside the driver, and a moment later the door opened and the familiar giant hand displayed the crutches that had been secured along with the rest of the baggage.

"Go ahead, son," one of the other passengers said with a smile and a shooing motion. "I daresay you're more anxious to get out of this thing than any of us."

So he *hadn't* succeeded in hiding his discomfort from the other passengers. Ah well, at least he hadn't disgraced himself with a bunch of moaning and groaning, even if his teeth would likely ache for days. "Thank you, Mr. Benfield. It was good to meet you and your lovely wife. Mr. Scott, Mr. Kennedy."

Their farewells sounded as he maneuvered himself into the doorway. They'd stopped enough times that he had this particular dismount down to one fluid motion. He gripped Luther's shoulder, let him brace his upper arm, and jumped to the ground, landing on his good leg.

"Thank you, Monty."

Luther smiled and motioned to the row of cabs waiting by the inn. After positioning his crutches under his arms, Phin led the way to the first one. Within minutes, they were yet again bumping along, and he was yet again clenching his teeth.

The fire of the sunset disappeared into the half-light of dusk as they gained the good section of town. "Almost there."

Luther studied the streets of brick and stone mansions and shot him a glare.

Phin sighed. Luther had known what he came from, but he supposed this first glance of prosperous Savannah brought it to life in a way words never could. There were similar sections in London, he knew, but Luther likely didn't frequent them. Even in free-as-the-air England, black men weren't greeted as equals. He no doubt had a nice little home in the Negro section, but nothing like this.

His heart felt its first thump of happiness when he spotted Dunn House. But it gave way to fresh disappointment when he realized there were no lamps lit in the rooms his family would frequent this time of day, only in the foyer. They were not at home.

He leaned toward the driver. "It's the gray one there, on the right."

The man turned the horses into the drive and pulled them to a halt at the front doors. No one rushed out the doors to meet him, as he had imagined they would do. No one was there waiting. Phin drew in a deep breath, let Luther help him down, and paid the cabby.

As the horses clomped away again, Phin stood for a moment and just looked up at his home, the place he'd been longing to reach forever now.

"Are you just going to stand there, or go in?"

Phin jumped at Luther's deep rumble. It had been days since he'd last spoken, days since he'd had the opportunity to. Grinning at himself, Phin turned to his friend. "I forgot you had a voice."

Luther snorted a laugh. "More like you *wanted* to forget."

"Nah. I find I almost miss your sermonizing. Almost. I may have missed it more, had it not continually echoed through my memory anyway."

With a chuckle, Luther motioned toward the stately façade. "Shall we, my lord and master?"

Phin narrowed his eyes even as he hobbled forward. "Sarcasm doesn't become you, Luth."

"Nonsense. It and I are the dearest of friends."

"Mmm-hmm." He made his way up the stairs and gripped the latch. It wouldn't be the first time he had arrived home unexpectedly and had to let himself in, but it hadn't happened often. Usually a servant was stationed at the entrance.

Not so tonight. He swung the door wide, stepped into the cool entryway of his home, and looked around. A staggering stack of calling cards sat upon the tray. More flowers than usual adorned the tables.

A servant screamed from the hallway and dropped a tray with a clatter and clang. Phin pivoted as best he could on his crutches and headed her way. "Old Bess! Are you all right?"

She'd followed the tray to the floor and kneeled there in the mess, a hand splayed over her chest and her dark eyes wide and incredulous. "Lawd o'mercy, protect me now from the spirit come outta the water to haunt me!"

Phin sighed, propped his crutches against the wall, and lowered himself to the floor beside her. Getting up would be a chore, but he'd think about that later. "Were I a ghost, Bess, this wouldn't hurt nearly so much."

The shake of her head looked trancelike. "No suh, that's just trickery. Mass Sidney, he got that letter from our boy's commander. He done got shot and fell overboard, so you ain't him."

"Logical." He rubbed a hand over his face. "Except the Lord saved me from the water, Bess—somehow. I washed up in Cuba.

I was in a real bad way, though, for months. Nearly died. But I wrote when I woke up—I assume my letter never reached home?"

Bess shook her head again, but some of the glazed fear faded from her eyes. "They never got no letter, no suh. That really you, Mr. Phin?"

"In the aching flesh." He held out a hand, let her grip it. "Is my family away for the evening?"

She grimaced. "They done gone to the Owenses' ball. Yo mama didn't want to, but yo daddy say she need to git outta the house. Since word come bout you a coupla weeks ago, she been a ghost herself."

"The Owenses'?" Though he tried not to frown, he felt his face pull down anyway. It didn't take any great genius to puzzle out why Delia's family would be throwing a ball so soon after hearing he was dead.

It seemed his fears were well-grounded.

"Let's hope they don't mind an uninvited guest." He tried to push himself up and succeeded only in wearing a bit more enamel from his teeth. "Monty, could you . . . ?"

Strong hands gripped his arms and lifted him.

He shot his friend a smile. "Much appreciated. Is River here? I should change before I go."

The servant clambered to her feet, shaking her head. "He done gone with yo folks, Mr. Phin. He been keepin an eye on Miss Sassy, what with all them soldiers flocking the city like moss on an oak."

"Ah. Perhaps Father's valet, then?"

Bess planted a hand on her hip and sent an arch glare over his shoulder. "Cain't this strappin fella here help?"

"Oh." He glanced at Luther, who nodded. "Of course he can."

The look Bess gave him was the same one she'd been prone to use when he was a boy, trying to hide some mischief he'd found. "You buy him from his massuh or somepin, to see ya home?"

Hopefully reaching for his crutches would excuse the vagueness sure to plague his affirmative hum. "His wife was sold somewhere in Savannah, and I promised to help him find her. Don't suppose you've come across an Eva? Would have arrived in the spring, about thirty years of age?"

Brow furrowed in concentration, she shook her head. "I keep me an eye out though, sho nuff."

"That would be good of you. And my apologies for startling you so, Bessie."

A grin emerged as she shooed him away. "Aw, ain't nothin. You git on upstairs now and git yoself dandied up so's you can go see yo Miss Delia."

He needed no more of a dismissal. He headed for the stairs quick as his crutches would allow, Luther falling in behind him. Once halfway up, he motioned his friend to draw even with him. "Old Bess knows everything that goes on in Savannah. If Eva stayed here any length of time, she'll soon hear about it and let us know. If not, then I'll start asking about sales in the last few months."

Luther nodded. "Nothing to be done about it tonight, Phineas, but I do appreciate your making it such a priority. Let's get you ready for this ball for now, so you can reclaim your Delia."

My Delia. That made his pulse gallop—or maybe it was the exertion of climbing the stairs. No, it was dread. Dread and determination, combined into a tempest set to rip him to shreds.

He wanted to see her, had to see her . . . and yet feared it more than he'd feared the barrel of that pistol aboard the *Cuba*. What if she had changed? Changed her mind? Or . . . what if she hadn't? What if she expected *him* not to have?

Lord, put your hand upon this meeting. I love her, you know I do. But when I asked her to wait, I never realized more would pass than time.

Which just went to show what an ignorant pup he had been just months ago.

His room was unchanged from the last time he'd entered

it, except that his mother had left one of her shawls upon his bed. The scent of her rose water still clung to it, which made him think it hadn't been here that long. Had she sat upon his mattress and mourned him? Cried into his pillow?

Chest tight, he turned to his wardrobe and pulled out the first decent suit of clothes he put his hand to. With hurried but steady movements, he changed from his bedraggled uniform into the fine worsted wool that hung a bit too loose now, requiring Luther's assistance only a time or two.

Then his gaze caught on the length of highly polished wood leaning in the corner of the wardrobe. He reached for it slowly, lifted it with a feeling of suspended reality. He'd bought the cane three years ago simply to be fashionable, had liked the hidden blade inside it.

Never had he dreamed it would prove genuinely useful.

Luther frowned. "That won't provide you with enough support, Phineas."

"We can't know that until we try, can we? I've been weeks on the crutches. My strength has improved considerably." He took a cautious step, putting his weight on the cane.

The exasperated toss of Luther's hand matched the roll of his eye. "If you fall on your face, don't expect me to scrape you from the floor."

Phin took another step and grinned. Partially at the lack of screaming pain from his leg, but largely from his companion's gruff tone. "But you would."

"Well, I *shouldn't*, if you're too obstinate to listen to reason." Luther waved at the discarded crutches. "Take those. The last thing you want to do is make a fool of yourself before your sweetheart."

"No, the last thing I want is to try to maneuver them through a crowded ballroom in search of her. This will work nicely."

"Phineas." Oh yes, Luther had perfected how to growl his name.

No doubt Phin couldn't imitate the rumble well enough, so he went for a simple, even tone. No-nonsense. "Luther."

The man sighed. "I think I preferred you unconscious. You listened far better."

"And could move far less." He headed for the door. "Come, my good man. Let's head downstairs so you'll be obliged to stop talking."

"Is there any point in my even going?"

"Certainly. I'll introduce you to River, who can be trusted with the truth. He can then introduce you to the others and see if anyone has seen your wife."

Luther straightened, which made him look far more self-possessed than the slave-appropriate clothing they'd found him would imply. "Very well, then. Lead the way, so I can scrape you up if necessary."

Between the railing and the cane, he managed the stairs with relative ease and soon discovered that Old Bess must have told the servants to ready his phaeton, for it waited in the drive. He needed Luther's help in getting up, but when he took those reins in his hands he felt, for the first time in months, in control of something.

Not life—he knew that now. But this one thing, this one carriage. If he steered it properly, it would do exactly as he asked. Small as it may be, it nevertheless brought him a breath of peace as he drove the familiar streets to the Owenses' house.

An unfamiliar boy met them outside and held the horse while Phin gingerly lowered himself down, then led her off to join all the other horses and carriages. Phin scarcely paid him any heed, his sights set on the familiar figure at the edge of the garden. "River!"

For a moment, his faithful servant seemed turned to stone. Then he spun, and the light from the gas lamps caught the hope that possessed his face. "Mr. Phin?" He took off at a run, headed straight for him. "Mr. Phin?"

"It's me, River."

Phin braced himself for the impact, but River pulled up a foot away and stared at him with a big smile but a shaking head. "I kin't believe my eyes, no suh. We done heard you was dead—kin't tell you how glad I am to see you, Mr. Phin."

"Can't be gladder than I am to be home." Phin slapped his free hand to River's arm and drew him close so he could speak in a hush. "The man with me is Luther—he rescued me. He's English, free, but pretending to be my mute slave—we're calling him Monty—so we can find his wife. We're going to need your help, my friend. Can I count on you?"

Myriad thoughts raced across his servant's face—question, confusion, jealousy, understanding. It settled on proud determination. "Course you kin, Mr. Phin. Don't even need to ask."

"Good. Take him somewhere you can't be overheard, and he can tell you all that happened to me, and about his wife. I must hasten inside before this ball draws to a close."

"Sho thing." River gripped Phin's wrist, gave it a squeeze that packed two-and-a-half decades of emotion into one move, and pulled away. "Whatevah you need. I take care of it, you jest leave it to me. Git on inside."

"Thank you." He turned away from the flicker of surprise in River's eyes—hadn't he thanked him often enough in prior days?—and faced Luther. To him, he need say nothing. He just nodded, then strode toward the house. Uneven as his gait may be with the cane, he felt steady enough with its aid.

At least until he glanced into the windows of the ballroom and spotted them. His mother, his father, Sassy. They all stood together, a black-clad island in the midst of a rainbow sea. Talking, yes, with someone or another he couldn't identify from the back, but even so they looked . . . separate. Apart.

His fingers curled tighter around the silver head of his cane. A few minutes more, that's all it would take for him to get inside and work his way through the crowded room. Then he could erase that line marring his father's brow. Lift the weight that seemed to bow Mother's shoulders. Tease a smile from Sassy, who ought never to look so serious.

And find Delia.

Drawing in a deep breath, he continued to the door. It opened before he could knock, and the servant's eyes went round. "Mr. Phin!"

"Good evening, Moses. I haven't an invitation—I do hope that poses no problem."

The servant stared at him, a more stoic version of Old Bess's shock in his eyes. "Uh . . . no, suh. Go on in, that's right fine."

"Thank you, I . . ." He forgot what he wanted to say when a whisper moved up his spine, and then a blue skirt swished out of the ballroom.

Even before he saw her, he knew. Somehow or another, he felt her nearness. The small waist, the perfect golden curls, the well-chiseled chin, those were just verification. Delia. His Delia.

But where were the roses in her cheeks? The lilt to her lips? She looked half ghost herself, her face too pale and her movement absent the buoyancy that had always set her apart. Had he done this to her with his absence? Or was she simply unwell tonight?

She got a step outside the door and paused, turned his direction.

Her father stepped up beside her before she could raise her gaze, a tall officer with him. Phin couldn't make out what they said, but Mr. Owens took Delia by the arm and led her down the hall, toward the library. To his eyes, she looked as though she'd have liked to bolt the other direction. But she wouldn't, not when her father led her somewhere.

The officer went with them, on Cordelia's other side. Looking down at her with a smile that struck him as predatory.

Phin squeezed his cane so tightly that his knuckles ached.

"Best git after em, Mr. Phin, be you ghost or man." Moses spoke softly, but with a note of desperation.

He got. Wished he could hurry more than he could. And wondered who the devil the fellow was who had the audacity to chase after his girl.

Chapter Seventeen

Delia's stomach churned and threatened to rise when Daddy motioned her into the library. The *library*. Of all places to force her with Julius, must he choose her favorite room in the house? Must he taint its hallowed shelves with a memory of *this*?

She wouldn't budge. Her feet moved, certainly, but on this, on Julius, she would not. Better to be an old maid forever, lost in the memories of a man who had actually been worthy of her love, than to spend her life beside a scoundrel like Julius James.

Warrior-king—ha! Definitely the cleverest of villains. He may have already deceived her family, but not her. She would . . . she had only to . . . Tears burned her eyes for the millionth time that evening.

She wanted Phin. If Phin were here, this would all just go away.

"Delie-Darlin, I think you know what this is about." Daddy, his voice gentle but unyielding, pivoted her so she faced Julius. "It's time, sunshine. Time to move on. Your cousin would like to court you properly, and I've given him permission."

"Daddy—"

"Hush." He touched a finger to her lips. "He knows you still have feelings for Phin and is willing to help you sort through them. But we're at war, Cordelia, and there isn't much time for dillydallying. Now, square your shoulders and be the strong young lady I know you are."

He was right about that much. She squared her shoulders, lifted her chin. And determined that if the only way out of this was to bring the war into this very room and fight with nails and teeth, she would do it. She would be an Amazonian princess—all right, so she had no intention of cutting off certain body parts so she might better wear her sword and shield—but she would embrace the *spirit* of an Amazonian princess.

She would fight.

"That's my girl." Daddy chucked her under the chin and smiled, apparently misreading her determination. Well, let him. "Now, Julius has requested a few moments' private audience with you, and knowing well his intentions, I have agreed."

A tapping sounded behind her, from the hall, though she noticed it only when it halted. When she realized it was a cane, and that it meant someone else was there, something—expectation? fear?—coiled inside her.

"Might I have the honor of cutting in on that audience, Mr. Owens?"

That voice! For a moment she stood paralyzed, certain it was her imagination. A delusion born of her desperation.

But why would Daddy and Julius turn in response to her delusion? Why would Daddy's eyes go wide with surprise?

Her heart thudded so, she felt as though it was the first it had beat in years. And each thump said *Phin, Phin, Phin*. She turned, telling herself to be calm. Telling herself to be prepared for disappointment if it were instead someone else who happened to borrow the exact cadence and tone of his voice. Telling herself that, even if the impossible had happened, she would handle it like a lady of breeding. With serenity.

But the second she looked up and saw his smile, all such thoughts winged away. "Phin!" The cry ripped from her throat even as her feet disobeyed her mind's order for calm and sent her running across the few feet between them. With an abandon she never imagined showing—certainly not in the company of her father and Julius—she threw herself into his arms. "Oh, Phin! You're alive!"

But something was wrong. He didn't wrap his arms around her, didn't swing her up and around. He loosed a sound halfway between a grunt and a moan and staggered into the doorframe. One hand encircled her back, but he didn't hold her close so much as grip her for support.

Rejection choked her for half a breath. Then she looked up and saw the pain undulating over his face. The hollows in his cheeks, the circles under his eyes. And his other hand gripped a cane. Horror at herself brought her hands to her mouth. "Oh, you're hurt! I've hurt you!"

"I'll be fine." Tension made his voice thready and low, but the hand on her back gentled, and his thumb made a caressing sweep of where his fingers had dug in. "Delia. I've . . . I've missed you so."

She forced a swallow and reached up to brush her fingertips over his cheek. A bold touch, to be sure, and under normal circumstances she wouldn't have risked such a move in company. But it wasn't every day one's love came back from the dead.

How many times had she dreamed of this? Yet she couldn't remember what she had imagined saying. "I . . . I saved the waltzes for you."

A grin rose through the pain on his face, then faded. "I daresay it'll be a good while before I can claim them, darlin."

Daddy stepped up beside them, put a hand on Phin's shoulder. His face was a strange mixture of emotions—incredulity, a touch of pleasure, but also a bit of . . . what was it? Not exactly disappointment—more like determination. "We heard you were dead. Shot."

"In the leg." Phin's larynx bobbed.

"And that you fell overboard."

He nodded. "Washed ashore in Cuba. I was in a bad way for months. Barely woke up. But as soon as I did, as soon as I could walk a bit, I started for home." He glanced back down to her, his eyes filled with all the emotions they should be, and a shadow of pain she'd never imagined there.

There were so many things she wanted to ask, so many dreams she wanted to question him about, but before she could open her mouth, Daddy looked down at her with a strained smile, then back to Phin. "Have you seen your family?"

Phin shook his head. "When I saw Delia coming this way as I entered, I followed her."

He did? Before even letting his mother know he was alive? Cordelia's heart was so full she nearly wept anew.

Daddy darted a glance at her face, his own shifting a bit. Indulgence took the place of the harder-to-identify emotion, though she still detected an undergirding of iron. "Well. You look as though you'd rather sit than brave the ballroom. Cordelia will keep you company for a moment while I fetch your family for you. Julius?"

Julius—she'd nearly forgotten about him, but now that terrible vision from earlier flooded her mind. She grabbed Phin's hand and urged him into the room so that, when Daddy and the villain passed by, she could remain between him and Phin.

And given the look her cousin shot Phin, she was glad she had. Not that he pulled out a weapon, but the hatred in that glare . . . Maybe it was her imagination. *Dear Lord, let it be so.*

"Delia." Phin spoke her name like an invocation, and his hand settled on her cheek. She turned her face toward his.

A shiver went up her spine at the intensity on his face. She could tell he meant to kiss her—the way his lips parted, the stroke of his thumb over her cheekbone—but it was different than that day in the garden. There was no tease, no half-lidded, lazy gaze. No smile to charm her. Just a demand, patient but strong, in his eyes.

Even as she went up on her toes, a terrible thought shot through her mind that this wasn't Phin at all. That she ought to turn and run before she could be branded by his kiss. But even had she been inclined to act on that, it would have been too late.

His lips barely touched hers. The lightest of brushes, so sweet it could have been called brotherly. Except that he lingered. Hovered. Managed, with that feather caress, to strum a chord within her that made her knees go weak. That made her think at any moment he might crush her against him. But he stayed just as he was, his hand gentle on her cheek and his mouth a whisper away more often than it was upon hers.

Receiving his lighthearted passion back in May had made her head spin and her mind go foggy. But sensing his tightly held restraint now made her tremble and lean forward, determined to set loose just a bit of whatever he held back, and yet afraid if she did that it would devour her whole.

"Phin." Her voice scarcely sounded like her own. It was too faint, laced with too much desperation. What had she to be desperate for now? All she'd wanted these long months was his safe return to her. Now here he was, in her arms. She ought to be the soul of contentment. Why, then, this yearning to . . . for . . . she didn't even know. She just *yearned*.

Perhaps he understood it better than she did, for he seemed to respond to that strange something in her tone. His hand moved to the base of her head, and he drew her closer. Parted her lips, deepened the kiss.

Just for one second. One glorious, heart-stopping, soul-searing second. This time the earth didn't spin—it seemed to expand. Her mind didn't go foggy, it crystallized. Clarified. As if she could see everything in a way heretofore unknown, if only she could think where to look.

Then he broke away and just rested his forehead against hers, dragged in a breath that sounded every bit as tremulous as she felt. "Delia, I . . . I don't know. You've haunted me. Thinking of you, longing for you. Realizing that I—thinking I should have done things differently. I should have told you how I feel. I should have—so many things I should have done. So many regrets."

"Hush." She lifted a hand and pressed a finger to his lips. "There's no need to waste time on regrets. You're home now. That's all that matters. You're alive, and you're here. You're . . ." He straightened a bit, enough that she could look into his eyes. A chill danced through her.

He was home. He was alive. But yet again she had to wonder if he was Phin.

Ridiculous. And yet she couldn't help but ask, in a low murmur, "What happened to you?"

His hand fell away, and he turned toward the furniture. "Nothing worth telling you about. I was unconscious or out of my head from morphine most of the last few months."

Nothing? She was supposed to believe that *nothing* had changed him so? She shook her head, but he didn't see her, as he was too busy lowering himself onto the sofa. He held a hand for her, and she sat beside him, keeping his fingers in her own. Perhaps he was a more intense Phin than he'd once been. But that was only to be expected. "You needn't spare me because I'm a female, you know."

"I'm not. There's just—" His shoulders jerked in a semblance of a shrug, and his face went hard. "There's no story to tell you, Delia. Nothing you can weave into some inflated, exaggerated tale to wax romantic about. We were betrayed. I was shot. Then I was unconscious. That's it."

That wasn't even nearly it. She needn't have any great insight to see that something had happened. Something that made him speak with such reviling, such disdain. To her—about her. Or about her stories anyway, which amounted to the same thing. Her spine snapped straight, her chin edged up.

Then she deliberately lowered it again. She couldn't act that way, the offended damsel. He *had* been through something, something obviously traumatic. A proper heroine would see beyond the harsh words to the pain underneath. Would soothe, draw him out instead of nursing her own slight wounds. She would bring him back to health and win his love anew.

Cordelia drew in a long breath and searched her mind for something to say that would demonstrate her gentle spirit and not possibly reveal any offense. "I . . . I prayed for you, Phin. Every day."

"I thank you for that—perhaps it is what saved me." Yet his breath of laughter sounded strange. "I didn't even know how to pray at the start of this."

"Nonsense." And why did she feel the need to defend Old Phin to New Phin? "You were always a proper Christian gentleman."

"No, my dear, I was a proper gentleman bred in a Christian home. I'm afraid it meant nothing more to me than that." He tapped his cane, and his gaze went distant. "It means far more now. I see now that faith is more than the church to which one belongs."

She opened her mouth without any idea what words she should speak. Only one question begged to be asked, but she had a feeling he would refuse to answer it. *And how did you come to this realization when unconscious?* More proof that *something* had happened. How could she convince him to tell her what?

His gaze refocused and swept over her, lingering, it seemed, on the extravagant detailing of her skirt. "How long have you thought me dead, Delia?"

Heat surged into her face. Why, *why* had Mama insisted she wear such a vibrant color? "I didn't. That is, we've known you were missing since July—your uncle was in Cienfuegos when the *Sumter* arrived without you. But your commander didn't send word about what happened until two weeks ago."

Somehow the lift of his brow made her feel the fool, and she wasn't sure why. "Yes, the letter about my getting shot and falling overboard. Yet you didn't think me dead?"

"I . . ." Her hope ought not to shame her. He was here, after all, proof that it had been well founded. Or at least divinely inspired. But when she considered telling him about those dreams, unease filled her stomach. "I imagined you were on some grand adventure. You know, wrestling alligators or . . ."

The sardonic smile upon his lips stopped her cold. "Of course you did. Well, I'm afraid such heroics will have to be left to those with two strong legs now. That gentleman in here with you a moment ago ought to handle it nicely."

Julius? The very mention of him made that heat surge again, far differently. "Ha! If it were my tale to tell, the gator would eat him."

Old Phin would have burst into laughter at that, not just donned a half-smile like New Phin did. But then, Old Phin would have mentioned Julius with a touch of jealousy, so that she could assure him . . .

No, he hadn't shown the slightest jealousy of Thomas Bacon that day in the garden. But then, she hadn't spotted Phin until she'd already dismissed Thomas, so he *could* have . . . she imagined he . . .

Even his half-smile faded. "I see."

She suspected he did. And had no idea what it was, exactly, he saw—only knew it wasn't to her credit. "Phin—you . . . I . . . I promised I'd wait forever. I meant it."

His eyes went soft, yet somehow still lacked in assurance. "I know you did. It was too romantic a notion for you not to. But, darlin—"

"Phineas? Phin?" Willametta's voice carried down the hall, along with the sound of many hurried footsteps.

But, darlin—what? Cordelia clung to his fingers. He couldn't mean to abandon her now, could he? When he was finally home again? No, that wasn't how it was supposed to happen. The grand entrance, the kiss—those had been perfect, but *this*, this sensation of loss she hadn't felt all the time he was missing, this aching, gaping hole that yawned open inside . . .

He didn't love her. That was the only possible explanation. His time away, whatever had happened, had changed him all the way down to his heart. He wasn't her Phin anymore. And he didn't . . . she wasn't . . .

"Phineas! My darling boy!"

Cordelia jerked to her feet as the Dunns stormed the room, habit pulling her up where despair would root her down. Phin stood, too, reclaiming his fingers from her, and moved a few steps toward the door. He held wide his arms, and his mother rushed into them.

What was on his face now? Pain again, at the enthusiastic greeting? Happiness? Reassurance? Would he be able to greet his family with more than he had given her? More of the Phin they would recognize?

She pressed her hands to her skirt, smoothing the fabric over the hoop even though it had fallen into place without assistance. And watched as Willamette and Sidney and Sassy all gathered round Phin. All embracing, all reaching out to touch, all talking at once.

It was as though a curtain had dropped between them. Invisible but impenetrable. She could hear only snippets of what they said. Something about hopes and fears and he-saids and what-abouts. But their voices all melded into one. Their brilliant smiles all seemed a galaxy away. The ringing laughter sounded distant and brassy.

What was she to do? Join them, forcing herself in where she obviously didn't belong? Or perhaps tiptoe out of the room and take the servants' stairs up to her bedchamber, neatly avoiding every unwelcome guest in the house?

A worthless question to ask, for she couldn't move. Even

swallowing felt like a foreign action, something done to her rather than by her own will. Maybe . . . maybe she wasn't really here. Maybe it was another bad dream, maybe she was still crumpled on her bedroom floor. It was all a delusion, the workings of her overactive imagination.

". . . Delia."

The sound of her name snapped her back, made the curtain part, made her lips turn up out of breeding and expectation, though she had no idea what Sassy had said. But her friend was smiling—no, positively beaming, her joy untainted by any confusion about whose hand she grasped—and inviting her into their little world.

"Of course." Willametta held out a hand for her, and Cordelia's feet moved her forward, her fingers reached for the lady's. Rote again, expectation, nothing more. "She has been a great comfort to us, and I am so eager for her to become my daughter. We can plan the wedding for—"

"Let's not get ahead of ourselves." Daddy's voice boomed from the doorway, clanging steel against the hope that had sparked in her chest when Willametta spoke, and when Phin had greeted the words with a smile instead of quick refusal.

What was her father doing? She looked over at him, not fooled for a moment by the congenial smile on his face. It looked carved from granite. "The boy has just returned from the dead, and much has happened in his absence. I daresay he and Delia will need to get reacquainted."

No. No, even if this wasn't the Phin she'd known before, the mere thought of turning from him made certainty resonate in her heart. He was still the one she wanted. "Daddy—"

"Now, darlin." He held a hand to her, brows lifted. Not a request—a command. "We don't want to impose upon the Dunns. You come with me and let them have some time to themselves. Clearly they'll want to celebrate, but Phineas hardly looks up to a ball."

She looked to Phin, praying he would argue, but there was a strange resignation in his eyes, and a muscle in his jaw ticked. "You are right about that much, sir. Though Delia would never be an imposition to our family."

"Gracious of you." Still, Daddy's smile was hard, and when she failed to put her hand into his palm, he reached for her arm. "Even so, I'm afraid Delia has only just made it downstairs and has some obligations to see to before the ball is over altogether."

Phin opened his mouth, but his father's hand landed on his shoulder, silencing him. "Of course," Mr. Dunn said. "If you could ask someone to fetch our carriage, we'll take our boy home. No doubt he's exhausted. A good meal, a good night's sleep, and tomorrow we'll call the family doctor for you, my son."

Daddy nodded his approval of that.

Willametta, however, wasn't so easily deterred as her husband. She reached for Cordelia's hand. "You and your family must join us for supper tomorrow, Delie-Darlin. I'll send round a proper invitation first thing in the morning."

"Thank you, ma'am. We'd be delighted." She shot a glance up at her father. "Wouldn't we, Daddy?"

He could hardly argue, given the situation. But she could see he wanted to. He jerked his head in a nod before tugging her out the door. "Of course. How kind of you to think of us amidst your joy. I'll let Mrs. Owens know to expect the invitation."

She didn't make a scene and fight her father, though she had half a mind to. She didn't do more than glance over her shoulder, but it was enough to see that the Dunns were all following them out, Mr. Dunn's hand still on Phin's shoulder. Steadying him—or restraining him?

For a moment, their eyes met, hers and Phin's. There were still far too many unanswered questions, too many words unsaid, too many stories untold. Worse, she could see in his eyes that he didn't expect to get the chance to put voice to any of them.

She could only pray he saw the hardening of her will reflected in her own eyes. She would *not* lose Phin now that he was home. And neither her father, nor Julius James, nor whatever horrors had changed Phin would stand in her way.

Chapter Eighteen

Salina gripped her basket tight, directed her gaze right to the ground, and whispered a new prayer with every footstep. Why hadn't she gone to Mass Owens? She ought to have, ought to have told him that his wife had sent her out here alone, so as he could put a stop to it. He would have, she suspected. Never in all her nineteen years had he permitted her to roam the city alone.

Especially not now, with it being in such a prolonged panic these months. Oh, it was right enough in the upscale shopping district she went to with the mistress and Miss Delia, but not on the outskirts, where the missus had sent her to meet up with Aunt Lila's boy. And not here, near the tent-dotted parade grounds.

But she hadn't dared go around the missus. Not with the hate-filled looks she sent her whenever their paths crossed. And besides, Mass Owens had been distracted seeing Miss Lacy off to Miss Ginny. There'd been theatrics aplenty around the house already that morning, and Salina had known better than to add any more to it.

She wore her drabbest brown clothes, a marked contrast to the other gaily clad colored folks strolling along the streets. Still, she wished she could somehow travel under the foot-deep sand of the roads. Better yet, if she could just snap her fingers and be back with Miss Delia.

They'll take wings and fly away. Fly away. Fly away.

A group of soldiers neared, a few laughing and a few more grumbling. Salina hurried to the edge of the parade grounds and hid herself as best she could behind a post. Which put her nose to nose with a faded, battered sign.

I AM A RATTLESNAKE, IF YOU TOUCH ME I WILL STRIKE.

A shudder clawed up her spine. She'd heard the other slaves talk of all the vigilante groups springing up round the city, determined to root out any Northern supporters and stem the tide of deserters, both white and black, from Confederate lines. She just didn't run into such things much. No, in their house the panic seizing the rest of the city thanks to all them encroaching Yankees had been focused instead on Mr. Phin.

Course, that *ought* to be over with now. She drew in a deep breath and shook her head. When she heard all that commotion last night about him coming home, she sure hadn't expected to find Miss Delia in more of a blue mood than ever. What was wrong with Mass Owens, ruining what should have been a joyful evening by separating them so quickly? Wasn't right.

"And why is my darlin cousin's pretty little maid frowning so at an old sign? Wondering what it says?"

She jumped, spun, and pressed her back against the post rather than get so much as an inch closer to the leering face of Mr. Julius. *Fly away. Fly away. Fly away.* "No sir. I just waitin for the troops to pass so as I can get home is all."

"Mmm-hmm." His gaze raked over her, from head to toe, lingering too long in places it shouldn't. "I'm surprised to see you without Delia. I thought she kept you right beside her. All the time."

Another shudder clawed. How could he make such innocent words sound so . . . so . . . ? "The missus sent me on an errand. Takin a few things to my cousin, who's delivering supplies from the plantation to our boys who are diggin trenches." She bit her tongue to make herself hush up. Then loosened it again. "They expectin me back now, though. So if'n you'll excuse me, sir."

"By all means." Yet he didn't move away. No, he leaned in, crowded her. Looked down at her with those icy eyes. "You must hurry home to Delia. Your mistress, isn't she? Her father mentioned she would come with a maid when she married."

Her hands took to trembling, so she gripped her basket harder to conceal it. And what would the master say to her becoming a white man's concubine? He wouldn't allow her to marry her own kind, but would he allow *this*? Or choose not to know, not to care?

But Miss Delia wouldn't have Mr. Julius, so it didn't matter. Wasn't an issue. He couldn't touch her, wouldn't dare, not unless she were in his house. Which she wouldn't never be. Never. Never.

Fly away.

He arched a brow, his glare going colder still. "I asked you a question, girl."

She forced a swallow and tried to paste on the false cheer her murruh had taught her as a child. "That's right, sir, when Miss Delia marries Mr. Phin, I'll go to the Dunns' place with her."

His spine snapped straight again, and his eyes narrowed to two blue slits. Were Miss Delia writing the scene, she no doubt would have had poison dripping from whatever words he next spoke.

"Salina girl!" *River?* She looked to her right and saw him running her way, shadowed by a man who seemed to go on forever, up to the sky. River wore a grin with more oblivion than she'd ever seen from him before. "There you be. Been lookin all over fo ya, sho nuff."

Mr. Julius growled low in his throat, like the dog he was. "You again. Haven't you anything better to do, boy, than show up wherever I am?"

River blinked, slow and dull. "Sorry, suh, I figured you be passin by, not actually *talkin* to a slave girl. If I be interruptin—well, then I real sorry. I just wanted to introduce Salina to my Uncle Monty." He motioned to the giant behind him.

She gladly stepped away, dipped her head. "So good to meet you, Monty. River's told me all about you." And if Mr. Julius tried to call her on that fib, she'd tell a story to match any of Miss Delia's.

Monty nodded, too, and smiled, but made no reply.

"He don't talk much." River motioned down the street. "We just waitin for Mr. Phin to finish lettin the navy-like folks in Richmond know he alive and git his orders."

She noted only then that Mr. Phin had been following behind River and Monty and had nearly caught up to them, moving slow and seeming in pain.

River nudged her with a playful elbow. "Sho would like to see you home, Salina girl."

Would he really, or was he just trying to rescue her?

Mr. Julius folded his arms over his chest. "You would trouble your master to go out of his way so *you* can see a girl home? I'm surprised he would tolerate such insolence."

The thud of a cane signaled Mr. Phin's arrival at their little group. Heavens, but he'd gone all thin, and his eyes looked right haunted. Maybe it was the pain. Maybe that's what made his jaw pulse as it did too. "You may speak to your own servants however you wish, sir, but I thank you for taking a kinder tone with mine, seeing as how they've done nothing wrong."

"My apologies." Mr. Julius sketched a bow that looked anything but humble. "We haven't been properly introduced, I'm afraid. Lieutenant Julius James."

"Phineas Dunn."

The skunk's smile was mocking. "The sailor thought dead, that's right. I've heard your name bandied about a time or two at the Owenses' table."

Salina huffed out a breath. "A time or two every minute, you mean." At the look Mr. Julius shot her, she added a low, "Sir."

"My Delia does know how to make a man jealous, artful creature that she is." He looked back to Mr. Phin and gave him a devil of a smile. "But we understand each other."

Mr. Phin's brows lifted in exaggerated enlightenment. "Ah. You understand, then, that she would happily feed you to the gators."

Pressing her lips together to hold back the smile, Salina inched closer to River. She'd heard of brawls breaking out in the streets between soldiers, and while she figured Mr. Phin was above such nonsense, she didn't have the same confidence bout that low-down lout across from him, no sir.

For now, though, Mr. Julius just paused, then let out a laugh that sounded far from amused. He glanced to Monty. "Fine man you've got there. Yours?"

Mr. Phin held that cane of his so tight, it looked as though it might snap right in two. "Mm."

"Interested in selling? I've a need for a good-sized Negro at my plantation outside Atlanta. Though of course I'd likely have to refugee him to keep him from being assigned to the trenches."

Mr. Phin's nostrils flared. "I'm afraid he isn't for sale, Lieutenant. And even if he were, I wouldn't sell him to you for all the gold in the Confederacy."

He took a step forward, eyes blazing. "And what exactly is that supposed to mean?"

Mr. Phin stared the snake down without so much as a flinch. "I know your kind, Lieutenant James, and you make a mockery of the honor you pretend to."

Mr. Julius lunged, arm moving, but Salina couldn't be sure what he intended to do. Attack Mr. Phin with a fist? Pull a weapon? Not that it mattered. Quick as lightning, River pulled her backward and Monty jumped forward, intercepting Mr. Julius's hand before it could do more than meet with empty air.

The beast struggled to pull free of what looked like an iron grasp before giving up and putting on that cloak of false dignity again. As if anyone would believe it real after seeing the rage that mottled his face two seconds earlier. "I see what kind of man *you* are, too, relying on your slaves to defend you."

Mr. Phin looked downright amused. "You pierce me through."

Trying and failing once more to pull free, Mr. Julius snarled, "Tell your dog to unhand me."

"Soon as you promise to keep your distance from Delia."

"Or what?"

Oh, she hoped Mr. Phin let Monty wipe that nasty look of superiority from the jackal's face! But he just grinned. "Oh, I don't know. I think I'd let Delia devise the *or*. She has the richer imagination."

Though he growled again, something flashed across Mr. Julius's face. Not quite resignation, but acknowledgment anyhow. Enough to make it clear he wasn't going to fight about it, not here and now. Monty let go his arm, and he spun away, tossing over his shoulder, "This isn't over, Dunn."

Mr. Phin sighed. "No, I didn't imagine it was."

Salina became aware of the fact that River's arm encircled her waist, and that she had tucked herself into his side like it was the most natural place in the world for her to seek refuge. For half a moment she let herself enjoy the warmth of it, the security she hadn't felt since the last time she'd been held, before Murruh got sick and passed on. Then she pulled away, careful to keep the smile she sent him grateful but nothing more.

His returning wink, though, seemed to say he'd enjoyed it every bit as much as she did. And he caught her fingers in his before she could retreat more than a few inches, nodding toward Mr. Phin and Monty.

Mr. Phin had turned to the giant fella—where'd he come by such a man, anyway?—with a frown. "Thank you, Monty. Though I could have handled him myself."

The man-mountain just raised his brows and sent a pointed look at the cane.

"Exactly." Mr. Phin lifted it. "It comes equipped with a blade inside, if I have need of it."

Now the big man folded his arms over his chest.

Mr. Phin sighed. "All right, so it may have been difficult to parry a blow without its support for my leg. Hence why I thank you—that and the fact that you obviously enjoy such intimidation, you who claim to be a herald of the gospel and its message of peace."

A grin seemed to be pulling at the big man's mouth, though he got it under control in the next instant. Could he speak into the master's mind or something? How did the two manage to communicate in such a fashion?

Mr. Phin turned away with a roll of his eyes. "Yes, yes, I know. '*I came not to send peace, but a sword.*'" He narrowed his gaze on Salina, which made her glad River still had her fingers after all. "Could you please help me figure out why the devil Mr. Owens has encouraged that scoundrel to court his daughter?"

Her shoulders relaxed . . . then kept on going down, all the way to a slump. "Apparently his plantation outside Atlanta is real close to Belle Acres, that the missus brought to the marriage. Together they'd own half the county or some such. Plus, Mr. Julius hides that side of himself well enough in Mass Owens's company."

"Hmm." He lifted his cane and pointed up the street with it. "Come, we'll see you home. The buggy is just up there."

She opened her mouth to protest, but he'd already started forward. Left her little choice but to follow with River. Monty stuck close to Mr. Phin's elbow, his gaze patrolling the streets.

Though after only a few steps, the master halted again and spun, irritation mixing with the pain on his features. "He must just be willfully blind, which I find inexcusable. That he would push her toward him, when she has obviously objected to it.

And push you along with her—how can he *not* know what he'll be sentencing you to with a man like that?"

Again her mouth fell open, though she had no ready reply this time. The only thought she had a hope of wrapping her tongue around was a question she'd never dare ask, no way, no how.

Still, she couldn't help but wonder. Why would he get so upset about it? She weren't nothing to him.

He didn't seem to note her lack of reply, just shook his head. "He obviously has no issues with the practice in general, but one would think he'd want better for his daughter than he forced upon her mother."

A squeak of protest came from her throat before she could stop it with the hand that flew to her mouth. "You know?"

His gaze fell on her like it might a child caught trying to pilfer a cookie with his mammy still a few feet away. "Do you really fancy it a secret? You bear more than a passing resemblance to the other girls, especially Delia. Same height, same build, same eye shape, same chin. By the deuce, you even have the same fingers."

She tightened them now around River's. "Don't say nothing, sir, please. Mass Owens, he wouldn't take too kindly to any whispers bout it. Especially since . . ."

His brows lifted. "Since what?"

Her breath came out in a whoosh. "Since Miss Delia done figured it out. You know how she loves her daddy—and no question she's always been his favorite. But since it came out a coupla weeks ago, they been scarcely speaking. She been—"

She buttoned her lips against any more words. Kind as the Dunns were known to be to their slaves, he was still a master. And if he knew Miss Delia had been thinking thoughts of freedom for her, he might reconsider a match. And endangering Miss Delia's chance at a happily-ever-after with the man she loved was the last thing Salina meant to do.

She cleared her throat. "She been real upset. Specially since it was the same day she heard about you getting shot. Been little more than a shadow since—though I reckon that'll change, now you're home."

Mr. Phin sighed. "Assuming her father *lets* it change, you mean. I have a suspicion that his ambitions for creating the biggest plantation in Georgia may outweigh his desire to indulge Cordelia's affections."

She had a suspicion he was right. But she wasn't going to speak such words—never knew when by the speaking of a thing you might make it true. And that was one sentence she didn't never want to see become reality.

Phin swirled the brandy around in his snifter, more mesmerized by the smooth motion of rich color than desirous of its taste. Cigar smoke teased his nose, but he had declined Father's offer of one of those entirely. The scent had taken him immediately back to Cuba, brought Rosario's voice echoing into his mind.

Not what he wanted to dwell on. *That* planter, at least, was out of his life. He just had to figure out how to meld back into the ones whose company he kept now.

"I'm at a loss, I confess it." Reginald Owens puffed on his cigar, then blew out a ring of smoke. "If I don't refugee my field hands, they'll all be sent to dig trenches, and heaven only knows if any will return. But all the neighbors who have attempted to send them inland, away from the government's grasp, have had rebellion on their hands."

Father took a slow sip of his brandy. "No great surprise. Family, community, is everything to them. When you break them up, not just immediate families but also extended ones . . ."

"I know." Owens massaged his brow, but in spite of the action, Phin didn't sense concern so much as annoyance. Frustration. "President Davis has tied our hands. We seceded so no one could dictate to us how to run our lives and our plantations, and what does he do? Demand we send our troops to Virginia and our slaves to dig, as if we haven't those plantations to run in spite of the war."

Father sighed and stared into his snifter. He said nothing, but Phin knew what he was thinking. He hadn't been a proponent of secession at all, had maintained that there must be a better solution. But he'd also stuck by Georgia and his neighbors—and hadn't wanted his concerns to be proven right.

Owens breathed a laugh and motioned toward Phin with his cigar. "One would think it would be enough that we send off our sons. Will they reassign you, do you think?"

His hand splayed over his leg. "The doctor sent his recommendation to the navy that I be discharged, on the basis that my year's term of service will be over long before I regain function of the leg—if ever I do. He recommended amputation, even at this point." The limb pulsed its rebuttal. "I refused that, of course, and intend to prove him wrong on his dire predictions in general."

"That eager to rejoin the ranks, are you?" Owens chuckled. "Back to the navy, or will you stay on land this time?"

"I . . . don't know." Didn't want to think about it, *couldn't* think about it. When the doctor had said those words—*amputate* and *never walk unaided*—it was like something had petrified within him. All his assumptions about his future, all his immediate goals had sunk into the swamp of reality.

The navy wouldn't want him. He'd be a liability to any troops he could raise. Spencer's betrayal had rendered him useless, forgotten.

And he hardly regretted it. Because he was none too sure he could stand shoulder to shoulder with his neighbor again and trust him not to run him through with a bayonet.

The furrow in Father's brow made him wonder if he could read Phin's mind as easily as Luther did. "You need not rush into any decisions, at least. You will have time to rest. Recover. Pray about what you ought to do next."

"Assuming the bill to institute a draft next spring doesn't pass." Owens puffed again on his cigar.

"Draft?" Phin straightened in his chair, setting his brandy aside. "There has never been a draft in North America. You can't mean to tell me that—"

"Leave it to our esteemed leaders in Richmond to be the first."

Father's nod echoed Owens's prediction. "I suspect it will pass. Enthusiasm is waning already. Men are deserting and fleeing to the Yankee lines by the score. At this rate, there won't be an army to fight if ever a large battle comes our way."

A cramp seized his leg, one that didn't ease by merely stretching it out. Phin pushed himself up, hoping it would relax with a bit of movement. Or perhaps it was the walk through the city that morning that had caused it. "I cannot say I am surprised to learn that the men turn tail and run when they realize war isn't all glory and prizes." He halted by the window, looked out over the darkened garden.

"Not all glory, no, but there's still honor in defending one's home." Father's voice was both soft and firm. "Whether that be in digging a trench or sailing the high seas."

"Honor." Phin gripped the head of his cane and leaned into the windowsill. "I used to think it innate in a Southern gentleman. Now I wonder if it exists at all."

A glass thudded against wood. "You may want to be careful sharing such an opinion in society, Phineas."

"He was betrayed, Owens. By a friend. Society will have to excuse him his questions."

Owens sucked in a breath. "A friend? The Yankees didn't just regain the upper hand?"

Phin turned his face back toward the older men. Neither, so far as he could see, had changed in the months he had been gone. Yet neither looked the same to his eyes. Father had always been so constant—it just hadn't mattered when the seas were flat. And Owens had always been so absorbed with his own concerns, his own ways, sailing his own course. But before he'd left, Phin had been hopeful that Delia's desires would sway him toward allowing a union, had hoped he could prove himself. Now, having learned of Julius James and Owens's obvious ambitions there, he was none too optimistic. Not given how the man had brought up James no fewer than half a dozen times during dinner.

Maybe that was what made him feel so heavy. Not just the remembered betrayal, but the knowledge that even when someone wanted to remain steady, like Delia, life didn't always leave her that choice.

"Betrayed, yes." His voice sounded harsh, flat, to his own ears. "By my closest friend—an *honorable* man, or so I thought." He snorted, turned back to the window. "Though who am I to say? Can a man lose honor through one action? Gain it again as easily? Is it as fickle as the rest of the world?"

Father cleared his throat. "Phin was a bit struck by all the changes in the city, you understand. When he left in May, it was still a hub of social life."

"And now it's a hub of militia and vigilantes, I know." Finally, Owens sounded concerned. "My wife refuses to leave so long as I stay—and I'm not ready to leave yet. My family helped found this town over a hundred years ago."

And the Owenses hadn't let anyone forget it in the century since.

Phin winced at his thoughts and forced a more pleasant expression onto his face. Then noted both men had ground out the nubs of their cigars. "Are we ready to rejoin the ladies?"

Father stood, eyes agleam. "A bit eager, are you?"

Owens cleared his throat. "Of course he is. Every young gentleman in Savannah is eager to see my Delia. I know I can scarcely keep Julius away from the house. It's a wonder his regiment even recognizes him." He chuckled at his own joke, though he was the only one.

The mere mention of Delia conjured up her image as she'd been at supper a half hour before. Directly across from him, curls shining like gold in the candlelight, roses flushing her cheeks, unlike last night. Beautiful enough to make his pulse quicken at the first glance of her. Whimsical enough to make him smile when his lips felt disinclined.

Simply *Delia* enough to make him wonder what words had been born from the fresh ink stains on her fingers. And pray they hadn't been about him. Better a sultan, a prince, a half-mad inventor—anything but a version of Phin that she'd no doubt paint the hero.

To her father, he offered a small smile. "She's always had a string of admirers. Delia is all things lovely and good."

Owens headed for the door, though slowly enough for Phin to keep pace. He wore the proud grin of a doting daddy, which nearly made Phin regret his choleric thoughts. Nearly. "She is that, isn't she? My sunshine. Fortunate is the man who will claim her as a wife someday."

His knuckles tightened around his cane. He'd been about to say last night that he'd marry her in an instant, as soon as it could be arranged, before Owens had interrupted. But clearly this wasn't a hint that Phin should ask his permission. It was instead a warning that it was a fortune he'd already decided should go to another.

And Phin had no idea how to convince him otherwise. Unless . . . "Indeed. And you can be sure, sir, that I appreciate your daughter for more than her lovely face—or even her stellar family connections." It was as close as he could bring himself to come to talking about her dowry. "It's her heart that gave me the strength to come home again. Her imagination. Her spirit. The things that make her Delia."

Just as he'd hoped, Owens's smile went even softer. As Salina had said that morning, there'd never been any doubt who was his favorite daughter.

Now came the risky part. Phin swallowed and said, "I'm not so sure this Lieutenant James fellow shares that appreciation and devotion though."

Owens's expression froze, hardened. "You're hardly unbiased, son."

"Even so." Phin hobbled through the door. "My opinion of him sank quite low after I saw him threatening Delia's maid today at the parade grounds."

Owens halted, eyes going wide and flinty. "Threatening *how*?"

Ah, so he did care. At least a little. Whether it was enough to make a difference remained to be seen. Phin glanced behind them, where Father had paused a few paces away, cloaked curiosity on his face, then back to Owens, with a shrug he hoped looked casual. "I wasn't close enough to hear what he said to her, but the poor girl seemed scared out of her mind—and no wonder, the way he had her backed into that pole. Looked ready to swallow her whole. I sent River rushing to her rescue."

The smile Owens dredged up looked false and pinched. "I can't imagine he was all that forward on a public street in broad daylight."

"Forward enough to make me wonder what he might have done under cover of darkness. I know his kind." Question was, was Owens in the same category of men? "He may keep his hands off so long as she's your property and he's courting your daughter, but if he succeeds in wooing Delia, if he were to marry her, if she brought the girl with her . . ."

Owens's hand fisted.

Phin tamped down a smile. "Not that that's any concern of yours, of course. Except I know Delia loves her maid, and if she were to discover her husband had—well, I hate to think how that would dim her sparkle. Don't know if she'd want to kill him or just . . . determine never to let him out of her sight."

Father let out a warning breath from behind them. Owens froze for a long moment, then tipped his lips up. "I do appreciate your concern for the happiness of my household. And out of a similar interest, son, let me caution you to watch how you speak to folks. Tempers are hot and nerves stretched these days, and if you're not careful, you'll find yourself called out."

Phin snorted a laugh and turned back toward the drawing room, where the ladies would be waiting. "You mean a friend may turn on me? Shoot me? Maybe even toss me in a handy body of water?" He strode forward, uneven but sure enough to make his point. "Cheers."

The thing that hath been, it is that which shall be; and that which is done is that which shall be done. And there is no new thing under the sun.

His lips twitched as he wondered what Luther would say if he realized his mind now provided Scripture to reinforce his cynicism. Nothing, probably—he'd be too busy trying not to laugh.

But all musings, cynical or otherwise, were sucked dry when he stepped into the drawing room. There sat Delia, grinning with Sassy, totally oblivious to the way seeing her made him feel as though all the air had left the room, all the light had focused solely on her. To the way his chest went tight, his stomach knotted. To how much he wanted to gather her close, kiss her senseless. Hold on forever.

Forever. She'd promised it. But she hadn't realized at the time that her father could well overrule her. She hadn't had any idea what could change in a few short months, let alone an eternity. Delia couldn't have known that pretty, romantic words had no place in the kind of reality upon them now. That promising something didn't necessarily make it so.

"Well, I don't care what you say, Delia, you'll not convince *me* to go into Currytown, not even if I had a posse of Yankees at my back." Sassy gave an exaggerated shudder.

Currytown? Delia had gone into Currytown?

Mother smiled. "We had an escort, Saphrona. We were perfectly safe."

"It was barely even an adventure," Delia added with her usual grin.

Phin swallowed, hard. Delia hadn't yet learned the lesson that sometimes adventure was just the gate to crisis. And that no amount of paper and ink in the world could rewrite it into something good.

"Still." Sassy shuddered again.

Delia laughed. Silver bells and sunlight, that's what it put him in mind of. Tinkling and gleaming in a world of rumbling and shadows. With no idea that both could soon be consumed.

She looked up, spotted him. Her smile was an arrow through his heart, an arrow with a cord attached to its fletching. Binding him to her. Connecting them, however it may hurt.

Forever. He saw that in her oh-so-green eyes, saw both the promise and the impossibility of it. He wanted it, craved it, needed it—but how was he to acquire it? How could he cherish her as she deserved if her father stood in the way? How could he protect her from Julius James? More, how could he protect her from the shattering of all those pretty fancies that had always made her Delia—like that stories still had happy endings? That anyone still existed who could be deemed a hero?

Somehow, through that same force that had molded him into someone other than Phin while he slept, he loved her now with an intensity that made his feelings in April nothing but an echo. But it wasn't enough. Loving her didn't make her his. He had to prove he deserved her.

And that was something he didn't know how to do anymore.

Beyond her, outside in the garden, he saw the movement of shadowy figures. The one too tall to be anyone but Luther, the other too familiar to be anyone but River. They'd been out this evening trying to scare up information on Eva. Find something, anything, that could lead them to her.

If it were one of Delia's stories, they would have discovered something useful. A key clue. But sometimes answers couldn't be found.

He managed only a nod for her, then made his way to the window. Drawing in a long breath, he rested his forehead on the pane of glass, let it cool and soothe. Luther and River disappeared from view.

Did Delia realize that sometimes the only people you could trust were the ones you could never admit were friends? Maybe. She had Salina, after all. But sharing that knowledge wouldn't make a way for them either.

She must have gotten up as he passed her, the swish of her skirts drowned in the laughter of their families. He didn't hear her, didn't see her. But he felt her approach like the tightening of a spring, and when she touched her fingers to his arm, it was a bolt of lightning.

His eyes slid shut. Did Delia realize that lightning could destroy you?

Chapter Nineteen

Cordelia flipped through a few pages of the book in her hands as she meandered down the hallway, not exactly thrilled about her selection—but then, she only had so many choices, and she'd read them all. Twice. At least. New books, it seemed, weren't the blockade runners' top priority for some bizarre reason. Though if something new didn't make it to Savannah soon, she'd be forced to resort to the only tomes in Daddy's collection she hadn't already braved—his economic books. Her face screwed up at the very thought of Adam Smith or the neighboring books in that shelf.

"I thought I'd made myself perfectly clear." Daddy's voice sounded from the entryway, bringing her feet to a halt. Not because it was loud, but because it was harsh. "No more letters from him were to be given to Delia—they were to be given directly to me."

"Yessuh. Sorry, suh." Old Moses? She couldn't ever recall Daddy chiding him for anything. And about letters for *her*? She edged farther down the hall, careful to keep her skirts silent. "I plumb fo'get things sometimes. Ol' mind ain't what it used to be."

Her brows knit. His body may be creakier than it used to

be, but never once had she thought Moses's mind was slipping. She slid another step, bringing them into view.

Daddy, visible to her in quarter profile, didn't look particularly convinced by the excuse either. He smacked an envelope against his palm, lips twisting as if looking for the next words to speak.

Delia's eyes focused on the envelope. She recognized the size, the shape, the particular shade of paper—Phin. Her breath fisted in her chest. Of course he'd been speaking of letters from Phin; they were only ones she received from a "him." And Old Moses had been slipping her the sweetest notes from him every day since he returned home nearly two weeks ago.

But Daddy had forbidden it? Truly? *Why?*

Never mind. She knew very well why, and it set her blood to simmering.

Old Moses glanced up, his gaze brushing against hers but flitting back down to the floor quickly enough that it didn't alert her father to her presence. He shuffled a foot, rolled his shoulders down in a show of regret. "I real sorry, suh."

Daddy huffed out a breath. "Don't let me catch you doing it again."

Was it her imagination, or did the corners of Moses's lips twitch up just a bit? "No, suh. You sho won't."

Her father pivoted and strode off toward his study, never spotting Cordelia in the mouth of the hallway opposite. Which was just as well, because had he glanced her way he would have seen pure fury on her face, and it wouldn't have won her any favors. She gripped the edges of the book in her hand and waited for the sound of his study door closing.

Old Moses was already scuttling her way, a look on his wrinkled face she'd never seen before. One flinty with determination. "Don't you worry none, Miss Delia," he murmured as he drew even with her. "I just tell the Dunns' boy to leave em with Fanny in the kitchen, to pass to Salina for you."

She opened her mouth but didn't know what to say. How to thank him. Why would he go to such lengths for her, risking Daddy's wrath? So in lieu of the right words, she reached out and settled a hand on his arm, giving it a squeeze.

His smile made the questions riot in her mind again. What was his story? His family's? What trials and joys and heartbreaks had brought him here, where he was willing to help her? Why had she never thought to ask him—or even to see the questions until now?

She frowned at her own blindness. She had always seen Salina as a person, as a friend, and now as a sister. But so many other souls moved about this house, invisible to her. She hadn't paused to think before of the lives they lived aside from her own. But they had their own stories, and they were the heroes in them.

And in their stories, what role did she play? She'd always been so focused on being worthy of being a heroine. But in their stories, that wouldn't be her role. It would be the exact opposite. She would be . . . would be a *villain.* Or a villain's accomplice, anyway. A villain's daughter.

Old Moses stepped close. "You a'ight, Miss Delia? You look plumb pale."

She blinked away the questions for now and looked, really looked into his eyes. In the decades he'd lived, he'd seen changes in Georgia—changes that must have broken his heart as the laws governing slavery grew ever stricter. He had a wife working here, too, but their children had long ago been sold or shipped to the plantations. How could he and his wife serve here with anything but bitterness?

One of these days she'd ask him for his story. Sit him down with a pad and pencil in hand. He spent much of the day sitting in the chair by the door, waiting for a knock to come. She'd just pull up another and sit beside him. Maybe tomorrow, even, while Mama and Daddy were out at lunch with friends. Why wait? He may not be comfortable telling her anything, but at least he'd know she cared enough to ask. "I'm all right, Moses. Thank you," she finally whispered.

He nodded, then continued toward the door. She focused her gaze on the opposite end of the hallway. Straightened her shoulders. Lifted her chin. Her father had something that belonged to her.

Usually she would approach his study door with normal steps, knock, wait for permission to enter. Not today. She kept her steps silent and, rather than knocking, opened the door the moment she reached it.

He started, though nothing as satisfying as guilt claimed his expression, despite the fact that he held Phin's letter in his hand, opened and unfolded. "Cordelia."

She slammed the door behind her. "Enjoying your letter, Father?"

He lowered it to his desk, eyes flashing. "I don't know what—"

"I heard you." She folded her arms over her chest, book still held tight in one hand. "Though why you would renege on your permission for him to write to me—and not even bother informing either of us about this new decision—I cannot fathom."

He lifted a brow. "If you can't understand it, then that itself speaks to the need for me to act on your behalf."

Would a proper heroine keep calm and collected or let loose the thunderclap of fury building in her soul? Oh, fiddle-faddle, what did it even matter? This wasn't about a story—this was about her *life*. She surged forward a step and gripped the back of the chair across from her father's desk with her free hand, resting her book upon it. "Have I ever disobeyed you? Have I been a troublesome daughter? Have I disappointed you in some way?"

There had been no calculation in the questions, only desperation. But she could see them strike her father, soften him. The lines of his face eased, and he sighed. "Of course not. You know very well you're the apple of my eye. Which is why I will do whatever it takes to achieve the best for you."

Her fingers dug into the leather upholstery. "The best for me—or for you? For your dreams of an empire? At least admit it, Daddy. This isn't about Julius as a man, this is about Julius as a landowner."

"Well, of course that plays into it." He set her letter down, eyes ablaze. "It's my responsibility to consider all things—what will be best for our entire family for generations to come."

Her breath balled up. "You'd sacrifice me, then? For your dreams of expansion?"

"Now you're just being dramatic." And he didn't sound amused by it. He reached for a ledger and set it atop the letter from Phin. "It is hardly a sacrifice to encourage a match with a man who clearly adores you."

"Adores me?" How? How could he see only what he wanted to? She shook her head. "That implies some genuine fondness on his part. Never when he looks at me do I get the feeling he even *likes* me. He's just a—a lion, seeking to devour."

"Now, Cordelia—"

"He scares me." She'd never admitted as much, even to herself. But there it was, the bald, naked truth. "I've seen his charm slip, and what hovers beneath is not pretty."

"You're being absurd. I've spent more time with him than you, and I've never glimpsed anything of the sort."

"Because you don't *want* to! And because you've never challenged him. But what if I'm right, Daddy?" A question that ought to make him rethink all his dreams, if he really loved her as much as he said. As much as she'd always believed. If he was really her father first, and then a Southern expansionist. "What if I marry him and he grows violent? Is that what you want for me?"

No reaction, beyond his fingers going tight around the pen he'd picked up.

She swallowed, forcing the next question out. The one that would bring up the subject she'd been avoiding with him for a month now. "Is that what you want for Salina? Can you trust him to respect *both* of your daughters, when I'm none too sure he'll even respect one?"

Daddy set the pen down with slow care. "Cordelia . . . this is a subject that goes well beyond your ken."

She shook her head. "I understand more than you give me credit for."

He looked up, met her gaze. She expected him to look away again, or even to dismiss her, but instead he kept his eyes locked on hers as he sucked in a long breath. "I've been waiting for you to demand a few answers. Why don't you sit?"

She didn't want to—largely because *he* wanted her to, and new rebellion made her every inch of skin go prickly. But she rounded the chair and sat primly on its cushion, never taking her gaze from him. When after a long moment he said nothing, she decided that since she'd given up avoiding the subject, she may as well take it by the horns. "You're not the man I thought you were."

He winced, looked away. His jaw worked for a moment before he opened his mouth. "I made a mistake. That's all."

"A mistake." He made it sound like one moment of passion—which would have been bad enough. But it didn't match the stories Salina had whispered to her over the past few weeks. The times she remembered her murruh coming into their room, crying. The way she'd clutch her close, time after time, and whisper prayers for something better for her daughter. Prayers Salina hadn't understood then but hadn't been able to forget. "You took a mistress. No, you *forced* a woman to your bed. You, who raised us to believe God's Word is truth and His commandments our law."

His face went red, though whether at her accusation or at merely hearing her say those words, she couldn't have guessed. "I did not *force*—" He interrupted himself, squeezed his eyes shut. "This is an entirely inappropriate conversation."

"What's inappropriate is the action that led to it." She leaned forward, tapping a finger on her book for emphasis. "You raised me to expect more, Daddy—from myself, from you, from my future husband. And you can argue all you want about Salina's mother, but the fact remains that she would not have *dared* argue with you. She was your *slave*. Your property. As is your own daughter now."

She sat up, blinking at the sudden burn of tears. She wouldn't cry, not now. It would just give him an excuse to go on thinking her nothing but a scatterbrained, emotional woman unable to understand anything of import. "Maybe that's all *any* of your daughters are to you. Bargaining pieces. Property. Chattle."

"Cordelia. How could you even say that?" He looked genuinely pierced by it.

But how could he be? "She's your daughter too. And she is your slave. There's no arguing that point."

"It's beyond my control." He hunched forward, leaning his head onto his hand, elbow on his desk. "I couldn't free her mother, I can't free her. It's the law."

"The law is *wrong*!"

"Hush!" He looked around, as if expecting President Davis to come rushing out of the woodwork and accuse her of treason. "I'll have no talk in my house that could be construed as abolitionist. The law is the law. End of discussion."

But that was how they'd gotten here, wasn't it? Having a conversation about how a man could end up owning his own child, in a state where a black man or woman was no longer allowed to be free under any circumstances, while war raged around them. Because when arguments were raised fifty years ago, a hundred years ago, they were shut down. Always shut down, because men like her father wouldn't give up their dreams of vast plantations, their fortunes made on the backs of others.

She stood. "I can't change the law. I can't change *you*. But I can promise you this, Father—I will *not* marry Julius James. I will not bring my *sister* into a house where she will be abused and mistreated and possibly even sold. I won't."

He stood, too, and she expected a quick, hard rebuke for her impertinence. Instead, he said, "Why do you think I promised her to you instead of Lacy or Ginny? I *know* you'll protect her. That you'd never sell her. I can't say the same for them." He leaned over the desk, closer to her. "But, Delia—this isn't just about Salina. And it isn't just about Julius either. I'm none too convinced Phineas Dunn is the man for you. He isn't the same fellow he was when he left."

A chill skittered up her spine. "I can see that. But he's a better one."

"Is he?" His eyes sparked. "I've been keeping a close eye on him, and he's been asking an awful lot of questions about a certain black woman, trying to find her."

He'd been . . . what? She clutched her book to her chest. There must be an explanation for that. Not that he'd made any mention of it in all those letters he'd written her.

"I'd hate for you to turn down a good man for fear of what he *might* do someday, for a man we have evidence is guilty of the same here and now." He pulled the letter from under his ledger. Crumpled it. Tossed it in the wastebasket. "Forget Phineas Dunn, Cordelia. If you promise me you'll do that, I'll tell your mother to let you invite Sassy to her garden party tomorrow. I know you were angry with her for not."

Because it had made no sense, before she knew Daddy had been trying to block her from Phin as well. Now, though . . . they were trying to cut all ties with the Dunn family. The last thing in the world she wanted to do.

But she couldn't promise to forget him—and she couldn't lie to her father about it either. So then, she would speak truth. She lifted her chin. "If your suspicions are grounded, then I would want nothing to do with him anyway."

Small lines fanned out on his face when he smiled at her.

"That's my girl. We can be glad he came back alive, and you can be friends with his sister—but that's all."

She wasn't about to agree. But she didn't dare argue. So she just spun around and left his study, her mind awhirl.

Luther loosened his grip on the reins, though it took deliberation to do so. Just as it took deliberation to unclench his jaw and direct his thoughts toward prayer rather than the moaning or railing to which he felt more inclined.

Two weeks they'd spent hunting down information on the *Bounty* and its passengers, on determining the name of the man who had "bought" Eva from Rosario. And what had they found? That the man had headed west, not due back until spring—and that no black woman had been reported traveling with him on the westbound train.

"I'm sorry." Phineas sighed and shifted in his saddle, though he'd said his leg wasn't hurting so much today. "We'll keep looking. There's a record somewhere of who bought her, where she was taken."

Luther hummed low in his throat. There *may* be a record. But it was so many months ago now, months of upheaval and unrest. Months when the people of Savannah had many more things to worry about than the arrival and disappearance of one woman.

Eva. Oh, Lord, where's my Eva? Lead me to her, I beg you. You got me into Savannah, closer than I've been to her since that monster stole her away from me. I know you'll direct me the rest of the way. Protect her, Father God, and preserve her until I find her. And then help us get out of this place before we lose anything more.

Shifting again, Phineas urged his horse a bit closer to Luther's. "I'm praying too. Might not carry quite the weight with the Almighty that your prayers do, Reverend, but I figure my addition can't hurt."

A chuckle came unbidden to his throat. Thus far, seeing the fruits of his months of nearly incessant reading to Phineas was the highlight of all this. According to River, with whom Luther was now sharing a room in a rough section of town, the change in the young master had sent quite a ripple through the household. He'd always been kind, apparently, but more than once Luther had seen a jaw go slack when Phineas thanked a slave for something. Or when they caught him frequently with his nose buried in a Bible.

Ferreting out the Scriptures that kept crowding his mind, he had said. Making sure Luther hadn't been filling his brain with nonsense.

Luther grinned at the thought. Had he known it would work so well, perhaps he would have tried inserting a few other well-founded ideas in the boy's mind.

"That's a dangerous grin." Phineas lifted a brow and reined his mount in, looking from the left—which would take them back to Dunn House—and then the right. The direction in which the Owens house lay. Indecision was clear on his face.

Luther lifted a brow. He knew very well that Phineas had a letter from his young lady even now in his pocket—a letter inviting him to come to a garden party today, but to do so stealthily, as her parents had only approved his sister's coming, not his.

The young man sighed. "I don't know what to do. I'll earn no respect by disobeying her father. But I risk losing her altogether if I accept his command to keep my distance."

Luther rolled his eyes and verified no one was near enough to be paying attention. "I'm rather surprised that *she* has crossed her father with the invitation."

"She says she needs to talk to me. Face-to-face." She had not, apparently, said about what, otherwise Phineas wouldn't look so anxious.

Luther sighed. "I'm never one to advocate disobeying one's parents. Or the people one hopes will become so. But it seems to me that you're right in your fears—if you do nothing, you've already lost her."

With only one last glance to the left, Phineas nudged his mount toward the Owens home. "I can't lose her. And yet the longer I'm back in Savannah, the more uncertain I am that I'm any good for her." His eyes were haunted, unsure. "Do you realize," he said in a murmur barely audible over the horses' hooves, "the risks of this plan of ours? If we're caught, you won't just be sent away this time, not with the political climate what it is toward slaves. We'll be lynched, both of us. At this point, I'm far more likely to be the cause of her distress than the key to her happiness."

Luther repositioned the straw hat upon his head. When he extracted that promise for his help in July, he hadn't much cared about the risk, certainly not to Phineas. But things had changed. And the danger was higher than he had supposed it to be. "You're right. You should stop searching, leave it to me and River—"

"No. I may not be good for much these days, but you were right that I'm the only one who has a hope of getting answers." He set his jaw. "I made a promise. And I mean to keep it."

Luther pressed his lips against a reply when he spotted a group of officers dismounting at the Owenses', that louse of a lieutenant among them. Phineas's knuckles whitened around his reins too—a reaction Luther well understood. Though his physical appearance was the opposite, something about the man reminded him of Rosario. The dark light in his eyes. The way he looked at people, whether slave or free, male or female, only in terms of what they could do for him. How he could own them.

He was another reason, Luther knew, that Phineas was willing to disobey Mr. Owens. Lieutenant James would be bad news to his young lady if he went unchecked and unchallenged. How could her father miss it? Though mankind did have a remarkable ability to be blind to what they didn't want to see.

Luther's eyes scanned the collection of young people as they drew near. Hoping, always hoping that amid the faces of the slaves on the fringes, he'd see Eva's. Though really, what were the chances that she'd be here, among Cordelia Owens's friends?

Phineas dismounted a minute later, careful to stay to the side as they drew near the garden entrance. Luther didn't spot Mr. Owens anywhere, but the missus was just inside the gate, chatting and smiling with another woman of about her age whom Luther hadn't ever seen before. Another mother, no doubt. There to act as chaperones for the twenty or so young people—most of whom were men in uniform. There were no more than six young ladies, all of them swarmed with attention.

Phineas hissed out a breath. "This was clearly a bad idea."

Not that he'd had any better ones.

Phin grunted acknowledgment of the unspoken observation. "I know, I know."

Luther's lips twitched, but he clamped down on his smile.

River met them between the stable and the garden entrance, a knowing gleam in his eye. "Startin to think you wasn't gwine come, Mr. Phin. Miss Sassy and me been here nigh unto two hours a'ready."

Phineas grunted and strained to look past his valet, to where Lieutenant James had made a beeline for Delia.

River looked up at Luther. "Any luck this mo'nin'?"

For now, he just shook his head. He'd give the young man details when they could slip away somewhere and be unheard.

He suppressed another grin when Phineas didn't even reach the gate before being nearly bowled over by a young lady with dark hair. She had a disagreeable look to her face, even when she smiled.

"Why, Phineas Dunn, I do declare! You've been a veritable recluse since you got home—and us all eager to hear your stories."

As River hid a chuckle behind his hand, Phineas's shoulders rolled back. "Miss Young. How good to see you again."

Her rehearsed laugh grated on Luther's nerves like nails on

slate. "Oh, fiddledeedee, Phin, you know well you may call me Annaleigh."

He sketched a bow. "With all due respect, Miss Young, I'd rather not."

This time River's snort of laughter escaped before he could contain it, earning a glare from the young miss.

She sniffed and raised her nose in the air. "Impertinent Negro. I do declare, it's near impossible to find dependable help these days, isn't it? What with all the coloreds running off the first chance they get. I can't find a dependable maid to save my life—and my current one will soon be of no use, being in a condition as she is. And Daddy is so determined to keep all his breeding females from running that he won't even let her out of the house with me anymore. Useless!"

Phineas turned back to River and Luther, gritting his teeth—no doubt to keep himself from saying anything too revealing about his opinions of Mr. Young. "The two of you are welcome to spare yourselves this torment and find your own entertainment."

The chit's mouth fell open, though she was quick to close it and cover her outrage with a coquettish giggle. "Oh, Phin, you are incorrigible!"

From the look in Phineas's eye, Luther couldn't help but think Miss Young caused him far more pain than his leg. He may have felt some pity over it, but a certain blonde was even now hurrying their way, fire shooting from her eyes.

"There you are!" Cordelia slipped out of the garden gate with a glance tossed over her shoulder. Probably to assure herself that her mother wasn't paying her any mind. Seeming satisfied, she slipped her hand behind Phineas's arm and nudged him toward the stable. "You wanted to see that new horse of Daddy's, didn't you? I'll show you."

"Oh, I do love the equestrian arts." Batting her lashes, Annaleigh took Phineas's other arm. "And your father always has the loveliest stock, Delia. Doesn't he, Phin? Not that any of them can compare to *your* mounts, though, I'm sure."

"Annie!" Phineas's sister leaned over the gate, the laughter on her lips not quite covering the calculation in her eyes. "Come back in, I need you. I was trying to tell Lieutenant Warner that story you shared the other day, but I can't do it justice. Won't you come? You tell it so much better than I can."

What a good sister Phineas had. One who clearly knew that flattery was the way to sway Miss Annaleigh Young. She looked torn for a moment, but Phineas gave her a smile. "You go on. And then you can tell it to me in a few minutes too."

"Well." The tilt of her head was part flirtatious, part demur. And utterly unconvincing. "All right. As long as you *promise* to join me soon."

"Of course."

Beside him, River shifted as Miss Young walked away. Pitching his voice low, he said, "You wanna tell me now? Or think we oughta play lookout for them two first?"

Luther held up two fingers. That brunette certainly couldn't be trusted not to crow for all to hear that Phineas Dunn was just outside the garden gate, and that would likely be all it would take to bring Mrs. Owens out, ready to boot him to the curb.

River nodded his agreement and leaned on one of the posts of the stable entrance. Luther took up the other while Phineas and Miss Owens moved a few feet into the stable, though by no means out of sight. She led him toward one of the stalls, where a white horse whinnied a greeting and came to sniff at them.

Luther directed his gaze back outside, but he couldn't exactly help hearing their words. The rushed assurance that each had been getting the other's letters. The young lady's apology that she hadn't been able to sway her father's stance.

"I've told him I won't have anything to do with Julius, but he won't listen. He refuses to see . . ." She paused, sighed. "And then there's . . ."

"There's what?"

"He said . . . well, he said you've been showing an undue interest in locating a certain . . . woman."

Luther stiffened. Only two weeks they'd been back—and already Phineas's inquiries about Eva had made their way back to Mr. Owens? That didn't bode well. He glanced over at River. Then over his shoulder at Phineas, whose glance flicked to him and then away.

"Monty's wife." It was all he said. Hopefully all he meant to. Because while clearly this young woman didn't agree with her father or Lieutenant James on some matters, there was no telling what her thoughts might be on the truth. She was, after all, a pampered Southern belle, the toast of the town. She'd have the ideals she was raised with, and no doubt shared the prevailing opinions on whether any black person could possibly deserve to be free.

Luther's fingers curled into his palm. He'd yet to hear her spout anything as irritating as Miss Young had a minute ago—but that didn't mean she didn't think it.

"Oh." Relief saturated her tone, and she looked his way, too, even sending him a small smile. "Is she here in Savannah? Can I help?"

"I really don't think so, Delia." He pulled away a bit, the look he sent toward Luther now one that said half a dozen things. Assurance that he could be trusted. Pain that she'd entertained even for a moment the notion that he'd been looking for a woman for base reasons. Irritation with her father. And under it all, that shadowed certainty that Luther had noticed building in him ever since they got home.

No, before that. Even on the way here. That he wasn't what he imagined this girl wanted.

This time her "Oh" carried no relief. If anything, frustration at being so summarily dismissed.

Phineas must have heard it as clearly as Luther did. He sighed.

"I don't want to get you in any more trouble with your father than I already have. And I daresay he wouldn't like you asking about for me."

"No. And Mama will probably find me out here any minute. I just—I had to see you. To tell you that your letters mean the world to me, and the servants all seem set on making sure I get them. I only wish it didn't require anything underhanded."

"*I* only wish that James fellow hadn't ever been stationed here." He said it on a breath of a laugh, but no doubt it was quite serious. If not for this "better" suitor, her father might not be so set on keeping them apart.

Luther saw a bonnet bobbing their way—the one the young lady's mother had been wearing when he spotted her a few minutes before. Looked as though their time had already expired. He cleared his throat. Nodded toward the garden.

"Look, Delia. You're probably better off without me. I'm not sure I can be who you want."

"Phin—"

"That said . . . as long as you keep giving me hope, I'm going to keep clinging to it. There's no one else for me. Never will be."

Mrs. Owens had reached the gate and was looking about, clearly irritated. Luther glanced into the stable, where her daughter had Phineas's hands clasped between both of hers and was looking up at him as if he were the only man in the world. Eva had used to look at Luther like that. *Please, Lord. Please.*

"There's no one else for me either. I'll wait, Phin. I'll wait until Daddy sees reason. Until the war is over, if I must. Until the very earth passes away. Forever."

Sweet, romantic notions. Luther had said a few similar ones in his day and meant every one of them. He could only pray that neither he nor Phineas would have to wait quite that long to claim their loves.

Chapter Twenty

NOVEMBER 13, 1861

The city writhed. Broiled with panic and dismay. Phin urged his horse through the first hole he could find in the crowds, but they grew thicker the closer to the port he drew. Tossing a glance over his shoulder to make sure Luther was still with him, he shook his head.

Why did Father choose now, of all times, to risk a trip to their plantation? Granted, he'd had no way of knowing that Hilton Head would fall to the Yankees while he was away. That most of their remaining friends would be packing all valuables—wives, daughters, and silver—and sending them inland. He hadn't realized General Lee would arrive during his absence.

Hadn't realized the talk that would spring up. Talk that Phin suspected had been started with Owens—and perhaps a certain lieutenant who had a vested interest in seeing the Dunn name tarnished in the eyes of Savannahian society.

"Whoa!"

He jerked around again at the unexpected sound of Luther's voice, and saw that a pedestrian brandishing a polished rifle had rammed his friend's horse. Phin managed to grasp the bridle before the beast could rear, and Luther soon had him in hand.

Still. Phin scowled at the gun-toting fool. "What the blazes is all the excitement about around here?"

The man turned around and proved himself to be no more than a boy, one with ginger hair and a face with more freckles than not. "It's the *Fingal*, sir! She made it past the blockade with a load of weapons, the biggest we've seen since those blasted Yankees came. They've got rifles, pistols, sabers, even new uniforms. It's a triumph!"

Phin hadn't even the chance to voice his opinion on this well-timed supply before an older man took hold of the boy by the arm and urged him onward, grim faced. "It won't matter, boy. You know what General Lee said—Savannah is not worth saving. All those guns will be sent to Virginia."

His hands tightened on the reins. *Not worth saving*. The words had been swirling through his brain since the general had dared utter them. Who was Lee to decide that? Perhaps Savannah was already overrun by their own soldiers. Perhaps the best of society had fled. Perhaps the Yankees swarmed the coastal islands—including the one the Dunn plantation called home. But did that mean they should give her up entirely? Hand her over to those who would destroy her?

Phin sighed. If this were one of the stories Delia had been including in her letters to him, the general would change his mind at the last moment and surge in for a sudden victory, making their hometown the new seat of Southern civilization.

But logic said General Robert E. Lee was right. Savannah was a lost cause. There was no hope of insulating it from the fleet off the Georgian coast, no matter how many stones they dumped in the river to try to keep the Yankees out. All they'd accomplish would be keeping themselves in.

Yet his heart cried that they ought to fight for her anyway. Fight for home, fight for family. Fight for what was theirs. Fight for the chance to make her worth fighting for again.

His leg throbbed at the very thought.

Luther cleared his throat and motioned toward the docks, where a familiar schooner had found a home. Phin turned his horse that direction and scanned the crowd for Father. He didn't see him at first, but he did see a blond head that immediately set his nerves on edge. Julius James? What was he doing here?

Or maybe it wasn't him. In the next shift of the crowd, Phin lost sight of the figure he'd thought he'd spotted. He was probably just starting at shadows. Shaking it off, he turned back toward their small boat and finally saw his father supervising the loading of a wagon. "Father!"

"Phin?" Father turned, frowned. "You didn't need to brave this madness to greet me today."

"Mother was worried." In days of old, Phin would have swung down and helped with the transfer of crates and bags. But dismounting was trial enough without swarms of people nearby to trip him up. "I've been coming all week to see if you'd made it back. We heard the Yankees have taken all the coastal islands."

The frown deepened on Father's forehead. He slid one last package into the saddlebag of the horse tethered to the rear of the wagon and vaulted onto its back. "It's true. Big Tybee was overrun. Not our plantation yet, but it's only a matter of time. I left the place in Caesar's care. He swore they would see to the planting and harvesting as always, but we shall see. I won't be able to risk another run to the island, hence why I brought all the valuables with me."

Phin's jaw clenched at the pile of parcels. It had been nearly a year since he'd last stepped foot on the plantation. What had Father brought? The silver, certainly. Perhaps some of the family paintings. Whatever gold may have been stored there, and the crystal. But he wouldn't have been able to bring the enormous magnolia Phin had played under as a boy. The beaches he and River had raced along, shouting with laughter as only boys can do. Or the hidey-hole between rooms that had been his pirate lair.

"You'll find that all your friends are sending their treasures away from Savannah too," Phin said, "and most are sending themselves as well."

Father picked up his reins. "They're leaving? Who?"

"Everyone."

"The Owenses?"

Phin's mouth quirked up. "Almost everyone. Owens still won't budge, though Delia said he's sending their valuables away. Lacy is, of course, already with their older sister at the Worth plantation, and Owens has been begging Delia and her mother to join them. I believe the Youngs are still here, given Delia's written tirade about the evil sorceress who refused to relinquish the city from her black spell."

Father breathed a laugh and pressed his heels to his horse's flanks. "Quite the young lady you have, that's for certain."

"There's no one in the world quite like her." If only he could *see* her for more than a stolen minute here or there. Letters were better than nothing, but he wanted to hold her. Hear her tell one of her stories with all the inflection and drama she always included. See the gleam in her emerald eyes when she looked at him. With a sigh, Phin guided his horse even with his father's. The crowds, thankfully, were shifting toward the other end of the docks, no doubt where the *Fingal* was moored. "I don't know how she can keep it up. The letter I received this morning had a complete fairy tale in it that she'd come up with. While I just look at the world and see nothing but a tragedy."

Father sent him a knowing grin. "And that's why you suit so well. You need that sunshine, Phin. Frankly, we could all use a good dose of it. We need happy stories in the midst of trials. They keep us going. Remind us of what we're struggling for."

"I know." It was part of the reason he ripped each letter open as if it were water and he was stranded on that Cuban beach again. "I just wish they could last. But it seems like happy endings aren't real. They're just moments isolated in time. After one crisis, before the next comes."

"Quite right." Yet Father sounded at peace as he said it. "They are pauses we all need. Those moments of beauty we can look back on, take strength from, when we're in the valley of shadows again." He sent a piercing gaze Phin's way, the very same he'd been spearing him with since he was a boy. "Those stories of hers are all that got your mother and sister through the worry this summer."

"Really?"

Father led them down a quiet alley. "When Beau let us know you were missing, I think we all knew it wasn't a matter of being a day or two behind. We all knew something had gone wrong. And we all would have given you up for lost if your Delia hadn't kept hope alive in us. I was rarely present to hear her stories firsthand, of course, but the ladies would retell them to me in the evenings. Stories of how you could overcome anything, anyone, and make your way home."

His father might as well have thrust a sword into him and twisted. "I'm no hero. The fact that she believes I am—"

"Son, no one expected you to wrestle alligators or charm savages. No one really thought you were single-handedly saving a marooned crew." Father smiled again. "But she made the impossible seem worthy of hope. And here you are."

"Through no skill of mine." For one moment—one single moment—he let his eyes slide shut. "I should have been dead, Father. The bullet should have killed me, I should have bled out. The water should have drowned me. Infection should have set in, gangrene should have eaten me up. A million things were against me, and there's no good reason for me to have survived, except through the prayers of the faithful."

"Prayers the faithful wouldn't have offered up if we thought you dead. That young lady—her faith kept ours alive. And Owens or no Owens, you need to get her down the aisle."

"I mean to. And . . ." He dragged in a deep breath and then heaved it out again. "And I'm terrified to. What if I disillusion her? I'm *not* a hero. And this world—it's falling to pieces. I don't want to be the thing that tarnishes it all for her. But if she can't even see the bad now, with all of this . . ."

"Not see it?" Eyes wide, Father shook his head. "You think she could have come up with the stories she did if she thought nothing bad possible? You think she integrated the worst of her imaginings into her stories for us? I suspect not. I suspect her dreams were filled with fears much worse than she ever put to paper."

"What good will that do me if your ship is blown to bits by cannonballs? Or capsized in a hurricane? Or attacked by a giant squid? Or . . . or eaten by a whale?"

Phin rubbed his eyes and drew in a long breath. With that imagination, Father was no doubt right. She could devise the impossible, and not just in the direction of lovely things. But the terrible too. "Giant squid." He shook his head.

"Pardon?"

"Nothing. Just . . . you're right. She would have feared the worst. And not just the reasonable worst, but the far-fetched worst. And if she did it then, no doubt she's still doing it now. It's not that she doesn't see the tragedy—she just chooses which stories to tell."

Father nodded, sure and decisive. They turned again, and the bustle of the port behind them faded. "The question, then, is how to move forward. Owens is set against you, and I'm not sure how to change that. But I know this—no success, be it in marriage or war or life in general, comes without a cost. If you want her for your wife, you're going to have to fight for her."

And she would be worth the fight. Phin cast a glance at the city, the only place he'd ever thought of as home. A place with flaws, with blinders, with a dichotomy that could very well feed its destruction. A place the Confederacy seemed determined to abandon. Delia was worth it . . . and their home was too. The question was whether he had a prayer of winning her before Savannah came down around them.

December 3, 1861

Luther plodded down the sand-packed street of Currytown, yearning for cobblestones. The familiar sound of Cockney voices shouting. London fog. They'd had a few blessedly cooler days . . . but only a few. Here they were, into December, and most days it still reached seventy degrees. It just wasn't right.

But the weather was the least of his concerns. *Lord, I am running rather short on hope just now.* Their last lead on Eva had run dry, and he honestly didn't know where else to turn. Phineas had been asking every family he could find whether they'd recently purchased a woman matching her description, but most of the families wealthy enough to own a houseslave had left the city. And among those remaining, all he'd received in response lately were doors slammed in his face. And increasing rumors that his intentions were less than honorable.

The boardinghouse that Luther had been calling home for the last two months loomed ahead, all dry, cracking wood just waiting for the next stray spark to set it ablaze. Every night when Luther laid his head on the miserable pallet on the floor, he prayed he'd wake up with a house around him in the morning. He couldn't count the number of times he'd dreamt himself home in Stoke Newington, his tidy townhouse around him, his Eva asleep beside him.

He couldn't count the number of times he'd awakened and wondered if it would ever be more than a dream again.

Turning in through the narrow front entrance, he climbed swiftly up the rickety stairs and aimed for the door to the small flat he shared with River and two other slaves—Jeremiah and

Tim-Tom, brothers who were both in their midtwenties. Low voices sounded within, so he assumed one or both were there, keeping company with River, whom Phineas had sent home an hour ago.

But when he pushed open the door, it wasn't either of the brothers inside with River. No, it was rather a young man who looked remarkably like him. And whose lips went silent the moment Luther ducked through the door.

River greeted Luther with a smile and motioned to the stranger. "Rock, this be Monty, the one I tol' you bout. Monty, this be my brother, Rock."

Luther opened his mouth but then shut it again. River's brother, yes. But did that mean he could trust him enough to speak? Usually here in the flat he didn't dare. Tim-Tom and Jeremiah were pleasant enough, but he didn't know them. Any conversations he held with River were hushed and in complete privacy.

But River chuckled. "I already tol' him a bit. You can talk. He won't say nothin to nobody."

Irritation sparked, fanned, burst over him for a few seconds. Who was River to decide who knew Luther's secrets?

Then he actually looked at Rock, met his gaze, saw the serious smile on his lips. "I got me secrets as big as your'n, Reverend. Mebbe bigger."

Reverend. It had been too long since anyone but Phineas had called him that. Careful to shut the door tightly behind him, Luther joined the brothers. And kept his voice at a bare murmur. "Bigger?"

Rock swallowed and darted a glance at River. "Came here to get a bit a help with it. The Dunns, they hire me out. I been a pilot these ten years, helpin folk navigate the tricky waters round the islands."

Luther sucked in a breath. He'd been overhearing more and more whispers about good pilots in recent weeks. From the slaves, who spoke of them in reverent tones as the only possible saviors for those who wished to flee to the islands and the Yankees on them. From the masters, who spoke of them with dread for the selfsame reason and cursed themselves for *"allowing Negroes to ever learn a skill so dangerous to their masters."*

But neither Phineas nor his father had ever mentioned to anyone that one of their slaves was counted among the number. "Interesting."

"He be the best too," River put in, a proud lift to his chin. "Only way Mass Sidney could get back from Tybee last month."

Rock ducked his head. "Riskier far getting back *to* Tybee."

"Wouldn'ta been, if you didn't have impo'tant cargo." He said no more. Just shot Luther a look that said he ought to know what that cargo was.

And so he did. He pulled out one of the roughhewn chairs at the small table and eased himself down on it. "That *is* risky business."

"Worth it though." Rock leaned forward, tapping a fingertip to the table. "And I have safety in the very thing I's doin. Kin't navigate the river nor the islands without a pilot, so the white folks kin't come after us. But if you help here, River . . . ain't no such safety."

"Help?" Brows flying up, Luther looked to River. "Help *how*?"

"Gittin folks to where he be."

Helping would-be runaways become actual runaways. Luther let his breath ease out from between his teeth. He admired the young man for taking the risk. And yet . . . the risk was greater for him than for others. "River. You know well Lieutenant James has been watching the entire Dunn household like a hawk, just waiting to catch someone in a misstep."

"He ain't gwine catch me." River's eyes looked as hard as his brother's name. "You got yo callin, Reverend. I got mine."

And Luther wasn't about to argue with him about it. But now

he had someone here who could answer a few of the questions he'd been having as he heard about the scores of slaves fleeing for the islands. He looked to Rock. "What do they do once there? Is it a stopping place or a destination?"

"Depends. Some move on. Most stayin, though, right now. It's safe, and still familiar."

That *familiar* was what Luther had been thinking about. "And what are their goals for after the war? Assuming the best, that they're granted freedom? What then? What do they hope to do, other than what they've always done?"

Rock frowned at him. "Don't rightly know if dey've all thought dat far."

And how could they? When someone had been trapped for his entire life, held down and kept deliberately ignorant of anything that could help him dig his way to a better existence . . . "In London, I ministered to many former slaves from the Americas. But it didn't take us long to learn that it wasn't enough to preach to them. We had to equip them for something more. Teach them to read, to write, if they didn't know how already. Give them the schooling they'd been denied. Is there anyone on the islands doing the same?"

For some reason, this just inspired Rock to lean back in his chair, cross his arms over his chest, and smirk at River.

River sighed. "Stop lookin at me like dat."

"You the only one I know who can read, River."

"I know *how*—don't mean I know how to *teach* it."

Luther's brows shot up again. "Phineas taught you?" He knew his young charge had changed during his convalescence . . . but was it possible he'd started at a better place than Luther had given him credit for? He'd just assumed he believed fully in the doctrines espoused by his culture: that a black man or woman *shouldn't* be taught such skills, and should be kept removed from any job where they could pick them up.

But River chuckled. "Taught me every lesson his tutors taught him till he gone off to college. Though I admit, I'd druther be outside playin than larnin letters and numbers."

It seemed Luther may owe Phineas a bit of an apology. "It's crucial that they be given schooling, whether at River's hand or someone else's."

River deflected the look his brother sent his way with a roll of his eyes. "If'n the time comes when I have to leave here, we talk den bout it. But right now, I ain't leavin Savannah. I can do good work *here*."

Rock snorted a laugh. "It ain't just the work, and don't you be sayin it is. It's that ooman you been talkin bout."

Luther smiled at that. River had been seeing quite a bit more of Salina than Phineas had been of Miss Owens, thanks to River's continued guarding of Miss Dunn. Given his own situation, Luther could hardly blame him for postponing a possible calling to focus on the one that kept him near her. Even so, it was critical that the runaways be given the opportunity to learn. Otherwise they'd find their freedom not nearly as full as it should be. Education, his father had always said, was the wings they were given with which to fly.

He looked from one brother to the other. "If there's anything at all I can do to help either of you, know that I'll do it."

When Rock looked at him, he had the strange sensation the bloke was seeing right past the words and down to the one thing he wasn't willing to do just yet. "I hope you mean dat, Reverend. Cause there be plenty."

Here. There was plenty here, in Savannah. And that was the plenty he meant to focus on until Eva was safely back at his side.

CHRISTMAS 1861

Cordelia stared down at the page before her, not seeing the familiar scrawl of her own writing or the words she'd just penned. Usually when she finished a story, a burst of satisfaction filled her—or of dissatisfaction, if she knew it still needed a lot of work. This time, she was altogether uncertain whether her imaginings about one of the shepherds who saw the Christ child on the night of his birth were worth the telling or should be tossed into the fire behind the grate.

Would this story make anyone rethink the arrival of their Savior? Their way of approaching Him? Would it *change* anyone? Did it have to?

With a sigh, she picked up her pen again and wrote a quick *Fin* at the end. She had no way of knowing whether it would resonate with anyone when she read it to them after dinner. But it was finished, regardless.

Her gaze darted to the bottom drawer of her secretaire. Under the stack of other stories and letters from her sisters rested a collection she'd have liked to protect with lock and key, if she didn't know that something like that would only garner her mother's interest. A stack growing by the day—the collection of stories she'd been writing down from the servants.

Old Moses. Fiona, his wife. Fanny, the cook. Martha, Mama's maid. Each had claimed, when she approached them, that they didn't have a tale worth the time it would take to tell it. And at first, no one would tell her anything beyond the stories of her own family, which she already knew.

But a week ago, Salina had pulled Delia into the kitchen one night when her parents were out, had sat down beside her and told her her murruh's story, there in front of the others. Cordelia had jotted down notes during the tale, listening intently, but her heart breaking a little more with every sentence. She had quietly thanked her sister for the trust she'd put in her, gone back up to her room, and written long into the night.

She hadn't dared venture to the kitchen again without being invited, but she'd given the story to Salina, and she had apparently read it to the others. A day later, Old Moses had been the first to ask if she might like to hear the story of his grandmother, who had made the trip from Africa, and of his daddy, who had toiled in the rice fields and tried, once, to run away. He'd said nothing of himself, but through those stories of his family, she had learned more about his heart and soul than she ever had through the decades of living here in the same house.

At his invitation, she'd ventured to the kitchen again to read the stories to the others. And since then, others had been seeking her out. They all had stories. Stories she was humbled and blessed to be entrusted with the telling of.

Stories of heartbreak and injustice, sometimes. Stories of love and family, always. Stories of redemption and sacrifice, more often than not. Stories of . . . humanity. Stories that had changed her as she heard them, as she wrote them. Stories that made her wonder if that's what stories were *meant* to do.

Her eyes fluttered shut. She'd never thought of the slaves as property, not like some did. But had she ever really paused to understand them as people? And that went not just for the servants in her own house, but for *everyone* outside the circle of those she loved. It was so easy to pass them by without a care. So easy to look no further than her own concerns. So easy to forget that they, too, were people with hearts just like her own. People affected by the decisions of others. Of men like her father.

Of her? Did she have a prayer of swaying anyone, ever?

"Cordelia! Are you still up here?"

She jumped at her mother's voice, doing a quick check of her hands to make sure they weren't covered in wet ink.

No—only dry ink, which she'd have no hope of scrubbing off entirely now. Perhaps Mama wouldn't fuss overmuch, given that it was Christmas.

A girl could dream.

"Coming, Mama!" She gathered the pages of her story and

tapped them into a neat stack, though that meant Mama opened her door before she could reach it.

She looked tired. Worry had dug permanent lines into her face, and even her hair seemed to have lost a bit of its golden luster. Was it the war that had aged her? The worry over their family? Ginny and Lacy being gone?

Was it Cordelia?

She made sure to give her mother a warm smile as she hurried over to her. Despite the fact that they didn't see eye to eye on much, she never had any doubt that Mama loved her. It seemed a good day to remember that. "I hope I haven't kept anyone waiting."

"Not yet." Mama glanced down to her hands, her eagle eyes settling on the ink stains for a split second. Then she, too, mustered a smile. "Not that there are many you'd be able to keep waiting even if you were late. It is a sad collection of guests we'll host this year."

"I know." All month Mama had been bemoaning how quiet it would be this Christmas. No relatives coming to visit, two-thirds of her daughters away, and precious few friends left in the city. But those who were still here were joining them for dinner. The Youngs, much to her dismay. The Dunns—even Phin, which offset her irritation over Annaleigh. Julius and a few of his closest friends, which was as unfortunate as the first. And their pastor and his wife, since few of their flock remained. "But those who are coming will appreciate your hospitality all the more, Mama. You've managed to bring a festive light to a dreary time."

Mama actually patted her arm in thanks and led her out into the hallway. "And you have a story to entertain us with later, correct?"

"I just finished it. Would you . . . would you read through it first? I haven't had time yet."

Mama blinked at her in surprise. She never *invited* her to read her stories, though Mama usually insisted on it, if she meant to share them with anyone. Perhaps the willing offering was what made her face soften. "Of course, Delie-Darlin. We'll go sit by the fire, and I'll read over it."

"That sounds lovely."

And may have been, had there not been voices at the door when they got to the bottom of the stairs. Cordelia buttoned her lips against a groan when she realized it was Julius speaking to Old Moses, here a full thirty minutes earlier than he should have been. There was no hope of avoiding him either. He was already looking their way, a smile on his face.

She murmured a Merry Christmas in response to his usual flattery of a greeting and glanced over at her mother. Mama was glancing at her, too, her eyes begging Cordelia to be welcoming. Practically shouting, *It's Christmas. Can't you forget for one day that you dislike him so much?*

A sigh built up in her chest. Why, why couldn't her parents give up this hope?

"I am sorry to arrive so early," Julius was saying, "but I was hoping to convince Delia to join me for a stroll around the gardens."

Mama's eyes widened just a fraction, her message clear. *Say yes.*

She could decline. Make an excuse. Go into the parlor with her parents as she planned. But her mother wouldn't now be happily reading her story—she'd be fuming at her stubbornness. And Daddy would see the strife and get that pinched look about his mouth that seemed to prevail lately any time he looked at her. And by the time the Youngs and Dunns arrived, it would be abundantly clear that while it might be Christmas, it wasn't exactly merry in the Owens house.

No. Better that *she* endure a bit of un-merriment rather than ruin the day for everyone. She held out the pages to her mother and smiled. "A breath of fresh air sounds like just the thing. Do I need a wrap?"

Julius blinked in surprise at her quick acquiescence but recovered quickly, giving her the confident smile she detested. "I'd say it's around sixty degrees."

She was wearing one of her heaviest dresses, so she ought to be fine. "Well then. Shall we?"

Mama beamed at them and promised to have Cordelia's story read by the time they came back inside.

Cordelia led the way to the door that let out into the garden—pretending not to notice the arm Julius crooked for her. She would be polite for Mama's sake, but she would *not* encourage him. When she stepped outside, she found the sunshine weak, the clouds many, and the wind a bit chillier than she'd expected. A good excuse to keep the walk short. "Have you had any word from home lately? Holiday wishes, perhaps?"

Julius kept pace beside her as she turned toward the dormant flower beds. "I had a letter from my mother just a few days ago, as a matter of fact. She was very glad to know that I'd be passing Christmas with your family."

Since she couldn't exactly agree with the sentiment honestly, she simply hummed and reached to urge a stray shoot of wisteria into its lattice. The gardens had been a bit on the wild side since Big Tom left.

She frowned as the stalk resisted her. Where was he now? Was he all right? She never knew him well, but she suddenly remembered the way she'd seen him looking at Salina. He, too, was a person with yearnings and dreams. A person who chased them far away from here. Had he found them? She whispered a silent prayer for him, wherever he was.

"Delia." Julius's hand brushed over her back, making her jump. She spun to find him closer than she'd like, his gaze intent upon her. "I have a question I'd like to ask you. A gift we could give your parents and mine this Christmas, if you'll but entertain the notion."

Oh no. No, not today. He *had* to know she'd refuse if he

asked her to marry him, so why would he even bother? Why was he drawing out a small jewelry box, lowering to a knee?

"Julius, please. Please stop." Her heart beat frantically, but not in the way she'd imagined it would at her first proposal. No, it was supposed to be Phin kneeling before her, a happy *yes* bubbling up inside her, not this panic.

But it was Julius, and he opened the box to reveal an antique emerald ring. "My mother sent this to me, along with her letter. I know you still favor Dunn—but hear me out, darlin. I can provide for you, for your whole family, when they have to leave Savannah. Dunn can't do that. His lands are already in the hands of the Yankees; they'll be decimated, and the Dunns will be ruined financially. Marry me and you'll have safety. You'll have the luxury to which you're accustomed. You and your parents and your sisters, too, if it comes to it."

Her throat went tight. Clever man—he knew well a financial appeal wouldn't move her, but to appeal to her sense of responsibility to her family . . . "And what else do you offer, Julius?" Her voice sounded strange in her ears. Cold and brittle, like it might shatter on the paving stones at her feet.

He frowned. "My devotion, of course. Is that what you mean? You have to know how I feel about you."

"I don't, actually. I know you like my dowry. I know you think me beautiful. But you always seem rather irritated when I mention the books I'm reading or the stories I'm writing. You never pay any heed to my opinions."

"You're being ridiculous, darlin." But he closed the box again and stood.

"Am I?" She lifted her chin. "And what about fidelity—would you promise that? That you would remain faithful to me always?"

"Of course I would promise it." His eyes sparked with that dark gleam that always ignited a flame of fear in her heart.

He would promise it, yes. But she wouldn't believe the words for a second. "I saw how you looked at my maid that day before the tableaux."

His laugh was dry. "You would refuse my suit because of one stray *look*? Darlin, I barely knew you then."

He didn't even bother denying it, she couldn't help but note. "Exactly my point. And do stop with the 'darlin' nonsense." She took a purposeful step away. "I don't mean to be unkind on Christmas, of all days, but I have no intention of ever changing my mind, so you might as well give up."

"I don't think so." His fingers closed around her arm. Not too tightly, but still. "Your father and I have an understanding, Cordelia. You don't want to disappoint him, I know you don't. This is the best thing for our families. The best thing for *you*. You think that slave-loving coward could make you happy?"

She jerked her arm free. "How *dare* you speak so!" As if it was a crime to seek the best for one's servants? To see them as people, to want to help them reunite with their families?

"It's the plain truth. Phineas Dunn has spent more time looking for that slave's wife than seeing after his own affairs. And his father is probably a Yankee collaborator—it's no coincidence he was on Tybee when the Yankees arrived."

"Now you're just being absurd. Of *course* it was a coincidence!"

"If he wasn't working with them, then how did he manage to slip back into Savannah, hmm?"

Cordelia nearly rolled her eyes. "With the help of a *pilot*."

"All the pilots are slaves—slaves who have turned mighty fast to the Yankees. So why would they help *him*?"

"I suppose because his people are loyal to him. Because the Dunns *care* about the men and women who serve them."

He leaned closer, towering over her. "Phineas Dunn is no better. He spends more time with his slaves than the gentlemen left in the city. Even the ones who had always been his friends are talking about how he doesn't appreciate his own kind anymore. How he's admitted he's too cowardly to ever serve with them again. Seems he thinks the coloreds are the only ones worthy of his attention these days—so it's no wonder he isn't paying any mind to *you*. Probably more likely to woo that maid of yours that you're so worried about. Maybe that's why his valet is always lurking around her. Maybe he's setting up trysts for him and—"

Before she could even think about what she was doing, her hand shot out and collided with his face. Partly for Phin, partly for Salina, partly just to make him shut his venom-spewing mouth. "How dare you insult the decency of good people."

He laughed and took a step back, not even lifting a hand to his cheek. "*He's* the one you can't trust, darlin. You'll see that one of these days. I just hope, for your sake, it's not too late when you do." He pivoted on his heel and walked back toward the door, whistling a Christmas carol as he went.

His cheek wasn't even pink where she'd struck him, blast it all. She curled her hand into a fist, thinking maybe she ought to have struck him that way instead. Or stomped on his toes or kicked him or spat in his face.

He had some nerve, saying what he did. So what if Phin preferred the company of River and Monty? She certainly couldn't blame him for that. *She* preferred Salina's, after all. She spun away, stomped through the garden toward her favorite bench under the live oak. There was no way she could go back in yet, not with this fury pumping through her. Her parents would see it in a heartbeat.

The cold of the wrought iron didn't make it through her skirt and petticoats, but when she leaned back, it certainly cut through her bodice, making her shiver. No matter. Better a chill than Julius James. How could he possibly believe he'd ever convince her to marry him? He understood her so very little.

The wind picked up, deepening the chill. She'd bear it a few more minutes before she gave up though. Let it cool her temper.

"Delia?"

"Phin?" His voice brought her back to her feet, the cold forgotten. She hadn't heard his voice or seen him in so long. But there he was, stepping into view much as he'd done at the barbeque last May. Except this time his smile was deeper, more solemn. And he held a package in one hand, a cane in the other. She rushed toward him, the joy of seeing him, actually *seeing* him, nearly bringing a sob to her throat. "Phin."

He held out his arms, and she couldn't refuse the invitation. No, she could only soak in the warmth as they closed about her, breathe in the scent of citrus that clung to him, relish the sound of his heart thumping under her ear.

This was home. It didn't matter if his plantation was lost. It didn't matter if Savannah would be. It didn't matter whether he went to war again or stayed home—wherever he was, that was where her heart would be. Why couldn't Daddy just bless *this*?

"Merry Christmas." It was the only thing she could think to say through the bittersweet joy.

Phin pressed his lips to the top of her head. "Merry Christmas. Old Moses said you were out here. Suited me fine. I brought you something."

She could feel the package against her back. And didn't care a whit what was in it. "You did. *You*. I can't put words to how glad I am to see you."

"My Delia, at a loss for words?" He shifted, urged her to move so she could look up at him. He was grinning down at her. "Though I do know what you mean. I feel like it's been a century. I've missed you so." He shifted again, moving one arm around to come between them. The package in its festive wrapping appeared under her nose. "But I did want you to open this while we have some privacy."

Certainly not jewelry, though if *he* were to offer anything with a question of forever, she'd agree before he could even finish the request.

He wouldn't though. Not without Daddy's permission.

She took the package and let him nudge her back toward the bench, waiting until he'd sat before she untied the ribbon and folded away the paper. The cover of a book met her gaze. And beneath it, another—and another. Her eyes went wide. "*Great Expectations*—all three volumes! Wherever did you find it?" While he laughed, she flipped through volume one. "I'd read the first installments of the serial last spring but hadn't been able to get my hands on the rest. Oh, I've been dying to know what becomes of Pip!"

"I assumed as much." Phin snuggled in closer to her side than he would have dared had their parents been out here. "I found it in Cedar Key and thought of you. I didn't imagine issues of *All the Year Round* had made it through the blockade."

"No indeed. A later one did, but I couldn't bear to read part five when I hadn't read two through four." She closed the cover, traced a finger along the embossing. "Cedar Key. You've saved it all this time for Christmas?"

He breathed a laugh. "Well, I would have gladly given it to you earlier, had I thought your father would allow it. I didn't imagine he could object too much today."

"You're a wise man." More, one who knew her so well. She ran a hand over the cover of volume one, relishing the feel of it. Imagining the hours of story-feasting within.

"There's more." He tapped the paper below the books.

No, not the paper—cloth that the paper hadn't totally uncovered yet. She lifted the books and drew in a breath at the beauty that met her gaze. Jet beads caught what little light escaped the clouds gathering overhead, contrasting brilliantly with the ivory silk of the Maltese lace. She let her fingers take in the feel for a long moment before pulling out the shawl. Then, of course, wrapped it around her shoulders. "Phin, it's stunning."

And intimate. No one but her family had ever given her an article of clothing before, and Mama would no doubt have something to say about it now. But she didn't care. Every time she wore it, she'd imagine his arms around her. "I have something for you, too, but it's inside."

"I don't need anything but this. Time with you." His fingers covered hers. Then a spark of mischief entered his eyes. "Well. Maybe *one* more thing . . ."

She met his lips without a qualm, savoring each second of contact. But all too soon he pulled away, leaving her sighing. "That is certainly not your gift from me, Phineas Dunn—that was every bit as much *for* me as *from* me. No, I put quite a few hours into what's waiting in the parlor for you."

He traced a finger over the ink stains and calluses on her hands and hummed a vague acknowledgment.

She laughed even as she gasped in horror. "She told you! Your sister can't keep a secret for anything!"

He laughed, too, and gripped her fingers again. "Don't be mad. I was bemoaning that your latest letters didn't include any stories in them, and she let it slip that it was probably because you were spending so much time recording some for me for Christmas."

Though she huffed, she couldn't exactly be angry with Sassy. Not today. Not when Phin was here, his fingers around hers. "I'd been saving up a blank journal and filled it to the brim. Some of them are old ones I know you liked. Some are newer. Though I haven't written much fiction since—" Oh, fiddle. She hadn't meant to say so much.

Phin's brows lifted. "Since what?"

She looked down at *Great Expectations* again. Would he judge her for the projects of late? Think her foolish, as she knew her family would, for transcribing the tales of their servants?

Or was he maybe the only one who would understand? "I've been writing . . . memoirs."

"Memoirs?" His fingers went lax in hers. "Of whom?"

She shouldn't have said anything. Certainly not the truth. It was asking too much of him to expect him to be inclined in this particular direction. Still, she cleared her throat. "Old Moses and Fiona. Fanny. Martha. Henry. Jill—"

"Delia." He stopped her with a finger to her lips. And his eyes—his eyes weren't condemning at all. They weren't accusatory. They didn't name her ridiculous. No, his eyes were warm golden pools in which she could well drown. "I love you. You're the most remarkable person I've ever met."

Forget the books. The shawl. Even the kiss. *That* was the best gift she ever could have dreamed of receiving this Christmas. "Oh, Phin. I love you too."

Chapter Twenty-One

FEBRUARY 17, 1862

Phin tried to focus on the words before him, but the small print in the Bible kept blurring. Or perhaps it was that his gaze kept tracking right, to the newsprint not completely obscured by the Scriptures.

Two forts fallen to the Union in ten days. Fort Henry on the sixth, and now Fort Donelson, just yesterday. And General Grant marched onward. Deeper into the heart of the South. The fleet on the coast was no doubt making its men cozy on the plantations dotting the barrier islands, the Dunns' among them.

His eyes moved again, this time to the map pinned to his wall. Sketching it had been drudgery during his school days, but now he looked at each carefully noted city and river and fort and was glad he had. Glad he could see that no matter how vast a land might seem when you're simply standing upon it and going about your day, it wasn't nearly big enough when the enemy drew near.

Fort Pulaski he had marked with a more extravagant star than had been necessary, and his teacher had taken a point off because of it. But he had thought it had deserved the attention.

After all, it was a mere fifteen miles from Savannah, the guardian to the city. Only one mile from Tybee Island.

Only one mile from the Yankees.

Who were only sixteen miles from the city.

They were coming. If not to Savannah itself, to the fort. If not now, then soon. There was no question about that. The question was whether the structure, deemed impregnable upon its completion more than a dozen years ago, would withstand its first bombardment.

And as if it wasn't enough to worry that his very home might be destroyed, they'd also just received word this morning that they were expected to send more slaves to dig trenches for the Confederacy. They'd have bucked against that order regardless, but with the plantation cut off, that meant the workers in demand were expected to come from their household staff. Which meant, in a word, River.

And Luther, since no one knew he wasn't in fact a slave.

Dear Lord. He closed his eyes, rested his head upon clasped hands. *Dear Lord.*

But he didn't know what to pray. Didn't know if he could accept what answers might come. *Lead me, Lord. Lead me in the paths of righteousness.*

He splayed a hand onto his Bible, where that most familiar Psalm lay open. The twenty-third—one of the few he had known even before Luther recited it to him again and again, over and over. Every day. Every night.

"The Lord is my shepherd; I shall not want."

I've wanted, Father God, you know how I have. All my life, seeking that next great adventure. Delia. Prize money. Glory, honor. I wanted . . . and always wanted. But I don't want all that anymore, Lord. I just want to be in your shadow. Help me want what you want.

"He maketh me to lie down in green pastures: he leadeth me beside the still waters."

You'll give me peace if I follow you. I see that in those who do. In Luther, though such trials have come upon him. In my father, who bears the burden of such loss with our property cut off as it is. And here I am, still aching. Not in the leg, but in the soul. I ache, Father, from so much thrashing about in my own mind. I just want to rest. No more troubled seas, just the still waters of your guidance.

"He restoreth my soul."

Restore my soul, O Lord.

His mind wouldn't let go of that verse. "He restoreth my soul."

Restore me, Father. Restore my soul.

He felt the waters wash over him. A mighty wave, strong enough to send a ship rolling, to make a deck pitch. Strong enough to wash a man from carefully fitted wood into the great abyss of uncharted waters.

His knees hit the floor, chair tumbling down somewhere behind him. But the gleaming oak of his bedchamber's planking gave way to the night-darkened deck of the *Cuba*. It bobbed, it tilted. And thunder filled his ears. That from the sky, and that from the weapons.

That from the hungry sea. Frothing and foaming, calling out to him.

He restoreth my soul. He restoreth my soul. He restoreth my soul.

Sucking in a breath only made him shudder, made the world yawn open. *He restoreth my soul.*

It crashed again, that relentless water. Submerged him into the deep.

Deep. So deep it called unto itself.

But not dark. His wonders were there. Though the depths may overflow, they didn't swallow him up.

There you are, Lord. There you have always been. If I take on the wings of the morning and make my home in the sea, you are there. If I descend into heaven or make my bed in hell, you are there. You restoreth my soul.

The torrents came, but the waters receded. Warmth of sun touched his back. Touched his mind. Touched his spirit. *Lead me, Lord. Lead me in the path of righteousness. For your name's sake.*

River.

It wasn't the name that filled his mind, but rather that familiar face, which he'd looked on far more often than he had his own. His eyes flew open to see the polished wood of his floor. His chest still heaved. "Lord?" His voice emerged as a hoarse whisper through his tight throat.

Never once had he felt pressure upon his spirit like this. Never had something, someone filled his mind so thoroughly in such a way.

No other direction came. But then, he needed none. Sucking in breath enough to withstand the painful climb to his feet, Phin staggered up, grabbed his cane from where it was leaning against his desk, and surged out the door.

He nearly bowled into one of the maids, who squealed and then slapped a hand over her mouth in apology. Her eyes, at least, danced with laughter at the near collision.

It was all he could do to force a smile. "My apologies, Tansy. Do you happen to know where River is?"

The laughter flashed into something else. Something he had no name for. "I think he be runnin an errand, Mr. Phin. Don't rightly know though."

An errand? Phin thanked her and turned toward the stairs. *He* certainly hadn't sent him on any errand. Though it was possible Sassy or his parents had, he supposed. They were so shorthanded these days, anyone could end up doing anything. Regardless, it meant there was no use looking for him around the house. Where, then?

Outside was the obvious first step, so he headed for the back door, breathing a sigh of relief when he spotted Luther shouldering a sack of flour toward the kitchen. "Monty!"

Luther paused, looking as though he barely noticed the fifty-pound weight, and turned to him with an arched brow.

Phin hurried over to him, as much as his limp allowed. He saw no one else nearby but still pitched his voice to a murmur. "River—do you know where he is?"

Something flashed through *his* eyes, not altogether dissimilar from what had sparked in Tansy's. What was going on? Whatever it was, the servants knew it. And clearly didn't want the masters to.

Phin hissed out a breath, that pressure on his spirit weighing all the heavier. He splayed a hand over his chest. "It's urgent. I don't know why, but I . . . I was praying, and his face flashed to mind, and now there's this *weight*. . . ."

Luther's lips twitched up.

Phin nearly growled. "Yes, yes, you can crow over the change in me later. For now—*River*."

Holding up one finger, Luther covered the remaining distance between Phin and the kitchen in a few long strides. He emerged again a moment later sans the flour sack and motioned him to follow.

Following, however, meant fetching horses from the stable, the wait for which was nearly his undoing. But at last they were mounted and heading at a quick pace toward . . . the docks. In days past, this direction could well speak of an errand from his father. But with the river filled with rubble to keep the Yankee ships out, there hadn't been any other shipping either. Father had long ago wrapped up what remaining business he had here. He'd barely made it back to Savannah as it was. If not for Rock—

Rock. Phin sucked in a breath and nudged his horse's pace up a bit more. Trading vessels may not be making it up the river, but small craft still could—if they had a skilled pilot. And there were none more skilled than River's brother. Had he come here to meet him? Why?

Unlike the last time he'd been down here, when the crowds had made it impossible to dismount, this time it was eerily empty. Gone was the hustle and bustle he'd always so enjoyed. The slips were full, but the ships all empty. By now the last of the holds had no doubt been emptied, and there was no point in loading them again. There would be no leaving, unless they sailed upriver. No doubt a few would, or already had. But the majority were stuck here until they dredged the stones from the river mouth again.

As he neared where their vessel was docked, Phin swung down from his horse and hitched him to a post. River and Rock could be anywhere, and the horses wouldn't allow him to search as many places.

Luther followed suit, but he didn't seem to have any other secret knowledge, since he didn't lead the way. Forced to guess, Phin turned in a circle. And caught his breath when he heard a raised voice to the right. With his cane in hand, he took a few hurried steps, not sure whether to utter a prayer of praise or alarm when he spotted River's familiar dark head—ducked before some sort of port official who was shouting at him.

What in the world had they gotten themselves into? They rushed toward River—and, yes, Rock was there too.

As they neared, he could make out more of the officer's words. "Do you think I'm stupid, boy? That I'd believe such a harebrained story? You ain't here on behalf of no one but your own self—or maybe a few ungrateful slaves you mean to steal away."

Stealing away slaves—helping them run? *Was* that what River and Rock were about? He looked from one of them to the other, then cast a glance toward Luther too. He was looking straight ahead, his face not giving anything away. Nor did the subservient postures of the brothers.

But that would make sense. Rock was able to move between Savannah and the barrier islands as few could—the islands, where the Yankees were in control, with their promises of freedom and more to any slave who came to them. The islands, to which it was rumored slaves were running daily. Were River and Rock their means of doing so?

His chest went tight. It took him a few more steps to realize it wasn't with frustration, wasn't with outrage, wasn't with disbelief. No, it was one part fear, given the attention they'd obviously gained from sectors they should have been steering clear of. And it was at least two parts pride in his oldest friend. He was doing something. Helping people.

Phin gripped his cane until his fingers ached. What was a family like his, on whose shoulders the burden of owning slaves sat so uncomfortably, to do? They couldn't free them. But the only other way to distance themselves from the practice would be to sell them—and that was something they couldn't countenance. Better to keep them, where at least they could be sure they were treated with decency and respect, than to send them to fates unknown, separating families and consigning them to possible whippings or worse.

The law had tied their hands. But Phin found himself mentally cheering River for slipping around it, seizing the opportunity the war had presented. Phin was by no means a fan of the Yankees—but he couldn't blame any slave for running to them.

River had been mumbling something to the officer that Phin couldn't catch. But he was close enough now that when the officer grabbed Rock roughly by the arm Phin could bark out, "See here, unhand my property!"

The officer spun, clearly ready to argue with him. He paused, though, when he took in Phin. He'd be seeing the fine suit of clothes, the silver handle on his cane. Or perhaps Luther towering behind him.

River's eyes flashed up from the ground they'd been focused

on. He'd know Phin used that particular phrase solely for effect, so no resentment gleamed there. But a bit of apprehension did.

All the proof Phin needed of what he'd been up to. And knowing that, he could pretty well deduce what else had been going on. He scowled, not at the brothers but at the officer. "What's the meaning of this? I send my boys down here to see to my business, and you're holding them up? As if running a business isn't difficult enough in these times, you have to make trouble for me. I ought to report you to your superior."

The stranger narrowed his eyes but released Rock's arm. "Business? Begging your pardon, mister, but there ain't no business being done here these days."

Phin breathed a laugh. "Not for the unenterprising, perhaps. But I, sir, have a good pilot here who's loyal to me. Aren't you, boy?" Praying they'd both play along with his charade, he reached out with his cane and tapped Rock lightly on the leg.

He'd never known Rock quite as well as River. But well enough. The young man looked up, then back down, shoulders slumped. "Yessuh, Mass Phin. Yessuh. We try an tell this fella we about yo bidness but he don't believe us."

At that, Phin lifted a brow at the officer. "Let's sort this out, then, shall we? You and I, so my boys can get back to work. Get on now, you two. Daylight's burning."

They didn't wait for the officer's permission—they spun and took off at a quick walk.

The man watched them go with narrowed eyes. "You can't trust no slaves these days, Mr.—?"

"Dunn."

"Well, Mr. Dunn, you can bet they'll run off first chance they get. Keep getting reports of slaves sneaking off to the islands, and they obviously pass this way. We've been told to keep an eye out for any suspicious behavior. And I was told to keep an especial sharp eye on those two."

Phin's spine tingled. "Told by *whom*?"

The man's brown eyes flashed, and his face went a bit red. As if he hadn't meant to say quite as much as he had. "Well, I only meant . . ."

"Let me guess. A certain lieutenant by the name of Julius James gave you that hint."

"How'd you know that?"

Phin forced a laugh. "Simple rivalry, my friend. We're both courting the same girl. He'd do anything to damage my business. But let me let you in on a little secret." He leaned close, though he knew well his eyes would be sparking warning more than secrecy. "We both know all the soldiers will be sent north any day now. Whatever he paid you or promised you, it'll soon be over. I, however"—he indicated his bum leg—"am stuck here for the foreseeable future. So, I can make your life hard—or I can make your life easy. You just tell me which way you mean to look when my boys are down here."

"Well now." The fellow took a step back, sizing up him and Luther again, clearly weighing his options. At length, he smiled. "I reckon I'll look whichever way you please, Mr. Dunn."

"Glad to hear it. And your name is?"

"McDonald, sir. Gus McDonald."

He made a mental note, nodded, pivoted. And flipped a silver coin over his shoulder. Not that he could afford to be tossing their precious silver around freely in general—but desperate times and all that.

Not knowing exactly where River and Rock had scurried off to, Phin simply headed back toward his horse, making it a point *not* to hang back and allow Luther to catch up to him until he was well out of sight. And even then, he only exchanged a glance with him, hoping his friend understood the show he'd put on.

Which, of course, he did—if anyone would at this point, it was Luther. And indeed, he smiled at him, pride gleaming in his eyes.

The brothers were waiting by his and Luther's horses. Phin let out his breath slowly as he approached.

River made a show of holding his horse's bridle. "Mr. Phin, it ain't . . ."

"I imagine it *is*, River. And I can't blame you for that. I'd be doing the same in your place."

River's brows shot upward. "You would?"

Nodding, Phin secured his cane in its loop alongside his saddle. "Frankly . . ." With Luther's gaze from a minute before still fresh in his mind, he nodded. "Frankly, I'm proud of you. Not that you need my pride or my approval. You're a man following your conviction and your heart. But even so—you have it." He reached up, gripped the saddle, but didn't put his foot in the stirrup yet. Instead, he looked at River until he lifted his gaze. Held it. "You're my friend. Always have been. That's not conditional. You do what you have to do. I only ask one thing."

River tilted his head.

"Stay safe. And . . ." He squeezed his eyes shut for a moment. That order he and Father had received that morning still glared in his mind's eye. He would *not* send River to dig. Never. "And take yourself to Tybee soon too. They mean to draft you into digging. I won't allow it, and I'm sure not refugeeing you inland. So, you just get yourself away from Savannah before they can force the issue. Hear me?"

His face hard, River shook his head. "I kin't leave yet, Phin. Not wifout Salina."

Phin. It was the first time he'd ever called him that, without a title ahead of it. Even through their shared childhood, that *Mister* had always been there. How could his name sound so different, so much warmer, without those two little syllables leading to it? "Well then." He put his foot in the stirrup and pulled himself up. "We'll just have to see she goes with you."

Cordelia ran her fingertips over the gold-leafed title as she closed the cover of *Great Expectations*, volume three, yet again. She'd already read the whole thing three times, and she told herself that was all the longer she'd hoard it up here in her room. Books were precious these days, and new titles hard to come by. It seemed cruel to deprive her parents of the pleasure of taking a turn with it, even if it *had* been a gift from Phin.

Her lips turned up at the mere thought of him. Of how he'd looked at her on Christmas. Those beautiful words that had whispered from his lips. He loved her.

Pulling the shawl he'd given her more tightly around her shoulders, she stood with a little sigh and gathered up the other two volumes of the book as well.

She'd no sooner slipped into the hallway than Fiona, Moses's wife, shuffled by with her dustrag in hand. She gave Cordelia a warm smile. "Mornin, Miss Delia. You sho made my day last evenin, tellin us dose stories."

Cordelia grinned back. She'd known Fiona all her life but had always thought her rather grouchy. Funny how things looked different when you knew someone's heart. She'd spent a solid three hours with the woman last week—and then, when Mama and Daddy went to Pulaski House for dinner yesterday, she'd offered to share all the stories she'd compiled thus far with the servants. Never had she imagined that an evening spent in the kitchen could be so much fun. "It was truly my pleasure, Fi."

She expected the old woman to keep going on past her. Instead, she stopped at Cordelia's side and reached a gnarled hand up to rest on her cheek, looking deep into her eyes as she'd never done before. "You done brought some light into these daa'k times fo us, Miss Delia. We grateful."

For a long moment, all Cordelia could do was draw in a deep breath and cover the weathered fingers with her own. "You don't need to thank me. I'm only sorry I had never taken the time before to realize you all had stories to tell."

Fiona chuckled and let her hand fall away. "You a chile befo, honey. Chil'ens don't never see sech thing, most times. But you done *now*. More'n most can say—white *or* black."

Maybe it shouldn't feel like the dearest compliment she'd ever received, but Cordelia fairly floated down the stairs and into the library. So peaceful was her heart that she didn't even scowl upon realizing there was no room anywhere on the shelves for the three volumes in her hand. No, instead she grinned at the packed bookcases, fair to bursting with countless hours of joy as they were. She'd just do a bit of rearranging, that was all.

It was only the fiction shelves that were so overcrowded. Daddy wouldn't mind if she expanded that section by a shelf, would he?

She glanced at the other bookcases, filled with various nonfiction—some of which she appreciated, given that she used them for research, and others she'd never touch in a million years. Then she glanced at the door. He might sigh at her, but he wouldn't *do* anything if she took over another shelf.

Decision made, she set about her task with gusto, stowing *Great Expectations* on a table for a few minutes while she set about creating a few stacks of books in the nonfiction section to take up less horizontal space and use all the vertical. Frankly, she kept telling Daddy it looked charming this way anyway. And he kept shaking his head at her and letting her do whatever she liked to the fiction section.

Half an hour later, she was sorely aware of how big a task she'd just made for herself. It seemed once she fiddled with one shelf, she had to do the same to the previous, and the one before that, and before long *all* of them. But she eventually reached the shelf full of economics treatises, which should be the last one she had to do.

She'd never so much as pulled these off in curiosity. The very name Adam Smith was enough to make her shiver in dread. How could Daddy ever have forced himself through that enormous *The Wealth of Nations* tome? With a shake of her head, she pulled out it and its neighbors.

And frowned. Two books were flattened against the back of the bookcase behind them, their scrolled back covers facing her. Had it been one, she'd have thought it nothing but an accident. But two matching volumes? No, this was clearly a two-part book, deliberately placed behind the most boring titles Daddy owned. Which could only mean he hadn't wanted her or her sisters or mother to find them.

Before she could even pause to think of *why* he might hide books from his family, she was reaching for the one on her left, pulling it out, flipping it over. Her breath caught. *Uncle Tom's Cabin: or, Life Among the Lowly* by Harriet Beecher Stowe.

Her eyes flew to the door, half expecting Daddy to appear there with thunder in his eyes. Well could she imagine why he had this book that, by all accounts, had played a major role in leading them to war—he'd want to be aware of what was enflaming the North against them. She'd heard him denounce the story as slanderous nonsense once, though she hadn't paused to wonder how he knew. But why had he kept it instead of getting rid of it, if that were the case?

Well, whatever his reasoning, she wasn't about to put the volumes back. Instead she replaced the economics tomes just as they'd been, quickly made her stack elsewhere to gain the room she needed, and finished her reorganization. Then, contraband hidden in the folds of her skirt, she raced back upstairs with heart pounding.

In her hands she held a novel that had changed the course of history. And she meant to discover how Mrs. Stowe had accomplished it.

Chapter Twenty-Two

Too many soldiers crowded the room. Cordelia tried to push aside the sense of overwhelm, to laugh and flirt like Sassy and Annaleigh and Maybelle were doing. It was, after all, the last these particular men would see of Georgia for who knew how long. Tomorrow they'd be marching to Virginia with General Lee. Savannah would be all but empty.

But she wasn't feeling festive, and smiling at all these men for the last hour had made her cheeks ache. She stubbornly clung to her seat now, even though Mama had been playing lively dances on the piano for the last twenty minutes and kept shooting her annoyed glances. Perhaps it *was* cruel of her to refuse to dance when she was one of so few young ladies present. Of so few even left in the city.

And perhaps she'd feel more inclined if her mind wasn't still whirling with the words from *Uncle Tom's Cabin*. Given that she had to read it in secret, when she knew no one would interrupt her, she'd only just turned the last pages that morning, two weeks after her discovery.

Her heart ached for those fictional characters—more, it ached for the real people she knew, some of whom had whispered stories to her that were not so dissimilar. Daddy could say all he wanted that it was slanderous. It wasn't.

Maybe all masters weren't cruel, but Mrs. Stowe hadn't said they were. Hadn't Mr. Shelby, in fact, been a kind man? The kind of master her father and all his friends claimed to be? But the fact still remained that when push came to shove, he'd sold Uncle Tom and little Henry to save his own hide. Sold them like horses or oxen or acres.

She stared at the collection of laughing, dancing couples. People who, even with war knocking on their very doors, at least knew they wouldn't end up on an auction block or in the hands of an unscrupulous slave trader. They knew that, win or lose against the Yankees, their lives would still be their own.

A basic comfort that would be denied Moses and Fiona and Fanny.

And Salina.

Cordelia's eyes slid shut. She, too, was a slave. Not her father's daughter so much as her father's property. Maybe he said he'd never sell her, that he'd give her legally to Cordelia, but she didn't *want* to own her sister. She wanted better for her. She wanted . . . she wanted *freedom* for her.

But did wanting that for her sister, for all their servants, change her own role at all? She was like Mrs. Shelby—not a harsh mistress, but complicit simply by *being* a mistress. She was part of the society that held them in bondage.

Salina and Moses and Fiona had trusted her with their stories and encouraged her in the telling, but for the first time in her life she had to wonder if that was enough. If caring was enough.

That question had kept her up far too late last night, and there was no one she could talk to about it but the Lord. He had never forbidden slavery in His Word, it was true—something she'd heard argued time and again. But Paul *had* given instruction, which she'd reread that morning, in Colossians 4:1. *Masters, give unto your servants that which is just and equal; knowing that ye also have a Master in heaven.*

What was just? What was equal? What was fair, remembering they had their own Master?

Only one answer settled in her spirit. If they were to do unto their slaves as they wanted God to do unto them, then that left nothing but the very things Americans had been taught to value above all: freedom and equality.

"You sure look lonesome, Cousin."

It took effort to open her eyes, but she managed it. And told herself not just to scowl at Julius, who would be marching north with the rest come morning. Thank the Lord for that blessing. Still, her smile felt pained when she looked up at him. "Not at all."

"You'll have to do better than that if you expect me to believe you." He sat beside her, pulling his chair too close and then leaning in. "The prettiest girl in Savannah shouldn't be alone at any gathering. It's just not right."

"Fiddle-faddle, Julius."

"Is it?" He braced his arm on the back of her chair and leaned in still more. No doubt it would look, to everyone else, as though he were merely trying to be heard above Mama's enthusiastic playing.

No one else felt that shiver of alarm course up her neck from where his breath fanned it though.

"You know well your father's never going to permit Dunn to ask for your hand. Your choices, my sweet Delia, are quite clear. You either disobey him . . . or you give me a chance."

She tried to shift away, but she had chosen a petite chair, one that left little room for her to wiggle, what with the volume of her hoops positioned just so within it. But she could turn her face away, at any rate.

The truth wasn't ignored so easily, however. Daddy had indeed made his decision clear, over and again these past weeks. To Julius and only Julius would he give his blessing.

She had made her stand clear as well—she would never consent to that match.

Which meant . . . what? Remaining unmarried or disobeying her father? Were those her only choices? And did it even matter, in light of the greater war waging its way through her soul?

Julius trailed a finger down her arm, from elbow to wrist. "I'd make you happy. Give you anything you wanted. A whole room full of books and paper. That's all you say you need, right?"

She pulled her arm away, clasped her hand to the place that seemed to itch from his touch. "You know nothing about me."

He somehow made a laugh sound like a weapon. It grated on her sensitive flesh, trying to rip and tear. "*I* know nothing about *you*? Have I not taken every opportunity to be in your company, tried so hard to win your smiles? Yet you spurn me at every turn. But please, not today. Come, my beautiful Delia, just one dance before I march to Virginia to defend you. One dance."

She sighed and glanced down at the hand he'd rested, palm up, on the arm of her chair. A refusal was on the tip of her tongue, but then she looked into his face. And sighed again. Much as she dreaded the thought of his company, it wouldn't hurt her to grant him one dance before he marched to what could be his death. "One—and only one. And don't think it's out of anything but pity."

When she set her fingers lightly upon his, he gripped them and pulled her up. His grin made her regret her decision in a heartbeat. Wolfish, that's what it was. Positively wolfish. And she'd never felt more the lamb.

But she couldn't pull away now—he'd already swung her into the group of other dancers, just as Mama transitioned from the reel she'd been playing to . . . a waltz?

"No." Much as she didn't want to make a spectacle, she couldn't give him a waltz. "Not this one. The next song."

His hand clamped onto her waist, the other holding hers far too tightly. With the sparks shooting from his eyes, she half expected the room to be set ablaze. "He isn't here to claim it, now, is he? Of course not. He isn't good enough for you, and your parents are smart enough to recognize it. He'd rather be rubbing elbows with the slaves anyway. Rumor has it he's even had a hand in helping a few runaways—which we both know means he'll end up swinging from a noose soon enough."

The dizziness that swamped her wasn't because he spun her too quickly into the dance. "What?"

He sneered. "That's right. He's knotting his own rope at this point."

She couldn't breathe. Couldn't think. Phin, helping runaways—was that true, or just what Julius would consider a nasty rumor? Was Phin in danger?

She squeezed her eyes shut. Or was he her hope of salvation for Salina? For Moses and Fiona? For Fanny? For any or all of them willing to risk the run to the islands?

Having her eyes closed made the dizziness worse, but at least it bought her a moment to try to sort it all out in her mind. She'd known Phin was different—loved that he was different. But she hadn't imagined he'd risk his own life. Was he though?

Julius pulled her to an abrupt halt and took hold of her chin.

Her eyes flew open and took in the hall that would lead to the library and Daddy's office. How in the world had he maneuvered her out here? Why'd she gone and closed her eyes like that? Had she been paying attention, she would still be in the safety of the group. Not alone with the wolf.

When she tried to pull away, his fingers tightened around her jaw. "Is that really what you're looking for in a husband, Delia? A man who can't defend what's his—a cripple? A man who prefers the company of blacks to his own kind?"

"Yes." The tears blurring her vision shamed her, but he was hurting her chin, and her wrist, too, where he still held it. "Let me *go*."

He leaned down, his tobacco-scented breath making her skin crawl. "I've been patient. I walked away when you refused me at Christmas. But we're out of time. Your parents and I have agreed. We'll marry tonight, Delie-Darlin. A quiet affair. Then you can take your mama home to Fulton County. She can see her sisters again, her brother, her cousins. Don't you want to do that for her? Make sure she's safe?"

She was already shaking her head, though obviously not in answer to the question. "Not like that. I won't, Julius. I will *not* marry you, not ever."

"Of course you will." His smile wasn't just confident—it was hard. "If you don't, your father said he'd send that pretty little maid of yours to Ginny."

"He wouldn't." Would he? Her blood ran cold. Lacy had probably told Ginny by now that Daddy was Salina's father. What if she reacted like Lacy had? What if she, like Mama, thought the best solution to the embarrassment would be to sell her? Be rid of her forever?

No. She couldn't let that happen. Couldn't let her best friend, her sister, endure such shame—and likely worse.

But would Daddy really ask *this* of her? That she sacrifice herself, the rest of her life? All for his dreams of a Southern empire?

Fury swept over her, fast and hot and fueled by a pain so dark it blinded her. Fury with Daddy. Fury with Mama. Fury with the state of Georgia and its impossible laws. Fury with this arrogant man before her.

She tried to jerk her chin free, but when he only tightened his grip, her vision went hazy with rage. She gathered her skirt in her free hand, pulled back her hoop. And then kicked him square in the shin so hard it sent a tremor all the way up her leg.

He released her with a string of curses, and she quickly backed away. When he sneered over at her, the mask of gentility slipped off, revealing a face that seemed mottled with hatred. "You'll pay for that, you little she-demon."

"Come a step nearer and I'll scream to high heaven." Would

it even matter though? Would Daddy care that Julius had just proven right her every fear about him—or would he blame *her*?

She wasn't about to find out. Instead, she gathered her skirts, spun around, and flew away.

Salina hummed along with the music drifting all through the house as she ran the cloth over the pane of glass, reached high as she could to get all the way to the corner. Heaven knew if she missed a spot, the missus would find it. Would come in here after the guests left looking for a fault to find, though she rarely stepped foot in the library otherwise.

And shorthanded as they were right now—as every grand house in Savannah was—there was plenty of work for Salina to do imperfectly. Plenty of chances for the missus to screech at her for not excelling at what she'd never been called upon to do before. Especially today, when the other staff were busy tending all those officers and ladies.

But why dwell on that? She hummed a little louder, reached a little higher. Until she heard a deeper hum join hers, match it point for point. Coming from outside somewhere. After glancing over her shoulder to make sure everyone was still in the drawing room, she raised the window to better look out it.

Didn't see no one though. Not in the garden, not near the stable.

The hum came again. From directly below her. She leaned into the windowsill and looked down so she could smile into River's face. "What you doin out here, River? Idlin?"

"Enjoyin it whilst I kin, yes'm." He grinned at her, but it wasn't just light in his eyes. It was side by side with something graver. "Yo even pretty upside down, Salina girl."

He lit something inside her, sure enough. She'd tried denying it, tried telling herself it was nothing but friendship, but the more hours he'd spent here, accompanying Miss Sassy, the more the truth had welled inside her like floodwaters. This man was more than a handsome face, never kept a string of girls, and looked at no one else like he looked at her. This man was something special, and every time she smiled at him, she felt the sunshine all the way to her toes. "Ah, get on with you."

He pushed himself up and turned around, but didn't stand. No, just found himself a seat on an upturned flowerpot positioned just under her window. Felt strange, looking down on him like that. Course, when he smiled at her in that way of his, all understanding and affection, she plumb forgot to notice.

Took all the restraint she had in her not to reach right out that window and rest her palm on his cheek. "Why you look at me like that, River?"

"B'cause I love you." He said it so simply, so sure. Without so much as a nervous blink or shuffle of his toe.

She, on the other hand, felt the force of it so hard it sent her upward—right into the window above her. Clamping her eyes shut against the agony of embarrassment and her lips against the cry of pain, she would have retreated into the house to go cry over ruining such a moment had strong hands not framed her face. Probed her head. And pulled her right back down where she was.

"You a'ight, honey?"

His tone soothed like the scent of roses, wrapping around her just like his arm had last fall, on the street that day. She opened her eyes and found his face close, stamped with concern. Least she could do was dig up a smile for him. "You oughta warn a girl before you go sayin that."

"Now, you kin't tell me you didn't know how I felt." His thumb stroked over her cheek, so soft and gentle she just wanted to curl up like a kitten and purr. "And it ain't like I 'spect you to say nothin back. I knows I ain't good nuff fo you, you havin Owens blood."

As if that did anything but lower her. "It ain't that, River, ain't a matter of goodness."

"Is in yo pa's eyes, I reckon."

She would have straightened again, had she not learned her lesson. And had his light touch not anchored her in place. "He ain't my pa. He's my massuh, and he's my father. But not my *pa*."

River searched her gaze, held it until she heard herself as he must have. She was about to apologize, assure him she wasn't as bitter as she sounded, but he hushed her before she ever spoke by brushing his thumb over her lips. "I sho wish I could give you a family, Sal. Let my pa be yo pa, my murruh yo murruh. Wish I could hold you close eb'ry night and raise up a couple babies wif you."

The ache that thudded in her chest at his words, at the sincerity in his gray eyes, was unlike any she'd ever felt. "I wish you could too." She'd tried so hard not to dream it. Not to want it. But the moment he put the words to it, she knew how fully she'd failed. She'd never wanted nothing much as she wanted this. Not just him, but a *life* with him.

He sat back down on his flowerpot, grasped her hands. "You do? I ain't no Big Tom—"

"Hush up, River. I don't want Big Tom and never did, so don't even think about him." Big Tom might have been handsome enough to turn her to corn mush, but she'd always known that wasn't enough. He'd never made her wonder what she had to lose by disobeying Mass Owens's commands.

And really, what *did* she have to lose? Wasn't like she had Mass Owens's respect nohow, nor his love. Wasn't like she could lose it if she followed her heart instead of his instruction. "Maybe . . . maybe someday. Eventually Miss Delia will convince her daddy to let her marry Mr. Phin. And then . . . ain't like he'll have no say then. Won't be nothing he can do. And Miss Delia would be happy for me."

But River just pressed his lips together, pressed their palms together, and stared deep into her eyes. *Not* saying something he obviously should be. Something that made her drag in a quick breath. "What?"

His larynx bobbed. "I kin't stay here no longer, Salina." The whisper was so faint she scarcely heard, had to lean halfway out the window.

And then nearly tumbled out the rest of the way when the words pulled her down like a stone. "*What?* You runnin?"

"Got to. Mr. Phin tell me to—it's that or dig. So . . . I goin to Tybee. Wif my family, and whoever else has flown thataway. To teach em to read, me and Monty. And I mean to make sure the plantation don't git run over by the Yankees too." He squeezed her hands. "Come wif me."

She sagged against the windowsill, wishing she had a chair, or even a handy pot like River's. "I can't. I can't leave Miss Delia."

His fingers tightened on hers. "She wouldn't begrudge it, would she?"

Begrudge it? She nearly laughed. Delia had been whispering of little else in recent weeks. But that was the thing. Delia always saw the world in terms of happily-ever-afters. Salina knew that wasn't likely. Not for people like her. It wasn't worth the risk of death or worse.

Or was it? Hadn't seemed like it, not until she stood here looking at River's earnest face.

Her eyes slid shut. "It ain't that. And she's already taught me readin."

"Did she? Then you could help. We gwine need all the help we can git." Now he wove their fingers together, which made hers feel small, delicate. Protected. "Sal. Honey. Think about it."

"Oh, you can be sure I'll do that." Getting away from here, away from the father who owned her and the mistress who hated her, fleeing with a man who made her whole soul take note, going somewhere she could belong, really belong, and be useful too . . . He painted a picture that called to her very being. "When you leavin?"

He went so still it made her breath catch. And when he answered, it was so quiet she barely heard. "Whenever my brother gits here. Could be tonight. Could be tomorra. Soon, either way."

"*Tonight?* And you didn't say nothin till *now*?" Panic seized her in two fists—she had to make a decision now, today. And whether she decided for or against, he'd be going. She'd have to say good-bye either to him or to Delia. The thought was enough to rip her right in two.

"Got to—but you could come later. Rock, he be makin reg'lar runs here. Eb'ry week."

She reached out the window, fisted her hand in his shirt, and pulled him up. Pressed her lips to his until she thought she might cry if she didn't let go.

He kissed her again and again. Once more. Then fell back onto the flowerpot with a little groan. "Say you marry me, honey. Someday."

She'd have suggested they sneak out tonight, if he weren't leaving. But that was no doubt a bad idea. She didn't want to end up like Vangie, with a fatherless babe—not when she knew well it would result in Mass Owens sending her far away, where she couldn't disappoint him. No, if she were going to marry River, it would be when she was with him. "Someday." Movement to the left caught her eye, and she strained to see who or what it was.

Mr. Julius strode through the garden toward the house, his face full of thunder and fire. No way he would have heard their low whispers, but still. When he turned her direction, her blood ran cold. He had a look about him, like trouble just searching for a place to roost. "You best get on now, honey, before that lion comes prowlin this way."

"You keep callin me honey, and I go anywhere you want." He stole another kiss, quick but full of promise, as the sound of a slamming door reached them.

"Go, go, go." Not waiting to see where he'd choose to take himself, she pulled her head back inside and lowered the window. Halfway, anyway—spring's sweet breeze would be welcome in this little-used parlor.

Another door slammed, this one close. Too close. She spun around in time to see Mr. Julius lowering his arm. His eyes blazed hot, with a million uglies roiling about inside them.

Fly away!

The lyrics struck her full-on, sent her stumbling and tripping. To her right, away from that devil and whatever evil he intended. He advanced, as she'd known he would—what with everyone at that gathering, this part of the house was empty. And if he was leaving soon, he'd have nothing to lose. But she couldn't let those thoughts slow her. Couldn't look over her shoulder.

No use trying to get around him, he'd likely catch her. Her best hope, her only hope, was the door hidden in the paneling by the sofa. She scurried that way, shoved at the piece of molding that would let loose the catch, then at the door itself.

A hand grabbed her by the turban, pulling on the hair underneath it. A scream ripped from her throat, her limbs flailed out. When her foot caught his leg, he grunted, cursed, and let go just enough for her to lunge into the dark passage.

She screamed again when fingers closed around her ankle, pulled her down. "Get off me!"

"I don't think so, sweetheart." His voice sounded like the rattle of a snake in her ears. "I'll have a taste of *you*, at least, before I go."

The passage was so narrow she couldn't fall far, just into the wall. If she could just shake him enough to get up and run, he'd get lost soon enough. She could come out in another part of the house and he'd never—

His hand slid from ankle to calf. "Go ahead and scream. No one'll hear you over the music. No one else is close enough."

She kicked, praying she'd find his head or something equally vital, not even knowing what words came from her lips. Cries, pleas, prayers, she didn't know. Didn't care. Just had to get away, get away. Take wing and fly. Fly somewhere else, somewhere safe.

He tugged on her leg, making her slip, grapple for a hold to keep herself upright. Her fingers caught on a hole.

The latch, the latch for Mass Owens's study, right beside the little parlor. She flipped it, pushed the door open. Toppled out of the darkness and into the room, whimpering now when her knees struck the wood floor.

She could feel him just behind her, knew he was close, getting closer. One hand braced on the floor, she tried to get to her feet, but he caught hold of the back of her dress and gave her a push. Try as she might to catch herself, she headed downward, and her forehead bounced off . . . a shiny black boot.

The click of a rifle cocking sounded like cannon fire in the room.

Those terrible hands let her go, and Salina wasted no time in pulling away, turning, standing.

Beside her father. Who had that rifle usually mounted behind his desk aimed square at Mr. Julius's chest, and a look of such rage on his face that it was a wonder the whole Union army didn't feel it and run on home.

He said nothing, just held his place and steamed.

Mr. Julius edged back a step, hands up, but apparently the way Mass Owens repositioned the gun made him rethink trying to get away. No, he instead tried for a smile, though the confidence of it wavered in the corners. "Sir, it's not—she threw herself at me. I should have walked away, I know, but I'm only a man."

Mass Owens narrowed his eyes. And his trigger finger twitched. "Do you think I'm deaf, Julius? Didn't hear her screaming?"

Salina inched closer to her father. "He attacked me, sir. I didn't do nothing—anything to invite it. I didn't."

The devil swallowed. Hard. "She's ashamed at getting caught, that's all. It was a game, sir. Just a—a—"

Her father stepped forward and jammed the barrel of the gun into his chest. "Are you calling my daughter a liar?"

His daughter. He'd just called her his daughter to someone else, to another gentleman. Claimed her, if only to save her.

"Your . . . ?" Yet Mr. Julius's gaze, after flicking between them, lost most of its fear. "You understand, then, Owens."

"Understand?" His voice was low, vibrating with fury. "I never forced myself on a servant. Not my own, and *certainly* not someone else's."

And Salina's heart sank back down into the pit of her stomach. Daughter in one breath, servant in the next. As she would always be. Thinking that just because Murruh hadn't screamed and fought—hadn't dared—that she welcomed his touch.

"I . . . I'm sorry, sir." Mr. Julius drew in a breath and pasted on that terrible excuse for a smile again. "I was out of my head after Delia rejected me again. That's all. Not thinking."

Though Mass Owens lowered the weapon, there was nothing forgiving about his manner as he did. And so it was no great surprise when he grabbed Mr. Julius by the collar and gave him a jerk away from the servant's door, then a mighty shove toward the exit of his study. "She was right about you. She tried to tell me, but I wouldn't listen. You best get out of my house, Lieutenant."

Mr. Julius regained his footing in the doorway, squared his shoulders, and sent a challenging look at him. "I'm the only hope you've got for all your plans. You dismiss me and you might as well kiss them all good-bye."

Salina glanced at her father, who gripped his gun so tight his knuckles were white, to match his face. "Get. Out." The breath he drew in seemed half a gasp. "*Now*."

"You know where to find me when you change your mind." With one last haughty adjustment to his sleeves, Mr. Julius turned on his heel. And plowed straight into a dark fist.

Salina squealed, then covered her mouth with her hands. "River, no!" Didn't he know what a fool thing that was? That devil-man could . . . would . . .

Mass Owens jumped forward, caught Mr. Julius with his arm pulled back. "You had it coming, Julius, and if you dare make trouble with him for it, I'll claim *I* did it. Just get on, now. Get out of here."

He left, spewing a string of vile words after him. But still, Salina couldn't force a swallow, not with the way her father then let his gun clatter to a rest against the wall. Not with the way his eyes went all unfocused and his hand clutched at his chest.

The panic just wouldn't let go. "Mass Owens?"

He didn't say a word. Just dropped to his knees, hand still clawing at his chest.

The scream tore up her throat again even as she fell to her knees beside him. "Help! Help! Someone *help*!"

Chapter Twenty-Three

Phin pulled up on the reins as they neared the parade grounds and looked over the sea of "able-bodied men" who had been called upon to come hear a speech given by a Georgian colonel. There had to be at least a thousand men there, maybe closer to two.

Phin shifted in his saddle and let out a sigh. It was a recruitment speech, nothing more. And according to his doctor, Phin wasn't able-bodied. But the men who had come to his door that morning and demanded his presence had no interest in his medical discharge papers. It was mandatory and enforced by men with guns and a look in their eyes that said they were spoiling for a fight.

So here he was.

"And so," the colonel bellowed from his place on the stage, "those who join up now, of their own will, before the draft is instituted next month, will receive a fifty-dollar bounty and a sixty-day furlough. These incentives await you men of conviction and courage, and I invite you now to walk three paces to the front and line up here." He indicated the space between the stage and the start of the crowd and stepped back with a smile, gaze roaming the crowd.

Not a single man pushed his way forward. Silence hung heavy as a curtain.

Beside him, Luther muttered, "Awkward."

"Shh." Phin shot him an amused glance.

The colonel stepped forward again. "Come now, fine sirs, don't be shy! Who has a hankering for that fifty dollars?"

Movement on the fringe caught Phin's eye, and the officer's too. A group of Irishmen made their way to the front, to the enthusiastic cheering of the crowd. The colonel jumped off the platform to exchange a word with them, then hushed the crowd. "These forty brave men step up as a new company, the Mitchell Guards. Now, who else will join them in service today?"

At the renewed silence of the gathered throng, Phin shook his head and leaned toward Luther. "I have a feeling we're going to be here awhile."

Luther returned the shushing and looked over to the edges of the crowd, where other uniformed men stood with weapons at their sides. Their message was clear—no one was leaving, not until the colonel had his men.

Slowly, a few volunteers trickled forward. One here, another there, until fifty or so stood beside the Irishmen. But it took an hour. A far cry from the response the colonel no doubt wanted, and even from the rear of the crowd, Phin could detect his frustration.

Did none feel the stirring within them? The desire to defend what was theirs? Or was it just that they didn't want to defend what was Virginia's? He shook his head. The eager ones had already enlisted, were already dying of disease in the trenches or marching north to meet the Yankees head-on. Those remaining in the city were either too incapable, too vital, or too cowardly to join them.

Loathing closed off his throat. These long months, he hadn't been forcing his recovery so he could rejoin. Wasn't sure he wanted to. But as he looked out over the familiar buildings of his town, he didn't want to be one of these men either. Maybe he didn't believe in everything the Confederacy stood for, but he sure believed in defending his home and the people he loved.

He believed in honor, even if too many didn't.

He believed in the right to fix what was broken himself, not let some politician in Washington do it for him, without the first clue how to do it *right*.

The colonel pointed directly at him and shouted, "You there, on the painted horse, with the giant Negro beside him. Won't you fight for your country?"

His pulse didn't even pick up. When he nudged his mount forward, the crowds made enough room to let him through, creating a path to the stage. Phin followed it until he emerged into that too-open area before the platform.

The colonel's gaze fell to the cane strapped to his saddle, then to the folded paper Phin held out. He took it, read it, and his features softened. "You, at least, have already fought. Georgia thanks you for your service, son, and for your injury on her behalf. You may return to your home."

"Thank you, Colonel." He took his exemption and half turned, but then looked back at the man. "It was an honor to serve. Will be an honor to serve again when I can, where I can." Just not blindly. Not for glory. For Georgia, for Savannah. For Mother and Sassy and Delia. Because they were worth fighting for, fighting for the right to live in whatever world emerged from this war-torn one.

He was halfway back through the crowd when the colonel called out, "Let's try it this way. Anyone with valid exemptions, step forward and show them."

Never in his life had he heard a roar of voices quite like the one that followed, or seen a crowd of people surge like an angry sea. His horse nickered, sidestepped, and it was all Phin could do to keep the animal under control. When he finally made his way through the roiling mob, his leg ached anew from clenching his mount so tightly. He found Luther just beyond the soldiers, looking at him anxiously.

Phin breathed a sigh and motioned toward the empty streets. "We'd best get out of here."

"Gladly."

They were silent so long as they could hear the crowd, but once back into the quiet of the all-but-abandoned neighborhoods, Luther looked over at him. "He made you think."

Phin rubbed at his leg. "What does the Lord expect of me? I could ride that note of exemption through the war. The doc already said he deemed me a lost cause and didn't want to see me again. But I'm getting better every day. Stronger. I may not always be crippled."

Luther darted a glance over his shoulder, his expression one of concern. "You want to join those men?"

"Those men? No." He curled his hand against his thigh, directly over the mottled, ugly scar. "The thought of marching to Virginia makes me realize I'm not quite as healed as all that. But they're leaving Savannah wide open. The Yankees could come from the coast, destroy it all."

"Phineas." Luther shook his head, then shook it again. Thinking, no doubt, of the skiff secured even now in the marshes, loaded with the supplies they had spent weeks gathering to take out to Tybee Island tonight. "You're a study in contradictions."

"No, I'm just the first to admit Georgia has its problems. Things that need to be changed. But the politicians in Washington aren't the ones to do it, Luth, they don't understand us well enough. *We* have to do it. Ourselves."

Luther just pressed his lips together.

Phin sighed. "Don't make the mistake of thinking the Yankees are any fairer toward your people than Southerners are. They might oppose slavery, but they don't consider you equals. Most abolitionists seem eager to ship all the black people back to Africa whether they want to go or not. No, this war is about money—money and the power it grants you."

At that, Luther sighed. "Isn't everything, at the root of it? But saying it's only about that is ignoring a very critical part—the freedom your people claim to value but deny to those who don't look like them."

"I won't deny the issue of slavery is key to this war. It's just not the *only* issue." They reached the corner, and Phin paused. His hands wanted him to pull the reins to the right, to head to Delia. Just to be with her, to hear one of her stories, to steal a minute with her in his arms. He missed her so much he could taste the longing on his tongue. "How have you survived it, Luth? Being separated from Eva so long?"

His friend drew in a long, thoughtful breath. "Prayer. Hour by hour, day by day. It's been almost a year, Phineas. A year without my wife."

His horse pranced a bit, but Phin held him still at the intersection. "But you're sure about this? About going?"

There was no hesitation, just a nod. They'd already talked it out at length, had prayed about it together. Phin had sworn to keep looking and would keep an eye out for the return of the man who'd brought her here. They'd hope she made her way to Tybee on her own, that the Lord would whisper it in her ear and provide a means to escape. And in the meantime, Luther could be doing good. Ministering, again, to those to whom he'd been called to minister.

He was just about to urge his horse toward home when a commotion drew his attention toward the Owenses' street instead. He frowned when several carriages clattered his way, their own among them. Before he was even aware he'd given the command, he'd nudged his mount toward the open phaeton. River was driving, and his face looked odd—taut, strained, pained.

Had Salina turned him down, then?

But no—Sassy looked every bit as upset. He drew up alongside them. "What's wrong?"

"Oh, Phin! It's terrible." Sassy leaned toward the side of the carriage, revealing red-rimmed eyes. "It's Mr. Owens—his heart, they think. He collapsed and is unconscious. The doctor is on his way, but we all had to leave, of course. Delia is an utter wreck."

"What?" His own heart thudded in sympathy. Much as he didn't like Owens, he'd never wish him any harm. And poor Delia. She'd always adored her father, and the recent strain between them was sure to make this all the harder.

He had to go to her. They'd probably bar him from the house, but that didn't matter. He'd find a way. Some way to give comfort. Without another word to his sister, he spurred his horse onward.

Other carriages and horses were still leaving the house, providing just enough chaos that he could slip into the stable without anyone noticing him. He led his horse into a stall and then stood at the entrance for a moment, strategizing. Did he dare go right up to the front door? Old Moses probably had orders not to let him in. He could no doubt sneak around to the back—but then what? Steal inside? Just hope Delia noticed him and no one else did?

"Have you a plan, Phineas, or are you simply going to climb the lattice and pretend you're Romeo?"

He jumped a bit at Luther's voice, quiet as a prayer behind him. He hadn't given any thought to whether his friend would follow. "I'm thinking."

"If I may make a recommendation—don't think too long. Moses saw you come in here. If he means to bar your entry, he'll send someone out here soon."

Phin dragged in a breath and nodded. If he'd already been discovered, there was no sense in being covert about it. He strode out of the stable.

And was met by Old Moses within a few steps. The lines

in the man's face looked deeper than usual, and the hand he raised in greeting had a tremor to it that wasn't usually there. "You hear already, Mr. Phin?"

"I just passed my sister." He looked to the house, as if he had a hope of seeing through the walls. "Has the doctor come yet?"

"Jest showed him in—he was only a coupla doors down, praise be to God. You wanna wait in the garden, I let Miss Delia know yo here. No sayin when she come out, but . . ."

He had no idea what he'd done to earn the help of the Owenses' servants, but he wasn't about to question it. "Thank you, Moses. I'll just settle in on Delia's favorite bench and pray for her father."

"I know she preciate it." The aging man led him toward the garden gate and opened it for him. But didn't step out of the way. Instead, he turned and met Phin's gaze with a serious one of his own. "Mr. Phin?"

He couldn't recall ever seeing that particular glint in the man's eyes. "Yes, Moses?"

"You watch yo back, now. That Julius devil—he leave jest befo Salina start screaming that the massuh need help, and he look mighty mad. If'n they had a fallin out . . . well, seems likely he blame *you*, if'n you know what I'm meanin."

"I do indeed." And his whole spirit went rigid at the thought. Today of all days, he didn't need Julius James's interference. Not when his two best friends were planning to run tonight or tomorrow, not when it all hinged on Rock making it safely to their rendezvous. "Thank you for the warning."

Moses said no more, just nodded and edged out of the way. Phin hurried past him. And then prepared to wait.

It was her fault. All her fault.

Cordelia gripped her father's hand, not even knowing how to pray right now. No words would come, just a silent sobbing toward heaven. He was alive—that was all they could say. He was alive for now. But he could slip away from them at any moment, and it was her fault.

She was the one who'd let her pain and frustration get the better of her. If she hadn't kicked Julius, he wouldn't have gone outside as he'd done. He wouldn't have seen Salina in the window. He wouldn't have come after her. Daddy wouldn't have had to save her. Salina's whispered explanation had included her *own* feelings of guilt, but she had it all wrong. She'd done nothing. It had all started with Cordelia.

But she hadn't missed the way Mama had looked at Salina, obviously catching at least a few of her tear-soaked words. *She* would blame her. And if the worst happened, if Daddy died, if Mama became the one making all the decisions . . .

She had to convince Salina to leave. Now. Tonight. If she didn't get away today, she might be sold by tomorrow.

A hand landed on her shoulder, and Cordelia started and looked upward. Dr. Wilkes stood at her side, his eyes kind. "He needs to rest now, Delia. You go on out for a while. Let your mama watch over him."

Mama sat in the chair on the other side of the bed, her face set in granite and her limbs unmoving. She didn't look in any better shape than Daddy did, truth be told. "Are you sure? I can stay. Watch over them both."

Dr. Wilkes's hand gave her shoulder a pat. "You're a good daughter. But right now rest is the best thing. You can check on him in an hour or two. All right?"

Numbly she nodded. Numbly she stood. Numbly she let him usher her out the door. But when it clicked shut behind her, the sound brought tears surging to her eyes.

What if he died? What if she lost her father and Mama sold Salina and they left Savannah forever? What if she had to live with this burden of guilt on her shoulders, this sure knowledge that she had brought her father to nothing? What if—

"Miss Delia." Fiona materialized beside her, though she couldn't have said where she came from. But she wrapped a firm, thin arm around her and steered her from the door. "What you need's a breath of fresh air, sweethaa't. G'on out to de garden a minute."

Though she shook her head, Delia had no real power to protest. Her feet just went wherever Fiona steered them. "I don't want to go outside. I should . . . I need to . . ." *What?* What did she need to do? Salina, she had to see to Salina. Had to convince her to leave. Had to say good-bye to her best friend, her sister.

But Fiona wasn't pushing her to Salina, and Delia couldn't seem to make her hands and feet obey her command to stop following. A minute later, the warm spring breeze was around her, the smell of magnolias so heavy on the air that it made her stomach turn. She meant to say something, swing back inside, but Fiona vanished and the door shut behind her.

She'd sit for a few minutes on her bench, gather her thoughts. Put words to her prayers. That was only wise anyway. Then she'd find Salina.

Her mind cleared a bit as sunshine and the spring breeze worked their magic. The burden didn't lift any, but a few of the cobwebs blew away. She turned the corner, her gaze going by rote to the bench—and she drew in a breath. "Phin!"

"Delia!" He was on his feet, surging toward her, and the next moment his arms were around her. "I'm so sorry, darlin. I met Sassy in the street, and she told me what happened. Moses let me wait back here. How is he?"

A simple question—if only she had a simple answer. She lifted her shoulders in a shrug and rested her cheek against his chest. "He's hanging on. But it's too soon to say anything more than that." She squeezed her eyes shut. "It's my fault, Phin."

"Nonsense."

"It *is*." She told him briefly of what had transpired that

morning—and by the way he went stiff, he saw her point. Perhaps he'd chide her for her role. She deserved it.

But when she braved a glance up at his face, he looked angrier than she expected. Then muttered, "That man—he can't march north fast enough. How can he claim to be a Southern gentleman when he treats a lady so?"

Her breath eased out. Had she been holding it?

Phin relaxed, met her gaze, cupped her face. "The fault isn't yours, darlin—it's *his*. He's the one who acted not only without honor, but with vile intent. You did nothing but defend yourself."

"Defending myself shouldn't mean harm to my best friend." It was the first time she'd dared admit her affection for Salina in the company of anyone else. But she had a feeling Phin would understand. She gripped his lapels. Dropped her voice to the softest of whispers, so it would be indistinguishable from the breeze to anyone more than six inches away. "She needs to get away from here, Phin. If Daddy . . . or even if he's just incapacitated for a while. Mama hates her so, I don't trust her not to sell her."

What was that emotion that flitted through his eyes? It was so unexpectedly bright she couldn't quite grasp it. But he nodded. "River was going to speak with her today. I don't know yet what she answered him, but . . ." He looked around the garden, no doubt for listening ears. "They're leaving as soon as River's brother makes it to the city. Heading to Tybee to help the runaways—teach them, provide some schooling. River and Luther are both going."

She frowned. "Who's Luther?"

For a moment, his face went blank—then he breathed a laugh. "All these months, and I misstep on his last day here. Thank God it was just with you. Monty, darlin. He's not really a slave I bought in Florida to help me get home—he's a freeman. From England."

As if conjured by the speaking of his real name, the mountain of a man slid into view, moving at a quick pace. For a split second, she feared he'd heard Phin's confession, was angry, and meant to have it out with him here and now.

But no. It wasn't anger on his face—it was excitement. Tinged with a strange shadow that looked like regret.

Phin's arms loosened around her, though he kept a hand on her waist. "What is it, Luth?"

Luther's step hitched a bit—no doubt at hearing his true name—but he recovered quickly. And actually *spoke*. "River just slipped back. Rock has arrived."

He spoke with a decidedly English accent, proving Phin's words true. Not that she'd doubted him, but still it made her lips part in surprise. "Were the two of you truly searching for his wife?" Or had that too been a fabrication?

The shadow went darker, regret deepening to pain. Luther's head sank. "Eva, yes. To no avail, I'm afraid. But I cannot tarry here longer or they'll force me to the trenches. I, too, shall go and trust that our Lord above will whisper to my sweet Evangelina to meet me on Tybee."

Evangelina? Cordelia's brows knit. Quite a name for a slave—and one that a master would no doubt change altogether or shorten. But Phin must have thought of that already. He'd no doubt not been searching for her only with her given name. And Eva, as Luther had first called her, was a far likelier nickname.

But not the only one. The moment he said *Evangelina*, she had a flash of a slave woman, sewing needle in hand, along with one of the tableaux costumes. Vangie. "When did she arrive here?"

"Nigh unto a year ago." Luther leaned against the trunk of the tree, looking overcome by that truth.

A year ago. Could it be? Probably not. How could Phin have missed that this long, if it were so? The Youngs were close acquaintances of the Dunns. They would have been among the first households he questioned.

But Mr. Young was also on a tear in recent months about protecting his workforce. Hadn't Annaleigh mentioned that he wouldn't even let the maids leave the house in recent months, lest they run away? Especially when . . . "Was she with child?"

She regretted the question, seeing the way it made the pain flare like a musket's charge over his face. "I cannot think so. In our decade of marriage, we have never been blessed so."

Unlikely—but not impossible. Wasn't the Bible, and history itself, filled with cases of the supposedly barren having a child when she least expected it? Still, she didn't dare blurt out her suspicions. Especially since the more she thought of it, the less sense it made that his Evangelina was the Youngs' Vangie. *She* certainly didn't speak with an English accent. "She, too, is English, I presume?"

But he shook his head, lighting the wick of hope in her again. "Not by birth, at any rate. She was born and raised on a plantation in Cuba. When she was a young woman, she bought her freedom and came to London."

So she was free—by law, not just through having run away. If that was true, and if it *was* Vangie . . . the Youngs could face serious trouble. Not only had they bought a slave illegally brought into the country, they'd bought a *freed* slave illegally brought into the country.

Phin tipped her chin up, his eyes alight. "What are you thinking?"

"I don't know yet." She could say nothing until she was sure, so she forced a trembling smile. "But I'll ask a few questions. In the meantime—Salina."

Phin nodded, face as serious as a Yankee invasion. "Send her to my house after dark. River can lead her to the skiff."

River. Her friend would at least have him. Cordelia hadn't missed the way her eyes lit up every time she mentioned him.

And from what she'd seen, his heart was hers as well. "They'll be together, then. I'm glad of that."

A smile broke through the fortress of Phin's sobriety. "And if they decide to get married, the good reverend here can help."

Reverend? She shot another look at Luther, who tipped an invisible hat. "The Reverend Mr. Luther Bromley of Stoke Newington, miss. At your service."

Reverend. She turned up her lips, though it didn't feel like a smile. "Good to meet you, sir. Might I impose upon you for prayers for my father?"

His smile faded too. "Of course, Miss Owens."

Phin's fingers stroked her jawline and then slipped down to tangle with hers. "I wish . . . I wish *we* could run off too. But I can't ask it of you. Not now."

"No." She squeezed her eyes shut, the fear rushing her again. "I can't leave him."

"I know. But someday, Delie-Darlin—someday, would you do me the honor of being my wife?"

He didn't drop to a knee. He had no lovely jewelry. The world was far from a place of orange blossoms and sunshine and rainbows right now. But somehow, the words still sounded sweeter to her ears than the most poetic of proposals possibly could have. Throat too tight to speak, she nodded. Swallowed. Squeezed his fingers till he probably wanted to shake her free. "Will you wait for me?" she whispered.

His smile said he remembered when he'd asked *her* that question, nearly a year ago. And he remembered his line. "Forever. And then some—however long it takes, Cordelia. There is no woman in the world for me but you."

The sound of a door opening invaded the joy of the moment, and Moses's voice snuck into the garden. "Miss Delia? Yo mama want you."

She didn't know when Phin might come back, so she wasn't about to let him leave without a kiss. As Luther turned back toward the garden gate, she stretched up on her toes and pressed her lips to Phin's.

A gentle embrace. But the promise was there. *Forever*. When she broke away, tears were stinging her eyes again. "I'll make sure Salina comes tonight. After dark."

And if that suspicion in her mind was God-sent and not her own wishful thinking, she'd be sending Vangie there with her.

Chapter Twenty-Four

The night was dark as tar, cool and damp and quiet enough to stretch Salina's nerves taut. She cast a glance over her shoulder to where Vangie—Eva—followed a step behind, her tiny baby nestled against her chest, secured with a length of cloth. Prayed, for the millionth time, that the little one would stay so content all the night long.

Not much farther now. She didn't dare speak, but with every footfall, the words thrummed through her mind. *We'll take wing and fly away.*

Hoofbeats reached her ears, and Salina darted behind a hedge, pulled Eva with her. But it must have been a street over. She gave it a moment, just to be sure, and to let her pulse hammer back down to normal. Then she touched Eva's arm to signal her to follow once more.

Dunn House was just there, she knew, where that single light shone in the window. Somehow, seeing it didn't bring the rush of relief she'd expected. Rather, it lit up a big ol' fire of second-guessing. Was she doing the right thing, leaving? Miss Delia had been so insistent that Salina had found herself carried away with the plan. But while it might save her own skin, given the dark looks the missus had sent her that afternoon, what about her sister?

She'd snuck out like Miss Delia had asked her to do, over to the Youngs'. Half hoping, half fearing that by the time she got back, the plan would have been abandoned. But when Salina had returned and whispered that Vangie had greeted her questions with wonder and affirmation, Miss Delia had been more determined even than before. There hadn't been no talking her out of it, no reasoning with her. And Salina knew she didn't really want to reason her out of it, either. There'd been something in her sister's eyes that resonated all the way down to Salina's soul. Something that said this was a step they both had to take. To be the women they both needed to become.

She crept now up to the back entrance of the Dunns', where the gate had been left unlatched. It swung open without a creak, and she and Eva slipped through quietly. No one had bothered to tell her where they were supposed to go once here, but she headed for the kitchen, figuring that the most logical place to find the servants.

A lamp glowed within, illuminating a blessedly familiar figure standing beside the table.

Eva rested a hand on her arm. "You're sure, Salina? Sure my Luther's here?" Her voice quavered, strained. Like any moment she might burst out either in laughter or tears. "If the Youngs catch me sneakin off . . ."

"They won't. And he is." She patted the trembling hand and reached for the door.

The moment the knob turned, River's head jerked their way, his hand going to his waist. Salina saw the gun secured there and was quick to step into the light. "You shoot me, River, and you can forget marryin me."

"Salina." Worry gave way to a grin, and he all but jumped across the space between them to pull her into his arms. "Please tell me you didn't jest come to say bye."

"No." She stretched up on her toes so she could bury her face in his neck. "I'm comin with you."

He held her so tight she thought she might melt right into him, then pulled away just enough to kiss her so nice she thought she might melt right into a puddle instead. His hands cradled her face when he pulled away. "We'll marry soon as we get to the island. Monty can do it, he be a preacher, sho nuff."

"Monty!" She pulled away, spun to the door. Eva hovered in the threshold, a sweet smile on her face. Salina motioned her in. "We found Eva."

"You found—*Vangie*?" River's eyes widened, his mouth fell open. "You mean t'tell me all this time she was with Miss Annaleigh, and we never made the connection?"

"Miss Delia did." Salina's lips pulled up. "Maybe you shoulda asked her sooner. Where's Monty—Luther, I mean?"

River's gaze had gone to the half-concealed face of the baby, still so small. "He and Mr. Phin are out checkin on something in the gear we stowed away. Oh, he shoot right to the moon with happiness, sho nuff." Then he frowned. "It's gwine be a tricky trip out to Tybee though, with the leely chil'."

Eva slid into a chair and wrapped her arms round the babe. "She be a good baby, quiet as a church mouse. We won't be no trouble."

A breath of a laugh shook the arm he had around her. "Don't reckon it'd matter even if you was. Monty—Luther, whatever he gwine by now—sho ain't gwine anywheres without you, now yo here."

Salina let the knapsack on her shoulder slide to the floor and snuggled into River's side. Slid her eyes closed and just took a moment. Breathed it in. She was really here. At the side of the man she loved, soon to be his wife. Ready to leave Savannah, her sister, her father.

Her father, who might not even be alive come morning. Didn't seem right, leaving him lying there like that, and on account of her. But what was she supposed to do? Mrs. Owens wouldn't even let her in the room to see him.

But she could pray just as well for him on Tybee as here. And Miss Delia had promised to get word to her about him through Rock, next time he came to the city.

And at least she'd go knowing that he loved her enough to defend her against that devil man. It was something. Maybe not enough . . . but it would have to be.

River's lips pressed against the top of her head. "How's Mr. Owens?"

Her throat went dry. "Bad. But still breathin, when I left. Miss Delia's going to make sure he don't hear bout my leavin till he strong enough it don't hurt him none."

Assuming he recovered. But they wouldn't speak of anything else. He'd recover. And she'd make it safely to Tybee. Marry River. Have a good life.

It wasn't gonna be easy—she knew that. Plantation life was always hard and often fatal, and she wasn't none too sure they oughta be trusting the Yankees on the islands to be any better than a Southern master in general, and sure not better than the ones she knew. And if the Union beat a retreat, all the runaways would have to either run more or face their masters.

River obviously wouldn't mind that day, what with having Mr. Phin's blessing and help. And Miss Delia wouldn't never try to haul her back here. Even so, the future was a big ol cloud of uncertainty.

But at least she wouldn't be facing it alone.

"That should do it."

Luther tied the bag shut tightly and nodded at Phineas. "It should indeed. You've done all you can to be sure we're safe and successful. River and I will take it from here."

The young man shoved his hands into his pockets, his face shrouded in the night's shadows. "I know. And you'll be fine. River's brother will meet you at the skiff, and there's no better pilot to be found. He knows every marsh and waterway between here and Tybee."

"I'm well aware of that, Phineas."

"Right. Luther?"

"Hmm?"

Phineas sighed. "It's going to be awfully quiet around here without your silent sermonizing."

Luther chuckled and tossed his hat onto the wagon's bench. "And I suppose I'm glad I didn't let you die on that beach. I'll be praying for you and your Miss Owens."

"And if Eva doesn't find you first, I'll find her, I promise. And send her to you." Phineas made his way slowly toward the front of the wagon. "Once you're together, don't feel obligated to stay on Tybee if the opportunity arises for you to head back to England."

"As the Lord leads." But for now, he felt a solid peace about this new task. And couldn't shake the feeling that his Eva would come to him soon. He strode to his friend's side. "A thought came to me today. I think you can take a lesson from the nation of Israel."

He felt more than saw Phineas cross his arms over his chest. "Calling me stiff-necked?"

"Well . . ." Another chuckle tickled his throat. "No. Rather, in this: Sometimes they fell away. Sometimes they wouldn't listen to their prophets. Sometimes the Lord sent another nation to carry them off."

Phineas leaned against the wagon. "Do you think that's what this is? That this war is God giving my nation over to the Yankees?"

Luther shrugged. "I can't know if this fractured nation is truly an echo of Israel in that way, much as it may seem like it to my eyes. I can't know how the war will turn out." He drew in a long, slow breath, let it ease back out. "But I *do* know that when the enemy comes—even when the enemy is one's own brother—that the faithful are not blamed for defending their homes. It's a man's right and obligation to protect what's his. Even when what's his has problems that need to be taken up with the Almighty."

Silence held for a long moment, and then Phineas's hand landed on his arm. "Thank you."

Luther nodded. "We had better get inside, rebel. River will wonder what became of us."

They strode together through the night, the warm glow of lamplight from the kitchen drawing them toward the house. Though he frowned when he saw multiple silhouettes moving about within. Old Bess, perhaps?

As they drew near, one silhouette took on more details and was definitely a younger figure. One that wasn't just standing near River, but in his arms.

"Salina." Relief sounded in Phineas's tone. "Delia convinced Salina to come."

Luther expelled a sigh of gratitude, too, and followed him into the kitchen. Noted yet another figure seated at the table. Froze even as his heart galloped. In spite of the unfamiliar turban, in spite of the rough brown clothes, he'd know her anywhere. That fine column of her neck. The oh-so-beautiful slope of her shoulders. And when she turned her head, that perfectly chiseled jaw, and the face—the face that had fueled his dreams for a decade. "Eva?"

"Luther!" She flew from the chair, tears streaming even as her smile beamed.

"Eva! My precious Eva." He caught her by the waist, lifted her, spun her around, then nearly dropped her when a mew sounded from between them. Setting her down, he stared at the tiny creature secured to Eva's torso with a length of soft cotton. "Who's this?"

She laughed, wiped at her cheeks, and lifted the wee child from its home. "This is your daughter, Luther. I've been calling her Amada, after Grammy."

He held out his arms, a wave of awe washing over him when she slid the mite into them. So tiny. So beautiful, just like her mother. But he saw himself in her too—his nose, his lips, his chin. "Amada. It means *beloved*, doesn't it?"

Eva nodded and then rested her forehead against his chest. As she had done so many times—as she hadn't done in so very long. He had to close his eyes just to take it all in. His wife, in his arms again. With a child, their child. A beautiful little girl for whom he'd long ago given up hoping. "I feel I must be dreaming."

Her laughter soothed over him again like birdsong. "I've felt that way ever since Salina came this afternoon. When she told me you were here, had been here for months. Oh, how I've missed you, *corazoncito*." Her arms wrapped tight around him. "Did Grammy get better?"

"No, my love. I'm sorry. Dr. Santiago and I did all we could, but . . ."

"I knew it somehow. Felt it." Though sorrow deepened her eyes when she looked up, peace lit them too. "Just like I knew you'd come. Soon as you could."

He wanted to assure her he had tried right away. Tell her all about that first trip, being refused entry and sent back to Cuba. He wanted to tell her of Phineas washing ashore, of Santiago and Rosario, of the months of prayer and care. Of the trip here at last, the endless search.

And he would. Later. For now, he pressed a kiss to the impossibly soft skin of little Amada's forehead and held her out to Phineas, who was watching from River's side. "If you would hold my daughter for just a moment, Phin, I need to greet my wife properly."

"Oh. Ah . . ." Uncertain enough to earn chuckles from everyone, Phineas awkwardly took her in his arms.

Grinning, Luther turned back to Eva. She wore that knowing smile he so loved, the one that said she understood every thought winging through his head, understood and loved him for them. Then he pulled her close, and it was like life's puzzle clicked into place. His arms had been empty too long, but no more. "My darling Eva."

He bent down until he could touch his lips to hers. Only a light kiss, given the audience, but she would feel the love surging through it, making his arms shudder under her hands too. She would know. She would know all that lay behind it.

Just as he could tell from her every movement, from the tears that wetted her cheeks, how much she had to tell him. She would tell him of the pain, of the indignity. But of the Lord's continued protection through this last year. Of the hope that had held on inside her, the comfort she had taken from the child she hadn't expected to ever carry. She would tell him of the tears she shed upon realizing that their daughter would be born a slave.

And he would assure her she wasn't. Remind her that she had never legally been a slave here, circumstances notwithstanding. Promise that when the Lord released them from their new work and provided the way home, they would return to Stoke Newington and Amada would grow up breathing in that English air that made one free.

"My Luther," Eva whispered against his lips. "I have missed saying your name. But I did not dare, knowing you would have to come in secret. I should have known though—should have known those whispers about the mountain of a man called Monty were really you. I just could not fathom you'd come with a white man. Salina says we are going to Tybee Island?"

He nodded. "We're turning the Dunn plantation into a colony of refuge, a school. We can minister and teach there until a way home presents itself."

"Good. I would not want to sail all the way home yet, with the baby so small." Smiling, she reclaimed their wee one from Phineas and slid her back into the sling once more. No doubt she was most content there, with her mother's heart under her ear.

"Speaking of which, we had better go." River urged Salina toward the door, his gaze lingering on her as if unable to believe she was there.

A feeling Luther well understood. He couldn't convince himself to let go of Eva entirely either, so he wove their fingers together.

Phineas opened the door.

Delia closed the cover of the Bible she'd been reading aloud to Daddy, her eyes heavy and gritty. It was nearing midnight. Salina ought to have made it safely to the Dunns' by now. Perhaps they were even on their way to the river already. She said a silent prayer for their safety, her hand splayed over the warm leather binding of the Bible.

Mama had finally been convinced to sleep for a few hours. The servants were all ready to take a shift sitting with Daddy, but Cordelia had insisted on the first one. She'd felt a bit strange at first, here in his bedroom, where she'd so rarely been. But that had nothing on the strangeness of seeing her strong father looking so weak and pale.

A soft moan escaped him.

Cordelia slid the Bible on the nightstand and surged forward. "Do you need something, Daddy?"

His eyes fluttered open. "Delie-Darlin? That you?"

"Of course it is." She reached for his hand and held it between both of hers. "How are you feeling?"

He attempted a smile, though it bore little resemblance to a real one. "I'll be all right."

She hoped he was right. "You've given us all quite a scare. Dr. Wilkes was here most of the day."

His hum bespoke acknowledgment, if not remembrance.

Then his expression shifted. "I should have believed you. About Julius."

She pressed his palm between hers. "I wish I hadn't been right."

"I know." He shifted, winced. "Is Salina all right?"

Though she opened her mouth, Cordelia didn't know quite what to say. Salina hadn't been exactly *all right*. How could she be, after being attacked like she had? And then at being informed she had better hurry to the barrier islands if she wanted to avoid the auction block? "She . . . suffered no injury."

For the space of a few breaths, Daddy said nothing. Maybe he was too tired. Maybe she shouldn't be engaging him like this at all. She was about to offer him a drink to help him settle back down to sleep again when he said, "That boy of the Dunns' that rushed in . . ."

Salina had mentioned that part too. "River?"

He nodded. "You tell him he's not welcome here anymore, even with Sassy. Salina's too good for the likes of him."

"Daddy." The admonition slipped out before she could think better of it. And now that she'd already earned his scowl, she might as well earn it right and proper. "He's a good man."

"He's black."

She huffed out a frustrated breath. "Of course he is. What does that matter? And how can you make such an objection without hypocrisy? Wasn't Salina's mother black too?"

"That was different."

"You're right. It was." She let his hand drop to the mattress. "She wasn't ever given a choice. But Salina should be—she shouldn't be judged for *your* sins. And she certainly shouldn't be refused happiness because of your convoluted ideas about your precious blood making her better than her mother, better than River. Because let me just tell you, Daddy, your blood doesn't have that power. There's only one man's blood in all of history that can make us better than we are—and you are not Him."

At least it brought a bit of color to his cheeks. "Watch how you speak to me, young lady."

She breathed an incredulous laugh. "Daddy, I love you. I will obey you. I will honor you. But that means caring enough about you—heart, body, and soul—to tell you when I see something that could cause you harm. And this . . . this stance of yours will lose you Salina forever."

His eyes flashed, and he tried to sit up, only to relent when she squeaked and pressed a hand to his shoulder. Pallor washed over him again. "Does she mean to run? I won't have it. I won't—"

"Daddy, stop. Please." Tears stung for the millionth time since that morning. Why was she yet again pushing when she should give way? He was in no condition for this conversation. "You're going to give yourself another episode."

He made a visible effort to relax, though his breathing was too quick for her liking. "She can't run. It's too dangerous. Tell her to stay here, where I can protect her."

"But you can't." Her voice broke on the truth of it. She reached for his hand. "From Julius, maybe. But not from Mama. Not from the fate she'd dole out if anything happened to you."

She watched as it sank in, degree by degree. Until he closed his eyes in what could only be termed defeat. "Was it that close? Whatever this was?" He lifted an arm like it weighed a ton, let his hand fall on his chest, and opened his eyes again to look at her.

Cordelia could only nod, sure she'd break into a sob if she dared try to say more.

He let out a long, slow breath. "I only want the best for her."

That much she knew. "What if your judgment of what's best isn't right, Daddy?" *Like with Julius*, though she knew she didn't need to say that. Not now. He was already thinking it. "What if the best is freedom? A husband? A family? What if it's helping others? What if it's something bigger than us?"

The fingers she held again went stiff. He said nothing for so long that she feared he didn't mean to speak to her again, ever.

Long enough that she had time to wonder what Salina's story would end up being.

Long enough to know that her own story might never be more than this. Paying the price for her decisions concerning her sister. Too afraid for her father's health to speak against him when it was for herself instead of someone else. Her own dreams forever out of reach.

But they weren't. The old dreams, maybe—the ones she'd spun yarns about. But she didn't need to be a heroine in some fantastic tale of derring-do. That wasn't what the Lord had given her.

No, He'd given her words. Words to live by. Words to create with. Words that maybe, just maybe, could change the world beyond her house as surely as they had changed the one within.

She didn't need to live some grand tale. She only needed the freedom to write whatever God put on her heart. If helping Salina gain freedom meant forfeiting most of her own—so be it. If that was the price she had to pay to avoid being a villain in anyone else's story, then she would pay it most gladly.

When Daddy shifted, she jumped in surprise. He looked tired again, but his mouth had its familiar set of determination. He lifted a hand and motioned toward his bureau against the wall. "The bottom drawer. Right back corner. There's a small box. Would you?"

She stood and moved to the piece of furniture, though she cast a curious look at him over her shoulder. He said no more, just watched her. She crouched down and pulled open the bottom drawer, feeling around among his socks until the edges of the box met her fingers. She pulled it out, nudged the drawer shut again, and took it over to him.

He accepted it from her hands and opened it up. Stared at whatever was inside for a long, long moment. She couldn't see within, could only watch his face as emotions flitted over it.

Sorrow. Longing. Regret. He touched a finger to the insides of the box and then held it out to her, still open.

Too curious to do anything but take it, she felt her brows crease when she saw the locket nestled into the pillow of cotton. It was open to reveal a miniature of a beautiful woman with Salina's face shape, chin, brow. Her murruh, no question.

Daddy cleared his throat. "I always meant to give it to her. But I was afraid of what would happen if your mother found it, so I've kept it these many years. Figured I'd give it to her when you got married."

Cordelia drew in a breath, let it hitch, let it slide back out. She closed the locket's gold face over the tiny portrait within and then the lid of the box over it all.

"Give it to her now. Tell her . . . tell her I only ever tried to protect her, as I promised her mother I would."

Her heart pounded in her chest. Salina would be at the Dunns' already. Or perhaps even on her way to the river. Maybe if she hurried—maybe—she'd be able to get this parting gift into her hands before she began the journey. But . . .

A tap sounded on the door, and it creaked open, Fiona's familiar face peeking in. "I's ready for my shift, Miss Delia. You get on to bed now."

She had to have been listening at the door, to know that Cordelia needed help in making a quick escape. And she'd thank her profusely for it tomorrow. For now, she just leaned down, kissed Daddy's cheek, and said, "I'll get it to her."

Two minutes later, she was running through the streets, the box tucked into her pocket. She hurried toward the Dunns', glad she'd at least let Salina help her out of her big hoop and corset before she left, since she'd have had a time getting out of it all on her own. She'd changed into a low-profile dress she'd never dream of wearing out of the house, but it certainly made darting after her sister easier now.

She'd never been out at night alone before, certainly not on foot, but she didn't have time to let her imagination run wild. The moment it tried to start at a shadow, she clamped down on it and focused all her energy on breathing in, breathing out, and pumping her legs down the familiar streets of home.

She'd walked to the Dunns' before—in the daytime, of course. She knew the way, but even so, it was different. Without the sun to warm her, the air was far too cool for comfort, and she'd paused to grab no heavier wrap. She'd been wearing the lightweight shawl Phin had given her for Christmas, but that was all.

She hoped Salina and Vangie had something warmer. And the babe, especially. They'd need the little one to be so cozy and happy she'd stay quiet from the sheer comfort of it.

Something shifted in the shadows she was ignoring, something that made her heart pound faster and her breath turn jagged and frayed. They were *moving*, those shadows, as if they were themselves living creatures. Moving like a great writhing snake. Moving like a ferocious beast crouched behind the buildings, waiting to pounce.

Moving like four people ducking down to avoid notice.

Shaking hands clutching her shawl tight, she watched for a moment, holding otherwise entirely still in a cloaking shadow of her own.

Four figures darted across the intersection, heading away from her. Four figures that could be none other than Salina and River, Vangie and Luther. She didn't know whether to be glad or frustrated that they were so close yet she'd still missed the optimal time to catch them. She couldn't exactly shout for their attention. What choice, then, did she have but to follow them?

As she trailed them toward the park, she couldn't help but think that this was a foolish errand. Why put herself—and them, likely—at risk for a locket?

Because it was a locket that would remind Salina for the rest of her life that her father loved her. That she had a family.

And if she never saw her again, if life took them in different directions from here, if . . . if Daddy didn't recover, then that knowledge could make all the difference in her life.

What was that sound behind her? She looked over her shoulder but saw no more living shadows. Probably just a stray dog or cat. Certainly not a wolf or . . . or a cougar. Or any other wild thing set loose in the streets of Savannah by some mad scientist.

She nearly hissed at herself. *Lord, I seem to have an inability to control this imagination of mine. If you would be so kind as to help me, help me to focus . . . and not to lose them in this night.*

Another noise from behind made her spin around, and she had to clamp a hand over her mouth to keep from screaming when a shadow loomed, separating from the others around it.

"Delia!" the shadow whispered. "What in blazes are you doing out here?"

Phin? She didn't know whether to laugh in relief or slap him for scaring her. So she did neither, just turned back toward the park. "I have something for Salina."

Phin slid to her side, and she could feel the disapproval rolling off him in waves. "It had better be something mighty important, to take such a risk yourself instead of just sending it with Rock next time."

Rock—she hadn't even thought of that option. Even so, she wanted to give it to Salina herself. She swallowed. "It is."

"Well, let's hurry. We'll catch them and then I'll see you home."

Before she could so much as agree, a sudden flare of light from the park drew their gaze.

Light that illuminated the four fugitives in stark relief.

Light held in the hand of Julius James.

Chapter Twenty-Five

Phin charged toward the park as fast as he could, praying with every footfall that the Lord would somehow redeem this night. It had seemed, half an hour ago, that everything had been going smoothly. But within minutes of the foursome slipping out of the well-oiled gate, the strangest feeling had overtaken him. He'd just intended to watch them out of sight. Convince himself the feeling was baseless fear, not some warning from on high.

Then he'd seen a shadow following them through the intersection and had known he'd better investigate.

Delia was certainly no threat to them—but James was another matter altogether. And a danger Phin wouldn't have known was lurking if he hadn't hurried after Delia.

Lord, help. They were the only two words he could think of as he tried to hurry on a leg still too weak to match the pace he attempted to set for it. He had to slow, just to keep from falling. Which at least meant he was approaching more quietly. James didn't seem to have noticed him yet.

The lieutenant had his lantern raised and was laughing—*laughing*—at the stricken faces of Luther, River, Eva, and Salina. But he was also swaying a bit on his feet. And when he said, "Well, well, what've we here?" the slurring told Phin why.

Drunk. Which might make him easier to take down . . . but it could also make him unpredictable.

Phin knew River and Luther had both spotted him as he came up behind James. And from the flicking of Salina's eyes to something beyond him, he had a bad feeling Delia was closing in on the scene. The only good thing, so far as he could tell, was that James appeared to be alone, and no one else from the area was rushing to the park to see what the commotion was about.

The worst thing, by far, was the pistol James had in his hand and was pointing in the general direction of Phin's friends.

"Wonder what your masters would say if they knew a bunch of their slaves were making a run for it?" Another cold, oily laugh slid out, and the wobbling gun took a steadier aim—at Eva. "Bet I know what *yours* would say."

Luther stepped in front of his wife, thunder in his eyes. "She has no master but Christ the Lord."

No doubt James was unconvinced by the argument—but the words themselves, the accent, seemed to confuse him for a moment. Enough that he lowered the gun a few critical degrees.

It was all the opening Phin needed. He lunged for the man's central mass, yelling, "Run!" to his friends as he knocked James to the ground. Phin's leg screamed in more pain than he'd felt in months as he went down hard with him, but he'd gladly suffer in his leg if it saved their lives. He heard pounding feet, but he could spare no more thought to them than that, not given the way James writhed underneath him, growling and cursing.

The gun hadn't fired, at least, which meant they might still avoid the attention of others in the area. And though it came swinging at his head, Phin managed to land a blow on James's arm, sending the weapon sliding along the path.

In his mind's eye, he was back, for one horrible instant, on the deck of the *Cuba*. A Yankee captain aiming a gun at him, his best friend playing a part in their betrayal. In that moment, Julius's face blended with Spencer's, and all the uncertainty came crashing in on him like the waves that had tried to take his life.

He tried to land a punch, but James bucked, threw Phin off him, and lunged. The waves crashed again over his mind, dragging him, drowning him.

Saving him. He blinked furiously, but still his mind couldn't quite process it when James seemed to rise under a power not his own, floating there in the air above him. Only when the man gasped, "Put me *down*!" did Phin realize hands had grabbed him and were holding him, suspended, by the throat.

Luther. And River was even now tugging Phin back to his feet. He met his old friend's gaze as he tried to catch his breath. "I said to run."

Luther snorted. "Since when do I listen to you, Phineas Dunn?"

Phin's laugh came out shaky and low.

James, however, didn't seem to realize the fight was over. He was still thrashing. And he reached even now for something at his side. Only then did Phin catch the glint of a burnished hilt by the fallen lamplight.

Delia stepped into the weak circle of illumination, arms extended and steady, with James's pistol clutched expertly between her joined hands. "I wouldn't do that if I were you. *Cousin*."

Luther must have loosened his grip a bit, because James was able to snarl and say, "As if you know what to do with that."

She lifted one golden brow in perfect mockery. "Every good heroine knows how to shoot a pistol with shocking skill. Test me. I dare you."

Instead, Luther dropped him back to his feet so suddenly he stumbled, though River was there to steady him—and plow a fist into his jaw. As the lieutenant slumped to the ground, unconscious, River shook out his hand. "I was hopin to git another one a-dose in."

Phin slid over to Delia, who had lowered the gun, following Julius's motion with her own. "Do you really know how to shoot?"

"Are you kidding?" She handed the pistol to him, her bravado slipping into a shaky exhale. "I've never even held one before."

He took the weapon and leaned over to press a kiss to her temple. "Well, you certainly looked like you did. Quite the heroine."

She shook her head, gaze still on James's prone form. "I'm not a heroine, Phin. Just a writer ready to tell other people's stories."

"Suits me fine. I'm not much of a hero either." He sent a pointed look to River and Luther. "Now y'all had better get moving. I'll make sure this one stays where he is."

"Oh! Salina, wait." Delia rushed over to her, giving the fallen man a wide berth. She tugged something from the folds of her dress and handed it to her. "From Daddy."

Salina took it with furrowed brows. "He sent you after me to give me something?"

"He didn't know you were gone yet. But he realized you'd be going soon. It's a locket, with a miniature of your mother. He's had it, saved, to give to you. When it was safe for you to have it."

Salina pressed the box, still closed, to her chest. "A picture of Murruh? Really?"

Delia nodded, then pulled her sister into a hug. Phin couldn't hear exactly what she whispered, but Salina nodded as she pulled away. "I will. I promise." Then she looked to River.

Phin clasped his and Luther's hands one more time. And then stood with Delia as they melted into the night.

"Now what?" She frowned down at James. "What are we to do with him?"

He wasn't entirely certain. At least not until an off-key song met his ears, growing louder by the second. A group of men, as drunk as James had been, clearly heading their direction.

Phin nudged Delia toward the deeper shadows under a tree whose trunk was wide enough to hide her. "Stay out of sight. I have a plan."

When the men drew nearer, he saw they, too, had lanterns—and they, too, wore Confederate uniforms. *Thank you, Lord.* It gave him the perfect excuse to hail them, not needing to feign the exasperation in his voice when he called out.

A minute later, they stumbled their way to him. "Can we be of assississ . . . astina . . . assistance?" one of them slurred.

It may have been amusing under different circumstances. Phin motioned toward Julius James, who even then let out a snore. "I believe you can. This fellow needs help rejoining his regiment."

"Say, it's Lieutenant James!" another of them said, then laughed. "Told him he'd had enough."

"Indeed." Phin backed up a few steps, not trying to hide either the wince or the limp, more pronounced than usual, thanks to the scuffle. "May I leave him in your charge?"

One of them toed James's boot, looking like he might decline the invitation, but his buddy nudged him with an elbow. "We'd better. We'll all pay for it tomorrow on the march if he wakes up here."

"He may need this on the march as well." He held out the pistol. Much as he hated to return it to the cad, he also couldn't in good conscience send a soldier to the front lines unarmed. "I'm afraid I had to take it from him when he lunged at me."

They didn't ask any questions about what made him lunge. But there was ample rolling of eyes and muttering. One of the tipsy men took the pistol, and the other two hauled James to his feet. He didn't so much as open his eyes, though he mumbled something entirely incoherent.

Phin lifted a hand to them in farewell, calling out a final thanks. Only once they were well out of sight did he turn back to the tree and Delia. Time to see his adventurous miss home.

Salina had never stepped foot on a boat before tonight, and her fingers dug into the sides of this one with every sway and undulation. She didn't quite trust it not to spill her out into the water. And though she knew her aunt hadn't been right about spirits living down there, she also knew this journey was one of the most dangerous she'd ever make.

The dark held as Rock maneuvered out of the tricky waters of the river. And when they reached the open waters, the moon slipped out from behind a cloud and shone down on them in silvery splendor. Beside her, Eva hummed a nearly silent lullaby, her little one yawning but settling right back down after nursing.

Take wing and fly away. She'd never dreamed she'd do it someday. Not through the air, but over water anyway. Rock let loose the sails now that they were away from the shore, and the little craft picked up speed. Flying, flying across the water. Flying on home.

She clutched the box she still held, then opened it. The moonlight caressed the locket inside. Beautiful. She couldn't tell in the night if it was gold or silver, but either way it was the costliest thing she'd ever called her own. She slid a nail between the two halves, her breath catching as it popped open.

The moonlight was too faint to give her a good look at it. But it was enough. Enough to recognize Murruh's precious face. She stared at it for a long moment. Then closed the locket, lifted it, kissed it. A few quick movements and she had it fastened around her neck, under her dress. It was safer there than in a box she had to carry.

When she looked up again, River was sliding to her other side. He'd been rowing when they were in the mouth of the river, but Rock must not need him so much now. He greeted her with a smile. "Soon, sweethaa't. Soon we be home. My family'll be yo family."

Home. She let her eyes slide shut and turned her face into the breeze. Yes, she was flying away. Flying away to more than she ever dreamed would be hers.

Cordelia squeezed Mama's shoulder and followed Moses's beckoning hand out of Daddy's room. He seemed better today than he was yesterday. His color was a little pinker. His voice a little stronger. Though he was still as weak as a baby and sleeping more than he was awake. But that was to be expected forty-eight hours after a heart attack, the doctor had said.

Moses closed the door behind her, whispering, "Mr. Phin's here. I had to put him in the drawing room, what with the rain."

Her heart kicked up. "Thank you."

"Go on, then. Don't wait for my old legs."

She grinned at him and then accepted his dismissal and rushed down the central staircase. Would he have news? Of River and Salina? She'd been on pins and needles all day yesterday, waiting for *something*. For word to come that their slave had been caught. For Julius to barge in, despite the fact that he should have been marching north to Virginia. For Phin to come with news of the boat sinking or being fired upon.

But it had been a quiet day. The worst actual moment was when Mama had demanded to know where Salina was when she couldn't find her to assign some new drudgery. All the servants had met her questions with wide-eyed shrugs, until finally Fanny suggested that "mebbe she done lit out."

Cordelia had expected an explosion. Instead, Mama had simply lifted her chin and said, "Good riddance, then." No mention of hiring a slave hunter to find her. No questions to Cordelia or any of the servants. Certainly none to Daddy. It was as if she'd welcomed the opportunity to forget Salina even existed.

The drawing room door stood open, and Cordelia rushed

through it, her gaze searching out Phin's face the moment he came into view. *Please, don't let him look sad or anxious. Please, Lord.*

He smiled, and that knot of worry inside went loose. Her shoulders sagged. "They're all right?"

He nodded, glancing past her, probably to make sure her mother hadn't followed her. Then he held out a hand for her to take. "Rock made it back last night and left a note for me from River. They're safe, settled. And welcomed with gladness when they laid out their plan to educate the others on the island."

"Oh, praise the Lord."

"Amen to that. Now, how's your father? That was my official reason for coming."

Cordelia squeezed his fingers. "Improving. It'll be a long, slow process. But Dr. Wilkes is hopeful that since he made it through the first day and night, he'll recover."

"He can't help but get better with you and your mother nursing him." The gleam in his eyes could fuel a million dreams of him. Had. Would.

"Miss Delia? You got nother visitor," Old Moses said from the door. "Miss Annaleigh."

Cordelia sucked in a breath. Though Annaleigh had been here countless times over the years, she'd never come on her own. Never when there hadn't been an invitation for some little lunch or tea or picnic. Never when not expected. But maybe she, like Phin's official story, was here to inquire after Daddy. She nodded. "Show her in, of course, Moses. Thank you."

With one more squeeze of her fingers, Phin let her go and put a bit more space between them, just in time for Annaleigh to glide into the room. The mean glint in her eyes belied the dimpled smile on her face.

"Well, Phineas Dunn, I do declare. I *thought* that was your phaeton I saw, but then, I haven't seen you around here much of late." She came toward them, skirts swaying and hand outstretched.

Phin took it, bowed over it, but even Annaleigh must have noted how stiff he looked. "Were it up to me, I'd be here daily, I assure you."

Obviously not the response Annaleigh was hoping for. Her simpering smile faltered and then fell away altogether. She reclaimed her hand from Phin and spun on Cordelia. "Well. I don't mean to stay long, I'm sure you're all busy with your father. I merely wanted to ask if I might speak with that maid of yours for a moment. Sally, is it?"

"No, it's not." But her palms went damp. Why in the world would Annaleigh want to speak with Salina? "And she's indisposed right now. Is there something I can help you with?"

"Oh, I very much doubt it." She sashayed toward the window. "My own maid seems to have run off—with her infant daughter—and Daddy is fit to be tied, let me just tell you. He's been questioning the remaining slaves endlessly since Vangie turned up missing, and this morning someone admitted to seeing Salina come by the other day. That's all."

Got her name right that time, Cordelia couldn't help but notice. She folded her arms over her chest. "I sent her over, yes. To return that pattern I'd borrowed last month. We were all scrabbling for something to do, and I knew she'd appreciate the walk."

Annaleigh batted her eyes. "Oh, I didn't mean in the afternoon. I meant that *night*. Unless you sent her on another empty errand at ten o'clock? I do find that infinitely hard to believe."

Cordelia offered a bland smile. "Well, I am full of quirks, as you've pointed out yourself often enough."

For a moment, her uninvited guest just stood, clearly fuming. Then she took a step forward, her curls bobbing with the slashing motion of her hand. "I *knew* you'd make excuses for her! I knew it! But she's run off, too, hasn't she? They both did—

together. Well, we're not going to stand for it, even if you mean to. Daddy's looking for a good slave hunter even now, and we won't rest until that ungrateful wretch is dragged back here."

Though a hole opened up in the pit of Cordelia's stomach, Phin didn't seem to be disturbed. Looking utterly calm, he said, "I wouldn't recommend it, Miss Young."

She started, as if she'd forgotten he was even there. "I beg your pardon?"

Phin reached into his jacket and pulled out a packet of papers. "I was planning on stopping by to visit your father today after I left here. I've come across some very . . . unfortunate information regarding that woman he means to hunt down."

Annaleigh's eyes narrowed. "What sort of information?"

Cordelia leaned forward a bit, too, not sure if he meant to weave a true tale or a false one. Curious either way.

He motioned with the papers. "As everyone has known—and been gossiping about—for months, I'd been searching for my man Monty's wife. Turns out it was your Vangie all along. Which we'd have known a lot sooner if your father hadn't all but quarantined her when it came out she was expecting."

"I don't see what—"

"She was brought here illegally." He unfolded the papers and held them out. From her vantage point, Cordelia only caught a glimpse of a seal, but it looked official. "And I can prove it. Your father purchased her from a man who had just arrived from Cuba—where *he*, in turn, had just purchased her from a planter named Rosario. I'm sure you know that international trading of slaves has been strictly prohibited for many years."

Annaleigh's cheeks went red. "Well, it's hardly *our* fault if that man misrepresented where he purchased her!"

"The law might not see it that way. Though if you want me to take this to them and see . . ."

Cordelia had to bite her lips to keep from grinning. This was probably what he'd been doing yesterday—finding the paper trail to back up the truth, now that it was all pieced together.

Annaleigh huffed. "What they've been saying about you is true, Phineas Dunn. You really do care more for the slaves than you do your own kind! And you!" She spun again on Cordelia. "You . . . you're not even *pretty*! I hope you die an old maid!" With that, she pivoted and all but ran from the room.

"My. I am so very insulted." Cordelia shook her head, even as the ridiculous curse settled on her shoulders. Daddy's opinion of Phin hadn't changed any just because Julius had proven himself a monster. So, an old maid she could end up being. It easily could be years before she could convince him to relent. Especially now when he suspected she had helped Salina run away.

Before she could turn back to Phin, Mama's frowning figure filled the doorway. "Was that Annaleigh Young? I declare, I'd have thought you'd have the sense not to make such a ruckus with your father so ill."

Phin stepped forward, though Cordelia wished he'd hidden somehow instead. "It was my fault, Mrs. Dunn. I shared some unfortunate news I'd just discovered about her maid, and you know Annie. She got a bit . . . vocal."

Mama nodded, but then narrowed her eyes. "And what, may I ask, are you doing here alone in a room with my daughter, Mr. Dunn?"

He cleared his throat. "Just inquiring about your husband, ma'am. We've been praying for him without ceasing."

"Mm." Mama didn't look angry. She just looked so very tired. No, weary. No . . . exhausted, and not just physically. She stepped to the side, a clear message that he ought to take advantage of the open door. "I'm sure Delia brought you up to date. And now, my darling daughter, you had better say goodbye. I don't imagine you'll be seeing Mr. Dunn again for quite some time. As soon as your father's well enough, we're leaving

Savannah for the duration of the war. And in the meantime, our house is closed to visitors."

Good-bye? No! She wanted to scream it, argue, cry out. But Mama wouldn't hear her. She wouldn't hear anything right now but her own worry, her own pain. So, Cordelia took a few steps and then turned to face Phin when her mother could only see her back. Mouthed *I love you.* "Good-bye, Phin. Thank you." *I'll write.*

He smiled. It was small, and it was sad, and it was filled with an understanding that went far beyond words. He knew she'd write. To him, whenever she could manage it. And more. She'd write every word the Lord allowed her, until she had something that would make a difference.

He lifted a hand, and then settled it over his heart. "Forever, Delia. And then some. However long it takes."

Chapter Twenty-Six

April 10, 1862

Another shell exploded, shaking the window as Cordelia walked by. Her heart pounded, her stomach rose closer to her throat. "It's miles away," she murmured to herself. "Miles. It's the fort they want, not Savannah."

Still, she heard Mama shriek down the hall, shouting at the servants to hurry up. They'd been packing ever since the first shells bombarded Fort Pulaski that morning, ever since Daddy had declared, "I'm well enough, whether the doctor agrees or not. We're leaving. Today. Anything you can't live without, get it ready."

They'd made as many preparations as they could for this day ahead of time. Still, it was no easy task, loading up a household. Cordelia told herself to stay calm. To be an island unaffected by it all.

Which would be a lot easier if one island weren't under attack right now, the batteries stationed on another. On Big Tybee. Where Salina was with her River. Where Evangelina was with Luther.

She eased onto the edge of her bed, her eyes trained on the window. The fort was well out of sight, of course, but it was in that general direction. Its stone walls meant to defend the city, the coast. Its brave men determined not to surrender, to wait out any siege. She'd even heard that a courier swam across the river every week to get messages back and forth without the Yankees knowing.

Another boom echoed over the city. The men could wait out a siege . . . but could they withstand the Union arsenal?

Her trunk yawned open at the foot of her bed, her favorite dresses, gowns, shoes, and gloves already packed. Her stories all neatly tied together with twine, her inks and pens carefully stored in their boxes. Daddy had told her she couldn't take but a dozen books, so she'd buried *Uncle Tom's Cabin* in the bottom. Resting on the top was *Great Expectations*, wrapped in the lace and jet-beaded shawl that she'd scarcely taken off this last month.

It had been such a quiet month. No visitors. No visits. No Salina. Just Cordelia and her words. Cordelia and her parents. They'd mentioned Phin a few times, to lay out again why he wasn't a good match, especially now, when his lands were likely in ruins. She never said a word in reply. Never brought it up herself.

For now, she'd simply love them. Care for Daddy. Show Mama that though they were different, it was no reason they couldn't get along. And she'd trust that someday, God willing, her own story might have some sort of happy ending.

But if not . . . then at least she knew she was spending her life well. She had a novel started, already so long that it took up a goodly portion of her allotted book space in her trunk. A novel about a set of friends that shouldn't have been. About a world that said they were too different, that one was the natural superior to the other. About hearts that knew they were the same.

The plantation would, at least, offer plenty of quiet for writing. And she knew good Moses and Fiona and the others who were traveling there with them would keep helping her sneak letters to and from Phin.

"Miss Delia?" A knock accompanied the call, the door opening to Fiona before Cordelia had time to bid her enter. Her eyes were wide. "You gwine wanna come wif me, baby. Yo Mr. Phin's here!"

"What?" She leapt to her feet. "And they're letting me see him?"

"Lettin you?" Fiona scoffed and waved her on. "Naw, they ain't send nobody up to fetch ya. But that don't mean you kin't at least *see* him. Come on. I take you behind the walls. I knows you at least want a last peek."

Cordelia tucked her hand into Fiona's and let her lead her down the back stairs and the servants' stairs—and then into one of the many passages she'd never entered, which allowed the servants to slip in and out of rooms without disturbing anybody.

How had she never written a story about *these*?

She hadn't time to shiver at the darkness though, nor to explore the maze. Fiona was leading her more quickly than she'd thought the old lady could move toward the faint echo of voices. Daddy's. Mama's. *Phin's.*

Longing made her throat go tight, and she gripped Fiona's fingers all the more. Then they were there, a sliver of light showing her the break in the paneling. It was cracked open—no doubt darling Fiona's work—so Cordelia could put her eye to it and peek into the room. She had to shift her position to see much of anything, but by doing so she could glimpse her parents, settling now onto the divan. And Phin, standing with his hat in his hands.

"Thank you for seeing me," he was even then saying.

Daddy's voice sounded back to normal these days, though his coat hung loose on him, clear evidence of a month of little appetite and less exercise. "If you're here to beg for Delia's hand again, save your breath, Phineas. We're getting her to safety."

"I know. And I didn't. I came . . ." He paused and drew in a long breath, fiddling with the brim of his hat. "I came simply to say that you're doing the logical thing, taking her inland. I can't blame you for it. And I know that right now all I have left to offer is what you're running from—a house in Savannah. Our plantation is lost to us. Maybe we'll get it back someday, maybe we won't. And that isn't enough. She deserves more. Even so."

He reached into his pocket and pulled out something small, held it in the palm of his hand. It was long, thin. Cordelia leaned forward half an inch. A key? "I don't have much anymore. But what I do have, I offer to you, and I swear to you I'll do all I can to protect it." Yes, a key. He held it out. "I know you don't value it very highly. And I know this key is just a symbol. But I want you to have it. To know that our home is always open to you or yours. That Cordelia is the only woman I would ever bring into it as a mistress. So." When they didn't reach for it, he set the key down.

Phin backed up a step with a sigh to heave his shoulders. "There's not much certain anymore. But if it matters at all, you can be certain of that. I love your daughter more than life itself. And it will be an honor to cherish her in my heart for the rest of my days, even if I have to do it at a distance."

Her own heart ached so fiercely she had to press a hand to it, and still it felt as though it might crack.

At her parents' continued silence, Phin nodded, spun around, and walked out the door, his limp not hindering the length of his stride.

Cordelia forced the crack in the wall wider, ignoring the squeak of protest from Fiona, who scrambled to remain in the darkness of the corridor. Mama and Daddy both jumped, their eyes going wide when she stepped into the room.

Daddy stood. "Obviously you heard."

She nodded.

"And I assume you mean to beg us to leave you behind with him?"

She shook her head. She *wanted* to beg. But she'd promised herself she wouldn't. "I just wanted you to know I heard."

Mama stood, too, her sigh long. But somehow, strangely, it didn't sound as weary as she'd come to expect. "Beautiful words he has—I know you appreciate that."

"It's more the beautiful heart that captured me."

A corner of Daddy's mouth actually turned up. "Your mother and I have been talking a lot about the two of you. All the more, I think, because you've been uncannily silent on the matter."

She spread her hands. "I knew I couldn't say anything more than I'd already said. I love him. He's a good man." The best of men.

Daddy exchanged a glance with Mama. "Savannah isn't safe. But then . . . we have no reason to believe the countryside of Georgia will remain safe when that of Virginia and the Carolinas hasn't remained so. These *are* uncertain times."

What was he getting at? She knotted her fingers together. "They are."

"But . . . if this is what you want. If you're certain. If you've taken this last month to weigh the reality against the dream . . ."

Was he . . . ? She nodded. Vigorously. "I have, Daddy. I have no illusions."

"So, if we put the choice to you—if we say you may marry him if it's your heart's desire—what would you say?"

She looked from Daddy to Mama, scarcely able to believe what he had asked her. Trying to take a moment so she didn't appear impulsive, trying to measure how much they needed her for the journey inland against how her soul leaped and soared at the thought of staying here with Phin. In the place that had always been home more than any other.

It would be difficult if they stayed. The war had reached them, and it was an ugly thing. She knew that. There could be food shortages, enemy soldiers swarming her streets. There could be desolation and death and injury all around her.

But still she had to draw in a long breath. "Would you be all right without me? I'd never forgive myself if something happened to you."

His eyes went soft. "I'm stronger now, darlin—and your sisters and mother will fuss aplenty. Don't make this decision because of me."

She looked from her father to her mother and back again. Could they really mean it? Were they really letting her make this choice? The thought brought joy bubbling up. "Then . . . yes. Yes, I would like nothing more than to marry him."

"Well then." Daddy turned to the door. "We'd best hurry if we mean to catch him. Are you coming, Mrs. Owens?"

"Now?" Mama gave him the same stern look she always did when he suggested she do something frivolous an hour before guests arrived. "I think I'd better go in search of the minister, don't you?"

"A wise idea, indeed. How about you, sunshine? Should I chase him down on my own? Maybe you'd rather unpack an appropriate dress to wear for your wedding."

As if she'd choose a dress over getting to see Phin's face? Unable to contain her laugh of joy, she surged forward.

Mama snagged her wrist on her way by. But her eyes were quiet now, no lectures lurking. She leaned over and pressed a long kiss to Cordelia's cheek. "I will never understand you, Cordelia Penelope Owens. But somehow . . . somehow, despite that, I think perhaps you are the best of us."

If ever a sweeter benediction had ever been spoken, Cordelia couldn't imagine it.

Phin pulled his horse to a halt when the road gave way to muddy ruts. But he could see Fort Pulaski on Cockspur Island from here, which was all the closer he needed to get. He could see the stones crumbling, the holes forming. He could hear the frenzied shouts of the soldiers within.

Rifled artillery. The Union had installed rifled artillery on Big Tybee, and the shells seemed to rip right through the "impregnable" walls. Another whistled through the air now, overshot the wall, and landed somewhere within the fort itself.

His hands tightened around the reins. *Lord, help them. Preserve their lives*. He wished he could do something, anything to help. But prayers were his best weapon right now. He certainly couldn't swim across the river and climb the walls. And even if he did, it wouldn't matter. Their guns were no match for the Yankees'.

The fort was going to fall.

Thinking of it made the scar on his leg throb and twist. Just as it had done when he read the report from Shiloh yesterday. So many dead. A few of his friends. One of his cousins. And countless, countless more. It was fast turning into a bloody, merciless war.

A bloody, merciless war that was knocking on Savannah's door.

Well, he'd be here to protect her. He'd stand firm beside the other locals who refused to leave. He'd do his best to preserve the home that he hoped to offer to Cordelia someday.

Eventually—perhaps not until this war was over, but eventually—he knew she'd be his wife. And in the meantime, he'd do whatever he must to preserve what she loved.

"Phin!"

He wheeled his mount around, not knowing whether to curse or whoop for joy when he saw the Owens coach trotting toward him. They couldn't possibly have followed him just to let her say good-bye, could they? He spurred his horse forward, hoping he could intercept them before they got stuck in the pitted road. Thankfully, Mr. Owens drew up as soon as he turned.

It didn't appease him much when another shell whizzed, whistled, and crashed with near-deafening force into the wall. His horse pawed the air, but Phin got him back under control and came up alongside Delia. "What the devil are you doing out here?"

"We saw you come this way." Her hand reached out and groped for his, her gaze on the fort. "Phin, it has a hole in it."

"I know." He caught her fingers and lifted them to his lips. He meant to look at her father, try to read his expression, but he couldn't take his eyes from the face he hadn't seen in too many weeks. "They're going to take it, darlin. There's no question, not at this point."

Owens blew out a long breath. "It was such a feat. An engineering marvel. I never thought . . ."

"No one did." He rubbed his thumb over her knuckles. Just to prove to himself she was really there—stupid as it may be to be *there*, now. "And you followed me because . . . ?"

Delia smiled, so bright and hopeful it almost blinded him to the destruction on Cockspur. Her father cleared his throat and looked their way. "Her mother and I have given this a lot of thought. And we both agree that the sort of love you two have . . . it doesn't happen often. And who are we to stand in its way?"

Cordelia's nostrils flared, and she pressed her lips together. He had the distinct impression those sentiments hadn't been shared with her before.

Though a smile started in the corners of Owens's mouth, it died again when the Confederates sent a blast of cannon toward Tybee. "Promise me you'll keep her safe, Phineas. To the best of your ability. I know only the Lord has the ultimate say, but . . ."

"You have my word, sir." Phin wove their fingers together, heart thudding. They all knew they were talking about marriage, and that it would have to happen soon—today, if at all possible. But he couldn't let it remain an assumption. "But what about you? I know Delia didn't want to be separated from you now, what with—"

"We had that conversation too. I'll be well enough. It's time she lives her own life."

But did Delia really agree with that? Phin's gaze moved to her eyes, digging deep until he was sure there was no second-guessing. He saw a bit of fear still, but that was to be expected. And it was eclipsed by joy. That was all Phin needed to know. "I'll do all in my power to see we're reunited someday, sir."

Owens's gaze went toward the farther island. His larynx bobbed. "And Salina? Have you—do you know if . . . ?"

More than the question and its implications, Phin noted the way Delia's face went soft as she studied her father. Phin cleared his throat. "We've received a few communications from the plantation. They're there, safe. She and River had what I'm told was a sweet little wedding with River's family all attending, Luther officiating."

"Luther?" Owens frowned.

Delia grinned. "That would be Reverend Luther Bromley of Stoke Newington, Daddy. Or, as you might know him, Monty."

He just nodded and swallowed again.

Delia put her other hand on her father's arm. "She's happy. As she deserves to be."

"She's on a plantation, Delia. If she works the fields, it'll kill her. And I swore to her mother she'd never know that kind of labor, that she'd have an easy, healthy life."

Delia drew her hand away at the mention of Salina's mother. Phin gave the fingers he held a soft squeeze. "She won't be working the fields, sir, I can promise you that. She'll be teaching the others to read and write."

Now Owens's eyes went wide, and he turned on his daughter. "Delia."

She gave him a sheepish smile. "How else was she to help me with my stories?"

Another blast from Tybee made the horses jolt and the carriage roll. Phin tried to keep his even with them and was ready to loose her fingers, but rather than release him, she stood to narrow the distance.

He grinned. "Perfect. If I tried to kneel in this mud, I may sink straight to China, but now at least we can pretend I am."

"Why would you—Phin." Though her eyes danced, her face remained calm. "I don't need any grand gestures. Not today."

With a shrug, he said, "Suit yourself." Then grabbed her around the waist and pulled her from the carriage onto his horse. Her squeal made the beast prance away, but luckily she had grabbed hold of him and found a seat on his lap, otherwise her weighty skirts may have pulled her straight down to that greedy mud. Phin chuckled and positioned her. "I'll just carry you away then, my princess, and force you to be my bride. Spoils of war."

More cannons boomed from the fort, and Owens took up his reins again. "Perhaps you two could continue your nonsense elsewhere."

Delia wrapped an arm around Phin's neck, that bright smile back in place. Lighting his heart and soul. "Daddy, you're ruining the moment."

"We have no more moments to waste. If one of those shells goes astray, we could be celebrating our funerals instead of your wedding."

While he backed the horses up to a drier patch of road, Phin clicked his into a walk and nuzzled Delia's ear. "There's always time for a moment. And you deserve it, princess. You deserve a story to tell our children."

She smoothed back a lock of his hair that had fallen onto his forehead. "And how shall I tell this one? Are you my mighty knight, come to my rescue, or a prince from some exotic land come to carry me away as a prize?"

"Hmm." He dipped his head to steal a quick, gentle kiss. "I fancy the knight—though I admit my armor is rather rusty. Prolonged exposure to salt water, you know."

She tucked her head onto his shoulder and motioned toward the fort. "And your castle is in need of some fortifications, it seems. I hate to see it so, Sir Phineas."

He urged the horse a little faster so she'd lose sight of it sooner. "I know. But I'll protect you, darlin. So long as God continues to honor me with that responsibility, I'll protect you."

Ahead of them, Owens maneuvered his carriage back in the direction of Savannah. "Can you ride that way? We ought to hurry. My mother will have everything ready for a wedding by now, I'm sure. Her plan was, I believe, to impose upon your mother for hosting the ceremony, Phin. Since we have a key to the place now and all."

"That's the best idea I've heard all year. Whatever will help in making Delia my wife is quite acceptable to my family."

"Your wife." Delia's eyes slid shut. "I began to think I'd never have those words."

"You'll have them, darlin." He nudged the horse a bit more to keep up with her father. "And my family will be overjoyed to welcome you."

"That sounds perfect."

"Cook will manage some miracle in the kitchen, we'll enjoy an hour or two with our family. By then, darkness will have fallen, and the shelling will have stopped."

She swallowed and opened her eyes. "We must pray for them, Phin. For the men in Fort Pulaski."

"We will indeed, darlin. We'll pray with my parents and Sassy, we'll pray together just the two of us. And then."

She pressed her lips together, love sparking in her eyes. "And then?"

"And then, my sweet princess," he said, hovering an inch away, feasting on the vision she made, "then you can tell me a story. One with adventure and romance and dastardly villains and a happy ending gleaming with hope."

Her smile put the sun to shame, and her trill of laughter drowned out the echoes of war. She nestled a little closer and rested her hand on his chest, right over his heart. "I have just the one."

Author's Note

Some books I write in a flash, getting the whole story down in a month or two before the editorial process begins. Others take years from first idea to holding those beautiful pages in my hand—and *Dreams of Savannah* is without question one of the second. I first wrote the book in 2011, and it was a busy nine years before I had the chance to place it into an editor's hands. Nine years that saw a lot of change in my writing, my career, and my country.

After writing so many books set in England, it felt somewhat odd to take my mind to another era, and back to my own nation. But I do love that I had Luther Bromley in this story to help me manage the shift. And I am so grateful to finally get to share Cordelia, my most imaginative heroine, with you. I hope you enjoyed the peeks into the rich fantasy life we novelists sometimes fall into.

Though those in the northern states consider me southern, those in the Deep South would no doubt term me a Yankee—this is the joy of being from West Virginia. But in truth, hailing from a state with such mixed loyalties during the Civil War gives me empathy for both sides of the conflict. When it comes to ideals, and especially the issue of slavery, I'm a Union girl through and through. But when it comes to states' rights and the slower way of life the Confederacy sought to preserve, I understand why they—even those who had never owned a slave—were willing to fight for it. And indeed, most of us would choose to fight to defend our homes when they're threatened. There were heroes—and villains—on both sides of the conflict. Most of all, there were *people*. People, as Cordelia discovered, with stories to tell.

Most of my research for what Savannah was like during this period came from the book *Saving Savannah* by Jacqueline Jones, a treasure trove of historical details about this quintessential Georgian city and how it changed so drastically with the war. Here, too, I was introduced to the unique Gullah culture that African Americans of that time and place were a part of. I spent many hours studying the language, beliefs, and customs, and I hope I did them justice.

But no matter how long I spend on the academics, there's also always the fear that I've done something wrong or will offend the very people whose story I wanted to tell a small piece of. And so I thank my editorial team for their loving eye, and my friend and fellow writer Toni Shiloh for working through the issues with me.

I pray that you enjoyed this little journey under Savannah's famous live oaks dripping Spanish moss, with the fragrance of magnolia blossoms on the air (though those don't grow in my neck of the woods, they were abundant in Annapolis, Maryland, where I went to college, and as I breathed them in each spring and summer, I always tried to put words to them). And I pray, too, that as you go about your day, interacting with the people around you who are just faces in the crowd, you pause, like Cordelia learned to do, to wonder what stories they could tell.

I'd love to hear yours. Feel free to contact me from my website, www.RoseannaMWhite.com, and tell me about your family.

Discussion Questions

1. Delia has a vivid imagination that leads her both to fancies and to fears. Do you have, or did you once have, an active imagination? If so, did it bring you joy? Get you into trouble?
2. Phin made the decision to fight for Georgia, even though he disagreed with some of their laws, because he felt it should be the state's own right to fix them. Do you agree with this decision? What would you have done in his place?
3. The English abolitionist movement took place in the early 1800s and resulted in a gradual removal of slavery—first by outlawing the slave trade and sale of slaves, then by instituting emancipation in 1833. How do you think this perspective influenced Luther and his views? Were you surprised by his character or history? About Eva's story?
4. Salina found herself caught between two worlds and accepted by neither. Have you ever felt as though you didn't belong? How did you cope and adapt? Do you think she made the right decisions throughout the

book? How would you have felt toward Delia in Salina's shoes?

5. When Phin returned home, he struggled with the idea that he wasn't the sort of hero Delia wanted or needed. Have you ever felt you weren't meeting someone else's expectations for you? Did you ever talk to them about it, and if so, was it true or your own misperception?
6. Who is your favorite character? Your least favorite? Why?
7. Delia comes to realize that her calling is to write stories to help people see things in a new light. Has a story ever changed the way you viewed the world or people in it? Which ones, and how so?
8. River, Rock, and Luther take a huge risk in helping runaways escape to the barrier islands, where schools were indeed set up to prepare slaves for a life of freedom. Would you have done the same if you were them? Is there a risk you feel called to take or to support others in taking today?
9. Delia is forever changed when she realizes that everyone around her has their own story, and that she may have been a villain in theirs. Have you ever played the part of antagonist in someone else's life? Does thinking of it that way shed any new light on their perspective? What about people who have been the "bad guy" in your life? Have you ever paused to wonder what drives them?
10. What do you think became of Phin and Delia, Salina and River, Luther and Eva after the war?

Roseanna M. White is a bestselling, Christy Award–nominated author who has long claimed that words are the air she breathes. When not writing fiction, she's homeschooling her two kids, designing book covers, editing, and pretending her house will clean itself. Roseanna is the author of a slew of historical novels that span several continents and thousands of years. Spies and war and mayhem always seem to find their way into her books . . . to offset her real life, which is blessedly ordinary. You can learn more about her and her stories at www.roseannamwhite.com.

Sign Up for Roseanna's Newsletter!

Keep up to date with Roseanna's news on book releases and events by signing up for her email list at roseannamwhite.com.

More from Roseanna M. White

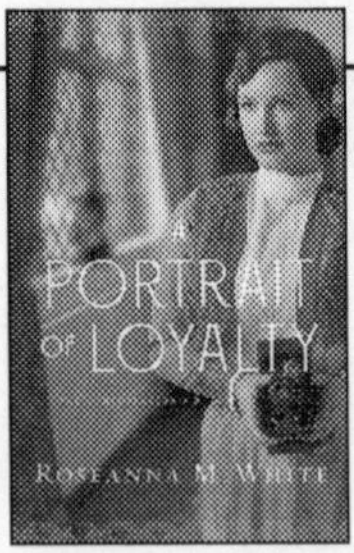

A skilled cryptographer, Zivon Marin fled Russia determined to offer his skills to the Brits. Lily Blackwell is recruited to the intelligence division to help the war with her unsurpassed camera skills. But when her photographs reveal Zivon is being followed, his loyalty is questioned and his enemies are discovered to be closer than he feared.

A Portrait of Loyalty
THE CODEBREAKERS #3

You May Also Like . . .

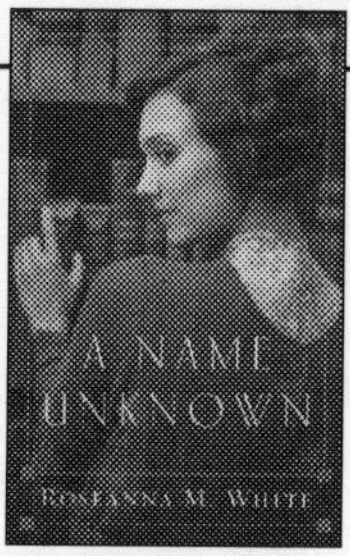

Rosemary Gresham has no family beyond the thieves that have helped her survive on the streets of London. Pickpockets no longer, they've learned how to blend into high society and now work as thieves for hire. But when a client assigns Rosemary to determine whether a friend of the king is loyal to Britain or Germany, she's in for the challenge of a lifetime.

A Name Unknown by Roseanna M. White
Shadows Over England #1
roseannamwhite.com

When Madysen Powell's supposedly dead father shows up, her gift for forgiveness is tested and she's left searching for answers. Daniel Beaufort arrives in Nome, longing to start fresh after the gold rush leaves him with only empty pockets, and finds employment at the Powell dairy. Will deceptions from the past tear apart their hopes for a better future?

Endless Mercy by Tracie Peterson and Kimberley Woodhouse
The Treasures of Nome #2
traciepeterson.com; kimberleywoodhouse.com

Nate Long has always watched over his twin, even if it's led him to be an outlaw. When his brother is wounded in a shootout, it's their former prisoner, Laura, who ends up nursing his wounds at Settler's Fort. She knows Nate wants a fresh start, but struggles with how his devotion blinds him. Do the futures they seek include love, or is too much in the way?

Faith's Mountain Home by Misty M. Beller
Hearts of Montana #3
mistymbeller.com

BETHANYHOUSE

More from Bethany House

After being robbed on her trip west to save her ailing sister, Greta Nilsson is left homeless and penniless. Struggling to get his new ranch running, Wyatt McQuaid is offered a bargain—the mayor will invest in a herd of cattle if Wyatt agrees to help the town become more respectable by marrying…and the mayor has the perfect woman in mind.

A Cowboy for Keeps by Jody Hedlund
Colorado Cowboys #1
jodyhedlund.com

Assigned to find the kidnapped daughter of a mob boss, Pinkerton operative Calista York is sent to a rowdy mining town in Missouri. But she faces the obstacle of missionary Matthew Cook. He's as determined to stop a local baby raffle as he is the reckless Miss York whose bad judgement consistently seems to be putting her in harm's way.

Courting Misfortune by Regina Jennings
The Joplin Chronicles #1
reginajennings.com

In 1946, Millie Middleton left home to keep her heritage hidden, carrying the dream of owning a dress store. Decades later, when Harper Dupree's future in fashion falls apart, she visits her mentor Millie. As the revelation of a family secret leads them to Charleston and a rare opportunity, can they overcome doubts and failures for a chance at their dreams?

The Dress Shop on King Street by Ashley Clark
Heirloom Secrets
ashleyclarkbooks.com

BethanyHouse